Words of Praise for "The Dead's Hero"

"Simply the finest piece of literature I have ever read.
And I'm a rabbi...so I've read the Bible from cover to cover!"
— *Rabbi Steve Foster...father*

"If you don't love this book you have something seriously wrong with your brain. And I'm a psychiatrist, so I know brains!"
— *Dr. Steven Sarche'...Danny's lifelong friend*

"I couldn't put this book down, but then again I couldn't pick this book up, or read it...because I am a Springer Spaniel. But I sure do love that Danny Foster."
— *Elvis...Danny's dog*

"Danny Foster's first novel delighted and thrilled me. It was so, so good. I promise you that you will find this book to be the best you've ever read."
— *Senator Joyce Foster...Danny's mom*

"Eh...it was OK...not great... average at best."
— *David Foster...brother*

"This book makes me like Danny a lot more than when I was growing up. He really picked on me a lot. But at least he knows how to write stories...I guess."
— *Debbie Foster...sister*

"Excellent first novel. But this will not get him out of taking out the trash and doing yard work."
— *Becky Foster...wife*

✳

D0916763

643

The Dead's Hero

Danny Foster

The Dead's Hero
Dead Books Denver Publishing, LLC
©Danny Foster, 2021
Denver, Colorado

ISBN: 978-1-7923-6334-4

Cover art, jacket design and book layout by Jena Skinner

Dedicated to a young man who made a promise many years ago.
Promise fulfilled.

Table Of Contents

And you need blind faith
No false hope
Do you have blind faith?
No false hope
Where is your blind faith?
No false hope
Open your eyes, open your eyes
Step into the light!!!

— Foo Fighters, "Congregation"

Important Note to Reader

On December 16, 1857 in the Basilicata region of Italy, southeast of Naples, a massive earthquake floored the province, killing over 10,000 people. Generally, earthquakes are a shifting of the tectonic plates beneath the Earth's surface, which de-stabilize the land above. Aside from a moment of sheer terror and panic for those experiencing an earthquake, usually the impact is no more than a few minor tremors, a crack or two in the ground, and a broken picture frame. They cause small inconveniences with little property damage and few injuries. However, at other times, like the 1857 Basilicata earthquake, they can cause massive land fractures, property destabilizations, and catastrophic death counts.

The Basilicata earthquake was written off by seismologists as an unfortunate natural catastrophe that had a high body count coupled with huge property losses. No different than the other earthquakes that impacted the region, such as the Sicilian earthquakes in the year 1169 or 1693, or even the cataclysmic destruction of the ancient city of Pompeii, just east of Naples in the year 62, when Mount Vesuvius blew her top. These were all simply natural phenomenon that didn't discriminate against the soon to be deceased residents of the area.

The only difference between the other Italian disasters and the Basilicata earthquake of 1857 was that the mountainous region had nothing to do with the shifting of Earth's tectonic plates. Had real seismology equipment even existed at the time, it would have been a mystery where the source of this earthquake occurred or why it happened. Nothing about it was consistent with a normal seismologic event. The fact is this was not a natural event triggered by the shifting of tectonic plates. It was a phenomenon associated with people and entities no longer connected with the living world as we know it.

On December 16, 1857, two ancient and very powerful orbs were buried in a cemetery in Montemurro, a small town in the province of Potenza, not far from the Basilicata earthquake's epicenter. The man who buried them, Corrado Tedesco, had hoped to settle an ancient dispute between two rival groups that exist in the Afterlife. One group, the Dead, compromise all humankind that die and search for a new plane of existence in a place of omniscience and growth. Contrary to popular religious or atheistic beliefs, when we die our souls continue to move on and grow and take on new forms of energy. Death is just a beginning and this new plane of existence is simply another level to our physical selves. Unfortunately for all of the Dead, and soon to be members of the Dead, there is another ethereal group that wants to preserve this plane of existence for themselves. They are not physical beings like humans but have many human desires that the Dead have: specifically the desire to harness power to grow and become omniscient. And in the Afterlife, just as in the living world, there is a never ending turf battle. This group at odds with the Dead is known as the Builders, because they continue to build a wall to keep the Dead out of their territory. The front line of this battle is known as the Divide and the Builders fight furiously to keep the Dead from breaching the Divide. They build and build their wall, but the Dead slowly, miraculously make their way over this wall and the Divide. But it gets increasingly more difficult year after year for the Dead to forge the wall and make their way into this Garden of Eden.

The goal for the Builders is simple: keep the Dead out! The Builders know that if the Dead keep crossing over into their territory that they will lose power. But if the Dead don't cross over into that territory, then the Dead have nowhere else to go and will never be able to evolve, grow or change. An eternity of malaise and deterioration. For the Dead they must bring down this wall and cross the Divide. For the Builders they will lose their power and territory if the wall comes down. There are no negotiations, no armistices, no settlements.

That fateful day in 1857 Signore Tedesco attempted to bury only two of the mystical orbs when in fact there was a third and final orb that needed to join the other two orbs to form an all-powerful triumvirate. A most coveted weapon that the Dead and the Builders each need to control the Afterlife. The three orbs have existed since the beginning of time. They were a product of the Big Bang containing incredible powers which broke apart into three small hand-sized pieces before the Earth was even formed. The orbs even had developed monikers over the years by those who possessed them. The MonteGresso (coined by an ancient Roman landowner who discovered it on his estate named The MonteGresso Bella), The PinonAstra (named by a courtier of an Egyptian Pharoah centuries before Ramses lived, who believed the orb had been delivered by a god of the same name) and The Mule (a 13th century English boat builder found it in a wet bog and called it The Mule for no other reason than it had the distinct features of a mule with a long snout and the peculiar ears of the animal. This occurred when it broke apart from its siblings).

Individually these orbs accomplish nothing and can help neither the Dead nor the Builders. Together, however, they tilt the existence of the Afterlife for whatever entity controls the triad. The orbs have surfaced and re-surfaced in the world of the living for millennia. The orbs however have never been reunited throughout their existence and yearn to be re-united to form this triumvirate. The only way to unite all three orbs is for a living human to find them all and bury them together and deliver them to either the Dead, or the Builders. Whichever entity controls all three orbs simultaneously would control the power to dominate the Afterlife. Just as the United States' development and use of the atomic bomb in 1945 was the greatest power on the planet and quickly ended the war in the Pacific, the triad of the orbs would be a weapon of unparalleled power in the Afterlife and ensure complete control to the entity in possession.

However, there is a catch. Burying one orb will do nothing but delay the formation of the triad and completion of the weapon. Burying the three orbs together will control the Divide and win the game. Unfortunately for Signore Tedesco, and the thousands of people in his wake, burying two of the three ancient orbs is the most dangerous thing a living person can do and causes quite a mess. Signore Tedesco was desperate in his plight and hoped he would be successful burying just two. Tragically he did not fully understand how the orbs worked, hence the destruction of Basilicata and the massive death count. Following this disaster the two orbs he buried, The PinonAstra and The Mule, would lie dormant deep in the Earth and eventually, slowly, re-surface through the Earth's crust, somewhere far away, wanting to be discovered and re-joined with The MonteGresso, which in 1857 was patiently waiting to be discovered. The Dead and the Builders would each need living, human advocates to find the orbs and unite them. The final end game would have to wait until the year 2020, another 163 years, and if the Dead intended to win, they needed a Hero.

Prologue: September 4, 1980

Briarwood Cemetery, Denver, Colorado

"Yitkidal, Vayitkadash, shmei rabah…" Rabbi Stan Berenbaum commenced with the ancient Jewish prayer called the Mourner's Kaddish, a prayer that has been recited millions of times over centuries. The prayer, connected with Jewish mourning and grieving for those that have died, never mentions death. Instead, it proclaims the sanctity and glorification of God. But to all who heard those ancient words it really meant that someone had died, and that person was being remembered.

Rabbi Stan, as he was known to his congregants, completed the kaddish prayer along with the mourners around the graveside. Rabbi Stan stepped up to a small portable podium that was assembled under a tent which sat adjacent to a grave that held a coffin sitting atop suspension belts, ready to be lowered six feet down into a dirt tomb. The family sat in the shade of the tent, in two rows, on green expandable seats designed for easy folding and removal. Rabbi Stan looked down at the grieving family, especially the parents of Mark Levin, the victim of a drunk driver and only twenty years old. Their tears flowed heavily and the sobs coming from the hundreds of friends, family and acquaintances surrounded the small tent structure designed to shield the immediate family members from the severe sun that beat down on Briarwood Cemetery that balmy September day.

"My dear friends, this is a hard day for all of us who knew and loved Mark. He was a beautiful young man in the prime of his life. Excelling in his studies and gifted on the piano. His life was cut tragically short due to the unnecessary and irresponsible actions of others and we are left to grieve. And especially you, Barry and Karen, the parents." And Rabbi Stan took a moment to look at the inconsolable parents sitting a few feet in front of him.

"The pain you feel now is real and palpable and it seems as if the grief will never go away. To bury a child is a pain that no one should ever know. But here you are. Unable to change the past and forced to figure out an uncertain future. But know this. We, your community, are here for you. And to his siblings, to lose your big brother, that is not an easy thing. I say this to you, Rachel and Kenny, that while Mark was more than ten years older than you, he felt very connected to your lives. And we as a Denver community are grieving with you. And understand that Mark, while his death was tragic and untimely, he did not die with his music still in him." At this point Rabbi Stan started to cry himself and needed a moment to gather his thoughts. He wiped his eyes with his handkerchief and placed it back in his pocket.

"Some people die having never tried anything. Having never ventured anywhere. Having never sang their song or written their script. But Mark was different. Mark was a talented artist who painted, wrote poetry and stories and of course was a gifted pianist. He excelled at his university. He was creative and talented, and we were all fortunate to get to experience his talents firsthand. And while we would have loved more for him, and more time with him, we can be grateful that God allowed him to live fully in his brief twenty years. Mark died having shared his beauty and music with the world, he did not die with his music still in him. Many people live to a ripe age having failed to share all of the music in their souls, but that wasn't the case with Mark. We were all lucky to have known and learned from Mark Levin. In twenty years, he lived a life that we can be thankful for. And while that doesn't ease any of the pain you feel, Karen and Barry, I know that when this cloud of grief and anguish has lifted, and believe me it will lift, slowly, ever so slowly, you will be left with the glow of the life of a remarkable person and it will fill your soul. Remember that Mark may no longer be with us in the flesh, but he continues to live in our hearts, and we can continue to honor Mark by being so kind and caring to the living—by forgiving those who have hurt us. And by providing love and charity to those in need. And we say Amen."

Rabbi Stan stepped back from the podium and turned to the operator of the small mechanical winch that slowly, painfully, eased Mark Levin into the ground. Each turn of the knob lowering Mark was another knife in the heart to Karen and Barry. His coffin landed gently in the cold dirt and then Rabbi Stan asked all family members and then friends to line up and take the customary shovel of dirt to pour onto the casket. Each time the shovelful of dirt landed on the wooden box there would be a muffled thump. Because no one uttered a sound each thump of dirt echoed painfully to all those gathered at the graveside. A sound that symbolized the end of a life and the closing of a book for all eternity.

The full mound of dirt next to the open grave was only partially used to insulate the casket. The rule at Briarwood in 1980 was that a cement block, or vault, was to be placed over the casket to protect the grass and landscaping above from depressions once the casket deteriorated and turned to dust. If the vault wasn't placed on top of the casket, then eventually the dirt above the casket would start to slowly sink and the headstones would eventually topple over. This was a common sight in the older sections of Briarwood Cemetery and at cemeteries throughout the world. Therefore, the ceremonial dirt was poured on Mark, but just enough to complete the ritual. The balance would be placed after the family left the grave and the crane was brought in to drop the thousand-pound cement lid. Then a team of groundskeepers would fill in the balance of the grave and place the sod. But that was not something that would take place for a few hours. Everyone briefly hugged the Levins, and shook Rabbi Stan's hand, then drove off to the Levin household for the commencement of Shivah, the seven-day period of mourning.

The grave sat there, only partially filled, void of mourners. Jeannie was watching from a distance. Carefully crouching behind one of the smaller crypts that adorned the 280 acres of the sprawling cemetery. The crypt, which belonged to the Richardson family, was adorned with cement cherubs and crosses. RICHARDSON 1909 was proudly etched into the cement above the old door that guarded the two caskets inside. There was a heavy padlock and chain that looked as if it hadn't been opened or disturbed in at least 50 years. She had watched the Levin funeral from a distance and did her best to hear what the Rabbi had said. It was hard because of the large crowd circling the family, but she heard enough to know that this was a painful death to endure for the family. Whenever a young person died the pain was always more severe, always. This was her best opportunity. Once the final car had left and it appeared there was no one left at the graveside, she cautiously approached the open grave. She scanned her horizon: Nothing but huge trees, bushes and rows and rows of headstones and crypts. The cemetery took on an eerie silence that chilled her soul. It was too quiet. Still, she had to take the chance. There would likely not be a better opportunity. She put her hand in her bag and grabbed the small blue orb. It was about the size of a tennis ball. Perfectly round, deep blue with shining crystals ebbed throughout yet it was completely smooth, lightweight and nondescript. That is, unless you held it high into the light to inspect it. When she got within five feet of the grave, she pulled out the orb and started to recite the words she had practiced a hundred times before:

"Lord and savior be my shepherd through the valley of death. I fear no evil for you are with me. Now and forever."

And she dropped the orb into the grave and saw it hit the dirt. She waited. And waited. Reciting the line over and over again. The orb sat there. She looked out of the corner of her eye; about 200 yards away she saw a black man dressed all in white, with a white beard and sunglasses. He started running at her. She had been seen. She began to panic. She had only a few seconds before he covered the distance. He was old but he had a little bounce in his step. She recited the line over and over again. And then, to her great relief, she saw the penetrating green lights encircle the orb and it started to take in the dirt of Mark's grave. She had done one part of her job. She looked up. The man was only a few yards away. She pulled out the gun in her bag, stuck the barrel in her mouth and pulled the trigger.

"Noooooo!!!!!" the man screamed as she fell lifeless on top of the dirt in the grave that now held two bodies.

Chapter 1 * The Bottom

Denver, September 15, 2020

The inevitable tragedy of the optimism of youth is impossible to see when one is young, and impossible to ignore when one gets old. Most children living in a stable environment are generally, with some exceptions, happy. They go to school, make friends, run, swim, get into low-level mischief and dream of an exciting future. Maybe they will be an astronaut, a veterinarian, or even a professional football player. They will have romances and adventures and feel there is nothing they cannot accomplish. And then, slowly, ever so slowly, the reality of the world starts to show its face. Failures, disappointments and regrets become the true baggage of one's life. Baggage that keeps them awake at night while listening to the restless snoring of a spouse who lost interest many years earlier, troubled by high school memories and long-ago embarrassments that never seem to fade. The impressions that are made in adolescence never leave, they just lie dormant, waiting until 3:15 in the morning, to come out and say: "Hey there fella, remember me? Remember how you dropped that ball in the regional playoffs? Or what about those people you thought were your friends, but didn't really like you? They mocked you. Remember those people?" The voices in one's head only dulled by the mercy of exhaustion that allows one to fall back into a restless sleep. Night after night, year after year.

Young people grow up hearing the term "mid-life crisis" and they don't comprehend that idea of a mid-life crisis—certainly not the young who are so pumped full of joy and optimism like steroids at a bodybuilder competition. Some may believe a mid-life crisis arrives like a deluge, fast and powerful and recognizable. Oh, but it doesn't. It comes on slowly. Like shifting tectonic plates. Like the atrophy of a mountain cut by a river. So very slow and meticulous. Leaving an immutable impression on the earth. Sure, the Porsche just showed up in the garage, or the plastic surgery just healed, but the mechanism behind the need for these things is a slow process undetectable to the human eye. Case in point: Victor Alan Jones.

When did he become so freaking pathetic? He was never pathetic, growing up; he always considered himself to be a fairly well put-together person with lots of friends and goals. He had his shit together. He might not have been an all-star athlete or valedictorian, but he was succeeding in life. There were tons of burn-outs, stoners, and delinquents at his school, but he wasn't one of them. Victor came from a well-adjusted family who provided him everything he could need: love, confidence, a sense of self-worth. When the hell did it all go downhill?

He distinctly remembered that in college he once told his parents that he believed he was destined for something great. Not necessarily greatness, per se, but he planned to accomplish something impressive and meaningful. The hopeless ambition and arrogance of the young. It seems so natural as an 18-year-old.

He often thought about that conversation he had as a college freshman, a fucking moronic freshman, almost thirty years earlier. He remembered it not because it was so stupid, but because it was entirely what one would expect of a coddled adolescent who had been nurtured to believe that he really WAS special, that he really COULD accomplish whatever he wanted. His destiny would be exciting, unique, filled with adventure and financial success, right? This was the textbook myopic thinking of an 18-year-old, an 18-year-old who had never known what it meant to suffer or go wanting. But Victor showed promise in his twenties and thirties. He had some direction, some good career trajectory and even a cadre of friends and romantic liaisons. He wasn't knocking it out of the park by any stretch, but he was doing better than some of his friends and acquaintances. But as the months turned into years, and the muscle atrophied and the hairline receded, it became evident that he would never live up to his boast he stated to his parents. He wasn't going to change the world or do anything great. He was losing his momentum in a very palpable way.

Thirty years after that discussion with his parents he sat on his couch in his house in a tidy yet unremarkable Denver neighborhood, and aimlessly flicked the TV remote. It was nearing 4 p.m. on a Sunday and this was his weekend routine. Sometimes he would stick for a minute on a channel and watch twenty minutes of some 80's movie he had seen a few dozen times, reciting lines by memory. Overcome by pangs of nostalgia and depression, he would look for something more contemporary to fill his time. Nothing satisfied him. He yearned to get up from that couch and move somewhere else, but he could not force himself. Not that he didn't want to move. He did. He really wanted to do something; he just didn't have anything TO do. He had fewer and fewer friends, fewer and fewer interests, and fewer and fewer ways out of his malaise. He was a man with interests a mile wide and an inch deep. He never wrote his novel, but he wanted to. He never learned guitar, but he bought one. He never competed in a triathlon, but he had purchased expensive running shoes. The list of failures went on.

At forty-eight, he was morphing into a pathetic and lost creature. Circling the drain. When did it go wrong? He wasn't sure if his conversation with his parents that fateful night was the catalyst for everything going downhill, and he certainly didn't want to blame himself for his youthful ambitions. After all, if one doesn't have dreams as an 18-year-old with his whole life in front of him, then what the hell did one have? An 18-year-old without hopes and dreams? That's what one calls a failure in the making. But even failures had rituals that kept them motivated. As he curled up on the couch trying to tear himself away from his fifteenth viewing of *The Breakfast Club*, Victor realized that his good days were behind him, and that at some point in the past thirty years he had gone from believing that he was destined for greatness to knowing the only thing great about him was his ability to daydream and fantasize, and the reality of his destiny would be disappointment, failed hopes, and unrealized potential. Pitiful.

Chapter 2 * Lists

Victor rolled off the couch at about 10:30 at night, having spent the better part of twelve hours immersed in his melancholy. During that time span he did the following:

1. Watched three full movies.
2. Watched parts of eleven different movies.
3. Ate a super-sized bowl of chicken ramen.
4. Ate an entire Meat Lover's Frozen Pizza Supreme.
5. Smoked eighteen cigarettes, but it would have been more if he had not run out.
6. Drank two liters of diet cherry cola.
7. Spent an hour writing down witty retorts for arguments with people that would never occur.
8. Took two naps totaling one hundred and fifty minutes.
9. Took one bowel movement that was a struggle and caused some rectal bleeding.
10. Completed half of a level one sudoku puzzle.
11. Scanned Facebook throughout the entirety of the day. Looking at the lives of those he was "friends" with, seeing them enjoying their lives, and wondering why none of his "friends" ever called him, ever texted him, ever gave a shit about him.
12. Started his List

For Victor, the List was much more important than anything else in his life. He needed to create a way to motivate himself. If he had a List, something to hold him accountable, then he was likely to follow it. Even if he created new Lists every few weeks, when his self-loathing was at its nadir, he needed new ones to help motivate him and get him out of his rut. The fact that making a new List actually made him feel better was probably not a terrible thing, in and of itself. At least it got him to stand up and exercise his brain for a few minutes. So his new List that he cobbled together on the back of a fast-food bag at 10:42 p.m. on Sunday night was going to be the ultimate of Lists:

1. Start working out, at least three times per week.
2. Reduce smoking to no more than ten per day for the first week, five per day the second week and one per day, at the end of the day, for the indefinite future.
3. No more than two hours of TV per day (this does not include watching videos on the internet).
4. Take work more seriously. Try to convince people that your opinions matter and that you are the right guy for this position and maybe get the district manager to bring you on board in a bigger role. Remember, you were meant to do something great!
5. Try to do something more than watching a movie. How about flying a kite at the park? Or maybe go for a bike ride?
6. Replace tires on bike; buy a kite.
7. Stop being a LOSER!

He decided that seven goals at 10:42 on a Sunday night was ambitious enough. He didn't want to overcommit and underperform. That was for the losers of the world. Victor was the worst kind of loser, a self-hating loser. He should have been more sympathetic to the losers of the world, but to do so would firmly cement him in that world of Loserville and he wasn't quite there yet. Maybe another few months, another few pounds, another few clumps of missing hair, he'd be there, but now was not that time and until he had reached full loser maturity, he refused to admit defeat. He was going to make his last and final stand. Like Davy Crocket and Sam Bowie at the Alamo, he had to fight until the bitter end. But unlike Crocket and Bowie, he wasn't planning on losing the fight and dying. He was going to beat it back against all odds.

Even though the younger, more handsome, more charismatic men of the world were making people like him seem obsolete and unimportant, he wasn't going to give up. Damn them and their fun ski weekends in Vail, to hell with their co-ed softball games and barbeques. He didn't care, he would fight like hell against obsolescence and come out a better man! Shit, this was the American spirit people always rooted for, the guy who went from rags to riches, the older boxer who won a knock-out against the tougher, younger man. He was going to be the quintessential American success story and second-chance person. He just had to have a little taste of success, a nibble, and then it would be all change for him.

Sure, he was a little fatter, a little balder and still unable to grow more than a wisp of a sandy beard, no matter how hard he tried. But those were only his physical attributes that he believed held him back. For good measure he was also divorced from a woman who found just about every other human being on

Earth more interesting than himself and he was inexplicably tied into a job at a nursing home in accounts management that was beyond tedious. He had to get out of the rut and be the man his mom always thought he could be. He was committed to his List and getting back on top. He had had enough setbacks and the pendulum was going to swing back in the direction of Victor Alan Jones. Tomorrow was the beginning!

Chapter 3 * Can It Get Worse?

"Victor, I am not sure this is working out. I mean, your performance this quarter has been less than what we had expected when we did our team evaluation in the summer. I wish I had an answer," Mike Guidry stated as soon as Victor came into his office at nine on Monday morning. This was not exactly how Victor needed to begin the life-changing sequence he had so eloquently laid out on the back of the McDonalds bag the evening before.

"Mike, listen, I hear you, but that's not entirely fair," Victor said with false enthusiasm (not that he believed a word of that bullshit statement). "I have made a lot of positive changes in my communication and scheduling; I really don't think it's as bad as you think."

"Yeah, well, I'm not sure what that really means," Mike replied. "It sounds a bit vague and ambiguous. Can you be more specific?" (Mike knew he was asking for the impossible.)

"Well, let me ask you, HOW exactly has my performance been less than expected, as long as we are being vague and ambiguous?"

Guidry did not see that coming; Victor had turned the impromptu performance review into a cross-examination thrust back on the executioner. He sat up in the red leather chair and kept his eyes sharply on Guidry.

"Well..." Guidry stammered, sitting up in his black $1,200 multiple-function reclining boss chair, "well...it's just not great, that's the best I can tell you without divulging confidences." Damn it! Guidry was not supposed to counter, and he knew he should have been armed with a few specifics as to why he wanted to terminate Victor, but that mostly had to do with the man's general lackadaisical mannerism, poorly-fitted clothing, refusal to lose weight or quit smoking, and most of all, the hair. Yes, hair was big to Mike Guidry. Guidry himself was forty-seven years old and had GOOD hair. People understood GOOD hair. Thick, straight, manageable, with deep veins of black mixed into this perfectly-timed gray. His hair was so nice you just wanted to grab it and hold it and be envious of it. Cuddle it close to you like a sweet little puppy. A little pomade, slicked back, incredible. And guys with GOOD hair dominated the world. They simply dominated. Think Ronald Reagan, Brad Pitt, and Elvis Presley. Sure, a few bald guys snuck in there, but they had to be like Bruce Willis or Michael Jordan. Super handsome and charismatic with features that were accentuated by the bald pate. But Victor wasn't Michael Jordan or Bruce Willis.

"Confidences?!?" Victor spit out with a gasp. A little, tiny, almost invisible drop of spit landed on the end of Guidry's desk that Victor didn't notice, but oh boy, Guidry did. He looked away, hoping it would evaporate. Victor continued. "I mean, Mike, really? I've been with this company for twelve years, am I not entitled to a drop of honesty?"

Guidry shifted in his chair, a sure giveaway of his uneasiness. "Victor, calm down, I can see you are a little anxious today." This was the ultimate power play, to tell anyone to "calm down" immediately switched the conversation and made the person being asked to "calm down" to become defensive, as if the person stating "calm down" had some unseen power to arbitrate who was calm and who was being a raving lunatic.

"*Calm down?!*" Victor stammered. "Calm down, what the fuck man, calm down, why are you telling me to calm down, who the hell are you to tell anyone to calm down?!!" Victor noticed that he had stood up and that Guidry was still seated calmly in his chair, looking at the spectacle that was Victor Jones. Victor reluctantly took his seat.

"Mike, I love Cherry Knolls. I love the people we serve. I think I am good at my job. I'm not sure what the problem is." Victor didn't mean a word of it. He hated Cherry Knolls, hated the concept of being old, stuck in a wheelchair staring blankly at the walls, waiting for death. And he knew he sucked at his work because he hated his life so much. But he couldn't afford to lose this job, especially since item # 4 on his improvement List was do better at his job and try to get a promotion. Right now, he was headed in the opposite direction on Day 1 of the new List.

Guidry stared at Victor, hoping his smirk wouldn't betray what he was about to say. "I know you love this place (lie) and I know you love the residents here (lie, lie) but let's face it, you hate working here (truth). You know you have other things you want to do (truth)."

Victor gaped. "Are you firing me?"

"Well, what other options do I have if I feel that my account management director is not getting the job done?"

"In order to help answer that question, I still don't know what I have done wrong." This was the first honest thing Victor had said that morning. Guidry sat back in his chair, put his hands together, fingertip to fingertip under his chin to provide the illusion of someone deep in thought, closed his eyes and deeply inhaled. Victor waited patiently for the exhale. It took a few moments. Guidry slowly exhaled as if the answer had finally come to him. He opened his eyes and leaned forward to speak.

"I suppose Jerri and you could swap responsibilities for a while, see if having her mentor you could bring your performance up to par. But that would mean taking a reduction in salary."

What in the HOLY FUCK was going on that morning? It took Victor every ounce of strength, reserve and courage to not dive across the desk and grab hold of that gorgeous mane of hair and slam Mike Guidry's face into the credenza that housed little silver picture frames with photos of his happy, perfect wife and children enjoying a ski vacation in Aspen.

"Jerri?" Victor asked in a controlled tone.

"Yes, Jerri, she seems to really understand the new Cosmix computer management software, hell, she even has been training some of us in operations. Talented young lady, you could learn a thing or two from Jerri."

"Jerri has been here for eleven months, Mike. She just graduated from college. This isn't a career for her, she is padding her resume while she looks for bigger and better opportunities. I've been here twelve years. Twelve years! Do you know how it will look if she is my supervisor? She's fucking twenty-two years old!"

"Well, Victor, that's the problem with you, you don't take this job as seriously as Jerri does. In fact, you need to act like you are padding your resume, because you never know when you will need to create a new resume." Ouch, that was harsh, even for Mike. He continued before Victor could attack. "I'm not saying you need to draft your resume, just have an open mind. This young generation is pretty advanced coming out of college. We could all learn a thing or two from them."

That line would've taken on more resonance if Victor had known that Mike had been nailing Jerri for the past few months, but thankfully for Victor he didn't, as that would absolutely have been the straw.

He knew he was defeated; he knew that his life was headed in the opposite direction he desired. "When do you need to know if I will agree to this DE-motion?" Victor asked.

"How about tomorrow morning, will that work?" Guidry said in a tone that appeared convincingly magnanimous.

"Sure, Mike, sure." And with that Victor stood up and left the president's office. Another arrow into his pathetic, waste of a life. He needed to exit quickly because the tears weren't going to wait for his fat ass to leave the office.

While Mike Guidry and Victor Jones engaged in their routine discussion something bigger, much bigger, was going on in the world. The orbs were communicating. The orbs had all surfaced after the Basilicata earthquake and were being held by three separate individuals. But the spheres were antsy. They longed to be re-united. They were dogs spinning in circles eager to be taken out for a run. Every day they weren't re-united they would become more rebellious. The people in possession of the orbs couldn't sense their excitement yet because they were too far apart. Forty years had passed, and they were just waking up. While their human possessors could not sense the excitement building in the orbs, there were two groups that most definitely could—the Builders and the Dead. Two otherworldly adversaries that were fighting for space and control of the Afterlife. Archenemies that needed a living, human advocate to gather all three orbs and bury them, together. Without repeating the mistakes of the past. Without burying them individually, or in tandem. No, all three needed to be buried together, and whichever group controlled all three orbs would control the destiny of all the people who would ever walk on the face of the Earth and most of those who had been dead for centuries. The chase was most definitely on and the battle raged between the Builders and the Dead to secure the orbs: The PinonAstra, The Mule and the most coveted, The MonteGresso. Time was ticking and blood would be spilled. Lots and lots of blood remained to be spilled.

Chapter 4 * New Friends

Grandma Lucy was being escorted into the last place she would ever live. Grandma Lucy didn't necessarily want to be here at Cherry Knolls, but Grandma Lucy was a pragmatist. She was eighty-four years old, weighed about ninety-eight pounds and sometimes, when she laughed, she would pee herself. Not very dignified for the former all-American gymnast from the University of Alabama, but even former all-Americans get old and start to pee themselves. Not much you can do about the inelasticity of an bladder.

"Come on, Granny, let me help you." It was her youngest grandson Taylor. He pulled her arm and despite the fact that she didn't need the help, she gave in. But she gave him that look, the one that said, "Don't pull me, let me hold your arm." Taylor immediately noticed the look and converted the pull to a hold. He smiled. She smiled back. The whole family had come to help settle her in. They weren't happy about this move. They loved Grandma Lucy. They knew, however, that Grandma Lucy needed assisted living care and Cherry Knolls was considered the finest adult retirement community in the city. Cleaning out Lucy's apartment was quite simple; unlike many people her age, she did not have lots of stuff. She was of the mindset that one could be sentimental about certain items and it was acceptable to hold on to some special keepsakes. But there was a fine line between sentimentality and hoarding, and she believed hoarding to be atrocious behavior.

So here she stood, in front of room 218 at Cherry Knolls, with only a few suitcases of stuff. There were 27 Cherry Knolls communities throughout the country and they routinely were ranked somewhere in the top third of retirement communities in the nation. That wasn't too bad. Anyone who read the literature, would almost want to retire there: *At Cherry Knolls, we love your family like you love your family. 24-hour a day service and loving care. Games, arts and crafts, cooking activities, music, dancing and fun are in store for you. The Young at Heart live and thrive at Cherry Knolls.*

Sure, there was no pool, but Grandma Lucy didn't swim. There were no uneven bars, but gymnastics was more than sixty years ago, so that didn't matter. There was no golf course, but Grandma Lucy had never picked up a golf club for fun, although she had picked one up a few times to use as a weapon many years ago. And there were no men who were even remotely enticing to Grandma Lucy, but then again Grandma Lucy hadn't the interest or the patience for a man in many years. Really, all Grandma Lucy wanted was some decent hot food a few times a day, a sunny room where she could sit in a rocker and knit, and clean sheets on her bed. She insisted on having clean sheets. She could live in a roach-infested icebox with lousy food and mean nurses, as long as she had clean sheets. That's all Grandma Lucy insisted on at Cherry Knolls. As she crossed the threshold, this was her thought: They'll probably fuck this up.

"Right this way, Grandma." Taylor, that precious 18-year-old, allowed her to lead and they preceded an entourage of grandchildren and children and Cherry Knolls staffers as they meandered down the second-floor corridor, bags in tow, slowly making their way to room 218. Her final resting place. Stephen Glick, the assistant manager of that community, quickly sidled by Grandma Lucy and Taylor so he could unlock the door and welcome her into the palatial room.

"Come on in," came a little voice on the other side. Stephen opened the door wide and Lucy looked inside. She scanned the room, exhaling uneasily. Her family all started to tear up. Lucy saw the western exposure depositing copious amounts of heat and light into the room. Veiled light filaments of sunshine paraded amongst the two potted plants, TV and her new roommate.

The older woman—Grandma Lucy's new roommate—peered over her magazine at the people in the doorway. Beverly was witnessing the all too-common sight of a family dropping off a loved one, relinquishing their duties, and knowing that once the drop-off occurred, the visits would become less and less frequent. But the moment Beverly caught sight of Lucy she felt an intense and powerful burning in her temples. She dropped her magazine and started to rub her forehead vigorously. Her glasses slid off her nose and landed on the floor. All she could see was light. A powerful light. Something she had never experienced before. She couldn't even utter a simple "Hello." Instead, she let out a loud moan. The entire group rushed to her side as it was evident she was experiencing some type of medical condition.

Stephen kneeled down on one leg and grabbed Beverly's hand. It was warm and slightly moist. "Beverly, are you OK? Talk to me." The others watched as Stephen tried to help Beverly. Was it a stroke? That was common for elderly residents. The light and burning quickly subsided and she regained her composure. She let out a slight, sympathetic chuckle. "Thank you honey, you can stand up, I just got a little heartburn out of nowhere," she lied. "I'm so embarrassed, that's not a proper way to meet someone for the first time." She couldn't take her eyes off of Lucy.

"Beverly, can I call one of the nurses?" Stephen asked as he handed Beverly her glasses. "No sweetie, that's kind of you," Beverly replied. "I swear it was just a little gas." Stephen seemed to accept the excuse and was happy he didn't have summon a nurse. Not a great way to settle the nerves of a new resident. Gamely, he tried to smooth things over with introductions.

"Lucy, this is Beverly Griffin, and Beverly, this is Lucy Black." Grandma Lucy took a long look at Beverly and stated, "Well, I'm pleased to meet you. Nothing like a little excitement, I usually don't have that effect on people." Beverly let out a little laugh. "Oh, I am so sorry about that, Lucy, I don't want you to think you are moving in with trouble. I'm usually always feeling good. Don't know what overcame me." But she knew exactly what overcame her. The moment she laid eyes on Lucy Black she knew this was an extraordinary person. Someone she was destined to know and who would prove valuable to her.

Beverly was a chipper eighty-five-year-old black lady with beautiful bright red hair. She would swear to her kids the hair was really the color she came out of the womb with, but that particular shade of red, bordering on Ronald McDonald orange, was not of this Earth. No human made hair that bright in color.

"I'm going to let you all have some time here," Beverly said as she stood up, aided by her walker. "Somewhere down the hall a game of gin-rummy is waiting for me." She pulled her shawl tightly over her slight, hunched-over shoulders and scooted out as fast as the little tennis balls on the bottom of her walker would take her. But before she left the room, she put her right hand on Lucy's face, closed her eyes and smiled. "Oh child, I'm so glad to have you here."

Grandma Lucy's family parted down the middle to let Beverly escape and smiled at her. "Oh, just like Moses, crossing the Red Sea, the waters parted," Beverly said with a smile as she made her way down the corridor to the Common Room. Lucy looked down the hall at Beverly's retreating form. She could still feel the soft skin of Beverly's hand on her cheek; it was warm, and she felt strangely liberated from her family and very much tuned into this strange old lady with the bright orange hair.

Chapter 5 ∗ Advertising Is Life

"Have you been injured through no fault of your own?!" the man screamed into the TV camera while he held a two-foot long custom-made samurai sword high above his head, his long goatee hair swaying in the wind.

"I will do to these insurance companies what they have done to you. I will make them suffer!" And with that Bingham "The Knife" Cutler unsheathed his sword and in one swift motion slashed a five-foot tall piñata of a man in a suit with a frown and evil pointed eyebrows with a sign across his chest, saying, "Insurance Company" and he slit that son of a bitch right in two. And once the insurance man was sliced in half, hundreds of dollars blew out of him, some being quickly taken by the wind, to the immediate concern of Bingham. "I will cut them in half and make them pay…you can always trust me…I'm Bingham "The Knife" Cutler, and I'll cut the insurance companies down to size. Find me on-line at TheKnifeLawyer.com."

"CUT!" Bingham screamed. "Whose fucking idea was this to do this scene outside on a windy day?" He pointed at his production staff, oblivious that he still had the sword in his hand. "There is money flying all over the place! Can someone grab those dollar bills, please!?"

"Um… Bingham, those are hundreds" stammered the production assistant as she ran around grabbing them as quickly as possible.

"Who in the fuck said to use hundreds?" shouted Bingham, chasing after the money. All the crew and assistants looked panicked as they plucked hundred dollar bills out of bushes, trees and video equipment on set of the shoot.

"You did! Jesus Christ, Bing, you said it would give an air of authenticity. Who wants dollar bills for their accident? They want hundred-dollar bills…I think that's exactly what you said." It was Sheila Evans, Bing's paralegal who suffered a lot, but didn't suffer fools. And her boss was the Fool's Fool.

Bingham was scared of no man, or woman, but damn if Sheila didn't rattle him to his core. "Well, why did we use so many? There's like $5,000 out here, hurry people!" Bingham pleaded now, realizing that frightening people wouldn't lead to their assistance, so as usual, he pulled an about face. "Thanks all for helping me get these."

"Um, we actually have $7,300 out there," the production assistant offered sheepishly, knowing things would get worse. "You said you wanted the explosion of the insurance adjuster to be huge and make a statement."

"For fuck's sake, please people, please hurry!" And just as Bingham said that a groundswell of wind shot in from the south and several thousand dollars made their way to Wyoming or Montana or maybe even Canada. As he watched the bills soar upwards, all Bingham could think was: gifts from your neighbors in Denver.

"Well, that is such a suck fest. Tell me you at least got the shot?" Bingham asked the director, "Pretty-Boy" Rob Anderson. Rob peered into his video screen and smiled and offered a thumbs up. Pretty-Boy Rob was sure handsome, but his timing was even better. Dude was the king of personal injury TV commercials, having shot them all over the country. He was the best in the business.

The director slicked back his perfectly coiffed gray hair and tied it together in quite a heinous man-bun. Even so, he was still "Pretty-Boy" Rob. A man-bun does not make you un-handsome, it only makes you look like an asshole. He wasn't an asshole by any stretch, but perceptions mattered.

"We got it, Knife!" Rob stated. Rob insisted on calling all of his personal injury lawyer customers by their ridiculous self-monikers. The Bear. The Shark. The Muscle. Big Red. Big Mike. The Barracuda. The King of Torts. The Insurance Assassin. The Grizz. Iron Arm Johnny. On and on these insane, clown names went. But his clients loved being called by their asinine names, and as long as they paid their bills, he would call them anything they damn well wanted. Most of these lawyers hadn't worked on a case, let alone seen a courtroom, in over decade, yet they minted money by peddling their half-assed lawyer credentials to a mass market of idiots who believed that Bingham "The Knife" Cutler would be a better choice to represent them in their serious motor vehicle case. Surely, someone like Cutler would have the ability to slice through a paper maché piñata of a vaguely indiscernible person titled "Insurance Company" and poof, thousands of dollars would magically appear.

"Hurry, get those little suckers before they get on the road!" Knife pleaded with anyone who could hear. He ran after the bills but forgot he was still holding an unsheathed, two-foot samurai sword, and barely missed decapitating his young production assistant.

"Whoaaa, Knife! Settle down, you don't want this commercial shoot to end in tragedy." It was Rob, looking cool and comfortable behind his aviators and tightly buttoned denim shirt. It was hard for Bingham not to resent the director's suave good looks. Damn, he should have used "Pretty-Boy" Rob's face in his advertisements instead of his own. "People, drop what you're doing and help collect that cash," Rob shouted to his crew. They rolled their eyes, shot a curt look at Rob, and chased after this idiot's money.

Ten minutes later Bingham clutched a handful of wrinkled dirty bills. He started shoving them in every pocket of his even more ridiculous leather Wild Bill Hickok coat that was besieged on all ends by long fringes and other accoutrement more appropriate for 1875 than 2020. He fancied himself a cowboy and wore cowboy attire. But the sartorial choice clashed with the samurai ninja thing he had going on. The Knife, a mish-mosh of clownish characters, had actually come to believe that he was some sort of modern-day Robin Hood, protecting the injured masses from the Sheriff of Nottingham.

"Thanks everyone for helping out," Rob yelled to the crew and Bingham's legal entourage. "You all earned some beer." He reached into the pile of ruffled money clenched in the hands of The Knife and yanked two of the hundred dollar bills free. He handed them to Charlene, his sound engineer. "Go over to Newman's down the street and buy the first few rounds," he ordered. He was classy too, that "Pretty-Boy" Rob.

Once she and most of the crew had scattered, Rob turned to Bingham. "So that went well, despite the money, I think we got most of it."

"I lost $1200," Bingham moaned. "Not to mention the $200 you just donated for drinks."

"Oh Bing, don't worry your pretty little fringes, you'll clear a million this year I bet, consider it donations to the needy," Sheila said without missing a beat. She turned to Rob. "The big question is when will this be done, along with the other three commercials in post-production? We need to get fresh material on air. We are starting to get hammered by Hank "The Hammer" Goldberg. His stuff is so raw and poignant." Sheila tried to muffle a laugh.

"Two weeks tops. And then we need to discuss next year's budget," Rob said. "I think next year we go huge. I'm talking two new commercials a month, along with a host of on-line ads. I think you need to step it up if you are going to compete with some of these characters." If Bingham "The Knife" hated being called a "character," he gave no sign. He was worried about money, not his TV persona.

"Yeah, well easy for you to say," Bingham said, his eyes downcast. "My investments haven't gone well this year. This year has sucked. The insurance carriers have been fighting back more and more and that's eating into my profits. I think I have to consider tightening up the budget." That's not what Rob wanted to hear, although several of his clients were saying the exact same thing. Bingham still had plenty of cash, but he was tight.

"My friend, that means you need to double down," Rob countered. "Now is the time to take over the legal TV advertising world. Corner the market. If you own the market it doesn't matter what the insurance companies do, they have to negotiate with you if you have all the business. Don't you see? Sure, you might have to settle the cases for a little less, but if you have all the cases it doesn't matter! And who can get them cash faster than The Knife?" Bingham sat and contemplated that message. He had to admit that Rob's hair was very nice all slicked back and tucked into a bun, and his teeth were white and looked even whiter with those sunglasses. Yes, Rob was a person who should be heeded. After all, handsome people were more successful and credible than their plainer counterparts. And being a forty-year-old short man with a goatee and a birthmark under his right eye, he would never be mistaken for a "Pretty-Boy." He knew it was important to listen to the good-looking people. He really wanted to be charming and beloved. But his personality was the opposite of charming. It was caustic and loud. And Bingham didn't exactly have a light touch either. He wanted to be seen as charming so badly that he would beat people over the head with his overpowering, look-at-me personality. It always backfired.

"OK Rob, you know best. Let's meet next week to talk about bigger and more obnoxious personal injury advertising. I'll double down. But I need good ideas from you. Something really stupid. Something that really makes lawyers blush and roll their eyes to know that they are in the same profession as me. Who would have thought that the only thing that separates me from the US Supreme Court Justices is a complete lack of interest in the law and 1,800 miles?"

What a joke he and the rest of the advertising lawyers were. They may have laughed all the way to the bank, but by and large they were the laughingstock of the legal world. Their kids were teased at school because their parents' ads were so offensive. The attorneys were never considered for any legal awards through the bar associations, and they were universally mocked by judges, law professors, and other practicing lawyers. Most advertising lawyers would say the money was worth it, but these days even The Knife was starting to think twice. It can get tiring being mocked. Maybe something, someday, would help him change the way people thought of him and instead of laughing at him, people would respect him. Well, maybe not respect, but at least his image wouldn't make people start laughing uncontrollably. He had to admit he caused a certain visceral reaction, and it was usually a bad reaction.

No one respected the advertising lawyer. Not even their parents. Yes, respect. One day he'd get respect.

Chapter 6 ＊ Resignation

It was early September in Denver, which meant that it was either really hot or snowing. One never knew what the weather gods would provide. What one did know was that the weather changed rapidly so if the weather was not to one's liking, the best advice was to go back inside, wait a few hours, and then voila! It would be better, or worse, depending on what it was one desired. Victor liked the cold. That wasn't much of a surprise. Overweight introverts with few friends generally liked the colder weather. It was an opportunity to wear a sweater, stay at home, and avoid people. It's not like Victor had a lot of people to see. No BBQ invites or volleyball games at the park awaited him. But in all fairness, Victor made no effort to get involved. So he prayed for snow. He was comfortable staying secluded in his den. It made life seem less disappointing.

On this particular mid-September day, the clouds had parted, and Denver was enjoying an 85-degree day. Dry and hot—exactly the opposite of what Victor was hoping for. He stared blindly at the computer screens in front of him. He was into day number two of his demotion and tutorship under the great and benevolent Jerri Hughes. Jerri was twenty-two years old, fresh out of college and apparently the master of the new computer database. How did his List get derailed so fast?

"So, doesn't that make sense?" Jerri chirped. "It's an account adjustment based on a Medicaid subsidy that is designed to true up the monthly balance. Type Control F and it will automatically download the current Medicaid subsidies for the month. It's completely automatic." Jerri smiled as she rattled off this formula from the Cosmix training manual she had all but memorized.

"Right? Victor? Doesn't that make more sense? Victor?"

Victor had been daydreaming and zoned out several minutes earlier. Now he turned to his side to look at Jerri, who had pulled her chair next to his desk and was rat-tat-tatting on his keyboard.

"Oh, yes. That makes a lot more sense. What was I thinking?" Victor had no idea what she was talking about. He could not stand this new computer system, Cosmix, it was so annoying. He imagined a Pac-Man chasing down Mike Guidry on the screen and gobbling him up. He smiled and giggled under his breath.

"What's so funny?" Jerri asked.

Victor quickly sat up and shook off his fog. "Oh, nothing, Jerri. Thanks for this update. I used to pull up the Medicaid subsidiaries directly from the Medicaid website for the state, but this Control F, wow. Now that is a difference maker! I think this Cockmix, uh excuse me, Cosmix program, yes that seems to be a game-changer."

Jerri blushed but ignored Victor's faux pas. He was the least threatening human she had ever met. "I think you are really getting the hang of this," she said. "Are there any other issues you want to discuss?"

Victor sucked up his pride, thought about item #4 on his list ("Take Work More Seriously"), and politely shook his head. "No thanks, not right now, Jerri. But I appreciate you helping us old timers. I remember when I started here, we had to actually call Medicaid and ask for the numbers. And if we got a busy signal, we had to stop our work until the line cleared."

"What's a busy signal?"

Victor knew she wasn't being a smart-ass; she really didn't know. Damn millennials, or was she Generation Z? It was all very confusing for a Gen-X'r. "Oh nothing, just something we used to have to deal with. Thankfully that's a thing of the past. I'll buzz you later for more help."

Jerri left his office and Victor shut the door. He went back to his chair. He could still smell the perfume or body spray or just cleanliness associated with Jerri Hughes. It lingered. But it lingered in a good way. A dreamy way. A woman like Jerri would never voluntarily sit next to someone like Victor and actually talk to him. Victor knew that if not for work they would never associate in any fashion. One might call that insecurity, but in Victor's world that insecurity was a reality. He hated the demotion, but working next to such a beauty blunted some of the pain. He might as well make lemonade out of his lemons—or hers. Hell yes, he would! The new Victor Jones was emerging, growing up. He even planned to take a jog went he got home, in the sun, in the heat. How NON-Victor Jones that was?

He leaned sideways in his chair and let a huge fart rip. He had been clenching his cheeks for about 30 minutes while Jerri sat right next to him. And just like that, he neutralized the lovely Jerri Hughes smell that had been wafting through his office. It was like his ass just did a full body take down of Jerri Hughes in less than one second. How sad. But not as sad as the fact that Jerri had left her notepad in his office and she walked right back in without even knocking.

The odor overtook her instantly. She froze. Her right eye jerked spasmodically and she frowned, as if repressing a powerful reaction. Touched by her tact, Victor jumped up, grabbed the notebook, and escorted her out of the office as casually as possible. Oh, nothing to see or smell here, officer. She beat it down the hallway.

Victor closed the door to his tiny office. At his desk, he contemplated writing a letter of resignation. Not only had he been demoted and replaced by a twenty-two-year-old right out of college, but she was very cute and now she had succumbed to his colonic issues. The only way it could have been worse was if she had actually heard him break wind, but the aftermath was pretty daunting, even without the audio assist. Maybe Mike Guidry was right, maybe it was time for a fresh start. Maybe passing gas was part of god's plan. Maybe he needed to look at this as an opportunity. A real chance to change things up. He was proud of himself. Get out of this dead-end career and pursue his passion, whatever that was. It wasn't the smartest thing to quit a job with no other job in the wings, but maybe it was time! Who else but Victor Jones could be inspired by ripping a profoundly obnoxious fart and having a beautiful young lady walk right into the cloud? Instead of the expected sadness and desperation, he was morbidly invigorated by it. This could be the kind of flatulence that would SAVE and CHANGE his life for the better. This tooting would not sideline him! Ask not what you can do for your colon, ask what your colon can do for you! This was the day of excellence.

Victor smiled. He thought about how he could tell Mike Guidry he was voluntarily resigning. That would feel better than being fired. He could leave with his head held high. But of course, reality quickly took over and the idea of being his age, without a job and very little in savings made him nauseous. Sometimes reality interrupted a really good daydream. As he started to clean up his desk his phone rang. "Victor, it's Stephen Glick."

"Yes Stephen, what's up?"

"Can you do me a favor? Yesterday we moved a Lucy Black into 218 with Beverly Griffin. It was an odd move in as Beverly had some sort of medical issue—"

Victor cut him off. "Medical issue? Is she okay?" Victor loved Beverly. He found her funny and sweet. Most of the guests were sweet to Victor because he treated them as adults and not like children.

"No, she is fine, she had a little gas," Stephen stated. Victor chuckled to himself, gas seemed to be everywhere at Cherry Knolls.

"Anyway, we want to have someone from administration go over a few forms with Lucy that she didn't sign due to the commotion. Can you handle that for me? The forms are up front at reception."

Victor didn't mind meeting with the guests, which didn't happen a lot, but he resented the managers always having him do things they were too lazy to do. However, it seemed like a nice way to escape the administrative offices for a bit and air out the room. Good karma could only come from this, and everyone needed a little good karma. "OK, OK, I got it. Room 218."

Chapter 7 ∗ Change Of Course?

Victor put down his pen, stood up, and gave himself a good stretch. It was almost noon and his stomach was grumbling. He pushed his chair out from under him and made his way out of the executive offices to reception and grabbed the paperwork. He headed to the residential wing of Cherry Knolls. This was the largest of all the Cherry Knolls facilities with over 800 residents.

Because this was the biggest of the Cherry Knolls communities, most of the national management team worked out of the Denver facility, running operations for residential facilities all over the country. There was a small New York City office where the CEO and much of the primary ownership team resided, but Denver handled the bulk of the work. It really was an impressive organization that made caring for senior citizens its mission and it did do a damn good job. Even if it made Victor crazy that Mike Guidry received all of that praise, the proof was in the balance sheet and more importantly, in the reviews they received not only from family members and residents, but also from state regulators around the country who consistently found Cherry Knolls to be among the best senior care facilities. This was evaluated by price, cleanliness, mortality (yes facilities lost points if their tenants died), activities and so on. So, while Victor couldn't stand the management, he was proud of his contributions to making these facilities run well, providing these residents some comfort while they were finishing up their final few holes on the golf course of life.

He turned the corner and approached the residential center. He saw a food cart pressed against the wall for deliveries to those residents who were too ill to make it to the cafeteria. He spied a container of green Jell-O and snagged it without anyone seeing him. He even managed to grab the plastic spoon all in one felonious swipe. He ripped off the foil top and inhaled the green substance in three bites and tossed the mess into one of the trash containers in the hall. He cruised the remaining expanse of hallway, walked up the stairs at the end of the hall and turned the corner to room 220, 219 and yes, 218. Ms. Black. Yes, Ms. Black. Cherry Knolls' newest resident. He hoped she was kind. Many residents weren't kind. But it was hard to blame them. Dropped off to live with people they didn't know, away from their families, stowed away, waiting to die. Of course they were cranky. Room 218's door was ajar. Lucy was sitting on her bed looking through some old picture book. Victor gently rapped on the door. "Knock, knock," he said.

Lucy looked up from her bed. "Come on in." She set the book down and turned to Victor. Immediately she was struck by a strong sense of déjà vu. It was the oddest thing. Victor saw the confused look on her face and he, too, was overcome by a sense that he had been in that exact same place before and had talked to Lucy Black at another time. But he knew that was impossible because he had never met Lucy Black, he was sure of it.

"Ms. Black, hello, I'm—" But before he could state his name, she responded. "You are Victor Jones. From administration." Victor was floored. How did she know this? "How did you know that?"

Lucy shot him a small grin. "Well, because Mr. Glick said he was sending Victor Jones from administration up here to have me sign some papers." Victor smiled and nodded. "Occam's Razor wins again."

"Who's Razer?" Lucy asked.

"Occam's Razor, it's the theory that the simplest explanation is usually the right answer." It was one of Victor's few strengths; he could recall bizarre trivia.

"I hate to be the wet blanket, but this ain't got nothing to do with no Occam's razer. This is destiny, my sweet friend." Victor looked over his shoulder to see who was talking. Beverly was standing right behind him, hands gripped on her walker.

"Hello there, Beverly. Nice to see you. Just came up to give Ms. Black some papers to sign." Victor handed the paperwork to Lucy, who immediately placed them on her bed without looking at them.

"Victor, the circle is now complete. We can go on to the next stage." Beverly walked past him and sat down on her well-worn rocker. Lucy and Victor both looked at Beverly with quizzical looks. Circle complete? What was that?

"Beverly, I know we just met, but what the heck are you talking about?" Lucy asked as she stood staring at Victor. She knew this man, but how? From where?

When Beverly gestured for Victor to close the door, he obliged. He too had no clue what was happening in that instant, but he knew something required an explanation. Beverly pulled off her glasses and spoke. "Victor Jones, I can't believe you have been here this whole time, I never was able to see that. But it required Lucy Black to join, to form the yin to your yang." She rubbed her eyes. "Stay with me, people, I'm not losing my mind, there is a point to this."

Lucy and Victor looked cautiously at Beverly. Was she having a stroke?

Was that what happened yesterday? Beverly sat upright. "You see, the world is more complicated than you have ever imagined. I suppose you are both looking at each other, wondering why you both seem so familiar to one another even though you've never met. Am I right?"

Victor could feel his own head throbbing. What was going on? But Lucy looked closely at Beverly, deeply into her eyes, and nodded. Her eyes were welling up with tears. Why? Something intense and unusual was happening. Beverly continued. "There are more mysteries to this world than any of us know. And I don't just mean the here and now while we live, I mean when we die. There are mysteries that we won't understand or comprehend until we are six feet under, or turned to ash, and that's not anyone's fault, it's just not what the universe intended for us. But believe me"—she paused for effect— "believe me when I say there is much, much more that you don't know but you will soon, you will." She rubbed her temples again as if she had a migraine coming on. "It wasn't until Lucy Black came into my world that the pieces came together. You two"—she pointed at Lucy and Victor— "you two, together, are the key. THE combination, forty years in the making, and who would have guessed?" Beverly emphasized the word "the" but that did not answer any questions for Victor or Lucy. They both stared at Beverly, their mouths slightly agape. Victor made an attempt to say something, but he was quickly cut off by Beverly.

"I know this sounds crazy, I know you are going to try and put me into the dementia wing of this place but believe me when I say that the two of you, together, will save the souls of millions and millions of people who have died and have yet to die," she said. "You both must be strong, and open-minded, and I promise you, the reward will be worth it." And with that comment she put her glasses back on and grabbed a magazine on the side table, starting to read it as nonchalantly as if she were sitting in the dentist's office.

But Victor was worried. Should he summon a nurse? That was about as strange of a speech as he had heard in a long time. He and Lucy looked at each other and raised their eyebrows. But they didn't say anything.

"You know what, Victor? I don't need a nurse, but I could sure use a nice hot cup of tea," Beverly murmured as she flipped through her magazine. Victor scratched his head. He would be happy to fetch her some tea, and maybe some Prozac.

"The thing is, Beverly, well, I'm not entirely sure what you are talking about, and I agree Lucy looks familiar, but I don't think I am the person you are looking for. In fact, I am thinking I may be leaving Cherry Knolls pretty soon. So maybe there is someone else you want to talk to?" Victor tried to be sensitive, to speak slowly and clearly, because many of the residents were starting to lose some of their cognitive strength.

"Don't you worry your precious little head about leaving Cherry Knolls," Beverly told him tartly. "We have more pressing matters and time is of the essence. That is, if you care about the fate of humanity, the existence of our Afterlife and our very souls. If not, then go ahead, quit your job, write your letter of resignation, and we will let the world cave in on itself, the billions dead unable to rest in eternal peace. A horrific fate for those who have died, all done forever and ever in the blink of an eye." Was she teasing him? No. And how did she know about the letter of resignation? Now she was frowning as she flipped through the pages. An awkward silence filled the room, then Grandma Lucy broke the mood.

"Oh honey, is it just me or am I going a little crazy?"

"You are most definitely not crazy or going crazy," Beverly replied, eyes still on the magazine. "You wouldn't be one of the chosen ones if you were crazy, believe me!" Victor knew Beverly well and he didn't think she was going crazy. In fact, she was behaving as she always did—with a solid grasp of reality. She had been a resident at Cherry Knolls for almost five years. She had few family members who came to visit so she spent most of her time knitting and watching TV. She was one of the most recognizable faces there, and she was not a resident with a dementia diagnosis.

"Ok, Beverly. You got me," Victor said, shooting his hands to the ceiling in a gesture of submission. "You know today is September 17th, not April 1st, right?"

Little Grandma Lucy tilted her head and looked at Victor. She guessed she'd play along as well. What a strange first few days at this retirement home. "OK, I'll bite," she said. "What is happening that will end the world and how can I, Lucy Black, an ancient southern belle, assist in saving the world?"

Beverly put down her magazine, removed her glasses once again, and summoned both Lucy and Victor to get closer. She kept her voice low. "If you are willing to believe me, or at least humor me a little, then Victor, I need you to pick up something for me, something on the outside." She motioned out the window, like she was a prisoner. "Bring it back here tonight, at midnight, and you will see what I am talking about."

Victor regretted saying that he was agreeing to do anything, but what could he do now? Well, he didn't exactly have a full social calendar, so he threw up his hands again in surrender. "Okay Bev, you got it. I'll come back tonight, at midnight. What do you need to me to pick up for you?" He couldn't believe this.

She reached into her shawl pocket and pulled out a small envelope that was sealed. On the front was written "Victor Jones." A shiver went down his spine as he reached for the envelope. Lucy shivered too. Inexplicably, goosebumps rippled across her chest. What an odd experience this was. Beverly grabbed Victor's arm. "Don't open it until you leave this place; the directions are all enclosed. And don't tell anyone about this." She squeezed his hand. "Do you understand?"

Victor stared back at her. "I won't tell anyone," he said numbly.

"I mean it, Victor, swear to me, swear to me the contents of that letter will be kept secret, and when you are done burn the note." This was getting ridiculous, but Beverly seemed as serious as a heart attack, so again Victor swore to her to keep this message secret and burn it after he read it. "Yes, Yes, Beverly, I promise." He held his hand up as if swearing on a Bible, but what else could he do to convince her? Beverly motioned for him to get closer. "Everyone needs to be tested to know they can handle their moment of crisis," she hissed. "You are a hero, Victor Jones; the world depends on you."

And with that she politely gestured for him to leave. And he couldn't leave fast enough.

Chapter 8 * Coffeeshops Are Dope

Bingham, Rob and Sheila decided against joining the rest of the entourage at Newman's and instead found their way into a quaint, hipster coffeeshop. The seats were mostly all taken at 3 p.m. by budding artists, writers, or entrepreneurs feverishly cooking up some app that would allow them to achieve financial independence and avoid the hard work that generally goes along with life. Bingham snagged one of the remaining tables and sat down, giving his order to Rob and Sheila. Rob needed a few minutes away from Bingham as the attorney was being more annoying than usual. Rob could handle annoying. Today, however, Bingham was caustic, rude, and annoying. The triple threat.

"Good lord, what is up your boss's ass today?" Rob whispered to Sheila as they stood at the busy counter, waiting to place their orders. "It was his stupid idea to load that piñata with hundred-dollar bills." Sheila shot Rob a knowing smile. Sheila Lucero was a fourth generation Colorado native whose family grew up in the beautiful San Luis Valley, about four hours south of Denver. Her father, grandfather and great-grandfather had herded cattle and horses on their ranch. They were Hispanic, proud and tired of the nouveau riche folks flocking to her state. She remembered when Denver had a slower pace and white people and Hispanic natives generally got along pretty well. It wasn't until the past few years that there was a scourge of prejudice against Hispanics. She found it funny that the assholes telling the Hispanics to go home hadn't lived in Colorado since 1880, as her family had. Most had moved to Colorado in the past 20 years from places like Los Angeles, Chicago and Dallas, virtually doubling the population of the state. Flooding into Denver, they caused the price of housing to skyrocket, jammed up the highways up to the mountains, and made even the simplest commutes around town unbearable. These foreigners literally took over Denver and acted like they had lived there for generations, but all they had done was caused a very chill and relaxed city to become another big, crowded metropolis full of whining millennials and microcraft breweries.

Sheila married a white man and took his last name, Evans, but she was a Lucero through and through. Her husband had died several years earlier of non-Hodgkin's Lymphoma but she kept the name Evans. She still missed him every day and had yet to close that door and experience the second phase of her life. She had beautiful black hair, light brown skin and was in excellent physical shape. No one who met her thought she was forty-five years old. She constantly was hit on, not just because she was a female, but because she was a smart, pretty, athletic, female. The true triple threat.

If Rob wasn't in a serious relationship, he would have asked her out a long time ago. Who knows, maybe she might have been interested. He was also the true triple threat: Handsome, funny and charismatic, man bun and all. People liked being around him, listening to him. He was trusted. That was something in short supply, especially since he made his money writing and directing commercials for probably the lowest rung of society: the lying, ethically-challenged, TV-advertising, ambulance-chasing lawyer.

"I don't know what his problem is," Sheila replied. "I've worked for him for ten years. He is an ornery son of a bitch. He just wanted to flaunt his money. That was his fault." Sheila knew Bingham inside and out. She couldn't stand him at times, but she thought deep, deep down he had a good heart. But that was pretty deep. Her boss lacked humor. It wasn't that he was too serious; she knew lots of serious people who also were inherently warm and funny. He either was too boring to be funny, or he just lacked that character trait. But he masked his sense of inadequacy by always having to be the smartest and loudest. That combination was painful to be around. He was also arrogant. He was arrogant for no particular reason other than he was wealthy. That's the worst kind of arrogance. Financial arrogance. Someone actually thinks because they make more money than someone else that their opinion is more valid, and their existence is more necessary than those of a lower income bracket. Sheila tolerated him because she was well paid, and she never could have made that type of money at any other law firm.

But it wasn't just about the money. She was able to direct a lot of firm resources to charities that she believed in and Bingham gave her free reign. Almost all the TV lawyers touted their charitable giving, it was the one way to make the average TV viewer partially tolerate the commercials. Usually, the commercials just made people physically ill, but there had been a recent trend, with the law firms touting all the charities they supported. Perhaps it was an attempt to make these hucksters appear a little more human. Bingham didn't donate a lot, but Sheila was in charge and she forced more and more money out of her usually tight-fisted boss every year. She had helped many multi-generational family farms in the San Luis Valley survive economic hardships with her donations from The Bingham 'The Knife' Cutler Family Trust. For that reason, alone, she would stick it out, but that didn't mean she liked the guy.

The guy behind the coffee counter had tattoos running up one arm, hair slicked back into a bun, skinny jeans and a Rolling Stones T-shirt. He was white, thirty-ish, and Rob pegged him as a liberal arts college graduate who would rather make $10 an hour serving expensive lattes in a coffeehouse than $15 to $20 an hour in a warehouse because he looked down on that type of work, considering it beneath him. Of course, working in a coffeehouse was not exactly the ticket to financial security. Annoying hipsters. The millennials were over-tattooed and underemployed and apparently it was everyone's fault but theirs. Rob saw a neck tattoo creeping up from the Rolling Stones T-shirt. That was a sure-fire way to guarantee one would work in a coffeeshop the rest of one's life. He rolled his eyes. "Three vanilla lattes, my friend."

The barista, aka dude who poured the coffee, wrote down that complicated order and turned to start the complex process of steaming milk and adding in vanilla syrup and espresso. Wow, Rob was impressed. This dude definitely deserved a fat tip. When Rob only deposited $2 into the jar, he caught a nasty glare from the barista. Like $2 was not enough of a tip. Maybe he imagined the smarmy look. Probably not. Rob made a mental note to ditch the man bun once and for all. He couldn't risk looking like this d-bag. They grabbed their overpriced coffee and sat down, huddled amongst the playwrights, novelists, wanna-be Instagram celebrities and other unemployed riff raff.

"Coffeeshops are dope," Rob uttered. "Where else can you find a large group of underemployed people who refuse to work hard for a living but think we are a bunch of assholes for not tipping thirty percent for a cup of coffee? They look down on us. Isn't that hysterical? People with jobs who aren't afraid of a little hard work. Good luck with your generation, pal." Rob sounded more bitter than normal. It had been a long day. Bingham found himself agreeing with Rob.

"They are all a bunch of entitled assholes," he said, "but hey, that's my market. As soon as one of them is in a car accident all their high-minded morals and ethics go by the wayside and it's 'fuck that asshole that hurt me. I want his money!'" The Knife might not have been the sharpest, but he knew his demographic pretty well.

"OK, so for your next series of commercials I think we start to get more of your former clients on tape," Rob said. "Let them sing your praises. Obviously, you have a large group of clients to draw from that would definitely be willing to go on camera and say how much you helped them and changed their life for the better. That is the new gold standard in the personal injury commercial world." Rob highlighted the word 'gold' with air quotes.

The director sipped his pretty fucking good latte and continued. "So, I've got this crew reserved for another week, can you please get me some clients? I can start shooting as soon as tomorrow. You don't even need to be there."

"Clients? Testifying on camera? Telling the world how awesome I am and how much I helped them? What about more outrageous antics from The Knife instead?"

Rob suppressed a shudder. "No more antics," he said firmly. "Getting clients to give references on air shouldn't be a big deal, you can get testimonials, right? Former pleased clients? I'd like to give this a try instead of the obnoxious Knife parodies, just to test it out." Rob suddenly sensed the tension. Sheila and Bingham looked at each other blankly, as if trying to recall any satisfied clients who would be willing to testify on behalf of The Knife. Bingham looked pained.

"Sure, Rob, that shouldn't be too tough," he temporized. "I think I need a few days though; I have to review confidentiality agreements and then narrow down the long list of great candidates."

Rob nodded. "Oh, and if possible, try and make these your good-looking clients, OK? People looking for attorneys want to be associated with good-looking people. Right? If good-looking people are happy with you, then less-attractive people will want your services. The less-attractive want to be a part of whatever good-looking people are doing." Rob talked as if he had a Ph.D. in human behavior.

"Even if those good-looking people are complete dumbasses?" Sheila responded. The fact that less-attractive people would be desperate to associate with more attractive people, regardless of intelligence, made her skin crawl. But of course, she knew that was the case. It wasn't just the society they lived in. It was straight up human nature and genetics.

Rob went on. "Oh yes. Basic psychology. Ask the barista up there; I'm sure he's studied it. And don't blame me, I didn't invent the concept of using attractive people for commercials. Find me one commercial that doesn't have reasonably attractive people."

"Not a problem. We will start the calls as soon as we get back to the office," Bingham exclaimed. He powered down the rest of his latte and stood up to leave. If he had to find satisfied clients, he had better get on the phone now and start calling.

The sun was starting to set. The earlier warmth of the day had dissipated; Denver was settling into fall. The Knife threw on his jacket and waved goodbye to Rob and Sheila, still sipping their lattes. Satisfied, attractive former clients willing to go on TV and lie for Bingham. This was not going to be easy. Bingham jumped in his car and hightailed it for his office.

Chapter 9 ✳ Confusion

Victor's mind was reeling. As he walked back to his office, he didn't notice anyone or anything. He had his hand in his pocket, firmly gripping the envelope. While he was suspicious of Beverly's comments, something most definitely happened up in room 218. It wasn't just Beverly's warning, but the intense feelings of connection with Lucy Black. And he knew she sensed it too. There was no faking that overarching sense of déjà vu. He noticed the time and realized he had several more hours of work before he could split and read whatever was contained in the envelope. And then he was expected to burn it of course.

He rubbed his hand through his remaining hair and made his way out a side door into the employee parking lot. He needed a smoke. He never smoked at work. He knew that people knew he smoked, but he didn't like to be seen smoking at work. People looked down on the day-smoker. People smoking at bars or parties was one thing. But the day-smoker who blasted out of the office four or five times a day to grab a smoke, even in the rain or snow, well, those people were addicts and people looked down on addicts. Yet the day-smoker, in certain settings, was privy to office gossip and other interesting details that were generated by other day-smokers. But Cherry Knolls didn't have many other day-smokers. Right now, he didn't care if someone saw him wrapping a belt around his arm and tearing a hole in his vein. He did not care what anyone thought.

Victor found an isolated wall he could lean against and lit up. The nicotine immediately calmed him and helped him gather his thoughts. What if the note was complete gibberish? Or what if Beverly wanted him to do something illegal? What did she mean by 'moment of crisis'?" He made a decision that if there was anything remotely improper or illegal in the note that he would simply burn it and not come back at midnight. He wasn't getting into trouble for anyone.

Victor took a long, final drag, tossed the cigarette butt into the parking lot and turned to go back inside. The side door was locked. You have got to be shitting me, he thought. He never went out that door because he never smoked at work even though he always kept his smokes on him. He had hoped to pop into the bathroom adjacent to the side door and wash his hands and try to disguise the reeking odor of cigarette smoke on his shirt and face, but he wouldn't be able to.

He started the long walk around the back side of Cherry Knolls where the employees parked. And what did he see there? Oh, it was Mike Guidry, and he was driving off at 3 p.m. Oh, and who was that in his front seat? It was none other than Victor's new supervisor, Ms. Jerri Hughes. Where were they headed? They were laughing it up in his Mercedes and he shot out fast as a rabbit. Neither of them saw him, but he sure as hell saw them. Was Mike having an affair with Jerri? Was that seriously what he just saw? And he just got replaced by Jerri. Oh, what a day. And yet this revelation was only the second most interesting and disturbing thing that had happened to him that day. He wondered about how long their affair had been going on for. Obviously long enough to find her fully capable of taking over his job. If only he had a nice set of tits and would go down on Mike Guidry, he too, could be taking the express lane to upper management. Oh well. That's the way the world has always worked. Powerful men having their way with people. And he wasn't a powerful man by any stretch. Being a day-smoker paid off.

He remembered the List he had just drafted a few days before. He intended to make lots of changes in his life but that was before he was demoted and had a bizarre interaction with Beverly Griffin and Lucy Black. He had no idea what Beverly was talking about, but her words were strange, and chilling and possibly very real, even if some of them were garbled nonsense. But his involvement seemed quite urgent and important. Yes, that will throw off one's "To-Do" List pretty damn fast.

Chapter 10 * Plans, Plans And More Plans

Victor sat at his computer trying to get through the balance of his spread-sheets and Medicare accounts, as well as the stupid Cosmix program. The minutes stretched into hours; the hours felt like days. Why didn't he just leave for the day? Still, he kept fondling the envelope in his pocket, his curiosity starting to get the best of him. He pulled it out and looked at the front of it again. It simply said, *"Victor Jones...Open after work, in private."* The script was calligraphy and looked like it took someone with some skills to make it look so nice. He didn't realize Beverly was a calligrapher. But what freaked him out was that she had been ex-pecting him in her room that day. She knew he would be there. He never went to the guests' rooms, or if he did it was rare. Stephen Glick had specifically asked him to go up there, was he part of this? How could he be? How did Beverly know he would be there, that he would patiently listen to her tale, and that he would accept the envelope and agree to come back at midnight? It was starting to drive him bananas.

After wasting most of the afternoon and accomplishing very little, he shut off his computer and left early. He couldn't take it any longer. He made sure to keep his office light and computer on in case Mike Guidry returned from his dalliance with Jerri Hughes, Mike would assume that Victor had just run to the bathroom. The oldest office trick in the book. He didn't need to get fired right now, especially since he needed to be able to come back at midnight.

Victor made his way to his trusty Honda Accord and sat down in the driver's seat. He pulled out of the parking lot and decided that since he had waited that long, surely he could make it back to his house before he opened this mysterious envelope. He was getting excited as he neared home. He couldn't actually recall when he had been so excited for something. And this could be a hoax, or some-thing entirely stupid, but life is made up of little excitements, and anticipations, like lily pads. One jumps from one to the next because it keeps the brain activated and provides motivation to get out of bed and keep going.

He drove as fast as he could and made it home in record time. He pulled into his driveway and jumped out of the car and went into his house and sat at his kitchen table. He pulled out the envelope and for some strange reason he looked around to make sure no one was watching him. Not that anyone would be, he lived alone. He looked at the calligraphy once again and then tore open the envelope and shook out a piece of paper. It started:

"Remember, Victor, heroes come in all shapes and sizes. Anyone can be a hero if they try. If they want to help. And help is desperately needed. Everyone needs to be tested to know they can handle their moment of crisis. We haven't evolved as human beings until we face our crises head-on. If you are the hero, we will see you tonight. At midnight. Not before, not after. Are you the hero? You see some people believe that, when we die, nothing happens to our souls. Some people don't believe we even have souls. Some people believe we are judged harshly by some type of god. And others believe there is no god or sentient being. Regardless of your denomination or faith or religion, it seems that maybe, just maybe, we have had it wrong. It seems that what happens to us after we die is nothing like we've ever been taught in Sunday School or seen in the movies or on TV. But then again to say that nothing happens to us after we die is also not the case. Something very much happens to us. And it seems that We, the living, are tasked with fighting a war on behalf of the Dead. A war that will impact us once we die. And if we don't win this war, well then, once we do die, we are going to suffer beyond anything you can comprehend. So, we must win this war for the souls of all of the Dead. And YOU, Victor Jones, play the most important role in fighting this battle and saving the world."

Victor had to put the note down for a second because the contents were too overwhelming and frankly entirely unbelievable. He, Victor Jones, was going to save the world and protect all the people who had died? Was she insane? Probably so. But it was a fun read. He continued to read:

"There are three celestial objects that are coveted by the legions of those who have died (the Dead), as well as their arch-enemy (the Builders). These entities have waged a brutal war for millennia and the Dead need our help to win. They need all three of these objects, or orbs, and if they gather them, all at one time, they will win the war and save the Dead to allow them to go on to a higher plane of consciousness. If, however, the Builders get the three orbs first, then it is checkmate, and the Dead will suffer an eternal purgatory. This cannot happen! You must be the Dead's Hero! And it all starts with The MonteGresso. It is awake after a forty-year slumber. It is hot and beaming and ready to unite with the other two orbs. And if you look outside there will be a delivery van arriving any minute to deliver a box to you. Do you know your social security number? Chop off the first 3. Good luck and see you tonight…Hero."

Chapter 11 ∗ The MonteGresso

October 15, 1908. Lamar, Colorado

    Death. The great mystery to the living. What happens when one dies? Is there an afterlife with heaven, hell and purgatory? Do people grow wings, play harps and sing with the angels or do they fry in molten lava while being stabbed with pitchforks by horned devils? If an afterlife existed, did it look like the scenes imagined by the Renaissance painters with cherubs and angels, devils and fire? Maybe reincarnation is what happens. When a person dies their soul goes into a new human, or animal, or plant, and lives a new life, thereby eliminating the concept of the afterlife. There was also the possibility that once a person dies, the soul comes back as a higher life form in a different realm or dimension that is something beyond the conception of man. Or there is also the possibility that absolutely nothing happens to people when they die. No afterlife. No reincarnation. No new paradigm. Just decomposition into the earth, becoming food for the worm and fertilizer for the soil. There are likely an infinite number of other conceptualizations of what happens once someone dies, each as unique as the person imagining it. Some conceptualizations give people hope and comfort regarding death, for others it stirs up fear and anxiety. But at the end of the day, there was no human on Earth who knew for sure what happened after death and if the soul moved on, or if it just ended. No one. Except Beverly Griffin.

    Beverly, the youngest of six children, grew up poor, like most African Americans in the 1930's. But her family withstood the economic calamities of the Great Depression, coupled with the complexities of being black in America, long before the civil rights struggle took hold. Her father was the owner of a general store in a part of Denver called Five Points. This historic neighborhood sat along a crisscrossing of main intersections in Denver; in the early 20th century virtually the entire Denver black community lived within spitting distance of where the five streets intersected. Beverly's father's store was simply named The Griffin Family General Store, a place where someone could find dried beans, rice, milk and other assorted sundry items on its shelves. Samuel Griffin was one of the first black entrepreneurs to purchase a building he worked in, and would continue to work there until the day he paid off the mortgage.

The Griffin family, all eight of them, resided in a three-bedroom apartment on the second floor of that old, brick building that had been built in 1898 as was evidenced by the thick chiseled '1898' engraved under the third-floor eave facing Welton Street.

Samuel had been born in 1894, on the wide-open eastern plains of Colorado in a little town called Lamar. In 1894, most of the native Americans had been herded onto reservations and the white settler's manifest destiny was almost complete. There were still small hold outs of Kiowa, Comanche and Cherokee that dotted the plains, but by 1894 most of the fight was out of these few remaining native American tribes, who had lost so much due to westward expansion. Samuel worked with his father on a sprawling 2,500-acre ranch, learning from a young age how to break a wild horse, place a shoe on a horse, clean and care for the animals and even learn how to hunt riding atop a 10-hand foal.

There was still a lot of wild game in the area, although most of it was small as the buffalo had been almost entirely eradicated from those parts of the western United States. Samuel would finish all of his chores and studies at home, with his mother, and then be allowed to go out with his three younger brothers to ride and hunt. It was an ideal way to grow up and due to the sporadic population in those parts, there wasn't much animosity or violence focused on black families. Sure, he was called a nigger from time to time by some of the other ranch hands and families that lived in the area, but there was no Ku Klux Klan in those parts and most of the violence was still centered on the remaining native Americans who had yet to take the government's offer to settle onto some shithole reservation.

Samuel thought he had it pretty good, especially compared to what he knew of many other black people in the south and even in the industrial north, where violence and lynchings were commonplace. Samuel's father had been born into slavery but once emancipation became the law of the land, Samuel's grandfather and a handful of other relatives left Kentucky as quickly as possible, heading west, until they knew they were safe in the Colorado territory. Samuel's grandfather died shortly after settling in Colorado, but he made sure his children were cared for as he had been lucky enough to find work on this same ranch, in Lamar.

Samuel didn't know much about the outside world and that suited him just fine. What else was there to need to know? He had a loving family, they had food and clean water, they had the use of horses to enjoy all the wide-open beauty of southern Colorado, and most important, they were free. The year 1894 was only thirty-two years after the Emancipation Proclamation and the concept of freedom, after several hundred years of bondage, was a relatively new concept for black people and white people. Samuel didn't have a concept of what it meant to be in bondage, but his father had passed down those lessons from his grandfather, who had learned many harsh lessons from the wrong end of a bullwhip.

Samuel's father was proud his children would never know that type of cruelty, but also wanted to ensure that they did all they could to assimilate into American culture and life. He constantly told his children that they would be enslaved if they didn't own their own property. And they would never be respected by their fellow American citizens if they didn't exhibit patriotism and loyalty to the American flag. Owning property and saluting the flag—those were the pillars of what it meant to be a good American. And of course, without having to even say it, they had to be loyal to their family and to God.

In late October 1908, Samuel, then 14 years old, had finished his chores, schooling and prayers. His father, suffering from the debilitating effects of a stroke a few years earlier, had stopped riding horses or doing anything that required manual labor. Therefore, Samuel's free time was extremely limited as he was responsible for organizing his siblings to get the work done. The ranch owner, Jameson Smith, could have evicted the Griffin family from the ranch once Samuel's father suffered the stroke, but he liked the family and knew the sons would continue to take care of the ranch as best they could.

It was about 4 in the afternoon on that late October day when Samuel grabbed his shotgun and jumped onto Sparky, his six-year-old horse, and decided he would try and grab a turkey or two before it got too dark. The turkeys were roaming aggressively that fall and he knew where the Toms hung out. He also knew they were careless, and he didn't think it would take much time to secure some dinner for the next few nights. He had ridden over a ridge about two miles from the ranch and due to the looming shadows cascading from the west, and the flat late afternoon light, his vision became a bit obscured. He crossed a small brook and maneuvered Sparky around some particular ugly cactus patches that flourished in the arid Colorado soil. He could feel a chill pick up as the wind increased in intensity. He fumbled for his coat, never taking his eyes off the horizon for fear of missing a shot. As he leaned over to button his coat, he dropped his gloves.

He jumped off Sparky, who stood proud and silent. Just then a gust of wind picked up one of the gloves and it started to cartwheel across the dry landscape, nothing to stop it for a hundred miles. Samuel ran after the glove but didn't see a small embankment where the land dipped down a few feet and he went crashing down on all fours, hitting his chin on a rock. Blood started to pour out of him, and he held his hand to the wound to stop the bleeding. He was able to secure that stupid glove and shoved it into his pocket. As he stepped back up over the small dirt ledge, he caught a glimpse of something blue embedded into the dirt lip. It stood out because it appeared to sparkle, but it was just the smallest sliver that he saw. He bent over to try and dig it out of the dirt to inspect. He and his brothers had found all types of interesting artifacts out in that prairie. Several old arrowheads, a few old earthen pots that must have been a hundred years old, and on one occasion they even discovered a fully mummified dog that had somehow died after falling into some substance that kept it from decaying. The entire body was dug up and they took it into town where one of the local ranchers bought it to sell to a museum back east.

But this particular item did not look natural, certainly not something that would have grown out in the dirt or been used by native Americans for cooking or hunting. He tried to pry the object out with his fingers but it was embedded deeply. He removed his pocketknife and started to scrap away some of the dirt but he couldn't make much headway. So he started to hack away at the dried clumps of earth and dirt until some of the overhang started to give way. He kept hacking and prying for almost twenty minutes but whatever that thing was had taken hold into the ground. His chin was throbbing with the exertion, but he was so focused on this he didn't seem to notice. He was oblivious as well to the droplets of blood that kept falling on his shirt.

Samuel started to make some headway with the digging, peeling away a lot of the layers of dirt. He could start to make out that this was a small, perfectly circular ball of some fashion. It most certainly did not appear "natural" based on its perfect circular shape, the color, the sparkly crystals and the gorgeously smooth exterior. It looked man made. He had removed the dirt surrounding almost three quarters of the ball and then he started to kick the ground to free it. It would not budge, but there was no way Samuel was leaving this now. His curiosity was piqued and the thought of chasing down a turkey had long vanished from his mind. The sun was starting to set in the west, and he realized he only had a few more minutes to get this out or else he would be home after dark, and that was something his father would never tolerate without warning.

The panic started to swell and he was violently beating on the remaining clods of dirt keeping this thing nestled to the bosom of the earth. He grabbed his shotgun, removed the shells, and used the butt to hammer the dirt. Finally, mercifully, the object gave way until it was tethered only by a small weed, or what Samuel mistook for a weed. He inspected it closer and he shook the dirt off the weed. It glowed brilliantly yellow and blue. A color he had never seen before. He didn't know how to even describe this color, but it was bright and warm and alive. Yes, there was something very alive about this weed and the yellow and blue light.

In the dusk, the blue glowed, illuminating the area. With one final hard tug Samuel detached the ball from weed. Immediately the light dimmed out and the weed curled back into the earth. Samuel jumped back. Did that just move into the earth? Samuel rubbed his eyes but that weed definitely was alive and receding. It was the strangest thing, but he didn't have time to inspect any further. He made a small mound of dirt and found a few sticks and other objects to mark this place. He had to come back and do a deeper dive into the weed, but for now he grabbed this perfectly round, hand-sized sparkly ball and shoved it into his knapsack. As he made his way back to the ranch, he hoped he wouldn't be in too much trouble for coming in after dark.

"Hey son, where have you been? You look liked you got into a fight with someone and lost," his father said from his comfortable rocking chair next to the fire in the room next to the kitchen. Samuel had completely forgotten about the bloody chin and only wanted to get to a place of privacy and inspect this new object. Something in the corner of his mind was telling him to keep this secret—something he rarely did. And in that small house with his large family, he couldn't keep a secret even if he wanted to, but he just had a very visceral feeling to keep his find private.

"Oh, yeah, the chin." He touched his chin. "It's nothing. I fell off Sparky chasing down a glove that flew out of my jacket. It was stupid. It don't hurt none. I'll go wash up."

As he made his way to grab the wash basin and fill it up, his father called, "No Toms out tonight? I thought for sure you would get one or two. You must be losing your edge." He smiled at Samuel and Samuel burned with guilt for not sharing what he'd found.

"Yeah, well, they weren't out and about where I thought they would be. To-morrow I'll circle back and get me a few. We'll be eating roast turkey tomorrow, I promise."

He took the lantern perched on a side table, lit it and carried it outside to one of the sheds. Alone, he sat down on the ground and pulled the strange object out of his bag. It was still caked in dirt, so he spit on it and used the bottom of his bloody shirt to clean it off. This ball was about twice the size of a hen's egg, but it had no imperfections or cuts or bruises or dimples. Entirely smooth and absolutely beautiful, its blue color reminded Samuel of the sky in late summer when the sun set low, filled with sparkles like stars. Out in Lamar at night, if there weren't clouds, he could see the heavens and stars and Milky Way. His father had taught him and his siblings where to locate the Big Dipper and Little

Dipper, as well as how to get home in the dark by celestial navigation.

These sparkles in the ball appeared celestial and reminded him of the planets. He studied the orb. Wasn't that Saturn? It looks like Orion over there. This was a spectacular find, but he had no idea what it was, where it came from or how long it had been trapped in that earthen bunker. And what was that green weed to which it connected? He was transfixed.

That night Samuel went to bed in the room with three of his brothers. Samuel shared a bed with his youngest brother, Jasper, who was fast asleep when Samuel climbed in next to him. He kept the orb in his knapsack and hung it on the corner post of his bed. That night, he dreamed hard—of slaves on the whipping post and being buried in mass graves. He dreamed of Apaches and Kiowa slaughtered and left to rot in the sun. He dreamed of white men in covered wagons being sabotaged by Comanche warriors, the men being hacked to death in gruesome massacres and the young white children being dragged off to live new lives as Comanche children. He dreamed of disease and tornadoes and drought. He dreamed of death. Those murdered and those who passed away due to old age. The people who didn't survive cholera or dysentery, and those who starved because the crops fell short. Death is death, regardless of how one died, they were still dead and joined the legions of the Dead that walked the Earth. Walled in a liminal space, that dimension between the living and another place beyond the realm of the living. Their voices and calls for justice and peace went unheeded.

Samuel tossed heavily, sweating beneath his blankets but unable to shake the visions that were so intense and vivid. He could see the Dead in the multitudes. In the hundreds, thousands and millions. They were walking outside his door, and on the ranch and in the town square and all the way up in Denver, over 200 miles away. He saw them roaming the hills of the Dakota territories and the bustling shipyards of New Orleans and Houston. He saw them marching in New York City and all the way down to Atlanta. The Dead. They didn't hurt the living. They didn't interfere with the living. They didn't frighten the living and they didn't give solace to the living. They existed in a world beyond Samuel's world. But they existed. They existed and they were lost. They existed and they needed to escape something. They were in need of help and guidance and they all seemed to want Samuel to help them.

Had Samuel been awake, he would have heard a faint chirping coming from his knapsack. Had he opened his knapsack, he would have seen the orb glowing bright blue and pulsating. He would have seen green lights coming out of the orb in wavy lines, searching for help and a kind hand. Like a dog that nuzzles up to his master and demands attention, the orb demanded Samuel's attention.

He was now the orb's protector and the one person to make things right for the Dead. The object in his knapsack hanging on his bedpost was the powerful orb called The MonteGresso.

Chapter 12 * Doesn't Anyone Love Me?

Bingham the Knife had been working the phones relentlessly for the past 24 hours. He had to find a few happy clients who were not only available to shoot a commercial, but also wanted to appear in a commercial too. That was the tough part, finding people willing to speak on his behalf. It was much tougher than he realized. Not only that, but he also had to find attractive clients.

Because he rarely met with clients, he had no idea what most of his former clients even looked like, let alone if they were good looking enough for one of his commercials. So he started as one would expect, by going through his files to see which of his clients had amassed the largest settlements. In the past twenty-four months, he had served over 1,000 clients. The average settlement ranged between $12,500 and $25,000. Sure, his law firm grossed a lot of money, but once the client was paid, the doctors were paid, the paralegals were paid, the radio and TV stations were paid, not to mention general overhead for rent, utilities and insurance, his cut was not nearly as much as he expected. He had no clue why he allowed himself to be openly mocked by the general public and ridiculed by his legal peers, just to net $700,000 or $800,000 a year. No doubt that was a considerable sum of money, but did if offset the pain of being mocked? Most attorneys who advertised on television accepted that this was part of the game. It was okay to make a fool of yourself on TV with outlandish commercials, promising people big bucks, because in the end anyone could endure the humiliation in exchange for a life of relative luxury. Bingham's classic analysis of Means justifying the Ends.

However, the competition for clients was getting fiercer and the cost for advertising was only increasing. More and more lawyers were going The Knife's route and further diluting the profitability of this venture. The Knife also knew that TV was the best option. It reached the largest mass market of people available. Sure, the internet was good, but the internet advertising was even more expensive than TV. In fact, "Personal Injury" was the highest cost per click of any targeted internet business. Nothing came close.

The Knife had started out advertising his face on bus benches and over urinals. Yes, urinals. But the amount of penis graffiti that was drawn over his face, or going into his mouth, or crisscrossing above his head was simply too much. He knew he had to stop with the bus benches when his mother saw a bench with twelve penises surrounding his face in the shape of a crown. No crown of thorns for this messiah; instead, a crown of dicks. It was modern New Testament. That was it with the bus benches. He stepped up his game, got a big loan from his bank, and immediately connected with "Pretty-Boy" Rob.

He had met Rob a year earlier at some plaintiffs' attorney conference. Rob had purchased a booth in the exhibition hall and made it a point to track down all the sleazy personal injury attorneys who were doing a half-assed job of mass marketing and convince them to step up their game to TV advertising, where he would make them the top sleazeballs in their respective markets. As soon as Bingham met Rob, he knew he liked him. He was charismatic as hell and he was saying all the right things. Rob knew about the bus benches and urinals, and he definitely knew about all the dicks that were constantly drawn on Bingham's face on bus benches. Regardless, he understood the business and he had made lots of other sub-par lawyers rich beyond their wildest dreams. Why not him? Rob and Bingham had drinks that night at the conference and Rob even came up with Bingham's moniker, "The Knife!" Bingham was hooked.

In just a few years he had eclipsed most of his contemporaries in the mainstream plaintiffs' bar as a top-client generator. Setting his sights on the three top TV dirtbags, Bingham wanted to be king. It didn't take long to be competing against all of those personalities and overall, he was happy. The Knife knew he wasn't a great lawyer and that most other lawyers mocked and resented him. After all, these TV lawyers were bringing down the reputation of all attorneys because the vast majority of people didn't know the difference. Joe Public generally thought morons like The Knife were the same as all other attorneys, so the non-advertising lawyers suffered with fewer cases and less money but were nonetheless lumped into the "ambulance chaser" genre. The Knife didn't care. He was making more money than he had before and was looking forward to one day profiting over a million dollars a year. He was very close, if he could just keep the expenses down.

But success came at a cost. Clients arrived by the bushel, but he was too busy to actually meet with them. He delegated his legal work to paralegals and associates, and he spent his days making obnoxious commercials and counting money. He was fond of spouting out inspirational lines such as "Sitting behind a desk your whole life ain't living…unless you're counting huge stacks of cash." How superficial could one person be?

He checked the list in front of him. So far there were thirty names with thirty red lines drawn through each one. Of the thirty people he called, no one wanted to help. They were either angry with him for settling their cases for too little money when he was pocketing such a huge fee, or others had no idea who he was because they never met him face to face and didn't feel comfortable expressing their opinions about how wonderful he was. The majority of the people he called simply didn't want to be connected with his sleazy advertisements and be seen advocating for Bingham "The Knife" Cutler. They were simply too embarrassed to associate with him. And what frustrated Bingham the most was that they didn't mind telling him that. One person even said, "That's a disgusting idea. I wouldn't want anyone I know to see me stand with a person like you. You're disgusting." And that was from someone who pocketed over $300,000. Granted, a reasonably talented and dedicated lawyer would have netted her over a million, but that wasn't his game. He found it ironic because all these people discovered him on TV.

"So I'm going to need a new list of names." Bingham said to Sheila on the office intercom.

"No one? Not even Joanie Mcacham?" Sheila was flabbergasted.

"Right, well, Ms. Meacham called me a"—he looked down at his notepad— "…a two-bit shyster scumbag. Or suck hole, or sum bitch. I don't really recall."

"Lovely," she blurted out sarcastically. "Well, maybe it would be better if I made the calls. Most of these people worked with me and I think I have a good relationship with them." Sheila hated doing the dirty work, but lots of people benefited from her doing the dirty work, so she would keep doing it.

"Oh, that would be awesome. Thank you, thank you!" Bingham said. He knew this was the only way to handle it.

"Alright, let me start with a new fresh list of people and see how things go. I'll call you later."

"Thanks Sheila, you are the best. Did I ever tell you that?" Bingham asked. He hung up before she answered.

Sheila combed through some additional names and kept scratching off possibilities. While she knew she could convince them to listen politely, once she told them they had to say nice things about her boss on TV, that's when she ran into problems. This shouldn't have come as a surprise. Bingham had a rating of one and a half stars on most attorney search sites, and his account had been flagged numerous times from the Better Business Bureau for sub-standard work. She was going to need a male client, and she was going to need one that would succumb to her charms. She scrolled through the recent clients and pegged a few possibilities: Johnny Cosgrove, Darius James and Victor Jones.

Chapter 13 * Nothing Good Happens In A Chapter 13

Barcelona, Spain

Kitta Schultz picked up the slumped over head on Mr. Joseph Avram Rabin. She felt for a pulse. Oh, Mr. Rabin was dead alright. She really didn't think she had applied that much force on his neck. But apparently, she didn't realize how brittle the bones in an old neck were. She placed his head gently down on the table and started to make an inventory of the apartment. It was an unseasonably hot day in Barcelona, that majestic coastal Spanish city. People were still at the beaches and walking on Las Ramblas, the exquisite mile-long stretch of gothic shops and buildings and vendors in the splendid Mediterranean city.

Mr. Rabin was probably in his late 80's but Kitta knew he maintained keen intellect and a sharp mind. He had obviously been expecting her because when she entered the front door to his small apartment, a make-shift spring-loaded contraption released and Kitta barely missed being stabbed in the face with an eighteen-inch blade. She had spied the booby trap as she opened the door and felt the unnatural tension on the door. She was able to dive out the way and save herself. Why Mr. Rabin wasn't sitting there with a shotgun she had no idea. Maybe he was concerned that he would fall asleep and he needed something to guarantee his safety in case she came while he was sleeping. Either way, the attempt to snuff her out failed and she had a chance to get Mr. Rabin to reveal his secret. She just failed to take into account how strong she was when she was inflicting the torture to his neck. She should have stuck to her tried and true method of cutting off a pinkie; that wouldn't cause death, but it sure got some-one's attention and increased their willingness to cooperate. She would have to search the apartment and hope the item she desired was easily found.

She went into his closet to toss around the clothing and then flipped over his bed. Nothing. She pulled out a knife and started to cut holes in the softer pieces of drywall and pried open any moldings around the base of the apartment where something could be hidden. Nothing. It had to be here. All of her study-ing and information indicated that Mr. Rabin, the survivor of Auschwitz, was for certain the last man who had the orb. She had closely monitored his apartment for weeks; he had journeyed out infrequently and no one appeared to have visited his apartment who could have taken possession. She knew she was close. It was evident that Mr. Rabin, a short blur of a man, knew she was hot on his tail. Instead of sneaking out, he'd decided to make a stand in his apartment. Idiot. He might have been sharp enough to know she was on his tail, and even deft enough with tools to create the booby trap but holing up in his apartment went against all logical thinking as it related to protecting the item she was seeking.

As she made her way into the back bedroom, she saw someone move and scurry into the corner, clearly hiding. Kitta placed her blade back in its sheath and grabbed her pistol. She didn't know what to expect, but she knew she was leaving that apartment alive and with the orb. She slowly approached the door, scanning the room side to side as she had been trained in her field operations.

"Come out, my friend, I know you are scared," Kitta stated in Spanish. When she got no reply, she switched to English. "Come on my friend, let's get this over with and I will leave in peace." Nothing. Finally, she raised her voice. In German she stated, "I will cut your heart out and hold it in front of you as you die. And it will be painful, I promise!"

"No. Please. Please." Kitta paused. Whoever was speaking sounded frail and vulnerable, belonging perhaps, to an old woman.. The voice continued in a pleading tone. "I will give it to you. Please just leave me alone."

"Come out, young lady, let me see you," Kitta responded in German, clearly the dialect of choice in the Rabin household. Babette came out from behind the bed at the opposite side of the bedroom. She was clearly too old and fragile to be move quickly, but she seemed to have a little spark left in her. Kitta, nearly six feet tall, towered over the old woman, who said, "I promised Avram I wouldn't give you the orb. Please take whatever it is you want in exchange." She went to her dresser and opened a box full of jewelry. "You may have all of this, plus money. I will give you my money. It isn't a lot but you are welcome to it."

"Oh, my sweet lady," Kitta said as she approached Babette and placed a finger on the woman's cheek. "You know that cannot happen. I do not have any needs or desires for your money and diamonds. I need the thing I came for. And I am not leaving here without it. We can do this two ways. And you know which ways those are." And she placed her hand in a death grip around Babette's throat. Babette started to cough and cry at the same time.

"But miss, I beg of you," Babette sputtered. Kitta released Babette's throat and grabbed her arm instead. Ferociously, she twisted it behind the woman's back until the sound of the brittle radius bone snapping was unmistakable. Babette let out a tremendous scream, which Kitta quickly muffled with her other hand. "My darling, my precious, would you like to have the other arm broken too? I'm happy to oblige."

With Babette's good hand she pointed out of the room. Kitta marched her over to where she apparently wanted to go—the kitchen. Gasping in pain, Babette opened a cupboard and pointed to a shelf of canned goods.

"Oh, my sweet. I'm not hungry either." Kitta applied more pressure on the broken arm. "No, in the can," Babette managed to say over the pain. "The corn, in the back." She held her head low. She had failed Avram and millions of others.

Kitta quickly let go of Babette's arm; she was of no use to her now and certainly she didn't pose a risk. Kitta looked at the top row of cans and with one swooping gesture pulled all of the cans down off the shelf. They crashed to the ground. Some hit her in the legs and feet, but she couldn't feel a thing. She was so close to her goal. She spied the one can that looked different, with lighter wrapping and a picture of corn on the cob that didn't seem natural. She bent down and grabbed it. She noticed it was one of those can safes that usually were reserved for jewelry and other special items. This orb was most certainly one of those special items. She twisted off the lid and stared at the auburn sphere. It had the sparkles from the crystals and was polished to a high gloss. Who would have thought this item had been around long before Jesus Christ? Mesmerized, she turned the can over, and the orb fell into her strong, waiting hand. She had been searching for over two years, killing and torturing many people to get this. Now her mission was almost fulfilled.

She gazed so intently on the auburn orb that she didn't notice Babette scurry away from the kitchen. It was then that Kitta felt a painful stabbing in her left shoulder. Babette had grabbed some kitchen shears and plunged them as deeply as she could into Kitta's shoulder. Kitta didn't make a sound. She just looked at the shears sticking out of her arm. Without dropping the orb that was secured firmly in her left hand, she twisted around and pulled out the scissors with her right hand. Then she turned toward Babette. The old woman seemed to be in shock, either from her injuries or the ones she thought she'd inflicted on Kitta.

"Oh, my sweet, sweet dear," Kitta crooned. "Aren't you just adorable?" She took the scissors, red and shining from the fresh blood, and deftly thrust them deeply into the side of Babette's head. Due to Kitta's strength and the ever softening of Babette's skull, the scissors made their way all the way through up to the handle. Babette didn't let out a whimper as she crumpled down and died on the cold linoleum kitchen floor.

Chapter 14 ✳ Strange Deliveries

Victor read the note again and started laughing. This was a joke, and he was the sucker. But it was funny. Now it was time to find something to eat and plop down on the couch. He had no plans to go back to Cherry Knolls at midnight. He was sure a whole bunch of employees would be there, waiting for him, to laugh at him. No thanks!

As he made his way to the cupboard, he noticed through his window a brown, non-descript van pull up outside. A lanky young man with blonde hair and a long-braided beard hopped out and was holding a black box the size of a microwave oven. He didn't appear to struggle with the object as he made his way up to Victor's door. Victor's heart raced. He looked at the note again. "*And if you look outside there will be a delivery van arriving any minute to deliver a box to you.*" Well, this joke was certainly planned out and very, very deliberate. He was sure Mike Guidry was behind all of this. Fine, he'd play along. He opened the front door before the braided beard guy could ring.

"Thanks much, I was going to have to put this down to ring your doorbell," the man said, a smell of tobacco wafting from his mouth. "I have a delivery for a Mr. Victor Jones." Victor opened the screen door to accept the package. The delivery man placed the box down on the ground and pulled a bill of lading out of his back pocket. "So, I need some identification, I can't just release this box to you." Victor showed him his driver's license. "This is me, Victor Jones."

The delivery man smiled. "Yup, so says your license. Now I need you to remove the inner box from the security box." The delivery man pointed to a numeric keypad on the top of the box. "Just punch in your six-digit code." Victor was stumped. Six-digit code? What was the six-digit code? "I'm sorry, I don't have a code. I didn't even know this was arriving." The bearded man reviewed the bill of lading, flipped to its second page and silently re-read it. "Yeah, I'm sorry, I can't release this without the code. I suppose you will need to call the sender. Says here the name is B. Griffin. That's all I have."

Victor asked the delivery man for a second and he went back to the letter. He looked at the last line: "*Do you know your social security number? Chop off the first 3. Good luck and see you tonight…Hero."* Victor thought for a second and went back to the delivery man. "I seem to have found the code," he said. He kneeled down to the box on the ground and as he did, he glimpsed a holstered gun under the man's jacket. He swallowed hard. He placed his hand over the keypad to shield it from the delivery man's view and typed in 16-7865. And he heard the sound of a lock mechanically opening.

"Perfect," the bearded man said. "Please open the door, remove the contents and sign this slip." He handed the bill of lading to Victor, who quickly scribbled his name. Then he pulled out another box, about the size of a bread box that was entirely red and closed the safe door. Inside the house, Victor locked the door, closed his shades and put the mysterious red box on his kitchen table. Wow, a lot of work went into this joke. He was almost flattered that someone wanted to fuck with him this much. And then something in the back of his mind made him think, for a second, that this could be real. And that thought froze him.

He sat at his table for what seemed to be at least an hour staring at the red box. He had yet to summon the courage to open it and see what was inside. He knew it wasn't a bread box. He had a strong sense that once he opened that box, he would either be proven a sucker, or more frightening, his life could be forever changed. It was his decision, no one else's. He could throw the thing out, or just return it unopened to Beverly. Either way he believed in self-determination. Nothing was predestined and his opening this box and taking possession of whatever was inside was his decision, if he wanted to do it. No one could force him, practical joke or not. He stood up from his table, went to the pantry and re-moved a bottle of whiskey. He rarely drank, but this seemed like an appropriate time to throw down a little courage. He poured himself a nice glass and tossed it all back in one shot. His throat and eyes burned.

It might have been the whiskey, or the effects of the day, but as he sat staring at the red box, he could have sworn he heard something emanating from the box. A low whine. He also thought he saw the box vibrate, ever so slightly. Was there a tiny puppy inside? No way. As he grabbed the box and shook it slightly, the whine increased in volume. The box—shuddered. Oh, something was very much alive in there. Well, that sealed the deal. He couldn't let an animal die. He grabbed a pair of scissors. The sound increased. He looked around his house again as if someone might be spying on him. He was alone. But then he realized the box could not be opened with scissors. There was a small fingerprint reader on the side of the box. He knew he never gave anyone his fingerprint, volun-tarily, but when he swiped his index finger, the light next to the scanner turned white and the box lid popped open. Obviously, a lot of planning had gone into this prank.

Heart racing, he slid his finger under the lid and pushed up on the top. Green lights, like fireflies, immediately spilled out of the box. And there was definitely something moving. He looked inside and pulled out a smooth glass orb. Blue, with crystals inside, it was emitting some green laser-like lights and was vibrating, or so it seemed. This thing was definitely alive. No other word for it. He picked it up and gazed at it. The green light coming from within moved over his face and hair and body. He was being scanned by this orb; that's how he felt. He was being evaluated and judged and measured. Was he the butt of a complex joke or the Hero? Was Beverly right? Was this a dream? The orb was slightly larger than his hand and weighed less than a pound. It was solid, beautiful and mesmerizing. He couldn't stop looking at it. But the lights eventually dimmed, and the sound ended, and he felt it was time to place it gently back into the box. Inside he saw a Zippo lighter nestled on a card, connected by a piece of tape. He pulled it out. It said: "Burn after reading." Victor had forgotten about the note. He picked it up, read it one last time, and flipped the Zippo. The smell of butane filled his nostrils; what a wonderful smell to a smoker. He turned the wheel, ignited the flint and released a big flame. He burned Beverly's note and watched the ashes ascend to his ceiling and then gently settle back down on his table.

He had made the decision. No one else. This was no joke. He realized that once those green lights scanned over him. He felt a great sense of fear. He was nobody's Hero. He recalled the words in Beverly's note: "Everyone needs to be tested to know they can handle their moment of crisis." He wasn't cut out to handle any kind of crisis. He was the master of his future and no one could tell him otherwise. He would head back to Cherry Knolls at midnight, just to return this ball, and go back to his mild, and irrelevant, existence.

Chapter 15 * Late Night Rendezvous

When Victor arrived at Cherry Knolls at 11:45 p.m., the parking lot was vacant. He had to use his card key to enter and was immediately greeted by Billy Stine, one of the night security personnel.

"Mr. Jones, what are you doing here so late? Did you forget you work in the daytime?" Billy laughed and shook Victor's hand.

"Hello, Billy. I just needed to grab some things and check in on one of our residents. Shouldn't be too long. You tell your family hello for me, would you?"

"You bet, Mr. Jones. Have a nice evening." Billy thought it strange that Victor would need to be there at 11:45 at night, let alone check in on a guest, but he didn't care. That was not his business. He got back to his rounds.

Victor passed a few of the night nurses who all causally waved at Victor and went about their business. Victor unlocked his office door and sat down at his desk. He cautiously removed the orb from the box and looked at it again. He wasn't sure what he was supposed to do with this thing, but he guessed Beverly would have an idea or two. He feigned typing something into the computer to give the appearance that he was working, but he didn't even log on. While his computer had remained on since he left earlier the day, the autotimer had logged him out. He just tapped on the keyboard and shuffled some papers on his desk. He took a deep breath, stuffed the orb into his pocket and made his way out of the offices, headed to room 218. He knocked on the door.

"Well, you are early, but we are glad you are here," Grandma Lucy said as she opened the door, welcoming Victor. "Are you feeling OK?"

"I feel good," Victor said. He glanced past Lucy and looked at Beverly, who was sitting her in rocking chair. "But I really just came to say this was a funny practical joke and I am impressed you could pull this off."

Victor was surprised to see both women in sweaters, with their hair neatly coiffed and their make-up done. It was an odd look for two geriatric residents, especially given how late it was. But maybe they had not had guests in a while.

Beverly stood up from her rocker and approached Victor. She didn't seem to need the walker and she seemed taller now that she wasn't hunched over. He was standing face to face with her; the deep ridges in her cheeks corroborated her long and hard years. She put both hands on his face and closed her eyes. Her skin was cool, soft and thin as crepe paper. Victor allowed her to touch him. She then opened her eyes, removed her hands and motioned for Victor to sit down on the bed across from her rocker. He resisted; he really just wanted to leave. "Sit down please, Victor. Relax." Victor obliged and Beverly sat down next to him. Lucy found her own chair and pulled in close to listen to Beverly.

"In 1908, my father, Samuel Griffin, found an object deep in the dirt outside of his ranch in Lamar. That's where he grew up. He wasn't looking for anything in particular, just some turkeys, but he found something that was beautiful and peculiar and powerful. It was just a blue orb, about the size of a tennis ball. He dug it out of the ground, cleaned it, and hid it away. He didn't know what it was, but he knew it was something special and likely someone, or something, had lost it many years earlier. You see, Lamar, Colorado, is a tiny town. In 1908, only a handful of humans had seen parts of the wide-open Southeastern Colorado plains. How could this object possibly have gotten there? He didn't have a clue. It didn't look natural, but it didn't look man-made neither. So, he hid it in knapsack on his bedpost. That night and for many weeks he had the oddest and most intense dreams. Dreams of dead people coming out of their graves and wanting the strange object. The dreams were almost always the same. The Dead were telling my father to take the orb, finds its partners, find a fresh grave, and deposit them back into the earth, together. This orb had surfaced after many long years and needed to be re-seeded into the ground. But the ground had to be sanctified for the Dead and ..." Beverly trailed off, stumbling on this last part.

"And what?" Victor gently prompted, sensing that this part of the story was painful for Beverly. Even if he had no intention of being anyone's Hero, he could still be kind and patient with this charming old lady.

Encouraged, Beverly forged on. "And when he found the remaining orbs he was to bury them back into the earth, he had to make a sacrifice to help the orbs take root. They wouldn't take without the sacrifice. Once the re-seeding of *all of the orbs* had been completed, then the Dead could rest, their battle would end, and peace would be achieved."

Victor tried to follow along but he was losing his grip. He hadn't heard any of this earlier in the day, and he didn't understand. What kind of sacrifice?

"You see, when we die, as you expect, our bodies turn to dust," Beverly said. "But our souls continue. Not like you might think though. There isn't a heaven or hell. But our souls do move on to another paradigm, another existence. We evolve, and keep evolving, even in death. I'm not sure what that looks like, or feels like, but I know it exists. Unfortunately, there is another force that doesn't want the Dead to move on to another existence. This force is not necessarily evil, but it wants to keep the Dead souls trapped in between death and moving forward. It gains strength and power from keeping these souls out of this new paradigm of existence. And this battle has raged since the beginning of time. It is a battle that has never had a winner. The two sides are in a perpetual struggle. One side, the Builders, want to keep the Dead from crossing over a physical barrier, a Divide, but the Dead need to cross this Divide. Members of the Dead are occasionally able to cross over; they find small seams and cracks and access points, but it a slow and painful affair. It should be a stream of humanity, but instead it's a dribble at best. The Builders keep pushing them back. But there will eventually be an end to this battle. And if the Dead lose this battle, then they will suffer for eternity in an in-between existence, a purgatory if you will."

"So, when is the battle being fought? And who are the warriors?" The answer wasn't obvious, he had to ask. Victor was unknowingly being eased into the mystery, like slowly submerging into a jacuzzi. It's hot at first and but then it becomes seductive.

"Well, my friend, the battle rages now as we speak. But there is a sense it is reaching a conclusion. There's nothing we can do about it except help the Dead, our Dead. They are trapped, and we're losing the battle, and that's because of my father, Samuel. You see, when Samuel received the instructions, he refused to believe that he, of all people, was to be a warrior for the Dead. He thought he was going insane with his dreams. It was complete insanity that he couldn't shake the dreams. The dreams came with voices that were insistent that he had to unify all three orbs and bring down the Divide. But if he couldn't manage that then he was instructed to just bury his own orb. The race was always on between people, like my father, versus the forces that fought against the Dead."

"The Builders?" Victor asked. "Correct," Beverly replied.

"Why the Builders?" Lucy piped in.

"Because they are building to keep the Dead from ever being released. And they build constantly. The more they build, the harder it will be to allow the orbs to take root and defeat them. If the three orbs are united and planted by a minion who knows what to do, then the Builders' great Divide will come crashing down and the millions and millions of the Dead will be able to finally make their way to their next phase. But if the Builders' minion plants all three orbs and gains control of this awesome weapon, then there will be no chance to ever bring down the Divide and the Dead will suffer in an eternal holding pattern." She started to cry.

"Why are you crying, Beverly?" Victor asked.

"Because my father, bless his heart, failed," Beverly responded, tears running down her face. "You see, in the event that a minion is unable to re-unite all three orbs, then it's just prudent to seed one orb by itself," she continued. "It won't fix the problem, but it will stall the process for a while, kick the can down road, if you will. My father was unable to find the other two orbs, but he tried. Believe me, he tried. He should have just re-seeded his orb and been done with it. But he failed and this has set us back years."

Her tears were not just due to the guilt she felt for all the Dead who suffered because of her father's failure, but also for her father. A good, honest, decent man who lacked the strength or courage to do what was needed. And who could blame him? It was a strange fairytale. Was it even real? Who in the prime of life just ends it all when they are healthy and happy and have a thriving family and business? By listening to the voices in your head, you can start to believe you are in fact going crazy—and Samuel thought he was going crazy.

Grandma Lucy put a comforting hand on Beverly's shoulder. She felt the pain that Beverly was suffering. She also feared for her parents and grandparents, and her sister, people she loved who had all died before her and were clearly suffering in some form of unimaginable post-life apocalypse. Grandma Lucy never had any visions, but she had heard enough to know that Beverly was not crazy and that something much bigger than any of them realized was at play.

Beverly continued. "The problem was that all his attempts to re-unite the orbs failed. And he probably lacked the courage to bury his orb when he was young and able to fulfill that mission. But families and careers and love affairs all come into play and just like any human being, my father wasn't ready to let it all go. When he was 86 years old, riddled with cancer and steadily weakening, he knew he had to just give up his quest to re-unite the orbs and simply bury his orb before the Builders found it. In his last attempt to stave off the Builders, he told me his plight. It was a burden that he carried with him since he was sixteen years old. I always knew that he maintained a secret but could never quite get it out of him. I was his only child, someone who wanted to listen and help. But he was too late. I didn't know how to help him. He never explained the details of his mission. He was so sick and had hallucinations all the time, but it wasn't until he passed away that I realized that his hallucinations were actually pleas from the Dead for help. They willed him to try and re-seed his orb that he had carefully hidden all those years. But someone found the orb and buried it before he could. My poor father."

She sobbed uncontrollably. Victor crept to the door to check outside to make sure no one heard; if a night nurse came by at this time, he would have a difficult time explaining what he was doing in their room. Even worse, whatever he was supposed to learn from the Dead that night would have to wait. Based on what Beverly was saying, there was no time to wait.

"Beverly, please try to hold your voice down, I know it's hard but, if I am caught in here, this could be a problem." He whispered. As Lucy continued to comfort and console Beverly, she finally tapered off.

"So what happened to your father Samuel?" Lucy asked.

"Well, he found the person who obtained his orb. He had been tracking her for some time. You see, he had lost his orb, or more correctly, it was stolen. And I knew who stole it as well." She paused, feeling familiar pangs of guilt.

"Who was it?" Lucy chimed in. She had not heard the whole tale yet.

"One of my dearest friends. Her name was Genevieve McIntyre, or Jeannie for short. We had grown up together. She was one of only a handful of white kids who grew up in the Five Points neighborhood where we lived. She suffered tremendous abuse at the hands of a bunch of black kids because she was one of the only white people they knew or interacted with. It wasn't her fault that blacks had suffered such persecution and abuse, but she was an easy target. I always felt for her. She had the most beautiful blonde hair. She would purposely cut it short and dye it brown so she wouldn't stick out so much. But that didn't really help her. I found her to be sweet and thoughtful and in need of a friend. I was that friend. We were inseparable throughout our teenage and young adult years. Even when we grew up and started our lives, we lived close by and had a cherished friendship. We shared all of our secrets as girls generally do. And as I learned of my father's secret, I felt comfortable knowing Jeannine wouldn't betray me. She was the one person I trusted with all my heart."

Victor was enthralled by the tale. He also grew up in Denver and had a little understanding of some of the racial problems that existed, and still did to that day, in this historic black neighborhood, especially as it struggled with increased property values, changing demographics, and the complexity of gentrification.

"So why did she steal the orb if she was your friend?" he asked.

"The Builders had to have gotten to her somehow. Mind control? Black-mail? I'm not sure," Beverly said with a shrug.

"Well, when you are considering the magnitude of what's at stake, it doesn't really surprise me how vicious this can get," Victor opined. Oh, the jacuzzi was so soothing. Why had Victor ever resisted at the beginning?

"Oh, my dear, vicious is an understatement," Beverly said. "I have no doubt that some of the bloodiest events in human history were connected to this nev-er-ending otherworldly battle." Her words gave Victor a chill.

"Okay, Beverly, so how did Jeannie gain her power, get the orb, and deal with your dad?" Victor was getting antsy for some answers.

"Again, I don't know how the Builders manipulated her, but they must have known she had information and access and could make a play for the orb. She must have seen some frightening visions in her dreams and gained a perspective that triggered her to believe that she was on the side of the good. I cannot imagine she would have ever done anything to hurt me and my family, not to mention endanger the souls of all those who had died. In 1979 or 1980, she was still very close to me. At some point she was able to convince me to reveal where the orb had been placed. She said she just wanted to see it. I believed her. I had no idea that she had been manipulated." The tears flowed again. And once again Lucy placed her comforting hand on Beverly's shoulder. "Go on, Beverly, you've done nothing wrong."

"Well, whether I did or didn't, the deed was done. I showed her the place deep in our basement, those 100-year-old stone walls where my father had pried open a large hole and placed the orb in a steel box and then meticulously covered up the dislodged stone and replaced it with a realistic-looking fake stone and placed a heavy cabinet in front of it. I told her all about the self-sacrifice my father was preparing for. If I didn't show her that she would never, ever have been able to find it. It was so well-hidden and my father kept it there for decades, waiting for his time to do what he failed to do earlier. The only reason I knew about it, and I was the only one, was because my father feared if he died before he could re-seed, then the opportunity would be missed and it could be decades or centuries, for someone else to find the orbs and do the right thing. His very soul, and the souls of many of his loved ones, demanded that he do his job and do it right this time."

Beverly stood up and regained her composure. "She stole the orb from me and my father one night when we were at church celebrating Christmas Eve. He sensed there was a problem and we rushed home. She had already fled, and we couldn't find her. But my father tracked her down through some contacts he had in the police department. He followed her closely, knowing he had only one chance to secure the orb. It wasn't easy for an elderly black man, with cancer, to break into a white woman's home. And even if he did, he had no idea where the orb was. I told my father that we had to use all means necessary, even violence. I might seem like an old, frail woman now, but I kicked a few asses in my day. I wasn't afraid." Of that, Victor had no doubt.

Beverly continued. "Father refused. You see, he was a minion for the Dead. And while there are many, many bad and evil people who are dead, the reality is that the Dead represent hope and light and peace. It is contrary and inapposite to the Dead to use violence or advocate their minions use violence. I don't know why, I don't want to know why, I just know that the Dead use cunning, and bravery, and compassion and kindness to do their job while the Builder's minions have used anything at their disposal, including torture and murder. But not our side. And not my father. The Dead's heroes are people they trust as good and kind and empathetic people. That's why you, Victor, have been selected to help."

Victor was shocked. He was hardly kind, compassionate, or empathetic. He watched too much porn, didn't donate enough to charity, and secretly couldn't stand lots of people. He considered himself to be petty and jealous. And he was a coward. He had no interest in being tested. He was hardly the kind of advocate Beverly described. He felt he was the opposite.

"I know what you're thinking, Victor. That you have fears and you have faults. Well, honey, we all have fears and faults. The question is do you act on your petty grievances and hurt other people? Can you face the test and stand up for the challenge? Some people have achieved a doctorate in hurting other people and cowardice. But you, my friend, are not one of them. You are braver than you know. People have had an eye on you for some time." This scared Victor. "Like whom? People have been watching me? Seriously? When I'm at home? How?" Beverly quickly responded. "Oh, everyone is watched. The Dead have more eyes than all the living combined. They aren't spying on you. Well, they kind of are. But don't worry, they aren't interested in your freaky side. I mean, we all have a freaky side." Victor blushed. Grandma Lucy blushed. "They are interested in your bravery and compassion." All Victor could think was that he was not brave at all.

Beverly continued. "My father finally tracked down Jeannie at the cemetery just down the street from here. He was going to confront her right before she buried the orb. He was going to talk to her. Explain why she was wrong. Try to rationalize with her. He was then going to re-seed the orb as planned in a fresh grave of a young man killed by a drunk driver. A horrifically sad story and well-publicized in the papers. It was a perfect grave. He had hoped he could at least deliver the orb to the Dead and stall the Builders' plans. But she beat him to the grave. She threw in the orb and blew her head off, as was required."

"What?!? She blew her head off?" Victor shouted. Grandma Lucy told him to hush, it was late, and he couldn't be found in their room. He lowered his voice. "She blew her head off? Why?"

"Because the re-seeding requires a personal sacrifice. And that is the problem. My father never had the guts. He dove into the grave after her. He was frightened of what would happen if the wrong person re-seeded the orb. The orb had quickly taken root. But he had just enough time to pry it free. He beat on the earth just like he had done almost eighty years earlier in the dust of the Colorado prairie. He willed the orb free. He knew that while he stopped the orb from seeding into the earth, he couldn't re-seed it again. It was too late as it had already hit dirt and a sacrifice had already been made, but he could stop it from helping the Builder's cause. The orb wouldn't be ready for re-burial for many years after that incident. With his last efforts he climbed out of the grave and came directly to me. He knew he had failed once again, but at least the Builders didn't have the orb. Who knows what would have happened if they had secured it?"

The self-sacrifice thing was stuck in Victor's brain. It was 2020 and people were seriously talking about sacrificing their very lives for some imaginary battle of the Afterlife? It didn't seem logical in any sense of the word.

"What happens if the orbs are not re-seeded by anyone? How long does this battle rage on?" Victor asked.

"Well, your guess is probably as good as mine. But the longer the Builders dominate the landscape, the more irreversible damage and control they will maintain over the Dead. And the Dead will eventually have no more options and their fate will be hopeless, irreversible. And then I don't know. But I fear that their fate will be horrific if they cannot be released from their purgatory and move on. And if we aren't successful then quite literally the fate of all humans will be forever doomed. How's that for pressure?"

Victor sat down now. This was some heavy truth she was dropping on Victor. "Beverly, forgive me for asking this, and if you've already stated this then I apologize, but how did you know all of this? And more importantly, how do you believe all of this? This does require a bit of blind faith, doesn't it?"

Beverly tilted her head and looked at Victor. "Fair enough. My father kept this a secret, as you know, throughout his life. He heard the messages. He communicated with the Dead. It was never me. In fact, I never noticed anything strange or off about my dad. Probably because he had lived most of his life with this secret. But in 1977 he was diagnosed with leukemia. He knew time was running out and he didn't know how much longer he would make it. He felt I was the one person he really trusted. So he filled me in with as much detail as he thought I could take. Believe me, it wasn't a one-time thing like I'm doing to you. He slowly explained and then gave me examples of what he had been doing. He eventually showed me the orb. And he summoned the green lights. That had an impact on me. Just like it did for you. I guess I just believe it. I have that blind faith you speak of. Of course, no one knows if I am right or wrong, but I sure as hell don't want to die and find out I didn't do everything possible to ensure my afterlife wasn't taken care of."

She backed up a few feet from Victor and walked towards her closet.

"Now you know I'm not lying about this orb, The MonteGresso. You've seen it with your own eyes. Ain't that right?"

Victor nodded. Lucy chimed in. "You've seen it? I've only heard Bev's stories today. How did Victor see it? And what's my role here?" She pressed Beverly.

"As soon as I saw you the other day, Lucy honey, something clicked in my brain. I know it clicked for you and Victor too. We are all three connected, and you were the missing piece. That's the Dead's power, not mine, not yours and not even the orb's."

Victor shook his head. "No. That orb, the MonteGresser..." Beverly shook her head. "The MonteGresso," she corrected.

"OK, The MonteGresso, it found me," Victor replied. "Is that what you are saying?"

"Nope. The MonteGresso and the other orbs don't have a stake in this thing. They are objects and don't take sides. It was the Dead who found you, and Lucy. They let me know about you two. So I arranged for the orb to be sent to you the moment Lucy completed the puzzle."

Victor spoke. "But my social security number? And my address? And the timing of the delivery? My fingerprint? It all seems so... so..."

"Magical? Yes, the Dead have that power. But again, it's the Dead's choice who they want to help them. Not the orbs'. They were able to program the safe the orb was locked in. They kept it safe while on Earth, but the time is now to use it."

"What about the green lights emanating from the orb?" Victor asked.

"It's just checking you out. The Dead can use the orb to communicate with you and investigate you. And by all accounts the Dead like you. So, Victor, let's see The MonteGresso. It's been too long, and it's been locked away from me. I had The MonteGresso locked away with a secure facility for years and finally gave them permission to deliver it. Victor had to admit, he had come in that evening content to return the orb to Beverly and walk away, but he was being pulled in, and he felt a sense of calmness, duty, and even bravery, all bestowed upon him by this little old lady with the fascinating story.

"And Victor..." Beverly added, "time is of the essence. The Dead are hopelessly trapped and need a Hero. This morning you asked me what happens to us when we die." Victor remembered his cheeky question. Bev continued, "What happens when we die?...Bad things...bad, bad things." Victor and Lucy felt the chills rip through their bodies, because they both knew Beverly was telling the truth.

Chapter 16 * Kitta Schultz

Kitta made her way through international screening at Heathrow Airport with limited problems. Her passport had been used so much in the past two years that she needed to get a supplemental passport. She had traveled extensively in her quest to find the three orbs and this led her from Hong Kong to Berlin, California to Mexico City, and even as far south as Patagonia in South America. She was nothing if not determined.

She had, finally, after painstaking research and surveillance, secured one of the three orbs in Barcelona and left as quickly as possible. She made quite a mess in the kitchen and didn't need to be stuck in a prison cell while the race was on for the other orbs. From her understanding of the mission, she needed to recover all three orbs, wherever they might exist, and then simultaneously re-seed them in a fresh grave and commit a personal sacrifice to ensure the orbs were properly placed into the earth. It had never happened before in all of humanity that all three orbs were simultaneously re-seeded. If this was accomplished, then it would be all over for the Dead. The Builders would have complete dominion over the Afterlife. They could create mass civilizations in the afterlife and rule completely, for all time. What that meant exactly, she didn't have a clue. But what she did know was that her child, her sweet Henry, taken at a young age, a victim of a nasty infection, would be well looked after for all eternity. He would be a king among slaves. That was the promise, and it was all that Kitta needed to know. She would kill and torture whoever stood in her way to get these three orbs and re-seed them, according to the instructions that she had been given.

Kitta was a 37-year-old blonde German who had striking physical features and was able to seduce men, and women. She was well trained in hand-to-hand combat, as well as an expert with knives and most firearms. She had served in the Bundesnachtrichtendienst, the German secret service, and had been used in missions throughout the world advocating on behalf of the German government. Much of what she did was deep cover espionage, and her training and experience made her an ideal candidate for the Builders. She came to the Builders' attention five years ago, right after her beloved three-year-old son, Henry, had died. Kitta's pain was relentless. She sank into a predictable depression. Kitta had never married and raised Henry on her own. His father was another German agent who was killed during a hostage raid shortly after Henry was conceived. She had left the German secret service after she became pregnant with Henry and never looked back. She vowed to forget the things she had done in the past on behalf of her country and focus on a more respectable life raising this child. But, as often is the case, the things one plans for do not always come to pass.

Henry was diagnosed with an unknown and never before seen strain of a bacterial infection that was immune to every antibiotic and other medication. He was seen by physicians from around Germany who were perplexed by this condition. They tried everything to save the cute little Henry, but it was not to be. He was buried within six weeks of diagnosis. The hardest part for Kitta, who sat at his bedside in the hospital for the entire duration of his illness, was the physical pain he suffered. Nothing, except for heavy sedating doses of morphine, would give him relief. So Kitta could not even interact with her child and read to him, or play games with him, or even hear his sweet little voice. If he wasn't sedated, he was in excruciating pain. It was unbearable for his mother who was so strong and vibrant to be so powerless to help him. Over those six weeks she grew bitter and angry at everyone. She had no idea how he contracted this infection but she railed against the medical providers and researchers who failed to provide answers. It was not uncommon for medical staff to be on the front line of a grieving parent's aggression, but Kitta was tougher and angrier than most parents. The medical staff threatened to prevent her from being with Henry unless she changed her attitude. She agreed, but she seethed. She seethed every night and vowed to discover who caused this sickness and do whatever she could to make them suffer like her Henry was suffering.

When she buried him on that bitterly cold Frankfurt morning in 2015, she changed. She stopped speaking to her few friends and former colleagues. She didn't have any other family because her parents had both passed away and she was an only child, so there was no one to offer her the comfort she so desperately needed. No one to help assuage the grief. She simmered. She was the perfect candidate for the Builders. She was strong, violent, smart, and motivated. They first came to her in a dream the night Henry was buried, although the Builders had scouted her for some time before. If no one else provided her comfort and solace and direction, the Builders certainly would.

The dreams started relatively mild. Visions of Henry in a peaceful rest surrounded by protecting angels. Those dreams allowed her to wake up feeling strong and confident even though the pain never seemed to dissipate. Then the dreams became darker, more intense. Visions of Henry being attacked by legions of the Dead. Those protecting angels were being attacked and swarmed by the Dead and they preyed on the vulnerable and the young children who had died. These dreams were vivid in color and sound and when she awoke, she was usually in tears, and angry and petrified that the dreams were in fact real. Someone was trying to reach out to her. The dreams felt too authentic and she had the same ones every single night. How could this just be her subconscious? She knew it was a message and she knew she had to do something.

After six weeks of these dreams, she was awakened in the middle of the night when she thought she heard someone whisper "Kitta" softly in her ear. It continued night after night. At first, she ignored these nightly callings and shrugged them off as part of her dream sequence. While they sounded real, she knew no one was calling her name. No ethereal presence was in her room trying to get her attention. She might be going mad, but she wasn't going crazy. The nightly callings intensified when she began to feel as if she was being shaken awake. Not violently shaken, but just enough to rouse her out of her sleep. And this generally happened when her dreams were at their most haunting. When Henry was being chased and terrorized and unable to peacefully move on to heaven. Finally, after succumbing night after night to the dream, and messages and the physical touching, she finally sat up one night in bed and decided to talk back. "What? Who is this? What do you want with me?" She said it quietly because to say it loudly would mean she was losing her mind, but to say it quietly would allow her to keep a foothold in reality, and also make contact with whoever, or whatever, was trying desperately to get her attention if they were waiting for her to respond.

The Builders responded immediately. They switched on her overhead light. It stayed on for a moment and then shut off again. Kitta jumped out of her bed. She had chills running down the right side of her body from her temple down to her toes. Was she awake or was this a dream that seemed painfully real? The lights flicked on and off again. Oh, this was real! She got back into bed and pulled the covers up to her chin. She might have been a trained killer and tough as nails but having an interaction with some type of ghostly presence was beyond anything she had been trained for and was certainly some freaky shit.

She started to see green lights emanating from her closet. They were brilliant, dancing around the floor and ceiling, across her dresser bed, walls and face. She felt a warmth overcome her and her fear quickly transformed into a sense of awe. Watching the dance of the laser green lights, she became entranced and sat up on her knees looking and communicating silently with whoever or whatever was making this happen. She started to laugh. Slowly at first, then harder and more aggressively until she was roaring with laughter and tears streamed down her face. She screamed at the top of lungs, "Hello! I've been waiting for you!!" The lights danced faster and faster. Her head started to pound, and she gripped it with her hands, rubbing her hair and blanketing her eyes. She stood up on her bed now and jumped in sync with the lights. Had she lived in an apartment she would have had neighbors pounding on the ceiling or walls, but she lived in an isolated house in a secluded Frankfurt neighborhood. No one was around to disturb her connection. It was as if all of the months of grief, tears, anxiety and fear related to Henry was being sucked out of her and re-filling her body and soul with confidence, direction, optimism and joy. It all occurred in a matter of minutes, and then the lights immediately shut off without any warning. No sound. No lights. Silence. Kitta passed out and slept for over a day. She would awake renewed, re-energized and filled with a new sense of purpose based on the magical and ethereal dreams and messages she had received. Thus began her journey as detective and warrior for the Builders.

Chapter 17 ∗ Strange Yellow Hues

Victor slept soundly that night. It was a miracle. He had been chatting with Beverly and Lucy for almost an hour in their room. They all saw The Monte-Gresso and despite all of his protestations, he came to the conclusion this was all real and he was to play a key role in some forthcoming saga. And though he yearned to trust his gut and play it safe; he couldn't turn off that tiny voice in his head that reminded him that his entire adult life had been a failure. A true disappointment. Maybe, just maybe, this was his path to redemption. Something that could make him proud. His chance to prove to himself that he was meant for something great in his brief time upon this earth. Yes, he would do it. He would take a chance and help this old lady, even if this was all crazy talk. He wasn't planning to blow off his head, but he would help Beverly even if it was just to humor her.

The problem was, Beverly didn't have much more information for him. She didn't have a well-thought out strategy on how to protect this orb, this Mon-teGresso, reunify it with the missing orbs, and complete the re-seeding. In fact, she wasn't much of a help as to how to find these other orbs. She just begged him to keep it safe, trust no one, and they would re-group the following day to start to hammer out some plans. That was good enough for him. When he got home, he was incredibly tired and while the shit he saw and experienced the day before should have ensured a hell of a bout of insomnia, that wasn't the case. He slept soundly and peacefully and woke at 8 a.m. without even needing the alarm. That was strange. He was a serial abuser of the snooze bar and to awaken without it, and feel fresh, was a unique and lovely feeling. He also usually had to pee in the middle of the night, a side effect of age. He would normally be deep into a dream of peeing in a toilet but not getting any relief. It was then that he would dramatically awaken, grab his crotch to ensure he hadn't pissed himself, and then head into the bathroom. He was saved from that experience as well.

He reached under his bed and grabbed his shoe and pulled it up onto his bed. He had stuffed a dirty sock into the shoe and in the sock, he had shoved the orb. It seemed that if someone broke into his house to look for this orb the last place they would want to look was in the smelly sock stuffed inside the nasty shoe. Hide in plain sight, right? That was his thinking. No one would touch his shoe; he felt it was as safe a spot as any until he could find a better location.

He pulled out The MonteGresso and stared at it. It was even more beautiful than he recalled from the night before. He held it up to the sunlight beaming through his bedroom window and looked at the complex levels and tones. It almost seemed alive. It probably was as far as he knew. But the real question was why was he being pulled into this and what the hell was he supposed to do with this thing? Why was he so special?

He walked into the bathroom to take a shower and turned on the light. When he looked in the mirror, something seemed very strange. He looked fine, and the room looked fine, but when he stared in the mirror, he saw a faint yellow glow across the glass. He rubbed his eyes and looked back at the mirror. There was the same slight yellow hue, subtle but definitely there. He splashed some cold water on his face, vigorously rubbed his eyes this time, and then looked at the mirror again. The hue was still present. He finally decided maybe he had not cleaned his bathroom in a long time. That was certainly the case since he was a bachelor and a slob. The two combined equaled disgusting bathrooms. If he ever had a woman over to his house, he would certainly have scrubbed a lot more. But that wasn't happening often, if at all.

Victor took a shower and got dressed. He went to brush his teeth but the hue on the mirror remained. He wasn't panicking, just yet. There had to be a reason for this. Maybe he was more tired than he felt. He finished with his teeth, tied his tie and went down to the kitchen to get something to eat. He popped some high calorie breakfast sandwich into the microwave. While his rations cooked, he held the orb and studied it intently. He held it up to the light again and grabbed his reading glasses to get a better view. It almost looked like there were tiny people in the orb. A tiny civilization with buildings and houses and cars and animals, and lots and lots of people. Why not? Nothing would surprise him at this stage. He was still looking at the orb when the microwave dinged. He put the orb into his pocket and looked at the glass microwave door. The dark glass took on a yellow hue, just like the bathroom mirror had. It was unmistakable, especially against the black backdrop. He rubbed his eyes and looked again. The yellow hue popped again. He decided to stop rubbing his eyes and came to the immediate conclusion that staring at this orb caused his eyes to somehow see a strange yellow hue on glass. He looked around the rest of the kitchen. Nothing out of the ordinary. But the yellow hue was still on the microwave glass. It was on the sliding glass door to his backyard too. He turned his gaze to the painted white wall and nothing. He looked back at the glass door, boom, yellow hue. He grabbed a coffee mug out of his cupboard and saw nothing out of the ordinary, no hue. Then he realized the mug was ceramic. He quickly grabbed a water glass—and the yellow hue was there as well.

He was no optometrist, but he quickly realized that this orb affected his eyes. He wondered why it didn't impact him yesterday when he saw it for the first time. Shouldn't that have created a yellow hue along his windshield? But it was evident that, when he looked at the orb in the light of day, especially with the sunlight beaming through his windows, the hue was there. A half-hour later it remained. So, this orb impacted what he could see on glass. Why was that? Beverly would know. She seemed to know everything, and he looked forward to talking with her and Lucy again. Just as he was getting ready to head into the office, his phone rang.

"Hello, this is Victor," he stated into his cell phone.

"Victor, my name is Sheila Evans. I'm not sure if you remember me but, three years ago, you were a client of our law firm and I was your paralegal."

Victor knew exactly who Sheila was. He'd nurtured a secret crush on her throughout his personal injury case. He'd really liked her and felt that she did everything on his case. The attorney, on the other hand, was a fraud and a huckster, but Sheila was A-OK in his book.

"Of course, Sheila, I remember you. How are you?" He was worried that something bad had happened with his old personal injury case. He wasn't sure why he was worried about it, especially in light of recent developments, but that was his nature, anxious and on-edge.

"I'm doing really good, Victor, thanks for asking. I assume you are feeling well?" She was referring to the old back injury he had sustained four years earlier in a mild, rear-end auto collision. She wasn't calling about the insanity of the previous day. Or so he assumed. But he was flustered.

"I am feeling good," he fibbed. Was he feeling good? Physically he felt OK, but emotionally he was a wreck.

"I'm so glad to hear that, Victor," Sheila replied. "So, I assume you don't know the reason for my call." Victor had no clue. She continued. "As you know, Bingham loves to advertise, and he feels that's the best way to help as many people as possible who need help and can't get it." She paused. The lie sounded lame—even to her. Her boss was a diehard ambulance chaser who cared mostly about the bottom line. She plunged on. "He wants to profile some of his former clients for whom he was able to help achieve a great settlement."

She waited, expecting Victor to immediately hang up as all of the other former clients did. One even called her a "piece of shit". But she hadn't heard a click yet and certainly Victor didn't call her a name.

"Um, what? Why are you calling me though?" Victor asked. He wasn't tracking with this call; his mind was in too many other places right now.

"Well, Victor, you received a nice resolution. And I think you would make a wonderful presence in one of Bingham's commercials. We are shooting this week. Can we count on you?"

Victor was still having a hard time understanding why anyone would want him, a washed-up, middle-aged-man to star in a commercial on a case where he didn't even make that much money. He sat there without answering for a minute.

"Victor, honey, are you still there? Are you Okay?" He tried to shake off the negative thoughts. "Oh, I'm sorry Sheila. I'm wondering why you want me. Honestly, I am not exactly TV material, and my case only settled for about $10,000. So why me?"

"Well, first of all you are a wonderfully charming person and I think people will connect with you. Second, we are looking for normal, regular people. We aren't interested in someone who looks like a movie star." She immediately wanted to reel in that last sentence. Way to go, Sheila, she thought, you had the fish on the line and you are going to lose this one for insulting him in the most innocent of ways.

Victor started to laugh. He appreciated her honesty. "Well, Sheila, at least you don't pull punches. You are one honest person. No one has ever mistaken me for a movie star."

"Oh Victor, that's not what I meant. I am so sorry." She blushed. "You are so sweet and kind. And real. I think authenticity is a critical thing to project to other possible clients." She hoped she salvaged this.

"No worries, Sheila, you don't have to apologize. That's very flattering."

"Thanks, Victor. But also you should know that your case settled for $50,000, not $10,000. Remember?"

Victor scratched his head and thought for a second. It was several years ago but he was sure he only took home $10,000. "What do you mean $50,000? I recall a $10,000 check."

Sheila immediately wished she hadn't said that either. Damn, she was screwing this up every which way. "Well, if you recall the case settled for $50,000 and Bingham's fee was forty percent of your settlement per the fee agreement. So that was $20,000. Out of the remaining $30,000 we had reimbursable costs of $1,500. That left $28,500."

"Yeah, I'm following you, so where is that other $18,500?" All of a sudden, the magical orb and the battle of the Dead for the control of the afterlife against a raging species called the Builders was not in the forefront of Victor's mind.

"So, Victor, if you remember we had to send to you to that doctor and the physical therapists and they got paid out of your settlement. They didn't accept the health insurance you carried. Their costs were $18,500." Sheila was silent for a minute. The silence from Victor's end was deafening. She heard some type of groan too. Her hopes of Victor agreeing to be in the commercial were fading and now she was worried she had opened up a new can of worms.

"You mean those doctors that occupy the second floor of Bingham's office building charged $18,500? And if I recall Bingham owns that building so he actually profits off this medical practice, right? I recall something about him owning part of that medical practice?" Victor was now heated and pretty frustrated with Sheila. He couldn't believe he was such a putz that he didn't pick up on this issue three years ago when they settled the case.

"Honestly Sheila," he continued, "I know this wasn't your responsibility, but doesn't your boss feel the least bit guilty about profiting twice as much as his client made in this personal injury accident? And who knows how much he got out of those quack doctors. What the heck kind of law firm do you people operate!?" He was now standing up and almost yelling into the phone. How did his day flip this fast?

"Victor, I agree that it seems unfair…" He cut her off. "Seems unfair? Unfair? This is unethical conduct. I realize The Knife has to pay for all those stupid commercials to con people into using his services, but then to screw them on the way out? That is wrong, Sheila. I cannot believe you are a part of this."

Sheila felt horrible. And she felt horrible not because her boss might suffer an ethics complaint, but she immediately felt a pang of guilt for knowingly cooperating in taking advantage of injured people at their weakest. When they needed help. And most of the people who visited her boss were not sophisticated people. They were average people who didn't have a long list of lawyers they knew. So, they turned on the TV and saw some yahoo with a huge sword kill a paper mache insurance adjuster and that image resonated with them. It was lowest common denominator stuff, and it made her sick. She felt terrible for Victor and she regretted trying to sweet talk him into participating in the charade of TV advertising, as well for being complicit all these years.

"Victor, I don't know what to say. I'm sorry. I thought you understood how these things work. Forget my request. It isn't a fair thing to ask."

Victor cooled down a bit. He really did have bigger fish to fry, but he was so miffed about being screwed over by his attorney, and the sweet Sheila Evans, even though he didn't think Sheila was responsible for Bingham's misconduct.

"Sheila, I apologize for my tone. I know you work hard for your clients. I'm sorry. I just am quite furious right now. I hope you have a good day. Goodbye."

Victor ended the call and regained his composure. He had other stuff he had to accomplish this day and he knew time was running short. If he wanted to help Beverly and Lucy and the rest of humanity, he needed to get his head on straight. He put Sheila Evans and Bingham out of his mind. He would deal with Bingham later. If there was a later. He filled his travel coffee mug and got ready to head into the office. He knew he had to do something with the orb. It couldn't be on him. He sensed that now he was in possession of the orb, some-one—or something—was likely tracking him down and might hurt or kill him. He had to make some fast decisions. He decided he would make a stop on the way into work.

Victor placed the orb in his front pocket and jumped into his car. Until he found a really safe hiding place for the orb, he would keep it in a soft cloth bag, tied tight and connected to his belt loop by a silver chain. It was not Fort Knox, but he felt better knowing it was on his person. Plus, he needed to discuss the strategy more with Beverly and Lucy, so he had to bring it with him. Maybe he would rent a security deposit box at his bank later in the day. But his sense was that if someone, or something, wanted this orb, they wouldn't be stymied by a common bank security deposit box. No, if what Beverly told him was true, then it would take cunning and creativity to keep this orb safe. A safety deposit box could never stop the violent forces at play to find it.

Victor prayed that this was a smart decision. He had no clue that the forces marshalling against him would stop at nothing to obtain this missing link that would change the life of everyone on Earth.

Chapter 18 * World War One

September 25, 1918-France

Private Samuel Griffin laid down as much crossfire as he could muster with his standard issue rifle, but despite all of his firing, he saw his comrades unable to marshal any real advance through the heavily-cratered death fields of Meuse-Argonne. The all-black 369th Regiment, also known as the Harlem Hellfighters, joined with the French troops in heavy fighting. The Hellfighters were one of the longest-deployed American units and they fought valiantly through France amid the violence and barbarism of the trenches. Samuel had volunteered to fight for his country even though many white soldiers had no interest in fighting beside black Americans. The US Army generally relegated the black soldiers to non-fighting positions, but there were some famous black regiments that did see heavy combat, and that's just what Samuel wanted. The French soldiers were fighting to save their homeland and their very existence. The United States still had the Atlantic Ocean to protect itself, but her European allies had nowhere to retreat. If the French and British succumbed to the Germans, then they would face a bleak future. The Treaty of Versailles would have been known as the Treaty of Berlin and to the victors go the spoils. Ironically, the Allied victory and the crushing terms of the Treaty of Versailles would help spawn Adolf Hitler and the Third Reich. Hitler's name would never be known had Germany won the first world war.

Samuel was fortunate to be assigned to this black regiment based out of New York, and despite his mother's wishes for him to remain on the ranch in Lamar, he felt an inherent need to serve his country. His father taught him about love of country and sacrifice. Those lessons were instilled in him long before he found The MonteGresso. He refused to sit idly by on the ranch when his country called. Samuel had enjoyed meeting all the Pierres and Henris and all the other fancy gentlemen who treated him as an equal while he fought as a Harlem Hellraiser. The Germans dropped propaganda on the black regiments, warning them they were pawns of the white man in America and they shouldn't fight to be part of a society that marginalized their race. While Samuel was no fool and understood there was some merit to that propaganda, he loved his country and most of the white people he knew had been kind to him. Maybe that was because his father had earned the respect of the white people of Lamar. But the racism he experienced in America was minimal and he fought to protect his family and to prove something to himself. To prove he wasn't a coward.

He felt a calling too. He had sensed he might find one or both of the missing orbs somewhere in the European death zone, which was the ideal place for him to make the ultimate sacrifice and save the Dead. He had been hoping for years that he would find the other two orbs and he could re-seed all three together. It was a feat that had never been accomplished in the history of mankind, but every day he didn't get his orb re-seeded was another day the Builders had a chance. Nope, France held the best chance for him to try and unite The Monte-Gresso's missing links and put an end to this battle.

From the intense visions that had visited him during his adolescence, he realized the Dead and the Builders were bogged down in their own trench warfare. There were three orbs that controlled a Divide between where the Dead existed and where the Builders existed. If one of the Dead's minions re-seeded an orb by itself, then the Dead would make some headway pushing against the Builders. But if one of the Builders' minions re-seeded a single orb, then the Builders would gain leverage against the Dead. After some time in the ground the orbs would re-surface, always looking for a chance to be reunited. If all three orbs somehow, some way, were re-seeded simultaneously, then the game was up. Either the Dead or the Builders would control the Afterlife for all eternity and the loser would face an extinction, of sorts. Samuel wanted to be the champion and find the other two orbs and make the sacrifice and save the Dead. If he was killed in action, and The MonteGresso was on his person, then The MonteGresso would be re-seeded and it would take years, if not decades, for it to re-surface. But at least it would delay the endgame temporarily until some other poor soul was tasked with uniting all three orbs. That's why he never went anywhere without the orb on his body. Just in case.

When he awoke that morning, he sensed that he could die that day. He had been having increasingly powerful visions and dreams during his time in the trenches. He felt the presence of one of the other orbs, but he couldn't quite grasp its location. At the same time, he also envisioned his own death. He was certain one of the Austrian soldiers had possession of this other orb and assumed this person had visions of him too. He wished he had someone to talk to about this, but no one would believe him, and he knew talking to other people could lead to his death and the loss of The MonteGresso. He could only trust in his dreams and visions, that was his only resource. And it had been that way for ten years, ever since he found this stupid thing and was burdened with its obligations.

The orb rested gently in his knapsack over his shoulder, nestled in a cheese-cloth bag. He had given himself six months to find another orb. It was like finding a needle in a haystack. He had decided that if he didn't find another orb in six months, then there likely wasn't one there. He would just keep The MonteGresso, and himself, as safe as possible until he returned to the United States and then continue the hunt. But he could not overcome the sense of dread that his demise was going to come quickly. Samuel checked his rifle again as it had jammed. He cleaned out the glob of mud that had worked itself deep into the shaft of his bolt action rifle and cleared the jam. He saw several of his buddies advance from the left, up and over the trench.

The bullets flew. The Germans were only 200 yards ahead of his position. The biggest thing in Samuel's mind was that, if he was going to die, The Monte-Gresso had to be with him when that occurred or else the orb may not properly re-seed. Charging the enemy line and getting killed was no different than putting a pistol to his own head. Both would be considered a sacrifice in the name of The MonteGresso. Might as well get a tin medal for his family if he was going to die. He felt the reassuring lump in the bag that hung over his shoulder. Just in case.

"Monsieur, hurry, vee must hurry across zee line!" It was one of the incredibly polite Frenchmen who was leading the charge into the void. Samuel had said his prayers and cried his last tears and prayed to his Lord. Few people survived trench warfare. The odds were stacked against him anyway and his death was inevitable, so it was now or never.

"I gotcha, Henri." Or was it Louis? He didn't know and he didn't care, it was time. The smoke was thick all around and the sound of bullets flying and grenades blasting filled his ears. The smell of rotting human and animal flesh was palpable. He could taste it. It was likely noon, but it could have been six or seven at night due to the haze of smoke, dirt and flies. He climbed out of the trench and started to make his way, along with 100 of his black and French brothers in arms, towards the Huns. There was a clear path forward as most of the barbed wire and bodies had been mashed into the ground. He slipped a little on the blood and mud, but pressed forward. His left hand held his rifle and he started to fire at the German line. He ran and fired and saw his comrades falling all around him. This was it. This was death. And just like that- BAM!!

Samuel's body flew up into the air about fifteen feet and he came crashing down on his head. He lost consciousness for a few moments and he saw many of his brothers lying beside him, torn to shreds. They had run right in front of an exploding shell. It may have been the Germans. It may have been the French. It didn't matter. He was hearing high pitches, screaming and felt another wave of soldiers leave the trenches and charge past them and over them and towards the enemy lines. He couldn't move. He couldn't think. Blood ran down his face and coated his eyes. Then the next thing he saw was blackness.

It would be two days before Samuel regained consciousness. He was lying on cool white sheets on a low bunk in some hospital far from the trenches and death zone. He had a bandage over his head and right eye. He saw that both of his legs were elevated by a pulley mechanism to aid in recovery and prevent inflammation. He hurt all over. There was not one place on his body that didn't scream in pain. He started to whimper and call out. Row after row, he saw wounded soldiers. He didn't know where he was, he didn't know what had happened, and he didn't know when the pain in his body and head would cease. But, after some time, a nice black orderly came by to administer some pain medication. His name was Jessie and he looked like an angel to Samuel.

"Did—did I do it? Did I bury it properly?" Samuel stammered out as he reached for Jessie.

"Well, Private Griffin, I'm not sure if you buried any of those dirty Krauts but you sure did do a number on your legs." Jesse gave a sweet, comforting laugh. Samuel was not the most injured soldier there and Jessie had seen some injuries that were downright gruesome. Death was better. "Why don't you take these, I promise they will make you feel better." Jesse handed Samuel a few white pills. He took them and placed them into his mouth. Jesse helped him drink his water as Samuel was immobile and just coming out of a deep state of unconsciousness.

"Did I do it? Please tell me. Are you an angel? Did I bury it? Did I sacrifice correctly? Is this heaven?" Samuel was starting to panic. What if this was the Afterlife he was trying to protect? What if this was all he had fought for and thought of for years? Unrelenting pain and immobility—this was not his idea of a nice death.

"Well, Private Griffin, aren't you a talkative one? Doctors didn't think you would be so talkative." And Jesse gave another short laugh. "I don't know about burying anything. I do know you ain't buried. You survived that death field. We lost over 5,000 people in that battle in the Meuse, but you, my friend, ain't one of them. You be all banged up, no doubt. But you gonna live, my friend. You gonna live. Now you just close your eyes and wait for that sweet, sweet medicine to hit your belly. "

Samuel started to feel a nice, relaxing sensation come over his body. His breath rate slowed, and his eyes became heavy. "But my orb, my orb...my..."

"Oh, ain't that nice? Well, I'll see you a little later." Jesse watched as Samuel's eyes closed and he started to doze off. He straightened Samuel's top sheet and helped change his bandage over his eye while he slept. He almost had lost his right eye, it sure looked nasty, but it would still be there. Jesse knew lots of other black soldiers in that segregated medical wing who had lost eyes, noses, ears, legs, arms and everything in between. Samuel was one of the lucky ones. He lived and would eventually survive and would be seeing his family again real soon. He was one of the lucky ones. Sure was. One of the lucky ones.

Chapter 19 ∗ Legal Regrets

"Bingham, we need to talk, I think I fucked up." Sheila barged into Bingham's office. His feet were up on the desk in his normal and customary style. He was playing some video game on a big screen monitor on the other side of the office. He had the associates and support staff to do all the work.

"Okay, Sheila, just give me a second." He looked past her shoulder to a sixty-inch video monitor that was supposed to be for conducting video depositions, but Bingham preferred to use it for on-line gaming. He was in the process of shooting a bunch of zombies that had infiltrated a war zone. Bam- Bam- Bam! The bullets flew. He was enjoying himself immensely.

Sheila didn't have time for his juvenile antics, she was trying to work. She turned off the video game console right when Bingham was about to get a high score.

"What the fuck, Sheila, I was crushing."

"You know, some of us have work here and some of us have to clean up messes."

"What mess?" Bingham sat up and grabbed a stack of message notes that had accumulated on his desk from obviously irritated clients.

"Do you remember Victor Jones? About four years ago we handled a soft tissue, tiny case for him." She already knew the answer, but she thought she would try.

He looked up with a shit-eating grin, a grin that said he didn't know and didn't care about any Victor Jones. Still, he tried to play along. "I honestly do not recall a Victor Jones. What happened? Was this poor sap unhappy he didn't become an overnight millionaire?"

"Actually, Bing, he was a sweet guy. Kind of a shlumpy dude. But sweet. He suffered a back injury. Not terrible."

"Yeah, sounds like half my clients. So how did you fuck up in a way that will come back on me?"

Sheila stared at Bingham for a moment and allowed her resentment to recede. He was a charlatan in a nice suit. He was successful only because the world was full of lazy idiots who took their advice from bigger idiots on television or internet chat rooms.

"Actually, I was recruiting him for one of your TV spots, because we cannot seem to find one good candidate to go on TV and brag about how awesome you are. This poor guy was like number 50 on my list. And when we talked, I reminded him how we settled his case for $50,000."

Bingham sat up straight and looked at Sheila. "For $50,000? That's great. For some bullshit soft tissue back injury. He should be kissing my ass."

"Yeah, well, after your tremendous 40% cut, and a reimbursement to the doctors who you are in business with, he walked with a little under $10,000. So, yeah, he forgot how bad he got screwed in this whole deal, until he was reminded."

"Too bad for Mr. Jones; the statute of limitations on filing a legal malpractice case has come and gone." Bingham smiled and reached over to turn the video console back on. Sheila immediately shut it off.

"Jesus Christ, he got screwed and you got rich and you don't feel bad about that? The statute of limitations may have run out on a legal malpractice case, but he could still file a complaint against you, and me, with the state ethics commission. Maybe even go public, call the news. This is just bad. I feel terrible."

"Listen Sheila, my dear, there are always disgruntled people in this world who complain about everything." He was right about that. "And I'm sorry Mr. Jones is having buyer's remorse four years later. But in all fairness, I have other clients to help, and I must focus on these important clients." He said it without a hint of irony. He honestly believed his own bullshit. "Now if there is nothing more, I have to get back to helping rid the world of killer zombies." And with that he turned the console back on and shooed Sheila out of his office.

Some days the work and headaches are just not worth it, was all she could think.

Chapter 20 ✳ Another One Down

Victor charged out of his car as soon as he pulled into Cherry Knolls and ran into his office to put his things away. He planned to immediately run up to Beverly and Lucy's room and get to strategizing. Time was the enemy and there was much to discuss. While he was frightened, he also had an incredible sense of energy and excitement, something he had not felt in years. He couldn't wait to discuss some strategies to help save the Afterlife for the Dead. He was especially intrigued by the visual yellow hue he seemed to have acquired from the orb. He had no idea why that happened, but he couldn't wait to get Beverly's take.

He dumped his jacket on his chair and made his way out to the residents' hall. He was moving past Mike Guidry's office when he heard his name.

"Victor, do you mind coming in please?"

It was Guidry sitting behind his ridiculously large and clean desk, with only a cup of coffee and his laptop on it. A smug office for a smug man. Fuck. That's all that Victor could think. The last thing he needed now was Mike Guidry.

"Yeah, Mike, can it wait a few?" Victor said as he poked his head into Guidry's lovely office.

"Nope, need you right now for a minute. Please. It will just take a second." Victor relented. The last thing he wanted to do was lose his job when he needed to be around Beverly and Lucy to strategize and keep them safe. So he came in. "Sure Mike." Victor grabbed a chair on the other side of the desk.

"So, you pulled a late one last night I understand." Shit, Victor immediately started to sweat, he didn't think Guidry would know he was here. Not that he wasn't allowed to be, but in the twelve years he worked there he couldn't count five times he worked past 5 p.m. That's probably why he had not advanced very far in his career. He took a moment to settle into his lie. "Yes, I wanted to spend some more time with Cosmix. I learned a lot, but I have more to learn. Yes, that Jerri Hughes, she's a smart one. I appreciate you connecting us." What a vomitous lie.

"Cosmix training at 11:45 p.m.? Wow. OK. I'm not sure why your computer wasn't accessed though. Is there a training for Cosmix that isn't connected to the computer?"

Damn. Guidry of course had access to the computer log-ins so he knew Victor had not logged in. Basically, he was setting a trap. Anything to fire him. He should have concocted a better story as soon as he saw all those employees last night. Of course, Guidry would have found out. He was just so consumed with the fate of humanity he didn't spend time worrying about little pissants like Mike Guidry who didn't realize that he was going nuts trying to save the Afterlife for everyone, including jerk-offs like Mike Guidry.

"Well, that's true. I had planned to address some issues last night, but I wanted to check in on Ms. Black as I didn't have a chance during the day to follow up on her room charges. I just wanted to tell her we would get it all worked out. Beverly Griffin started sharing some stories and Lucy showed me pictures of her grandkids and we all had a nice chat. By the time I finished talking to them, it was too late to start working on Cosmix so I went home."

There that ought to hold Guidry for awhile, Victor thought. That was a damn good lie; Victor was proud of himself.

"Well, I understand you spent at least twenty minutes in their room, Victor. That seems awfully long to spend that much time in a female resident's room, especially at night."

Victor shot up. "Just what are you implying, Mike?" He went from feeling defensive to feeling pissed. "Are you implying I was engaging in unethical conduct with two octogenarians? We were having a regular old ménage a tois? Are you kidding me?" He never had called Mike out like that before, but he had never been accused of doing something so perverted either.

"I'll tell you what, Victor, you are not to go into any residents' room unsupervised again. I'm not going to be the executive who gets sued because one of his staff was diddling a little old lady. So that's it. You stay at your desk, you stay at your little computer, and you do the tasks you're paid for. If you so much as talk to one of the residents without my permission, you are done. Do you understand me?" Mike was red with rage and was hardly going to be talked down to by someone as subordinate as Victor Jones.

Victor considered the gravity of this situation. He knew he needed to continue to have access to Lucy and Beverly if they were going to see this thing through, whatever it was. He couldn't be prevented from talking to them. He needed to be there to strategize and, more importantly, to protect them. Now that the orb was in his custody and Beverly knew he had it, she could be in danger. He wouldn't let her or anyone else die on his account.

"I'll tell you what, Mr. Guidry. How about you leave me the fuck alone? I'll do what I need to do here to help the residents." He pointed to the framed photo of the happy Guidry clan in Hawaii or Bora Bora or wherever this dishonest family photo was shot. "And if that's a problem, I'll just call Mrs. Guidry and get her take. Maybe she will be interested in her husband screwing around with a twenty-two-year-old assistant who was promoted over her more senior, but not nearly as attractive, co-worker. You know I snapped a few pictures of you and Ms. Hughes doing something in your car yesterday. How cliché, by the way, at least take her to a motel." Victor had not seen them doing anything but he sensed they were about to. Guidry didn't even protest, he was so taken aback. Guidry's face went white. He was speechless. Victor took that as a cue to exit the office.

After leaving, Victor breathed a huge sigh of relief. He had just blackmailed his boss who was having an affair and Guidry didn't fire him or even say a word after he dropped that bombshell. Victor had seen people do that in the movies, but he could never have ever envisioned a time when he would not only have to do that but have the temerity and balls to actually *do* it. This was something he needed to place on his LIST under "mission accomplished."

He was feeling pretty proud of himself as he strode out of the executive office suite and made his way down to the residents' wing. He wasn't sure about the next move, but he felt there was something to this tall tale he heard the day before. Finding the orb certainly solidified some of his feelings, but he still had tremendous doubts and concerns. He knew he needed to coordinate with Beverly. He was sure Beverly would have a well-thought out plan. When he started to walk up the staircase, he heard an alarm go off and saw several nurses sprint past him up the stairs. It wasn't unusual to see an emergency at Cherry Knolls because they had so many elderly residents, but the alarm scared him. He never heard that when he was sitting comfortably behind his desk going over spreadsheets. At the top of the stairs, he realized with horror that the nurses were in room 218. He ran down the hall and tried to look in.

Two female nurses were leaning over Beverly, outstretched on the floor beside her bed, arms askew. A male nurse was on the right side literally on top of Beverly, giving her chest compressions. They had an oxygen mask over her face. And several other residents, curious about the emergency, were milling about in her room. They all knew that, at any time, it could be them lying on the floor, getting emergency care. Lucy was standing in the corner of the room crying. Victor went over to her and immediately placed his arm around her to comfort her. Where was the ambulance? Why wasn't it here by now?

"What happened?" Victor whispered to Lucy, who seemed to be in a state of shock. She had only lived with Beverly for a few days, but in that short time they had become quite close. They had become fast friends and now it appeared to be over.

"I don't know," Lucy said between sobs. "We had just had breakfast in the cafeteria. She said she wasn't feeling well at all. She told me to call for help." The sobbing continued. "So I yelled for Nurse McCormack down the hall and she came running. Next thing I see, Beverly is lying on the floor unconscious. Oh, my God." She buried her face in Victor's chest. He held her tight. In another minute as the nurses continued chest compressions, there was a rush of excitement at the door. Three firefighters and two paramedics crashed in and, after giving Beverly an injection, immediately took over the CPR, this time with a mask over her face.

"We got something. It's faint but we got a pulse." It was one of the paramedics. He motioned for the pram to be wheeled in. Quickly but gently they loaded Beverly on. As they started to belt her in, she weakly raised her left hand and tried to pull off the mask. The paramedics tried to restrain her, but Beverly, struggling against them, somehow prevailed. With a last bout of strength, she ripped the mask off. "Victor, Victor," she rasped. "This is all on you now, my sweet boy…"

"Shhh, Ms. Griffin, relax," Nurse McCormack said, busily taking charge. "Shhhh, the paramedics need you to save your strength." Victor leaned down to listen to Beverly's words.

"Victor," she hissed insistently. "Use your new vision. Anyone who has held the orb has the vision. Find the other two. Bury them." She wheezed. "Save us."

The firefighters tried to shove Victor out of the way as they hustled Beverly out of the room and down the hall, but Victor stayed by Beverly's side, running with the firefighters.

"How, Bev? How do I do this alone? I don't know what to do!" he pleaded with her. This might be his final chance for any direction. He was scared to death he was going to be all alone without any idea how to handle the Herculean task ahead of him.

"You're not alone my child…use your new vision…your vision will help you find the orbs…the yellow light can be seen only by the orbs' holders…. you're not alone."

"I am alone. Who can help me?" He prayed she had an answer. "You have them," she replied, pointing to the ceiling. Victor looked up. What was she saying? "Who, Bev, who?"

"Trust your dreams. Use your new vision…glass…yellow…trust…" She stopped talking as the firefighters loaded her into the ambulance. They buckled her in. Victor tried to board the back of the ambulance, but they wouldn't let him.

"Thank you, Victor," he heard her say. "You save the world now, my sweet child, keep The MonteGresso safe." And with that the paramedics closed the door and the ambulance screamed off, lights and sirens blaring. What did she mean? He had no idea what do, who to talk to or how to save the Dead. The only thing he knew deep down in his bones is that he would never see Beverly Griffin alive again. She lived long enough to pass the burden to him. She would die on the way to the hospital. He also knew, that if the Dead were counting on him, the Dead were royally fucked.

Chapter 21 * The PinonAstra

London

Kitta was energized as she cleared customs and boarded the 747 for the United States. It was her third trip to the United States in the past year, but she had never come away with anything. Her visions were getting stronger, and she knew the Builders were helping to guide her, but she also knew she had to do the investigation on her own and find the clues to get the job done. She didn't understand the rules that seemed to be at play. If the Builders, or the Dead, for that matter, were so knowledgeable, then why not just tell the minions where these things were and get it over with? But she didn't have anyone to ask that question. That must be why these three orbs had never been united in all of human existence.

She got lucky in Barcelona. Her vision that led her there was of the Dachau concentration camp in Germany in 1944. The height of Hitler's 'Final Solution', when Jews and other undesirables were being eliminated at an astonishing rate. Mass murder, coupled with German efficiency, was a combination of unparalleled horrors that would forever change the face of world Jewry and the geopolitical fates of Europe, Asia, and the United States. Kitta had grown up years after the War and, like most Germans who were two generations removed from that nightmare, was educated about Germany's terrible past and made to feel guilty whenever she traveled outside of Germany. She wasn't responsible for the Hitler horror show and the pain caused by the Third Reich. Neither were her friends who were all raised in that bloody shadow. But the inescapable truth was that death and carnage ran through their bloodlines. All of her friends in Germany had parents or grandparents who either were afraid to speak up, or worse, supported Hitler and his vicious empire and participated in the genocide. Anyone who came of age in Germany in the 1960's, 70's or 80's, had relatives who had blood on their hands.

Her vision of Dachau led her to a Lieutenant Karl Weiss. He was one of the assistant wardens at Dachau and had been a staunch member of the Nazi party since Hitler took power in 1933. He had served in the first World War as a young corporal fighting his way west through France. That was visceral bloodshed. Visions of death he never could truly erase. He saw his brothers and comrades killed by the Allied forces and after the loss, they suffered again under the crippling sanctions of the Treaty of Versailles, which made losing the war even more catastrophic. The Allied forces had demolished Germany, turning the Fatherland into a pile of rubble with a decimated economy and a de-moralized national spirit. However, he found solace with the words and vision of a charismatic man who was a failed painter. This man had charisma and drive, and he let his followers know that the world had unfairly punished Germany and was being assisted by the worldwide Jewish menace.

Before Karl Weiss became a lieutenant in the Nazi machine, he pined for glory fighting for his country in the trenches of France. In June 1917, Weiss was part of an engineering battalion that dug and reinforced the comprehensive trench system that defined World War One. He was a digger and helped secure the trenches with thick railroad ties and cement. One rainy evening as he walked alone through his trench and was busy reinforcing some siding, he saw some auburn lights emanating from a crack between some of the railroad ties. He was sure his eyes were playing games because nothing that beautiful and vibrant lived in the trench. He looked around to see if anyone else saw this intense light, but no one was there. He grabbed his shovel and started prying at the hardened trench wall. After a few minutes the lights became clearer and brighter. He was sure someone would have seen this, but no one approached him. He stuck his hand deep into the muck and lo and behold this brilliant auburn orb filled his hand. He was transfixed. This was something special. It was beautiful and had to be valuable. What in god's name was this and how did it end up there?

He quickly yanked it free from a weed that also seemed to glow green but shriveled up and receded into the dirt once the orb was yanked free. He cleaned it off and took it with him to his sleeping bag so he could have some time to look at his new jewel. It had to be worth thousands, no, millions, of Deutsch Marks. If the war caused a lot of loss and sadness, at least it just re-paid him by making him fabulously rich. What a find!

Karl Weiss survived the war and the violence of the trenches. He kept the orb close to him everywhere he went and was not foolish enough to show anyone. He would have had to give it up to the high command or else someone would steal it. No, this was special. And it came with surprising components. He began to have bizarre dreams of other otherworldly battles, as well a newly acquired vision problem that caused him to see light yellow hues on glassy surfaces. He wasn't the sharpest man, but he could tell that something was trying to get his attention. When he did his best to ignore the dreams, they became more and more vivid. He had envisioned the other orbs but never felt a drive to gather the remaining orbs for the purpose of re-seeding them. His only interest was motivated purely by greed. If those other orbs did in fact exist, then he coveted them for no purpose other than self-enrichment. Karl Weiss wasn't the type of character to make any personal sacrifice for anyone or anything. That was his nature. As for the yellow hue, he assumed it was caused by chemical agents he encountered in the trenches. It didn't bother him, it was just an annoyance. He never connected the new vision to the orb. It's startling that the Builders chose him because he couldn't help them fulfill their immediate goals. But it was possible the Builders had a longer game plan and Karl Weiss was just a cog in their machine.

After the war, Weiss tried to find a market for the orb, but he was too scared to try and sell it. He knew the German people were reeling and someone with this type of portable wealth would be taken advantage of by some Jew-swine diamond broker. No, he would wait. He would wait for the right time to sell. Despite the nightly dreams, he pushed on. And as Hitler's power grew, Karl Weiss became Lieutenant Karl Weiss. Riding the coattails of the German high command, he was able to gain favor with the Nazi leadership. One day, when this new world war concluded and the Third Reich began its thousand-year reign, he would find a way to bring this to the Fuhrer. The Fuhrer had a passion for antiquities, and this was definitely an antiquity. Until then, he would wait. He would never leave it alone. And as he ascended into leadership ranks and became an assistant warden at Dachau, he kept it close to him.

Like all cruel leaders who benefited from slave labor, Weiss used a young boy to clean his house at the camp. This young boy was Weiss's personal valet and, despite being a dirty Jew, he was good at cleaning. Young Joseph Avram Rabin, only thirteen years old, took care of all of Lt. Weiss's needs in his house. One day when Weiss was out, likely overseeing a deportation of Jews to Auschwitz, his favorite thing, the lieutenant was careless with his beautiful orb. Joseph saw it sitting in a drawer in a safe that was left ajar. It was odd that Lt. Weiss would leave his safe ajar, very odd indeed, but here it was. And Joseph saw it, held it, was mesmerized by it. It moved him, just like the others throughout history who had been fortunate enough to see it. Joseph knew it was special. He also knew if he was seen touching it, he would be executed on the spot. So he carefully replaced it and closed the safe. He made a mental note that, the day he was saved from this brutal hell, he would exact his revenge on any Nazi he could find remaining alive and steal that orb.

Joseph did not have to wait too long and he was motivated. He had witnessed the execution of his father by one of the guards who one day felt an urge to murder an old Jew. He witnessed his mother and sisters be shipped off by rail to some unknown yet frightful location, never to be seen again. He witnessed his fellow Jews in the camp, many of whom he would not have associated with except that they were brothers-in-arms, collectively suffering under persecution and constant threat of death by bullet, maggot or starvation. He wanted revenge. He yearned for it. It was the only thing he lived for, the heat that motivated him and the hope that he would be given the opportunity. If only once.

It was the spring of 1945 and Joseph had been Lt. Weiss's valet for over a year. It had been almost six months since he had first seen the orb. It was the first and only time he saw it, but he was acutely aware that it remained in the safe. He had dreams and visions unlike anything he had before that day.

Ironically, Joseph had wonderful dreams before seeing the orb. He would often dream of swimming in a lake near his family's house in Berlin, enjoying picnics and parties and other joyous events with his family and friends. Of course, when he awoke from these dreams, he entered into the reality of the nightmare that was his life. Hunger, pain and depression filled his every waking hour, but solace came during the night. Sometimes he would awaken next to a corpse, the person's vacant eyes staring at Joseph as if to say, "I am sorry this is how you had to wake up. I'm sorry this happened to you, my sweet friend. I will see you soon. You know I will see you very soon."

Yet after seeing and feeling the orb, his dreams turned darker. He dreamed of battles amongst some pernicious entity and his family. All he had lost. His grandparents and great-grandparents. His cousins and siblings. They were fighting a new battle. And the imagery was vivid. It felt real and palpable. He could sense his grandfather talking to him. Spewing out numbers, the same numbers every night: 12-32-41. He had no idea what the numbers represented but they were implanted into his brain. He often saw his mother making a delicious iced tea for him and then before serving Joseph, she would grab a box of rat poison, take a heaping spoonful, and stir it in. When Joseph reached for the deadly concoction she slapped it away and he saw the tea spilled onto the floor as droplets landed on Lt. Weiss's face, who was sleeping soundly in a comically large bed with soft pillows and warm luxurious blankets. Lt. Weiss never seemed to notice the tea dripping on his face, he just slept soundly and happily. Then Joseph would generally awaken. It was the same bizarre dream night in and night out.

In the spring of 1945, he sensed a tension in the camp. He had overheard rumors from other inmates, and sometimes from his eavesdropping on Lt. Weiss, that the Americans were bulldozing towards Berlin from the west, and the Russians were charging from the east. It was just a matter of time until they would show up at the gates of this Hell on Earth to rescue the remaining skeletons who had somehow, beyond all odds, survived. That's when the Nazis stepped up their efforts to evacuate the Jews from Dachau and either march them into the forest to shoot them or load them up onto railway cars for extermination at Auschwitz. The Nazis didn't attempt to hide the genocide at this point in time, it was self evident. One just had to look at the mass piles of dead that seemed to fill every nook and cranny of the camp. It was a reality that Joseph did not even seem to notice any longer.

How a young man, barely old enough to shave a whisper of a moustache, could walk by a pile of corpses, people he had known, rotting in the sun, day in and day out and not suffer permanent insanity would become one of history's most interesting psychological studies. Many survivors committed suicide and others were unable to assimilate back into society; the grief and guilt of surviving too overwhelming to conceptualize.

Joseph only thought about survival. He never gave up, no matter the beatings, hunger pains, or humiliation. He avoided looking at guards, he made himself indispensable to Lt. Weiss, and he even succumbed to many of Lt. Weiss's barbaric sexual demands without a whimper. He did so because his dreams told him to. His dreams, as horrific as they were, gave him hope. And he waited patiently. His dreams started to crystallize. He knew what he had to do, and he knew how to do it.

His visions gave him a date and a plan, and he hoped he had the courage to do what needed to be done. On April 25, 1945, the time had come. He knew this because he could hear the distant explosions of munitions, the Allied planes flying freely over German airspace, the heightened anxiety of the guards. This all led him to believe that now was the time.

Lt. Weiss sat at his desk and barked orders at someone on the phone. The papers and ledgers on his desk were uncharacteristically scattered and disorganized. There was also a metal garbage can next to his desk where he was burning papers. He had not shaved for days, he wore just a T-shirt, black pants and jackboots. His fat belly hung uncomfortably over his partially zipped pants. He was smoking cigarette after cigarette and he likely had not slept in two or three days. His gray whiskers were pouring out of his chin and his eyeglasses were partially askew. Joseph knew this was the dangerous and unpredictable time, but the right time.

He went into the kitchen and grabbed the tea from the icebox. He poured a large glass and added a large scoop of sugar that Lt. Weiss had commandeered from someone, despite the severe rationing. He then looked over his shoulder to make sure he was alone. The coast was clear. He went to the pantry and grabbed the yellow box of rat poison that he was accustomed to using due to the disgusting rat infestation at the concentration camp.

Joseph put two heaping teaspoons into the tea, along with a little more sugar just to be safe, and vigorously stirred the deadly cocktail. He also placed some cheese and bread onto a plate and carried it to Weiss.

As expected, Weiss did not say thank-you or show even the slightest appreciation for the meal that Joseph brought to him. Why would he? Joseph, lower than the rat, was his personal slave and sex toy. Either due to exhaustion, stress or a combination, Weiss wolfed down the food in a few voracious bites. Joseph had gone into the other room and peered carefully around the corner. Lt. Weiss grabbed the drink while still chewing and barked into the phone. Grabbing the glass, he didn't even give it a second thought. He drained the glass in one tremendous swig and shouted at Joseph for a re-fill.

Joseph ran to the table to get the glass. Lt. Weiss let out a loud belch and scratched his underarm. He slammed down the phone yelling, "Fools!!" to no one in particular. Joseph held his breath. This psychopath would either keel over and die a horrific death or else summon help, get taken to the infirmary, recover and then torture Joseph for trying to kill him. When Weiss suddenly stood up and started clawing at his throat, Joseph looked on with eagerness.

"Help me, Joseph! I can't breathe!" Weiss said in a choked voice. "Come here! Do something!" Sweat poured off his brow. "Aaachh…Jew bastard…acchh help me…" His voiced trailed off.

Joseph stood motionless, watching the lieutenant curled over in pain. Weiss fell onto the desk; papers went flying, the phone fell off the hook, and he gasped pointlessly for air. Joseph carefully replaced the phone on its base so as not to generate concern from anyone monitoring the switchboard. Weiss finally fell face first on the desk and continued his struggle for precious air. Blood and vomit seeped from his mouth, a sight that filled Joseph with delight because it didn't just signal imminent death, but an imminent painful death for someone deserving of such a fate.

Joseph laughed as Lt. Weiss fought for breath. He was still conscious enough to see Joseph laughing. Joseph made silly faces at Lt. Weiss, taunting him.

"Excuse me, Lt. Weiss, did you happen to see the rat poison? I did. You just drank it." Joseph leaned down, face to face with Weiss, eye to eye, so he could watch the suffering up close.

When Lt. Weiss made a final lunge for the phone, Joseph gingerly removed it from his hand. Without a struggle. Lt. Weiss even tried to reach for his Lugar that was on the other end of the desk, but Joseph beat him to it and pressed the barrel against his forehead, but he was no fool as to shoot this man and alert people. Plus, why would he relieve him from his suffering? Tears streamed down Lt. Weiss's face.

"Good-bye Karl Weiss, the Jew won." Joseph whispered into his ears. He was careful to sit there for a few minutes to ensure the breathing had ended and that Hell had a new guest. He quickly ran into Weiss's closet and went for the hidden safe. He realized that the numbers he dreamt of had to be something useful. He knew it was worth a shot, so he turned the safe's wheel to the left…12, then to the right, 32, and finally back to the left, 41. The tumblers fell and the safe opened. He hastily rummaged through the cash, jewels and other stolen goods until he felt the orb. He pulled it out. It was as beautiful as it always had been. Time was wasting. He also grabbed a small pouch that he believed must be filled with diamonds or some other jewels. These might come in handy if liberation was close at hand. He shoved the orb and jewels into his pocket, careful to conceal the bulge in his pants. The one benefit of working inside a warden's house was that you got cleaner, less tattered clothes. The better to conceal ancient, glorious treasures.

He then went back to the very dead Karl Weiss, grabbed the glass, and returned it to the kitchen. He placed the box of poison back into the pantry and shoveled as much cheese and bread into his mouth as he could handle. He then left the warden's house and walked back towards his barracks. He had accomplished two of three goals. He killed the Nazi, he secured his beautiful orb, and now he just had to survive. That would be the hard part. There was no guaranteeing what the Nazis would do as the inevitable end of their reign of terror approached. They could kill them all, show mercy, or die in a blaze of glory fighting the Americans. Joseph hoped for options two or three, but he and his fellow Jews expected and feared option one.

Through sheer cunning and luck, Joseph avoided any questioning associated with the recently departed Lt. Weiss. It was evident none of the remaining Germans cared about Weiss. They only cared about themselves. Many had run off with whatever booty they could carry, while others planned for the defense of the camp. As far as Joseph knew, Weiss rotted on his desk for four days before anyone even saw him.

Due to the pandemonium and chaos in the final days of Dachau, an autopsy wouldn't be performed and, even if someone did see Weiss before the Americans arrived, they would just suspect he died of a massive coronary or that he swallowed a cyanide capsule since that little pill was the dessert du jour for most in the failed Nazi leadership. To Joseph, they were all a bunch of cowards and bullies, and they didn't deserve a fast cyanide death. They deserved endless torture, pain, and humiliation. They deserved to be dumped into a pit of fire while they screamed for mercy. But beggars couldn't be choosers and Joseph was just happy they were dead.

On April 29, 1945, four days after Weiss had a rat poison concoction, United States Lt. Colonel Felix Sparks and the soldiers of the 3rd Battalion liberated Dachau and witnessed the atrocities of the Nazis first-hand. Joseph was saved. He had been given a new lease on life, and he would always be thankful to the power of the orb for giving him the courage and motivation to survive.

Immediately after the liberation, Joseph would relocate to the land that would soon be known as the Jewish State of Israel. He would join with the Hagenah and fight against the Arab nations, who all intended to finish off Hitler's work and drive the small group of Jews and Holocaust survivors into the Mediterranean Sea, ending once and for all the Jewish menace. But the Hagenah proved to be formidable and, with a ragtag bunch of soldiers and second-hand weapons, they fought like lions defeating the Arab nations bent on Israel's destruction. Joseph settled on a small kibbutz near Tel Aviv, raised a family and spent his free time immersed in learning the jewelry trade. He still had his diamonds from Weiss's safe as well as the magical orb. He had tried for years to find the other orbs that he knew existed, but aside from visiting antique stores and jewelers, he didn't have much to go on. He had continuous visions and dreams, but he was unable to find the remaining orbs. He knew his primary job was to keep his orb safe until one day someone came to help him find the other ones or a clue appeared that gave him a lead.

He began to have visions of the Spanish artist Gaudi. He knew nothing of Gaudi and had never traveled to Spain, but he decided the time was right to follow this lead. He thought clues could be located in La Sagrada Familia Cathedral, the behemoth building that had been under construction for almost a century. Perhaps there was something hidden in the elaborate carvings that occupied the massive exterior. While Joseph loved his new Israeli homeland, he felt he would be better off following his instincts. His children had all grown up and moved away, so he and his wife Babette resettled in Barcelona. He spent years combing the libraries and intricate Gaudi exhibits looking for clues, but he never seemed to gain any traction.

It wasn't until a few days before his death that he spotted this blonde woman several times. He had been sketching patterns in Gaudi's intricate engravings on the outside of the cathedral. He had set up an easel, along with lots of other artists, in the park directly across the street. While the other artists were sketching or painting to capture the beauty of the unfinished church, Joseph was sketching for patterns or clues. It was at the beginning of September when the woman caught Joseph's eye. Normally she was exceptionally adroit at disguising herself and avoiding her subjects; however, she had followed him onto the Las Ramblas one busy afternoon during a heavy lunchtime crowd. Las Ramblas occupied many blocks of prime real estate just a few minutes from the Barcelona shoreline so she thought the crowds would protect her. Joseph had sensed someone was following him and he had been warned of something in his dreams. But the dreams, as usual, were short of specifics. Then he saw her. She failed to pull back in time and he turned quickly, sensing he was being followed. Joseph figured she knew her cover was blown, and she would have to make a move quickly. The following day, he constructed the elaborate booby trap and ordered Babette to leave the city. He would do his best to stop this person and give his wife a head start on an escape. Babette had been packing her bags, getting ready to flee down the back entrance to their apartment, but Kitta made her move faster than he had planned, killing Joseph and Babette and securing the magnificent orb, known by its name: The PinonAstra.

Kitta had found Joseph through painstaking research. Her visions led her to a young Cpl. Weiss, who became the ruthless Lt. Weiss. But the visions didn't place the orb anywhere after that, only telling her that it had not been re-seeded. She traced Weiss's time in Dachau and eventually learned through interviews and some torture that a young boy had worked in his house. Due to the Germans' impeccable record-keeping, she eventually discerned that Joseph Avram Rabin, from Berlin, was Karl Weiss's valet/slave in his house at Dachau. That had to be as good a clue as any. If this Joseph Rabin didn't know where the orb was, then her trail would be cold. Traveling from Germany to Tel Aviv, Kitta did her best to get people to believe she was doing Holocaust research on behalf of Germany's Holocaust Museum. That's how she gained access to old Nazi files and how she earned the trust of the Israelis who had once known Joseph. Told he had moved to Spain, it did not take long to track him down through some easy research and a few bribes. Once she got close, she knew she had him. Her senses became acute and she had a laser focus on her target. Once she had landed in Barcelona, it was only a matter of days until she had dispatched with the Rabins and held one of the three most important instruments in the history of mankind. Her next stop was America, where she suspected the other orbs were ready and waiting for her. The flight from London was the first time she had slept in days and she would need her energy to fight the final battles that were ahead of her.

Chapter 22 * Aloha Senorita

It was a sad time for Victor. Within 48 hours his world had been turned upside down and the only person who could help him had died. He could now only rely on his visions and Grandma Lucy, who didn't know much more than he did. That was it. He decided to do what he did in college to help him clear his mind and come up with some answers: take the rest of the day off, go for a long walk, and get high. What else would one expect from a burn-out? He'd had some epic weed-smoking days in college and after he graduated, but as he got older, he found he couldn't handle being high. He became paranoid to the point of panic. He thought people were making fun of him or talking about him behind his back (sometimes the paranoia was justified). Sometimes his heart would start racing and he was convinced he was only minutes from a major cardiac event (very unlikely, but the fatter he got the more likely), but mostly being high just demotivated him.

But Victor also knew that weed didn't always lead to lazy days on the couch for everyone. He knew many successful people were potheads and their creations were weed-inspired. Some of rock's best music was written by marijuana aficionados. Wasn't Thomas Jefferson known as the drafter of the Constitution as well as being the founding father of funk and weed? Carl Sagan and Bill Gates were also famous potheads. Maybe that was the answer. He was desperate and maybe, just maybe, some good ganja would help him have a breakthrough or, as the native Americans called it, a vision quest. If anyone was in need of a vision quest, it was Victor Jones.

Colorado had long been the pioneer of legal marijuana in the United States. During the coronavirus pandemic, the government allowed marijuana businesses to remain open to serve as an essential function (more so than restaurants, bookstores and salons). It was funny that within a few short years, possession and distribution of marijuana went from being felonious behavior to an "essential business activity." So it stood to reason the best bud in the world would be developed and grown in Denver's plethora of legal greenhouses. Maybe they had something for him.

He drove to one of the many dispensaries in his neighborhood and went inside. There used to be a stigma about going into a weed dispensary, but nowadays it was as socially acceptable as bringing your dog into a restaurant. Everyone was doing it. Victor entered The Frosted Bud and inhaled deeply. The skunky smell of strong marijuana permeated his nose and clothing. After showing his identification, he was personally assisted by a budtender. For real. A budtender. So much for originality.

"Hey buddy, how are you doing today?" asked a 25-year-old man with tattoos on one arm. His jeans so tight Victor wondered how he could bend over the display case. "What are you interested in? Can I help find you something tasty?"

Victor swallowed hard, trying to gather his thoughts. The array of edibles, pipes and other accoutrements made his head swim. The budtender chirped on, undaunted by Victor's silence. "My name's Chester by the way, what's yours?"

Why on earth did Victor need to give Chester his name? The liquor store clerk could care less what his name was. Budtenders were Gen-Z's response to the millennial barista; they all thought they were better than the ordinary retail or grocery store clerk. Sure, they made less money than a grocery store clerk, but they wouldn't be caught dead working in a grocery or liquor store. After all, budtenders and baristas had college degrees!

"Name's Victor, nice to meet you." He said just to be nice. But he wasn't sure what he needed. How could he ask for some type of marijuana that would help him decipher his dreams and learn the true power of the mystical orb? Was there any plant available he could use in the epic fight of the Afterlife between the Dead and the Builders? Was there some weed for that?

"Whatcha looking for? Something to chill with? Something to get you really numb? You like gummies or do you prefer to smoke?"

"I like gummies, but those edibles freak me out. I once ate three all at once and I couldn't feel my face for like five hours. So I think I'll smoke something."

Chester rubbed his little chin goatee. "Ouch, yep, three gummies at once will knock you out." He thought for a moment. This was exactly why he got his psychology degree and spent five years at Colorado State University. "So that's interesting. Okay. Well, the different varieties are Indica, which is a chill weed. Or Sativa, which is not so much a chill weed. What sounds good?"

"So, Chester, here's the deal. Does anyone ever say they need to smoke weed to solve a problem? I mean, I need something to help me, you know, to help me think through a complicated problem. You got something for that?"

Chester was really glad he got his minor in English; this seemed like a particularly focused question which would utilize all the information and resources his $110,000 education had to offer. "Sure Victor, are you writing a book or something?"

"Well, not exactly. I need to solve some riddles. I know this sounds stupid, but I need to…" He paused, "…I need to interpret my dreams. I know it sounds stupid, but is there anything you'd recommend?"

"Dude, I don't think you're being stupid at all. In fact, you came to the right place. The literature on weed and the subconscious is significant." He emphasized this by pointing both index fingers at his frontal lobe. "Weed is the key to the door of your subconscious and can help you see things you never thought to see in the daily grind of life. But if you really, really have a sticky situation may I suggest… a dose of acid." He whispered this. After all, drug dealing was frowned upon, especially in a marijuana dispensary.

"No, I don't need that," Victor answered quickly. He was too old and too paranoid to have a real hallucinogenic experience. "But what items here can you recommend?"

Chester thought for a second. "I think I have the perfect remedy for what ails you. I have a strain called Aloha Senorita. It's the best of the best to help loosen up the thought process. I highly recommend. It's a blend of Sativa, Indica and cannabinoid oil extract. A few tokes and you will have answers."

"Sold." He didn't feel like hanging out there too long for fear he might bump into someone he knew. Like many people of his generation, he still felt very, very odd, maybe even a little guilty, purchasing drugs from a dispensary. Victor pulled out his wallet to pay for the pot. It was sold in 1-gram units. He opted for the full 7 grams, which was the most a person could legally purchase at any one time. Just in case he needed extra help and his time was running short.

"Excellent choice, my friend. I hope you get the answers you are seeking. And I hope to see you again soon, Victor."

Victor thanked Chester and realized that he was a nice enough guy. He feared for the future of the country if these dipshits were in charge, but he guessed he was likely as much of a clown as Chester was when he was fresh out of college. He just hoped Aloha Senorita did the trick or else he'd be saying Adios Amigos to millions and millions of the Dead who were counting on him to figure out some serious shit.

At home, Victor tossed the weed onto his kitchen table. He planned to smoke and then take a nice long walk. Hopefully he'd come up with some answers. Hopefully he would learn what to do. He threw off his suit and put on some jeans, sneakers and a baseball cap. He then grabbed the Aloha Senorita and popped the top. It sure looked potent and it smelled quite good. He could see deep threads of purple and silver sparkling throughout. This was not his college weed grown in someone's crawl space using illegal hydroponic lights. No, Aloha Senorita was serious stuff. And, for a moment as he looked at one of the buds, it looked eerily similar to the inside of the orb. Was that a coincidence? He pulled The MonteGresso out of his pocket and compared the two. It definitely had some resemblance. He put some into a pipe he purchased, lit, and inhaled deeply. The toke was followed by a five-minute coughing spasm. It felt like blood and metal were in his mouth. It had been a long time since he smoked weed and the effect was much different than a cigarette.

He took a few more hits and in a matter of moments he was high as a kite. Oh my, he thought, I just waaaay overdid it. He started to giggle to himself. Wow. He felt good. He grabbed a soda from the fridge, the Aloha Senorita and double-checked that The MonteGresso was well secured in his pocket and walked out the front door. He decided to just walk and think. Ideas would either come to him, or not, but at least he would get some exercise and that might be just as helpful as an epiphany.

The Aloha Senorita was doing a nice job of making Victor feel good. It was a delightful fall afternoon, the sun was strong, but it wasn't too hot. There was a nice breeze just made for walking. And walk he did. He thought a lot. He thought about his parents who were getting close to needing Cherry Knolls and he knew it was only a matter of time until he was fighting for their souls too. He thought of his failed marriage to his ex-wife and was happy that, despite the error of those nuptials, there were no children who had to suffer. He thought about his job and his failures in life and how he would never be a player like Mike Guidry. Not in the sleazy, infidelity way, but in the successful, rich, charismatic, charming way. He would never be that kind of guy. And he thought of that asshole Bingham "the Knife" who sold his personal injury case out and probably acted unethically, if not illegally, in taking so much money for himself. He thought of Bingham's pretty and sweet paralegal Sheila; she would never be interested in an someone like himself and was probably just being nice on the phone today because she was paid to be nice. And he thought of poor Beverly who would go to her grave petrified that if he didn't do his job properly that she would forever be stuck in some horrific in-between world, suppressed and punished by some mysterious force called the Builders. Yes, this Aloha Senorita was doing the trick if the trick was being overly paranoid, frightened, and depressed all at once. It was sure doing the trick, thanks a lot Chester, you hipster fuck!

It was about 4:30 in the afternoon and Victor had noticed he was walking near the Briarwood Cemetery, about three miles from his house. He was surprised he had walked so far. He had not even planned to walk east, he thought he was moving south. But here he was at the front entrance of the most beautiful arboretum cemetery in the entire Rocky Mountain region. Its hundreds of acres of well-manicured grounds, and hundreds, if not thousands of 40-foot and taller trees of all varieties, welcomed people. And obviously the rows and rows of headstones. They were so interesting to inspect, all cut in unique shapes and sizes with no discernible pattern of placement, especially in the older sections.

There were also crypts of varying sizes and designs. He thought about the stories of the thousands of people buried there. Some as long ago as 1850- a full twenty-six years before Colorado even became a state. As he sauntered up and down the ornate rows and sections of the cemetery, he wondered what was happening on that land when the person died. He found a headstone with a heavily faded engraving showing a date of 1812-1865. It looked like the name was Abraham Huston, but the markings had eroded in the limestone. The headstone was also slightly askew from the shifting of the dirt below the headstone. It wasn't until 1970 that the cemetery mandated that a heavy slab of concrete be placed on top of the coffin, because as the coffin aged, and the worms worked their way through the body and structure of the coffin, it would disintegrate. This caused the coffin to cave in, shifting the soil above it, causing the headstones to become slightly off balance and in many cases tip. That's what gave old cemeteries their creepy, aged look. The cemetery staff was tired of replacing ancient headstones with owners whose great-great-grandchildren were not alive any longer. So, in some cases, they just removed the headstones. In other cases, with particularly interesting guests, they would place new headstones, mostly for the purposes of enticing future residents to buy plots in the well-maintained cemetery.

Victor sat for a while looking at old Abraham Huston's final residence. Had he fought in the Civil War? Did he vote for Abraham Lincoln? Was he a victim of a Comanche massacre? Maybe he was an old silver miner who struck it rich in the Rocky Mountains and then was killed in a shoot-out over a poker game in a saloon? Good lord, that weed was strong! Nonetheless, he was curious. It was likely old Mr. Huston was probably just some poor laborer who had moved west long before the Civil War. He'd probably struggled to make ends meet under the harsh conditions of the territory before there was organized law and order, when one was more likely to die of dysentery, measles, or smallpox than being scalped by a Comanche warrior. Who knew? What Victor was more interested in was what was happening to Mr. Huston at that particular time in the year 2020. Was he being prevented from passing on to a different reality? Was he trapped in his coffin, stuck in some horrific purgatory awaiting a savior who was high as the Goodyear blimp and standing just six feet above him? Had he made it out of the in-between and moved on before the Builders locked down the Dead?

Was this all some cosmic mind-fuck put to him by a woman with an overactive imagination? What the hell did he know?

It was starting to get dark. The Aloha Senorita was wearing off and he had to get out of the cemetery. And it was starting to get a little chilly. He didn't have any major revelations that day, but at least he had a pleasant day off. He left the older section of the cemetery and saw a few people visiting their loved ones, as well as people walking their dogs through the cemetery. These grounds attracted lots of recreational visitors who enjoyed the gorgeous trees and lush landscaping, and also a few creepy goth people strolling among the headstones, all dressed in black and macabre as hell. He was coming out of the predominantly Jewish section when he saw a young man, about twenty years old in a nice blue suit who was squatting over a small headstone deep in thought. He had both hands on the headstone, with his eyes closed. He didn't look particularly sad. He looked like he was stretching before a jog, but in a nice suit. Walking past him, Victor tried not to disturb his solitude.

"What do you think happened to this poor fella?" the young mourner said. He wasn't talking to Victor though, so Victor just kept walking.

"Don't you even have a guess?" the mourner said again, this time a little louder. Victor stopped and looked around self-consciously. Was he supposed to answer this guy?

"Um, excuse me. Are you asking me?" Victor asked as he turned in the mourner's direction.

"Yeah, you. Who else would I be asking? You think I come to cemeteries and talk to myself?" And he laughed a little. Victor thought he was being a bit of a rude asshole, but he was probably grief-stricken so he thought the better of saying anything rude back.

"Well, I don't know," Victor replied. "I assume you know." At this point the young man stood up and turned partially towards Victor, so that Victor could just make out a trace of his face.

"Yeah, I know what happened to him. I just didn't know if you knew." And he actually pointed at Victor when he emphasized the word "you." He wasn't pointing in a hostile manner, but the whole discussion was making Victor a bit uneasy. If the guy wasn't in such a nice suit, Victor would have taken him for some crazy, potentially dangerous vagrant and high-tailed it out of there.

"I'm sorry. What was his name? When did he pass away?" Seemed like a fair question. Victor took a step towards the man and the headstone, curious.

"Says here the poor fella was named Mark Levin. Born June 15, 1959 and died September 1, 1980. 21 years old. That's a bitch, ain't it? Whole life ahead of him."

Victor peered over his shoulder to see the writing on the headstone. Yes. That appeared correct.

"Was he a relative of yours?"

The man laughed a little. "Nope, he wasn't related to me exactly. I understand he was tragically killed by a drunk driver. Some selfish prick left a bar with a blood alcohol level three times the legal limit. Hit poor Mark as he was crossing the street on the way to see some friends one evening. Damn shame."

Victor was intrigued. "That is so tragic. Can I ask how you know this?"

"Well, Victor Jones, I was hoping you'd ask me that." The man turned toward Victor to face him head-on. He was a handsome young man with dark eyes and dark lustrous hair. Olive tone skin and roughly six feet tall. Victor felt a furious chill rip through his entire body; goosebumps popped up all over his arms and around his neck and ears. How did this guy know him? And did he really want to know?

"Did you just say my name? How do you know my name?" Victor asked, but he already knew.

"Well, Victor, if you don't mind me calling you Victor."

"Well, that's my name, please feel free."

"Victor, let me introduce myself." As his eyes turned all white and his grin literally stretched from ear to ear, "My name is Mark Levin, and you and I are about to become really close friends."

Chapter 23 * Mark Levin

For the first time in his life, Victor Jones fainted. This wasn't just a light-headedness swoon, but full-on, straight-out-of-Hollywood faint. His knees buckled, he saw black and when he came to, he found himself sitting up against a headstone. He rubbed his temple where he apparently hit it on the side of some tree or headstone, causing a minor bruise, but not a lot of real damage. He tried to stand up, but he was woozy and sat back down.

"Wow! Now that was something to see!" Mark said, as his pupils returned and his smile receded back to normal size. Victor looked around; he heard the voice but didn't see anyone. "I'm right here!" Mark said again, leaning over the headstone's top. Victor jumped and crab-walked backwards. He tried to stand but his knees began to buckle.

"Well, now, just slow down there, buddy, you just had a very hard fall. Don't be jumping all around. Take a few minutes. Let your blood pressure return to normal. Take some deep breaths."

Victor stared down Mark. "You know it would be much easier to calm down if you weren't scaring the shit out of me!"

"Me? Scaring you?" Mark said incredulously. "Seriously? Why would I want to scare you? I need you. We all need you." And he cast his arms wide and opening them to all the people buried at Briarwood Cemetery.

Victor began to feel his pulse lower and his blood pressure was heading back to normal (for an overweight, middle aged male, that is). "I'm sorry, I'm not used to talking to…to…"

"Yeah, spit it out…dead people? Is that what you wanted to say?"

"Yes, dead people. It's not something I'm accustomed to. So I apologize for causing a scene." Victor seemed genuinely apologetic. He found it odd he was apologizing to a ghost, or a dead person, for being startled by their presence. Wasn't that the normal reaction?

"Well, I can understand, Victor, I really can. By the way, do you know how long you were passed out for?"

What a bizarre question at this time, but Victor played along. "I don't know five minutes, ten minutes? I wasn't exactly looking at my watch."

"Thirty seconds. That's it. Isn't that interesting that when you pass out you don't realize how short of a timeframe that is? But again, as you said, you weren't looking at your watch. How's your head by the way? That's a nasty cut."

Victor rubbed his right temple and gasped. The bump was starting to get bigger and there was a little blood. But overall, he felt physically fine. Mentally? That was certainly another story.

"Okay, Mark Levin, you got me, I don't know how, but you got me here. How can I be of service to you?"

"Well, I think I can be of service to you," replied Mark, sitting down a few feet from Victor with his legs crossed. And he pointed at Victor. "But, before I am of service to you, would you care to reach into your right front pants pocket and pull out what you have there?" At first, Victor thought he wanted the orb, but that was in his jacket pocket.

Victor reached into his pocket and felt the marijuana bowl and a small chunk of Aloha Senorita. He also felt the lighter. He pulled the items out of his pocket. "Are you serious? You want to smoke weed?"

Mark looked at the paraphernalia in Victor's hand and eagerly grabbed it, put the bud into the bowl and held the bowl up to his mouth with a lighter about to spark. "Do you mind? I can't believe how rude I am being. I just plucked this out of your hand. It's been a really long time." Mark's hands seemed translucent yet had the ability to touch and hold things. Strange, Victor thought. But he had never met a ghost before, so what did he know?

Victor gestured for him to help himself and Mark immediately lit the bowl, taking a big hit. He held his cheeks together like a chipmunk's but quickly started coughing and laughing. "Oh my, that is tasty. As you can imagine, my lungs aren't really conditioned for this. It's been a while." He took another long toke and this time he kept the smoke down and exhaled a long white cloud of marijuana smoke into the air. "But it doesn't take long to get the old lungs raring to go!"

Victor grinned. As far as ghosts went, this guy seemed pretty cool. He supposed things could always be worse. He leaned to his side and pulled out the pack of cigarettes in his other pocket and put one into his mouth. He motioned for the return of the lighter from Mark.

"No sir! That shit will absolutely kill you. You know how many idiots are buried here because of those cancer sticks? Lots! I need you healthy."

"Give me a break. I think right now is as appropriate a time as ever to smoke a cigarette." Victor snagged the lighter out of Mark's hand and lit up.

"Ironic that you are face to face with a real-life ghost, a member of the

Dead, a person who knows something, especially about how people die, and you are ignoring this advice. Suit yourself." Mark took one final pull on the bowl. "Okay, Victor, that's some really nice weed. Too bad it didn't get legalized until almost thirty years after my death. But I can see how Chester, that weed clerk, did do his homework and found you the right stuff for your vision quest. Am I right?" He laughed. "You didn't think you would actually have a vision quest, but here you are, sitting cross-legged in a cemetery sharing your marijuana, and nice conversation, with a member of the Dead. Someone who, according to that headstone, has been dead for over 40 years. Isn't that simply fucked up? Crazy?"

They both laughed. Victor thought he might be going crazy. But crazy people didn't usually question their reality. If Victor was crazy, he would think this meeting with Mark was normal. And this was anything but normal. Therefore, Victor felt comfortable that he was NOT in fact going crazy, but simply having a discussion with a ghost. Sure, that seemed entirely ordinary. Ho hum, just another day chatting with a member of the Dead. The thought made his already throbbing head hurt worse.

"Listen, you wanted a vision quest and you damn well got one. I want to get right to it, what can I do for you, my fine living friend?" Mark leaned comfortably against the tombstone. his jacket and tie fastidiously neat, a broad smile across his face.

Victor went for it. "I don't know what I'm supposed to do. Beverly Griffin, she told me everything. I assume she is dead. I wouldn't doubt that those things, the Builders, had her killed so she couldn't help me. But I really don't think I know what I am supposed to do or even why I am the chosen person." He sounded confused. Mark nodded sympathetically.

"Bev held out until she found you. She was a sweet woman. Lord knows I've watched her work for years. Because the orb was fouled by the improper burial, forty years ago, everything was on hold for a long time until it was ready to be properly buried. In the last few years, she has had to try and find a champion. She's tried to find someone but the few people she had contact with were not deemed suitable. But you, my friend, had something special."

"What? That I'm a sucker?" Victor asked honestly.

"No. You cared. You were kind to her. You believed her. And even if you didn't believe her entirely, which is entirely understandable, you didn't mock her. That shows heart. And this task will require all of your heart and courage."

"Heart? Courage? You sure you have the right person?"

"Oh shit, my man, my brother from another mother, yes, you are! Bev Griffin was smart. And she needed a champion. And she held out until she found one. You should feel good, even if she put a giant heaping pile of shit on your plate, you were the first and only person to listen to her and not blow her off. Well, you and Lucy. When Lucy appeared that first moment it all clicked for Beverly. Lucy and you were meant to be a team to get this job done. But Lucy is just an assistant. The Dead didn't think she was capable of handling this task solo." Mark leaned forward. "Do you have any idea how often old people, especially those in nursing homes, are ignored, blown off, mocked, ridiculed and worst of all, pitied?"

"Pitied?"

"Yeah, pitied. They are pitied by the young, or at least those younger than they are. They are pitied because they are seen as having played their round, finished their game, sewed their oats, you name it. And now sitting in a nursing home…" Victor picked up his thought. "They are just waiting to die."

"Precisely. They are pitied and people who are pitied are never listened to, let alone believed. But you did and mazel tov to you my friend. I think Bev, and all of us, have found a champion!"

It was starting to get dark and cold, but the elements didn't seem to bother Victor one bit. He looked at Mark Levin. The first human being to call him a champion, maybe ever, in his life. "In actuality," Mark continued, "Bev didn't really need to find a champion until recently. You see, her father Samuel stopped an improper seeding right here 40 years ago. I know Bev told you that. What she didn't tell you was that this caused The MonteGresso to be useless for a long period of time until it gathered its strength again."

"What is it with the number forty? Forty days on Noah's Ark, forty years wandering in the desert, forty seems to always show up? It's very biblical," Victor said, recollecting his old Sunday school days.

"Go ask a priest, I don't know. I'm trying to talk over here and give you advice. Head back in the game, Okay?"

"Yes, sorry."

"Anyway, the 40 years just recently ended, and Beverly got to meet Ms. Black."

"Grandma Lucy!"

"Yes Victor, imagine that. An 84-year-old woman who also happens to be a grandmother, imagine the coincidence."

"You are a sarcastic son of a gun, aren't you?"

"Spend forty years in the dirt and you might get ornery too. Anyway, as I stated, it was the combination of you and Grandma Lucy, together, that the Dead were waiting on. The fact is we've had our eye on you for some time."

Victor couldn't help but feel a little proud. "Wow, I don't know what to say." Mark rolled his eyes and sighed deeply. "Yes, congratulations! You are now in charge of this mess. We worked to coordinate with Beverly to get you The MonteGresso and you need to protect it and do your job. So you need to keep The MonteGresso safe. Really, really safe."

"Yes, that's the name of the orb, right? That's what Beverly called it."

Mark nodded. "Yes, The MonteGresso, otherwise known as the number 1 orb, or sphere, or globe or ball. The one you possess is named The MonteGresso. It is one of only three spiritual and powerful orbs in the universe that form a trifecta of power. Incredible power. I know Beverly filled you in a little on what it is, but she doesn't know the full story. You cannot lose it or else we are fucked. Really fucked. So I hope it's in a safe place."

Victor instinctively started to put his hand into his jacket pocket. "Oh, you bet, I put it…"

"NO!! Do NOT say where you put it. I don't want to know. Do you already trust me enough to tell me where you put it? Or even show it to me?"

Victor was now really confused. "Why not? You're on my side, right?"

"So you think I am. But ask yourself, what if I wasn't? You would have not only been killed quickly, but you would have turned over the most critical item in the existence of humanity to the wrong person. That would cause unbelievable suffering. So do NOT trust me or anyone, with the whereabouts. Do you understand?" He stood up and pointed at Victor to emphasize his point.

Victor removed his hands from his jacket and looked downward, ashamed. "Yes. I'm sorry."

"You're sorry, for what?"

"I am sorry for almost revealing the location of The MonteGresso, that was dumb of me and I will trust no one."

Mark sat back down, happy to have that out of the way.

"Now, you need to acquire the other two companions to The MonteGresso. One is auburn in color and it is called The PinonAstra. The other is jade in color, it is called the Mule."

Victor laughed. "Are you serious? The MonteGresso, The PinonAstra and The Mule? What the fuck?"

"Dude don't ask me. It's The Mule. I didn't name the damn thing. It probably has a formal name, like QuzPacka, or some strange shit, but around these parts it's known as The Mule."

"Okay, The Mule," Victor agreed. "I need to find The PinonAstra and The Mule. So, first of all, how do I do that? And more importantly, why am I doing this? I swear to Christ, I don't get it"

Mark thought of a way to explain it quickly and in a format that Victor, a mere living human, could understand.

"So, I know Bev explained it a little. She did a decent job. But Bev never had the depth of visions you have had. Her father, Samuel, definitely had the visions. He had them for so long they almost drove him mad. But here goes. Before the Earth formed and there was just debris in the atmosphere, a way, way, way long time ago, there was a battle in another dimension among entities that are not human or even physical in nature. You can't even envision them because they don't have a form discernible to the eye. Regardless, they all battled for territory. The fight for land and territory is as old as the Big Bang."

He stood up again to make his point. "But a chunk of the debris from this battle collided with other otherworldly particles during the Big Bang and settled on the Earth. Three chunks in particular."

"Don't tell me, The MonteGresso, The PinonAstra, and The Mule," Victor guessed. "You learn fast. Whoever called you stupid was stupid," Mark replied.

"Who called me stupid?" Victor barked.

"Shut up. Listen. The entity desiring the three orbs are known as the Builders. They need these all together. The Builders block the Dead from exiting their dimension and crossing over into a new place where they transform into omniscient beings. It was the way it was designed. The Dead are supposed to cross this Divide and transform. But the Builders do not want the Dead to invade this area. They block this entrance, so to speak, otherwise known as the Divide. The Dead have slowly made a trickle through this Divide and many have moved on, but the vast majority of the Dead can't get through. Literally every single soul in this cemetery, for instance, has been stuck. No one here has made it through yet."

"You mean their bodies should have disappeared?" Victor asked. "No. The bodies remain and slowly deteriorate into dust, but the souls are very much alive and they are trapped." Mark responded.

"Well, that totally sucks," Victor chimed in. He thought of old Abraham Huston and realized he knew exactly where he was now.

"Tell me about it," Mark said. "However, if someone on Earth is capable of gathering all three of the orbs and burying them together, with a sacrifice, then they can literally go to the Divide, blow it up, and the Dead can move on."

"But I assume that's easier said than done?"

"Obviously, Mr. Jones. If the Builders are able to have their minion on Earth do this first, then the Divide will be permanently sealed. No Dead will ever move on. Ever. And forever is a long, long time." Mark stopped for effect.

"Well, what's happening now? Aren't you all able to move on to other places?"

"Good question. I can speak for many of them. Yes. Many have passed on to this other place because the three orbs have never been reunited and simultaneously re-seeded by one of the Builders' minions. And as long as they aren't, the Dead can move on, albeit slowly, and with limited movement. It's better than being prevented from any movement for all eternity, but it is hardly ideal."

"But if one of the Deads' minions buries all three together?"

Mark pointed at Victor. "As I stated, if *YOU* are able to do this, it will break the Builders' grip on the outer plain and the Dead will pass to another dimension. It is what billions of the Dead have been waiting for. It's the Shangri-La of the post living world, my friend and one day, when you die, if you accomplish this feat, well, you will be a hero the likes that have never been known."

Victor liked the sound of that. But if this has been a million-year-old battle, how on earth would he be the man to help? Really? Victor Jones?

"What happens if one of these orbs is buried on its own?" Victor persisted. "Beverly said something about the orbs being buried independently. Couldn't I just bury it and be done?"

"Yes, you could," Mark replied with a frown. "And it would only delay the inevitable fight for someone else down the road. The orbs have all re-surfaced and The MonteGresso's forty years of inactivity has recently ended. Therefore, the other two orbs are likely very active right now. Almost like animals in heat. They are calling to each other for the first time in thousands of years. This is going down soon. We don't have time to spare and we are so close we don't want to wait any longer. If you re-seed The MonteGresso on its own, now, it will hurt us."

Victor could feel the lump of The MonteGresso slightly purring in his jacket. For an inanimate object, it had been very animated. Mark went on. "The Builders may figure out a way to permanently seal the Divide even without the triad. So we need to win this battle now, no more delays."

"But didn't the Builders allow Beverly's girlfriend, Jeannie McIntyre, to bury The MonteGresso by itself?"

Mark furrowed his brow. Clearly, this was a painful thing for him. "Jeannie McIntyre. Oh Jeannie. You see, Jeannie screwed this all up. She stole The MonteGresso from Samuel and tried to re-seed it on her own, without understanding the true obligation. She fucked everything up."

"Beverly said the Builders got to her," Victor interjected. "That they helped her steal it."

Mark crossed his arms across his chest. "The Builders had nothing to do with it," Mark insisted. "Beverly told Jeannie all about The MonteGresso and the need for a personal sacrifice. Bev couldn't bear the thought of her beloved father making the sacrifice, so she told Jeannie she was going to take the orb and do it herself. She had all the plans laid out. She was going to re-seed The

MonteGresso on her own, by itself. She wouldn't be saving all of humanity, but she would buy the Dead some additional time." He brushed an imaginary speck of dirt off his lapel and went on.

"But Jeannie cared too much for Bev and made an impulsive decision to steal The MonteGresso and re-seed it, thereby saving Bev and Samuel. But she wasn't chosen. Samuel was chosen. And by lineage, Bev was chosen if Samuel failed. Jeannie, on the other hand, was not chosen. In her attempts to do something selfless, she in fact unwittingly did something very selfish. And of course, she did it in my grave. She poisoned my earth. It was a mess. And that's why I'm here talking to you right now because I don't have any place to go."

"So what happens to you, assuming I reunite the orbs?"

"Me? Well, I'll likely just fade away. My role here would be done. But I wouldn't be able to move on. A small price to pay. Unless—"

This was too much for Victor. He had just met Mark Levin and becoming instantly fond of him. "Unless what?"

"Unless I am able to have my remains scattered in Varanasi, along the Ganges River, in India. It is the only legitimate exit for someone in my position. Don't ask me to explain it to you because it won't make sense, but the Indians for thousands of years have cremated their dead in great funeral pyres along the Ganges River in Varanasi. At night the funeral pyre lights burn bright and heavy and can be seen for miles. That's why so many elderly Indians need to move close to Varanasi because they must have their bodies cremated there. It is actually quite beautiful to see. Very mystical. But not a typical burial for a Jewish kid from Denver."

"So, I assume your parents wouldn't be convinced to exhume your body and have you transported to India?"

"Well, my mother succumbed to cancer a few years after I was buried. That's her right there. Hi Mom!" Mark waved at the headstone next to his, indicating that a beloved mother, daughter and wife, Sheila Levin, rested in peace there.

"My father, on the other hand, is pretty old now, over 80. He has suffered from dementia and related illnesses for a few years. I also don't think my siblings would consider doing this either. Could you imagine knocking on their door and explaining that their dead brother's body needed to be exhumed and taken to be buried on the Ganges River? Holy shit, I would like to see their reactions! That would be hilarious! My sister Rachel actually is the conservator of my estate. She's a bit Looney Tunes, but a good soul nonetheless."

"So that's a drag. I'm sorry for you. How could I help?" Victor seemed sincerely sorry for Mark.

"This isn't about me," Mark insisted. "I only told you because you asked. This is about generations of the Dead throughout the world who need your help. And even if I was exhumed and scattered in the Ganges, it would be moot if we don't get all three orbs re-seeded properly. So why don't you first of all stay alive, re-unite the orbs, re-seed them properly, save the entire Afterlife existence for all the Dead, end the tyranny of the Builders once and for all, and then we can talk about what you can do for me. Sound good?"

Victor fought the impulse to giggle. Mark was a nut! Be serious, he told himself. "So, in the meantime, how do I find The PinonAstra and The Mule? Do you know where they are?" It seemed like a fair question to Victor.

"That's where I cannot help. For whatever reason I can't see where these are, but neither can the Builders. Even in the world of omniscience the orbs' location are unknown. The orbs' location eluded everyone alive, or dead. So, all you searchers, or minions as you're called, need to find them on your own."

Victor threw his hands up. "That's seriously fucking stupid. How the hell am I supposed to do that? As far as I know the other two are buried under the ocean somewhere. It's like finding a needle in an ocean full of haystacks. And even that seems infinitely easier." Suddenly he felt very tired. "Am I just supposed to open the phone book and start calling people? 'Um, hi, you don't know me, but do you happen to be in possession of one of the two remaining orbs? They look like colored snow globes?'" He laughed a laugh of resignation.

"Now, now, Victor, don't get frustrated so easily. Of course, it's not easy but a few things have happened that make it easier for you than most people. For one thing, we all know that the other two orbs are revealed. That means they have been discovered. That's a start. We don't know who discovered them, or even when, but we know they are not buried. How do we know this? Great question, glad you asked. We know this because the orbs have a presence in the Afterlife that is powerful. We can see them and feel them when they are buried. And the Dead will find these buried orbs and push them to the surface to be found. The Builders do too. The Builders and the Dead use the orbs to communicate to their minions."

Victor looked weary. "Sounds like a game of capture the flag."

"Not too far off, actually. More like hot potato. These orbs get moved into the ground, they re-emerge in the paradigm of a different dimension, where all the Dead and the Builders reside, and then the Dead and the Builders play a vicious, no-holds barred game of find the Orbs. Once they are found they are pushed back up through the crust of the Earth to be found. And if the Dead find the orbs, they find their own minions on earth to fulfill the destiny. But, if the Builders find the orbs, they will also find a minion to fulfill their needs. The orbs don't care who possess them, or who wins our ancient battle. They just want to be re-united."

"Well, once again, what about Jeannie? If the orbs don't care who possess them, then why did Jeannie screw this all up for you and the Dead?" This was all too confusing to Victor.

"Fair question, Victor. Because the Dead did not choose Jeannie, she would never have been a valid guide. She was trying to play a game she wasn't invited to play. Had Samuel failed to snag The MonteGresso when he did, then it could have been another million years before the orbs had a chance to re-unite. The Dead have chosen you and Lucy. You are the only rightful owners who can use The MonteGresso as it is intended." Mark knew this was a lot of information, but he needed Victor to pay attention, so he emphasized that last point by pounding his fist into his other hand.

Victor was starting to put this together in his mind. "Okay, so if the Dead's representatives, whoever they are, are pushing The MonteGresso onto me, I assume The PinonAstra and The Mule have similar advocates?"

"Alright, now you are catching on. Yes! The Builders have long been pressing the fate of The PinonAstra. It resurfaced in 1917 or 1918. We know that much. The Builders have a stronger bead on it than we do because they surfaced it. If their true minion still had it, then they would know exactly where it was. But since it's 2020 and it still hasn't been re-seeded, then it is safe to assume it fell into someone else's hands who didn't know exactly what to do with it. But no doubt the Builders' minion has clues we don't have."

That made sense to Victor. At least as much sense as any of this.

"So, let me see if I get this straight," Victor said. "There are three orbs. These three orbs have all been located in your Afterlife, or dimension, and they have all been pushed to the Earth's surface to be found."

"You're doing good, keep going, and toss that bowl over here, I need another hit." Victor obliged and Mark lit up and took another deep hit of Aloha Senorita.

Victor smiled with pride. "The MonteGresso was pushed to the surface by the Dead in 1908. Samuel Griffin was the Dead's minion. But, through a series of errors, he was unable to properly re-seed the orb. And his daughter, Beverly, had a friend who tried to re-seed the orb, but she did it incorrectly, hence you were cursed with having your soil poisoned. But the orb remained in the possession of the Dead until 2020, when somehow the Dead agreed that I was the proper minion to handle the re-seeding."

Mark applauded. "Look at you! You paid attention. Okay, now finish it up. What happens next?"

Victor had a broad grin, he liked puzzles, and this was one hell of a puzzle.

"Okay, so, I have The MonteGresso, and it is likely, although no guarantee, that one of the Builders' minions has The PinonAstra. Which leaves The Mule. You never told me who pushed The Mule to the surface, or when it was pushed to the surface."

"That's only because you didn't let me get to it, or because I'm really high." Mark laughed. "Either way, let me tell you. The Dead pushed The Mule up in 1967. We don't control where it ends up. It could end up on the top of Mt. Everest, or at the bottom of the Marianas Trench. But that's very unlikely because the orbs have a power too. And they want to be found. The orbs know a human being will never find them at the bottom of the lowest point in the ocean. So, they would resist surfacing there."

"Yes, you'd need Aquaman to find that."

"Precisely. So almost every orb is found around people, or around where there is a likelihood it will be found by the right people. In 1918, The PinonAstra was found by some German, or Austrian, who became a Nazi. How appropriate. In 1908 The MonteGresso was found outside a beautiful ranch in Colorado by a man who was the salt of the earth. Again, exactly what we wanted."

"Okay, okay, so where is The Mule? How do I find The Mule before the Builders do?"

"The Mule surfaced in 1967 and was found by one of the Dead's minions somewhere in the Far East. Hanoi, Vietnam. A place filled with a history of violence, anger, distrust and bloodshed. But also, a place full of kind and compassionate people whose country was being torn apart by a horrific civil war."

"Great! Vietnam, that's not impossible. Who has The Mule so I can call them?"

"Not that easy. The Mule was discovered by our minion, a young girl named Han Po, who found The Mule in a rice paddy on her family's farm. But before she had the ability to do anything with The Mule, her family's farm was decimated by the Vietcong. Young Han Po died in a 1968 attack on her village and The Mule seemed to vanish. We have not been able to pick up a lead on it."

"What are you saying?" Victor said. "The Mule is lost?"

"Yes. Once it is on Earth and out of the minion's possession, it's lost to us. Unless the minion—"

"Has secured another minion that you accept," Victor jumped in.

"You got it. So, you need to find these other orbs and get them before the Builders' minion kills you, steals The MonteGresso, and tracks down The Mule. Sound fun yet? Have a great adventure!" He started to laugh, realizing how impossible this all sounded. Not to mention dangerous.

"Sounds like a blast," Victor noted. "I do have another question for you."

"Shoot," Mark replied.

"Well, you've talked about visions and Beverly told me to trust my dreams. What's up with the dreams? Doesn't anyone call or write?"

Mark knew this was a key thing for Victor to understand so he spoke slowly. "Victor, dreams are just communication devices. There are many ways to communicate. Déjà vu is one way. Have you ever sat in your car thinking of a song and BOOM, it comes on the radio, like, immediately?"

"Of course."

"Well, whatever that is called, that's a way to communicate as well. Dreams are the easiest for the Dead and the Builders because you are relaxed, and your defenses are down. You need to start looking at this world differently. I know it's strange and uncomfortable, but you've got to listen to what they say."

"Can I talk back?" Victor asked.

"Dreams are one-way communications devices. But if it makes you feel better you can always talk back. Kind of like praying. You hope God hears you."

"Wait, is there a God?" Victor couldn't believe he hadn't asked yet.

"Another discussion for another time. Any other questions?"

"Yes, how will I do this? And what do you mean by personal sacrifice? You've stated that a lot. How will I make this happen, Mark? I don't want to fail you or anyone."

Mark looked Victor straight in the eye. "You are a warrior, Victor. Believe it. But you are going to need courage. And stamina. And most of all, help. You will need to find people to help you accomplish this task of finding the orbs." And then he paused for a second before delivering the second answer. "And the sacrifice is actually a human sacrifice. Someone needs to die."

Victor shivered, overwhelmed with a sense of dread.

Chapter 24 * Help

Grandma Lucy sat in the garden of Cherry Knolls with Taylor, her grandson. Taylor was the kind of grandson who made other grandchildren look bad. He genuinely cared for his grandmother and looked forward to visiting her, calling her and most importantly, listening to her. Lucy's other grandchildren often teased Taylor about being the favorite grandchild. Out of 14 grandchildren, that was quite a feat. His siblings and cousins would often come up with a list of Grandma Lucy's favorites, from top to bottom. Taylor was always a gimme first place, but other grandchildren would ascend or descend, depending on what they were doing. If one of her grandchildren called her to check in, then they would automatically seed themselves higher in this fictitious poll. If someone graduated from high school, or got a new job, they would move up. If they forgot to write her a thank-you note for a sweater, they would slide down, sometimes passing other people on the way down. If, however, someone had a child, making Grandma Lucy a great-grandmother, well then, they were certain to pressure Taylor for top spot. However, none of her grandchildren were ready for a kid.

"I'm so sorry about Mrs. Griffin. She seemed like a lovely woman," Taylor said, patting Lucy's hand. "I can't believe she died today."

"Thank you, honey. I didn't even know her very long, but we became fast friends. Almost like I knew her my whole life." Lucy rocked in the late afternoon sunshine in an outdoor rocking patio chair. It was just the perfect fall temperature.

"I'd treasure those moments, Grandma. I'm sure you gave her much comfort in her final days." Even as he spoke, Taylor felt at a loss for words. What did he know about life and death?

"You are such a sweet boy, Taylor, have I ever told you that?"

Taylor nodded. He'd heard it a few hundred times before. He also knew that he was mercilessly mocked by the other grandchildren for being a suck-up, but he didn't care. That's what made him a genuine person. Even though he was six foot two inches tall and starting to fill out, he was still her little grandbaby. He brushed the long blonde hair out of his eyes and continued to lean forward, holding Lucy's hand.

"Taylor, can I ask you a question?" Lucy asked.

"Sure, what do you need to know?"

"Well, it seems kind of silly, but what do you think happens to us when we die?"

This was a particularly unnerving question for Taylor because it wasn't the sort of question a parent, or grandparent, asked a child. It was usually the other way around. Taylor also took it as a sign that Lucy was struggling with the concept of her own mortality. Obviously, many people at Cherry Knolls had to struggle with that concept as they waited to wrap up their lives.

"Wow, how about an easier question, like why is the sky blue? Or why do zebras have stripes?" Grandma Lucy laughed at that one.

"I know it's not an easy question, but surely you must have considered what happens?" She was genuinely interested in his opinion.

"Well, Grandma, I clearly don't know, but I suppose something happens to us after we die. I just don't think we dissolve into dust and that's all there is."

"Do you believe in heaven?"

"I want to believe in heaven, but I suppose you don't get a heaven unless there is a hell. And I sure don't like the idea that someone could spend an eternity in a blast furnace with devils and pitchforks."

He continued, "If there is a heaven and a hell, then there must be a god or other heavenly being who determines who goes where. And if there is this deity, be it the white, bearded god of the Judeo-Christian world, or Muhammad, or Buddha, or whatever, I just don't see that deity holding someone prisoner in a pit of fire for all eternity because they cheated on their taxes, or their wife, or didn't believe in the deity. I know from when I've been to church, Reverend Charles has said he who does not accept Jesus Christ as his savior is destined to spend eternity in hell. I just cannot fathom a loving being doing that just because they didn't have faith."

Lucy considered this carefully. "You are a wise child. I agree with you. I have known many, many people who have died and I know many of those people were not perfect by any means, and many were not Christian. I can't imagine the Jesus Christ I believe in would allow someone to burn in hell just because they were gay, or Jewish. That never made sense to me."

"Grandma, why are you asking me my opinion? I know you are sad about your friend, but you are healthy and still very vibrant. You aren't going anywhere for a long time." Taylor started to choke on his words a little. The idea of losing Grandma Lucy was too powerful for him to conceptualize.

"Oh honey, I appreciate that. I don't plan to live another twenty years. Are you kidding me? I've had a wonderful, charmed life. I was a southern debutante and collegiate gymnast! While my marriage was hardly charmed, I did get all you lovely grandchildren. I am blessed."

The truth is, Lucy was very concerned about her own mortality. Not because she was getting old, but because Beverly had seemed so alive and vibrant, and as soon as she shared the secret of the orb with Victor, boom, she was gone. Was Lucy next? She didn't know much about this Afterlife battle, but if Beverly was correct, then the Builders had minions designed to snuff out the Dead's minions and steal their orbs. She had no idea where Victor stored the orb, but if they connected Victor to her, then she could be at risk. Someone could try to force information out of her. She didn't have Beverly around any longer to talk to and reassure her, and she felt particularly vulnerable.

"Taylor, can you do me a favor?"

"Sure, anything you need."

She leaned close to him, whispering so the others sunning themselves on the patio couldn't hear her. "Taylor, I need some cash. Here is a check for five hundred dollars. Can you take it to get cashed, keep two hundred for yourself, and bring me three hundred? I need it today." She pressed a check into his hand.

"What?" Taylor said, a little too loud. Lucy immediately shushed him and looked around. None of her geriatric neighbors seemed to notice, or hear, or care.

"You heard me. I know your mom doesn't want me giving you guys money, but I'm getting old, Taylor, and I want to give out some gifts. So, can you do this for me? Today?"

"Grandma," Taylor whispered. "What's the matter? Is everything alright? This is odd." Lucy laughed. How many teenagers would debate getting cash from their grandparents? Only Taylor. But the fact was she needed some fast cash. As soon as she learned of the dangers associated with this orb, she knew she needed some protection, and one of the waiters at Cherry Knolls indicated he could get her a small pistol. It was an awkward conversation, but because the guy had a big neck tattoo, she sensed that he was a good person to ask. If you're gonna have a neck tattoo, Lucy thought to herself, get ready for some inappropriate questions and comments. She needed the gun quickly; she wouldn't feel safe without it.

Chapter 25 * New Lists

Victor took a taxi home. It had been a wild day and the marijuana had long worn off. His head was spinning with the revelations he had that afternoon with the long-deceased Mark Levin. He would have stayed another hour or longer, but it had gotten dark and the rules of the cemetery were clear: no visitors after sunset. He had been contacted by one of the friendly groundskeepers and told that he had to leave. Of course, this groundskeeper couldn't see Mark Levin, who was sitting right next to Victor. The groundskeeper only saw Victor leaning against a headstone and animatedly talking and laughing to himself. Oh, the people one saw when working in a cemetery!

Mark wished Victor good luck and told him to trust his visions. Now, more than ever, the visions would become clearer and more focused. Because all three orbs were surfaced and in play, it was anyone's game. Mark did advise Victor that he had to be careful not to lose The MonteGresso, and to hold onto it as long as possible. The MonteGresso was to be re-seeded by itself only in the bleakest of circumstances. And Mark let him know that for it to take hold, there had to be a personal sacrifice. It wouldn't work without it. That was Victor's biggest concern, the sacrifice. He hadn't exactly set the world on fire in his lifetime and his life was unlikely to be one that was remembered by anyone. But he wasn't ready to die. He wasn't ready to put a bullet in his brain on the off chance he was helping save the afterlives of millions or billions of people.

Of course, what was a sacrifice? A sacrifice was doing something selfless for the betterment of others. But he just wasn't ready. And he certainly wasn't planning to do it just with The MonteGresso. If he was going to kill himself as a personal sacrifice, it was going to be while he re-seeded all three orbs. That he would do. Because at least in that instance, assuming the tale he heard was true, he would be saving the afterlife of the Dead, allowing them to move on to another plane of existence. Just seeding The MonteGresso alone would only delay this fight for another day and it could of course jeopardize his own soul.

By the time he got home, he was starving. He popped a frozen meal into the microwave and grabbed a beer. He had earned it. He sat down on his couch, TV dinner on the coffee table, and he wolfed down the Salisbury steak in record time. He then grabbed a yellow legal pad to create yet another List. At least this time he wasn't using a McDonald's bag.

TO DO LIST:
1. Every night sleep with a yellow pad to make notes in case I wake up and need to remember a detail.
2. Talk to Lucy about strategy. Even though I don't know what help, she can offer.
3. Keep doing your job well at Cherry Knolls. Now is not the time to get fired!!!!
4. Find The PinonAstra!
5. Find The Mule!
6. Buy a gun…maybe…we will see.
7. Re-seed all three orbs.
8. Become a Legend!!!

After he finished the List, he went to bed and he quickly fell asleep. The dreams didn't wait too long to start. He saw visions of vast amounts of people- thousands, tens of thousands, millions- pressing into a barrier. Beyond the translucent barrier appeared to be endless space and stars and other celestial entities. There was also a massive group of blocks or mountains that were just on the opposite side of the translucent barrier. It seemed the people were trying to escape through the barrier, but they were struggling to get over or through the mountains. They succeeded at a very slow rate. Few would make it past the mountains, many were helplessly lost, struggling to pass through this seemingly impenetrable barrier. The people were stacking up on the wrong side of the barrier and they appeared to be suffering. And just like that, Victor willed himself awake. Sweating, he sat up in his bed. He turned on the light and immediately grabbed his yellow pad. The dream seemed so real, unlike any dream he had ever had before. He wrote out what he experienced. It was evident to him the people pressing the barrier were the Dead. Had to be. The mountains, or mountain-like entities, were the Builders. They were massive and imposing figures that looked like mountains compared to people. But they were very much alive. They didn't have human features, but they moved, they spoke, they breathed, they lived. And they were preventing the escape of the Dead into the celestial paradigm. If Mark hadn't explained this to him, he wouldn't have had a clue. But this seemed very real. He needed to help eliminate the barrier that would allow all the Dead to escape at once and render the Builders impotent.

He could only assume that those who died centuries ago might only be making their way through at this point in time. He could only imagine that

Beverly was in the very rear of that mass of humanity. She may never get a chance to cross.

He looked at his clock. It was already 7 a.m. He felt like he had just gone to sleep. It didn't make sense to go back to bed, so he got up, showered, and got dressed. His goal to exercise every day would have to wait a little longer. He had noticed that when he looked in the mirror, or other glass, the yellow hue was still there, but it didn't seem to bother his eyes as much. He was starting to get used to it. He then had an epiphany. If this hue was only visible to those who have had contact with an orb, maybe, just maybe, he could use that in some fashion to try and communicate with the others in possession of The PinonAstra and The Mule. He would have to be careful because he didn't know who, or what, was in possession of these orbs. If he connected with the wrong people, would they torture him to locate The MonteGresso? Would he be able to withstand torture? What an ugly thought and a terrible way to start one's day. He was relatively certain that The PinonAstra was in the possession of one of the Builder's minions. But he wasn't sure about The Mule. If The Mule was held by one of the Dead, or a Dead sympathizer, then maybe that person would be prepared to re-seed all three orbs and commit the sacrifice. Why did he have to do it? Unfortunately, the pessimist in him didn't think that was going to be the case. He knew, deep down in his bones, that he was going to have the razor-thin opportunity to re-seed all three orbs and make a decision to kill himself. But would he have the guts?

He filled up a large travel mug of coffee, smoked a fast cigarette, and jumped into his car. His head was still a little sore from hitting the headstone, but his eye looked pretty good. No one would likely notice. His first stop would be to visit with Lucy and fill her in on the excitement of the previous evening and pick her brain on options. On the way to work, he turned on the radio and a song by the Doobie Brothers was finishing up. Thankfully. He loathed the Doobie Brothers. In fact, he loathed most 70's soft rock, especially the antichrist Steely Dan. If he heard Rikki Don't Lose That Number one more time, he would probably drive his car into a brick wall and just end it. As soon as the song mercifully ended, the commercials started:

"If you've been injured in a car wreck don't waste your time haggling with the insurance companies. And don't trust another law firm to get your case its maximum value. Call me...Bingham "The Knife" Cutler. We will cut up the insurance companies and put fat stacks of cash in your pocket. Remember, The Knife is Life. Go to TheKnife. com and learn all about how I will help you!"

The sound of The Knife's voice immediately reminded him of that disheartening phone call with Sheila James. He had put it out of his mind completely, but this annoying, bullshit huckster advertisement did place something firmly in his mind. The Knife might serve a purpose after all.

Chapter 26 ✳ Trekking The Midwest

Chicago

    Kitta got off the flight from Heathrow and made her way through customs at O'Hare International Airport in Chicago. The eight-hour flight had been smooth sailing all the way over the Atlantic. The PinonAstra was tucked safely into her carry-on, along with a few pieces of clothing, some shoes and assorted sundries. She only traveled with a carry-on as she needed to travel light and mobile. Her weapons could always be purchased on the road through a dozen safe and discreet dealers. If she needed different clothes, she would buy them and dispose of them after use. Her budget was unlimited; the Builders had provided her plenty of resources where money and other valuables were located. Similar to the Dead, the Builders had human connections from people who had died. Many people had untapped bank accounts, hidden treasures, and other valuables throughout the world. Both sides seemed to have equal access to cash. And in this battle, cash was not the end reward, but a means to accomplishing critical tasks.

    Kitta sailed through customs and headed to the rental car kiosks to rent a car. Her first stop would be to a friendly arms dealer on the north shore of Chicago who would help her out with a Glock 9mm and plenty of ammunition. She loved Glocks. After all they were invented by Austrians. The dealer would also provide her with several knives of varying weight and lethality, as she often found she could get a lot of information from people by simply threatening to cut off a finger. She had only had to do it a few times. It was a particularly nasty and bloody event, so it wasn't her favorite form of torture. But it was amazing what a person would volunteer when they saw their pinkie severed off and sitting in a puddle of blood.

    The weather was windy and rainy and Kitta struggled to keep her windshield free of water as she sloshed around the north shore suburbs. She landed in Buffalo Grove, a sprawling suburb forty minutes northwest of the city. Manicured lawns and two-story mid-1960's houses dotted the landscape. It was a typical American suburb—safe, clean and boring as hell. Kitta would rather cut off all her own fingers than spend more than a few hours in this glorified slice of post-World War Two Americana. Sure, if one needed a chain retail store or a franchised restaurant, Buffalo Grove was the perfect kind of town. But for excitement, culture, and unique food options, then downtown Chicago was probably, next to Manhattan, the best place in the United States. It was amazing how bland life could get just forty minutes northwest of one of the best cities in the world.

It had been several years since she was at Joe Sanchez's house, but it was memorable. Joe was a retired Army veteran who had lost his wife to cancer in 1999. He was only 65 years old, but he worked out every day, was a black belt in Tae Kwon Do, and knew everything there was to know about pistols, riflery, and hand-to-hand combat. Joe, like Kitta, had started to receive strange messages in his dreams shortly after his wife had succumbed to a particularly aggressive form of lung cancer. He was distraught as he had also lost his only daughter to a deranged boyfriend just a few months before his wife's diagnosis. No kids, no wife, and not much to live for, he was extremely susceptible to the Builders and they used him to help arm and aid their minions searching for the orbs. He never was asked to chase the orbs himself, but he knew he had a purpose. Instead of putting a gun in his mouth, he chose to help those who would help his wife and daughter, and that gave him something to live for. He had been manipulated, just like Kitta, while at the lowest point in his life, but the thought of one's family suffering in an eternal purgatory was all the motivation this combat veteran needed.

Joe was waiting on his porch when Kitta pulled up in her non-descript gray car. She walked out of the car, walked right past Joe and into his house. He followed her inside. Immediately they threw off their clothes and fell upon each other with relish. Kitta didn't need sexual release with a man any longer as she was so driven in her mission that nothing else mattered. But Joe had just enough masculinity left, and he was big, strong, and was her partner in this epic battle. She knew Joe wanted to fuck her the first time they met, and she was happy to oblige. He must have popped a Viagra shortly before she arrived as he had incredible stamina and focus, especially for a man on Medicare

After their romp they showered together and then Joe prepared a charming meal including caviar, imported ham and prosciutto, canapes, and Russian vodka. Kitta kissed the back of Joe's neck as he stood in his kitchen preparing the feast.

"A little culture in this god-forsaken wasteland," Kitta said as she poured down a shot of particularly good vodka and savored a few bites of caviar and toast. "So, what do you have for me?" asked Kitta, who was clearly in charge.

"Well, I assumed you wanted a selection of fine cutlery and a little horse-power." He motioned to a suitcase on the counter as he kept working on lunch. Inside were three different knives and a black gleaming Glock 9mm. She took the semi-automatic pistol out of its case, felt its weight, loaded a magazine, and pointed it around. Then she put it down and fondled the knives; they were perfectly balanced, sharp, discreet. He had a good sense for what she liked.

"These will do just fine. You know me so well."

"I just follow orders. But that six-inch blade, oh, that's a dandy. It is so properly weighted. Cost me $800, but it will be your new favorite."

Kitta grabbed the smaller of the knives, twirled it around, manipulated it in a variety of stabbing motions, and then put her left arm around Joe's neck. With the right, she held the blade up to his temple.

"That's one way to get yourself killed, Kitta," Joe said with a laugh. He knew she was one tough chick, but he would have dismantled her as he held a blade of his own in his left hand as he prepped the food. He made a fake stabbing motion and she pulled back.

"If I killed you, I would be stuck having to pleasure myself from now on. I would never deprive myself of that," Kitta stated as she grabbed his crotch. He laughed, turned around and kissed Kitta again. In the bleakness of his life, Kitta had been a bright spot. She had connected with Joe on a single's dating website which had been orchestrated via the Builders. They'd both had recurring dreams of connecting on singleandhorney.com; it didn't take long for them to find each other.

She walked away and looked longingly at Joe's garden. Even in the rain, even at the end of summer, it was beautiful. She would never be a gardener. That was for domesticated people. When you have taken more than a dozen lives and tortured more than a few dozen people, you've waived your right to settle into a simple life of domesticity and gardening. But she could certainly admire Joe's garden.

"What's your plan? Got a lead?" Joe asked as he observed Kitta looking at his azalea bushes.

"Bloomington. I know where The Mule is," Kitta stated without turning around.

"All this time and The Mule is just a few hours south of here?" He stopped chopping his radishes. "I can't believe it. Whereabouts?"

Kitta now turned to him. The rule was the possessor of the orbs did not acknowledge anything. You could never be too safe or trust anyone. The stakes were simply too high. She almost regretted saying Bloomington. But it just slipped out. Joe was her only real confidant in the United States and she knew she needed help to pull this off.

"Indiana, actually. But, sadly Joe, that's all I can tell you. You know."

"Hey, I have been in this with you almost from the beginning," Joe said, growing annoyed. "I have two people I loved very much whose eternal fate rests in the success of this mission. Why don't you open up to me? Two heads are better than one."

Kitta realized that he was too eager. She always worried about how much he had helped her, but what if he really was working for the Dead? What if he knew she had The PinonAstra right now, in this house? He would slit her throat as fast as he could, or at least she thought that could happen. The problem was the Builders didn't really promise that everyone's loved ones would be saved from the wrath. She assumed that, if Joe succeeded in getting all orbs re-seeded, his family would be royalty, and her precious child would forever rot in a hellish purgatory. She wasn't sure if everyone associated in her mission's success would reap the rewards. It only seemed fair that Joe's family would be treated as royalty too, but she wasn't taking any chances. She couldn't trust the Builders. Shit, for that matter, she couldn't trust herself. She was likely going to have to kill her friend and part-time lover, especially if he kept making her feel uneasy.

"I hear you, Joe," she hedged. "But every person who knows opens themselves up to unspeakable torture and death just by having some information. I don't want to put you into that situation." She was partially honest. She knew that information was dangerous, and people would cut off appendages to get even a little bit of it. She also didn't need to constantly be looking over her own shoulder. She would not hesitate to protect her interests, which could include killing Joe.

"I can handle myself, Kitta, you know that." Joe said.

Kitta nodded in agreement, but she still wasn't giving away any of her information.

"I'm heading down after lunch," she said. "I promise to keep you in the loop to the extent it is safe. But before I go—" Kitta led him off for a little more fun. Joe was happy he took a full dose of Viagra that day.

Chapter 27 ∗ The Mule

Kitta was loaded with weapons and motivation. She was one-third of the way to her goal and she knew where The Mule was hiding. The MonteGresso would be her final task, but she was quite certain she had obtained enough visions to know that a Samuel Griffin was the last true minion of The MonteGresso. That tid-bit of information came from Jeannie McIntyre's error. Once an orb was re-seeded, the entire Afterlife saw it through an explosion of light that culminated throughout the entire death dimension. It didn't matter that she shouldn't have been the one to have buried it. It was there for everyone to see. Like the big screen at the Super Bowl, whoever was in the stadium saw it.

All of the Dead and the Builders knew The MonteGresso was seeded by Jeannie McIntyre that sunny day in September 1980 in Denver, Colorado. The only problem was that Samuel Griffin dove in to chase it. Clearly, he had plans to reunite all three orbs and saw his plans wither away as soon as Jeannie poisoned the grave. Samuel would have to wait forty years before the orb could be re-seeded and, by that time, he would be dead and buried. The problem that eluded the Builders for forty years was where Samuel Griffin kept The MonteGresso after he saved it. His face and identity were revealed. He was an open book as far as anyone searching for The MonteGresso was concerned. He should have easily been tracked down, tortured, and forced to reveal the hidden treasure. But it didn't work that way, to the chagrin of the Builders. The Dead were able to hold The Monte-Gresso in safe keeping. It was, after all, their find. They were able to place it into escrow, held by a community of safekeepers who looked after The MonteGresso until the Dead found their new, true champion. And it wasn't until Victor Jones and Lucy Black popped into the picture that it became evident that they were the worthy minions. While Victor's identity was not known to the Builders, Samuel Griffin's most assuredly was. Kitta would follow up on that lead, as soon as she rescued The Mule.

The legend of The Mule was different than that of The MonteGresso and The PinonAstra. The Mule courted danger. It had been possessed by warriors and shamans, sociopaths and daredevils. It just gravitated to that type of person. In

Vietnam, in late December 1967, a young girl named An Ho lived in her family's house in a small village adjacent to the Ho Chi Min Trail.

On the last day of December 1967, An was tilling the soil in her family's rice paddies. It was a hot, strenuous and demanding job. Farming rice was all her family had known for generations, so she did not have any understanding of what she was missing by toiling all day in the paddies. She had five siblings ranging in age from 22 down to 2 years old, and she was stuck right in the middle. Her older brother Dao, then twenty-two, had been conscripted three years earlier by the South Vietnamese army. Since the day he'd been pulled out of the village, her family had only received one letter from Dao. Having her brother in the army made life very dangerous for her entire village. If the Vietcong believed her family was aiding the Americans and supporting the despicable reign of South Vietnam President Nguyen Van Thieu, then they would either be killed and have their rice stolen, or else they would have to swear allegiance to Ho Chi Minh and turn Dao over for torture and execution.

The Americans rarely knew for certain which villagers to trust. If the Americans came into her village, they could be treated as allies or enemies. And if they were seen as enemies, well, it could be that some of her family would be arrested and taken to South Vietnamese jails. It made no sense to An and she just longed for a day when the fighting ended, and her family was re-united. She prayed for Dao's safe return and that her family would end up alive at the end of the conflict. Considering that over two million civilians would die in the Vietnam War, the odds were not in her, or her family's, favor.

It was close to the end of the day and the sun was setting. An was clearing away some weeds from an isolated part of one of the paddies at the farthest edge of the farm. She dug her hoe deep into the ground and her hands immediately felt a terrible vibration as if her steel hoe had collided with another steel object. At first, she instinctively thought that the item was an unexploded bomb. There were plenty of those in and around her region. She had seen young children ripped apart when playing with these vessels of death. She jumped back several feet, but then realized that nothing had exploded, and she was alive. An pulled some of the weeds out with her hands and created a small pathway for the water to siphon off out of the berm. She scraped viciously with her hoe until she saw a green object with hints of pink and gold, about the size of a mango fruit. She bent down and grabbed it. It was stunning. She had never seen something like that before. It was not very heavy, maybe it weighed about one kilogram. It was circular but there were several protrusions that sat on its surface. It appeared to be made of crystal or glass but there was definitely something metallic that allowed it to maintain its strength. She peered deeply at the three protrusions;

they looked like a donkey's long snout with two pointy ears. There were no legs or eyes, and the object was mostly round, but the ears and nose reminded her of a donkey or a mule. Its most striking feature was that it gently glowed and slightly vibrated; it was alive. Had she been close to The MonteGresso or The PinonAstra at that same time, she would have seen all of them suddenly light up and come to life. All three were now recovered and were looking for each other.

She sat down in the wet dirt and marveled at this discovery. From where did it come? How old was this thing? It was slightly opaque, but you could still see crystals and other jewel-like features inside of the body. It gave her a chill that started in her neck and went down all the way to her toes. She didn't realize she had been sitting and staring transfixed at this object for over an hour when she heard her younger brother Pham scream at her to come home. It had grown dark. Her parents must have been frantic because she'd been gone so long. But this object moved her in a way she had never felt before. It felt magical to her and dangerous all at the same time.

She decided to put the object into her dress and not show anyone yet. It would soon settle down and the humming and lights dimmed considerably, but this thing lived. There was no doubt. Normally there were no secrets in her home, but something told her to keep this quiet. At least for a bit. She would have to spend more time in the light to really inspect this sphere to see what it was all about. And then maybe she would show her parents. However, knowing how honest parents were, they would bring it to the village elders to see if it belonged to someone else. An knew this was not owned by anyone. If so, they could have never kept this find quiet. And if her parents told people about it, someone would be sure to claim it as their own. Or they would try to steal it. Considering that money was difficult to come by during the war, anything of value could easily be stolen. People were desperate. And then there was the whole risk of the Vietcong learning about this. It had to be worth a lot of money, and they would take it to feed the war efforts. No, she would keep this to herself for the time being. That was the smart thing to do.

The first night she slept she experienced a similar series of visions that Samuel first experienced almost 60 years earlier- intense and frightful and very, very real. These continued in earnest for over a month, The Mule releasing its secrets to her as it had for other possessors. Unfortunately for An, she would never be able to begin the quest for the other orbs because she was living smack dab in the middle of a raging war.

On January 30, 1968, all of her hopes, dreams, visions, and plans abruptly ended when members of a Vietcong battalion descended on her village, prepared to attack the American Marines who were in close proximity. It was the night before the Tet Offensive, one of the largest escalating campaigns of the war. Without warning, over five hundred Vietcong cleared out her village, took all the rice, and committed numerous atrocities against An's friends and neighbors. The Vietcong had long considered her village to be sympathetic to the South Vietnamese and therefore open game on killing anyone located there. The American Marines stationed nearby were quickly under attack as of the next morning, with bullets and mortars zinging throughout An's village. Her family searched for safety in a series of old caves nearby, but in their haste to leave, An had been unable to grab her satchel where The Mule was hidden. She tried on numerous occasions to go back and retrieve it, but her parents wouldn't let her leave. They didn't know about The Mule, and even if they had known, they would not have understood the significance of the object since An had been silent about it.

It wouldn't have mattered. An and her family were discovered just outside the cave, along with many other villagers, all victims of a mass execution on January 31, 1968. Their bodies were left out in the open as a warning to other villagers who failed to cooperate with the Vietcong. The Mule dimmed considerably.

Most of the remaining villagers found that it was too precarious to remain at that location. They knew they were stuck in the dangerous middle between the Americans and the Vietcong. It didn't make sense to stay. So most left, leaving only a handful of people remaining. Within days, an American platoon came to this desolate village, where the remaining wary inhabitants just wanted to be left alone. They were fortunate that the American in command, Sergeant James "Jimmy" Bilks, was a good person. He ordered that the remaining villagers were to be provided aid. Bilks knew this could encourage future attacks against this tiny village, but Bilks was a Pentecostal preacher when he was at home in Indiana and he couldn't see this amount of suffering and not assist.

Sgt. Bilks had his men talk to the villagers to find out what services they needed and gather any other useful intelligence that could allow him to press forward in the bloody campaign. Bilks' men were tired and stressed from several days of fighting. He personally lost ten men in the preceding two days and tempers were taut, although Sgt. Bilks had an easy way about himself and was usually able to use his mild and engaging personality to keep his men focused and upbeat, even in the worst of times. And this was certainly as bad as he had seen it in his thirteen months of service. He approached the town elders about allowing his platoon to sleep in the village that evening. They had a well-fortified perimeter, and it didn't appear as if they would be expecting any more enemy company in the immediate future.

His request was granted with this caveat: they were not to interact with the villagers. That seemed like a fair proposal to Sgt. Bilks, who ordered his men to establish camp there that evening and provide rations to the villagers whose rice and livestock had been "donated" to the Vietcong.

One of the village elders indicated that there were several huts available to sleep in because the families had been killed. Bilks was profoundly grateful for the offer and divided his men into several groups to sleep in these huts. Bilks and several other infantrymen were quartered in the hut previously occupied by the Ho family.

It was about 10 p.m. and Bilks was trying to find a comfortable position in his sleeping bag. He was so tired but for some reason he could not sleep. He didn't know what was bothering him aside from death, mutilation, carnage and endless human suffering. But sleep was not generally elusive. The other soldiers were snoring and clearly enjoying a night of dry sleep and cots. Even an old cot in an old hut was infinitely more comfortable than a sleeping bag, in a bunker, usually in the rain.

Bilks turned on his flashlight to look around. Nothing particularly unusual about this hut. He had seen many since he had been in Vietnam. But he did notice a slight malformation in the base of the hut's wall that was no bigger than a loaf of bread. He went over to the wall and pried at it. It started to immediately give way and he saw that there was a makeshift hiding place. He pulled out his knife, felt for the ridges in the wall and was able to pry open a small patch of earth. Inside was a small satchel. He looked around to see if any of his comrades were awake, but all he saw were five sleeping people. He opened the satchel and looked inside. There was something that felt glass-like with odd protrusions. It was about the size of a baseball. He pulled it out and looked at it. He put his flashlight to it and observed beautiful, layered crystals and green depth throughout. There was slight pink hue to it, but he couldn't tell for certain because it was dark in the hut. But it hummed and lit up. It startled Bilks. He dropped the satchel and the humming simmered down. No one else noticed they were all too tired. Bilks had never seen anything like this. It was fascinating. He could see a face, or what looked like a face. Maybe an animal, he thought. Was that a horse or a donkey? He couldn't really tell, but he held it and admired it until he felt sleep overtake him and the placed the orb into the satchel and slid it into his backpack. He planned to hand this over to the village elders before he left. His night was filled bizarre dreams.

The next morning, the platoon packed up and headed out into the jungle. There was word that a small dispatch of Vietcong was still active in the area, so they had to leave before they were sitting ducks. It was going to be another rainy day, and no one was looking forward to it. Bilks thanked the elders and left what few rations he could. He wished he could do more. He tucked his blonde hair under his helmet and had all of his soldiers pull out. He had forgotten all about the orb in his bag.

They had trekked a mile into the adjacent jungle before they were under a strong attack from multiple directions. Bilks screamed for his men to take cover. Lightning flashes of heat and fire flew everywhere. Bilks' soldiers fired in every direction because there was no clear sight where the enemy was hiding. It wouldn't have mattered. They were outmaneuvered and out gunned. Only a few dozen of Bilks' men would survive that carnage and Bilks, the kind preacher from Indiana, wasn't one of them. He had taken three rounds in the back. It could have been from friendly fire, or enemy fire. The truth was inconsequential as bullets were flying in all directions. The fact that his body was even recovered and flown home to his grieving parents was nothing short of a miracle. The Mule, which was buried deep in his backpack and was counted among Sgt. Bilks' possessions, was untouched by the rounds and got a flight to the United States courtesy of Sgt. Bilks' flag-covered casket.

In a small box at Sgt. Bilks' parents' house, on a farm in southern Indiana, The Mule rested. It had only been unearthed a short time earlier. But now it continued to rest dormant, undisturbed, and out of mind. Its lights and humming were muted. Since both of the people entrusted to its care had been snuffed out, it went into hibernation. Bilks' father Cy refused to look at any of the items in the box for over a year due to the pain and anguish connected with Jimmy's personal items. But then one day he decided to summon up the courage to look through the box and The Mule caught his eye. The light was dim in the orb but he, like others before him, found it fascinating and beautiful. It didn't speak to him, as it had spoken to others, so Cy was not troubled by visions and dreams.

Cy decided that he needed to get rid of many of Jimmy's things. Constantly looking at them reminded him too much of his loss. So, he turned to an antique dealer he knew just down the road in Bloomington because he did not know what the orb was and maybe it had some value. He could certainly put any money to good use. Jimmy would have wanted that.

It was a scorching August day in Bloomington, almost twenty months after Jimmy had been killed. Cy visited Haggarty's Fine Antiques, located just off the main town square. The courthouse rested in the town square on a beautiful bed of manicured grass that sat lazily in the summer humidity. There were four streets that ran adjacent to the town square and there were a variety of shops, bookstores, restaurants and bicycle shops that surrounded the town square. Small town America at its finest.

Cy parked his car on the street and found his way to Haggarty's store. He had to dodge two young kids in denim shorts riding a bicycle and eating ice cream cones. One boy pedaled and the other hung on the back as they screamed down the sidewalk, each laughing and trying to gobble down the ice cream before it melted. Cy jumped out of the way and jealously looked at these children innocently having fun during their summer vacation. It made him miss his Jimmy.

He opened the door, and a customary jingling rang out as the door tripped a small bell. Eugene was sitting at the front counter, reading a book. His long beard had turned mostly gray and it contrasted deeply with his dark skin. Eugene was one of only a handful of black people in this predominantly white, southern Indiana town. Times were changing and Cy was sure glad they were.

"Well, look at you, I think you've gotten grayer since I saw you last." Cy pointed to Eugene, who looked up from his book and smiled.

"Yeah, well, I don't know anyone as fat as you are sir, could I see some identification?" Laughing, they shook hands. They had known each other since they served together in World War Two. Both had somehow managed to end up stateside, assigned to work at a government office that oversaw the production of tanks and other field artillery.

In the antique shop, there were all kinds of vintage pictures, books, and other odds and ends one would generally find in such a place. Haggarty's wasn't some high-end place you would find in New York City; this was a nickel and dime shop, but once in a while something interesting showed up. Today was the day.

"So how is the family? You all well?" Cy asked, honestly curious.

"Oh, we're all hanging in there. I am sure sorry about Jimmy. I haven't seen you since his funeral. I am so sorry for you. It breaks my heart."

Cy took out a handkerchief and wiped at his eyes. He had cried so much over the past twenty months that he didn't think he was capable of any more tears. But he quickly learned that the Lord provides an endless supply.

"Thanks, my friend," Cy said. "Hold those dear ones close." He started to sob a little more and Eugene teared up as well. He came around the counter and put his arm around his old friend.

Cy got a hold of himself and patted Eugene's arm.

"So, Gene, my son had this object in his bag when he came back from 'Nam. It was apparently in his personal effects. I put it in an old box in the house, couldn't bear to look at it but decided it was time. I don't have any idea what it is, where it came from, what it's worth. But I figure you might. I was hoping you might even be able to find a customer who would like to buy it." He handed The Mule to Eugene, who held it up in the air to admire the features. He scraped a little something off the side with his thumbnail and quickly determined this was some old, dried blood. He hoped Cy didn't notice.

"Wow. This is absolutely stunning, Cy. I love the horse face. It is so interesting. And it almost seems like it is glowing." Eugene could swear he felt it lightly vibrating in his hand, but that couldn't be. It was just a rock of some sort. Must be the neuropathy in his hands. "I have to tell you I have never seen anything like this before. It certainly looks like it wasn't manufactured by a glass blower. It almost looks like it is a natural formation of some sort. Like some quartz or other stone." He held it up to his lamp and looked deeper.

"See these crystals inside?" He pointed to them with the tip of his pencil. "Those have to be some type of amethyst or onyx quartz. I think they could even be some other gemstones, like broken pieces that were fused by something."

"You think it's worth something? You think you could sell it?" Cy became a bit anxious. He knew this was a nice piece but wasn't entirely sure. Eugene's reaction lifted his spirits.

"Well, I am sure this has some value. Certainly, to a collector. Maybe to a university. I don't know. I can't tell how old it is. I've not seen anything like it. But I wouldn't put this in my display case; I don't think you'd make any real money having some old Hoosier lady pop in here one day looking for a cute knick-knack. But, hmm…"

Cy leaned towards Eugene. "But what? What are you thinking?"

"There is a gem show that comes through the state in the fall. It's called The Ruby Ashling Gem and Diamond Show. Big-time dealers who travel the country. Some of them are very bright and I've met a few of these people. If the piece has real value, it could end up at an auction house. Could yield you some decent money."

"Well, that's great. How do I get it entered?" Cy asked.

"I would take a few pictures of it and place it into the sales program. Then, if there are interested parties, we could take it to the show in Indianapolis and see what it fetches. Could be lots, could be nothing. I just don't know." Eugene replied. Cy nodded.

Eugene pulled out an old hulking 35 mm Kodak with a huge flash bulb to try and get the best picture quality available. He took several photos from numerous angles, and in a few Cy held The Mule to give the item some size perspective. After he was done snapping the pictures, the two old friends shared a few more pleasantries and wished each other well. Eugene would contact him once the item was listed in the catalogue. The seemingly innocuous posting of this item into the Ruby Ashling Gem and Diamond Show catalogue would be the one remaining clue Kitta would use, five decades later, to try and secure The

Mule as part of the trifecta for The Builders and conclude their goal of locking down the gates of the Afterlife to all the Dead and secure complete domination of the Afterlife until the end of time.

Chapter 28 * The White Wax Pencil

Victor pulled up to Cherry Knolls, immediately ran to his office and rummaged through his drawers. He found what he was looking for. He then ran to room 218 to check on Grandma Lucy. He was scared for her and wanted to ensure her safety. He also had a plan, he hoped, to find at least one, if not both, of the remaining orbs. He had jumped the stairs two at a time to get to her room, he was slightly out of breath. A few nurses and caregivers glanced at him, but after his discussion with Mike Guidry, the day before, he didn't think anyone was going to cause him any grief.

He knocked on the door. "Lucy, are you awake? Lucy?" He panicked after she didn't answer the door immediately. Of course, it was only eight in the morning. Which, for most octogenarians, was like noon.

"Hold on, I'm a-coming." Lucy threw on her bathrobe and opened the door slightly to peek out the crack. When she saw it was Victor, she opened it wider.

"Oh, I'm glad it's you. I am worried." She looked a bit disheveled as she turned away from the door and back towards her chair.

Victor noticed her put something into her pocket. "What's in your pocket, Lucy?"

She pulled out a small caliber pistol, innocently smiled, and placed it back into her robe pocket. "You can never be too careful."

The sight of the gun alarmed Victor. This thing was moving very fast. Should he have a gun too? He did not like guns and just seeing one gave him a shiver.

"Where did you get that? You know residents can't have weapons." He said this very quietly, aware that any weapons infraction could get her kicked out of Cherry Knolls.

"Don't worry where I got it. As long as I keep it hidden away, no one will know. And don't look so surprised. You think this old southern belle doesn't know how to handle a pistol?"

"Well, don't get caught with it. And whatever you do, don't leave it in your robe! If you fall asleep and a nurse pops in and sees that gun, you are gone." Victor was definitely speaking the truth on that issue.

"I'll be fine. But I am concerned. I don't know what happened with poor old Beverly. Did she just happen to pass away as soon as she had released all of that information to you? Or was there something more sinister at play? It seems odd." Lucy's southern drawl, one that had been gone for years, kicked in when she was stressed and the word "odd" came out as "aw-ed."

"I don't know what happened to her, but I have to hope that she stayed alive along enough to ensure the orb was passed off to someone who could do something with it. You've heard of stories of old, sick people who somehow stave off death until all their children can be by their hospital bed to say goodbye. Maybe she willed herself to hang on?" Victor didn't believe it for a second. He definitely thought something, or someone had gotten to her, but he didn't know for sure. And frankly, it didn't really matter at this stage. What he did know was that he had a narrow window of time to reunite The MonteGresso with The PinonAstra and The Mule, before someone with evil intentions beat him to it.

"Listen, Lucy, I do believe you are safe. At least I hope so. Me, on the other hand, well, I could be at risk just because I am in possession of the orb. So, it is critical I find the other two orbs and handle this job once and for all." Lucy smiled and offered her gun to Victor; he thought about it, but politely refused with a wave of his hand.

"Suit yourself." She slipped the gun back into her robe pocket.

"So, without going into too much detail about my day yesterday, I think I have a plan to find the other orbs."

"Go ahead, dear." Lucy was ready for any plans he had.

"Something has happened to my vision since I've come into possession of The MonteGresso and I need to locate the other two orbs, The PinonAstra and The Mule."

"The Mule?" She laughed out loud. "*The Mule*? Like a donkey?"

"Actually, mules are the child of horses and donkeys, but yes, like a donkey. Anyway, my vision has changed a little."

Lucy was still giggling; it was nice to see a little smile on her face. "What do you mean, 'your vision'? Like your overall understanding of the situation? Like your eyes are open?"

"No, I mean my literal eyesight, how I see. Ever since I came into possession of The MonteGresso, I can see a type of yellow hue whenever I look at glass objects. It's not distracting, but I can see things I couldn't see before."

Lucy took a moment to ponder that. "So do your eyes hurt?"

"Not in the least. But I want you to do something for me." He reached into his pocket and pulled out a white wax pencil that he'd dug out of his desk. He went over to her window that overlooked the beautiful gardens at Cherry

Knolls. He took the pencil and wrote in large, twelve-inch letters "HELLO."
Then he walked back to Lucy about, who was ten feet away from the window.

"What did you do to my window?" The idea of drawing on a wall was abhorrent to a southern belle.

"Tell me what I wrote on the window," Victor demanded, in a curt tone.

Lucy put on her glasses and peered at the window. "Hello. You wrote Hello.
Of course, your handwriting isn't so good."

Victor smiled. He ran into her bathroom behind Lucy and she peered over
her shoulder, wondering what this peculiar man was doing. He grabbed a few
tissues from her bathroom, walked back to the window and wiped off the word
HELLO.

"Well, thank you for cleaning up. What was the point of that?" Lucy asked,
clearly confused.

"What does it say now?" Lucy looked up again with her glasses on her nose.
"Well, I don't see anything now. It's clear as day."

"OK, that's what I thought. Now, Lucy, you go over to that window and I
want you to write any word you want. Make it large. I am not going to look. But
write it. Then I want you to wipe it off clean, like I just did. Okay?" He handed
the pencil and the tissue to Lucy. He wasn't sure this would work, but he sensed
that it would.

Lucy had no clue what he was getting at, but she played along. In big block
letters she wrote "ALABAMA." Victor could hear the wax pencil squeak a little
on the glass.

"Okay, I wrote it," she said to Victor's back and he turned around to ensure
he couldn't see the word.

"Well, erase it with the tissue, don't use any water or anything, just wipe it
off."

Lucy scrubbed it off. "Okay, I erased it."

"Now, Lucy, before I turn around, I want you stand next to me and I want
you to put on your glasses and I want you tell me if you can see any writing on
the window, Okay?"

"Sure thing, honey." She looked through her glasses and all she could see
were blue skies and sunshine pumping through. There was no evidence of either
word. "Okay, I don't see a thing. It's shiny and clear."

Victor turned around and looked at the glass. A huge smile creased his face.

"Roll Tide! Sweet Home Alabama!" He started laughing and gave Lucy a
hug. "Lucy, I think I have a plan!"

Chapter 29 * Gem Show

August 30, 1969

Eugene Haggarty didn't have to wait long before the calls started to arrive on The Mule. The Ruby Ashling Gem and Diamond Show catalogue had created a nice demand and Eugene had hopes that he could make a good sale and deliver some nice return to Cy.

The catalogue was in color, which was rare for 1969, but it didn't do The Mule justice. The picture was grainy and small, only about one inch by one inch. Further there were hundreds of other specimens that competed for space in the catalogue. Most of these items contained a brief one-line description and an opening price. There was a lot number assigned to the item that a purchaser or interested party could use when trying to connect with the seller. It had to be routed through the Ruby Ashling Gem and Diamond Show's main line to ensure the company got its cut of the sale.

Eugene wasn't sure what compromised The Mule. He just knew it looked like a horse or donkey. He described the item as "jade with pink and gold hues, unique partially opaque rock and quartz formation loaded with crystals of varying hues. Features natural formations with a horse face. Slight glow. Immaculate gem carving. Exquisite piece." He didn't want to use the term donkey because he thought that sounded a little crude, but "horse face" was regal. He was deliberately vague about the composition of the object because, frankly, he had no idea what it was. And he definitely didn't mention the slight vibrations, which seemed to be less noticeable and he wasn't sure if that was even coming from the orb. He listed an opening sales price of $1,500. Surely that would get someone's attention because the average price for an item in the two-hundred-page catalogue was about $15.

The catalogue went to approximately 25,000 dealers and enthusiasts across the Midwest in late August 1969. It touted that the Indianapolis Hilton's ballroom would be packed with thousands of items and hundreds of dealers the first weekend of October. Dealers were urged to reserve their spaces immediately as the ballroom had capacity restrictions. Eugene wouldn't have to wait until October to spark interest; by early September he was getting at least three calls a day from people intrigued about the object. Their queries were always the same: what kind of stone was it? But despite his inquiries with several geologists, not one person, even the head of the geology department at Indiana University, could properly pin down just what this object was. The one universal opinion was that it was exceptionally beautiful, and not synthetic. The head of the Indiana University geology department had inquired about purchasing it from Eugene, but when he heard that the starting price was $1,500, he had to back out. He had a limited budget, and he didn't feel like taking this request up to the dean of the school. While it was a neat object, it likely wasn't worth much, aside from its aesthetics. There were millions of natural compounds that made all types of unique structures, and this was likely just another odd amalgamation of minerals that made you wonder. Plus, Eugene was not able to prove its ownership and that made it a hard sell to a public institution.

Regardless of Eugene's inability to specifically note the origin and composition of The Mule, he continued to discuss it with interested buyers. Many asked if they could come in and view it prior to the Show. He had convinced Cy to allow him to hold it in his safe and he would take it out whenever there was a curious buyer. Most would be charmed by the horse face, although sophisticated equine enthusiasts thought it resembled a mule. After many showings, and many negotiations, he finally landed a buyer in late September, which allowed him to take it off the entry list at the show. The buyer was an elderly lady from Cincinnati who collected all kinds of curiosities. She wasn't particularly interested in its origins or composition; she just found The Mule charming and she liked how it seemed to glow.   In fact, she had a large collection of equine figurines and thought this piece would be a nice compliment to her collection. The vibrations were not evident at all any longer. She negotiated a fair price for The Mule and brought it back to her home high on the hill in Cincinnati overlooking the Ohio River. And there it sat in a display case along with hundreds of other specimens that she loved. Her friends and family would take look at these objects when they came to visit, on Christmas and Easter, and for high teas and other events. But she never handled The Mule. It sat in glass. And no one in particular cared much about it because she had so many other lovely items. And then, when she died in 2015, her estate was liquidated, and the proceeds spread to a variety of charities because she had no heirs.

The Mule was not a coveted item. And it wound up, eventually, sold along with many other items to a young, 25-year old collector, Frank McDuffy, who came to an estate sale in 2015 after Ms. Riggs' death. Frank worked on computers by day and collected gems and stones by night. He lived with his parents in rural Tennessee, just east of Memphis. He took a real liking to The Mule, and unlike the previous owner, he handled The Mule, a lot. He looked at it through different lights and researched its material composition. And unlike many of the prior owners, it did impact his dreams. A young man, Frank put little stock into the strange dreams he experienced, but he took a keen interest in how his vision had changed since holding The Mule. It was if he had X-ray vision at times. Whenever he looked at glass objects, he saw an unmistakable yellow hue. He didn't connect this to The Mule. He thought it was due to all the time he spent in front of a screen. He visited several optometrists and physicians, but the source of his new vision problems was entirely undiagnosed. He just assumed it had something to do with an iron deficiency and time on the computer. But he loved his computer. And like most young men, he loved internet videos of all shapes and sizes. Whether they were sports, music or political, he loved watching videos and playing video games. He especially loved political videos and chat rooms. He was an opinionated social media advocate and considering that his political beliefs curved so far to the right that they almost came out on the left, he fought with just about everyone who crossed his path.

Frank thought the police were corrupt and would kill anyone. But he also thought black people killed by cops deserved it. He hated Israel because it was the safe haven for Jews. But he hated Muslims too. Frank was so fucked up in the head that he would be angry when he saw footage of radical Muslims shooting up a building—unless that building was a synagogue. Then he felt okay about it. The enemy of my enemy is my friend. He railed against illegal immigrants and their "anchor babies," but he wanted cheap fruit and vegetables and he knew that illegals were the only ones able to harvest this produce cheaply. He believed in Making America Great Again, and was happy to stroll into a Wal-Mart and buy tons of pro-USA merchandise that all happened to be made in China. Hypocrisy was a concept he didn't truly understand. Frank considered himself enlightened, special and advanced. And he was a grown man living in his parents' basement. Irony is another concept that eluded the enlightened mind of one Frank McDuffy.

Frank ignored his dreams as much as possible. He didn't trust the dreams. And, more importantly, he didn't know what he was supposed to do. He was nothing like Samuel Griffin, Joseph Rabin, or even Kitta Schultz. He suppressed the thoughts and visions and commands and kept them at bay with plenty of whiskey and weed.

The Mule sat in his safe in his basement where he had a workstation for his computers, surrounded by other rocks and items he thought might be worth something one day. He didn't believe in keeping his money in a bank as he thought banks were untrustworthy and all the information he read on the internet told him to keep his wealth in gold and other tangible items. The Mule had to be worth something, someday. He had paid $150 for it at a massive estate sale from a rich bitch who croaked in Cincinnati and a rich woman wouldn't own a bunch of worthless nonsense.

Frank had not traveled much outside of Tennessee, so his concept of the world was small and almost all of his friends were on-line. It was no wonder he harbored bigoted viewpoints. He was becoming radicalized in his cocoon. Most psychologists would say that Frank McDuffy was one Twitter comment away from shooting up a school or synagogue or mosque. If there were any Jews or Muslims in that part of rural Tennessee, they wouldn't stand a chance. He owned all kinds of guns and knives and he even had purchased a little homemade plastic explosive from a gun dealer he knew. Or maybe it was from that tattoo artist. He couldn't remember. But he kept that in a safe, along with some old Nazi memorabilia, an original signed copy of *The Turner Diaries* and a $1,000 in cash that he was either going to use to buy another gun, or a tattoo, he couldn't decide.

In the meantime, Frank would try his best to beat the computer in a game he had recently downloaded called "Battle the Beast." Immediately after turning it on, this game became Frank's favorite. He had not enjoyed a video game this intense, gory and violent in a long time, but it was so hard to maneuver up in levels and he knew it would be impossible to defeat Jorba the Beast. He often read blogposts about video games and other technical stuff. He even subscribed to the YouTube page of some young turd who was a self-described god among men when it came to video games. The information this blogger put out was actually pretty funny and damn accurate. There was a reason that over 10 million people followed his page on Instagram and YouTube. What else was Frank going to do when living in his parents' basement?

Chapter 30 ∗ Commercials

Victor Jones left Grandma Lucy's room and went to his office. He spent some time crafting some notes on a piece of paper, scratching them out, and trying again. He wrote and wrote until he finally liked what he had come up with. He got on the phone:

"Good Morning, law offices of Bingham Cutler" the sassy receptionist said. Or at least she sounded sassy.

"Good morning. Is Sheila Evans available?" Victor crossed his fingers.

"She is. May I ask who is calling?"

"Let her know it's Victor Jones and it's important."

Sheila got the page from the receptionist and heard that the call was important. She gulped and knew that she was going to get an earful. Well, you know what? This is Bingham's fault, not mine. I didn't do anything wrong here. Well, maybe a little. But he's the boss. He's the one who makes all the money. Why do I need to be attacked over this? She girded herself for the reaming.

"Víctor. Hello, how are you?" She thought she sounded too peppy.

"Sheila, I want to shoot the commercial. I will agree to participate."

Sheila was shocked. "Really?" She sounded too surprised, so she changed her tone. "Really, that's wonderful. Thanks for calling me."

"Well, I figure Bingham got me some money I would never have received on my own. I'm still a bit angry about how he did me, but I suppose that's the business."

"Well, we want all our clients to be happy," said Sheila, relieved that she'd dodged a bullet.

"I would like to have a little input in the process though. Would that be OK? I mean, I've always wanted to write and direct commercials and let's be honest, his commercials are really stupid anyway. Am I right?" He laughed and Sheila did too.

"I'm sure the director will consider your input." She knew Rob had a very specific way of shooting commercials and she would let Rob deal with Victor.

"Well, Sheila, I sure hope he does. Because to be frank, it's the least Bingham can do. I mean, I was really close to calling the office of Attorney Regulation Counsel yesterday and I thought some additional money would be appropriate under the circumstances. But I figured maybe this is all for the best and this could be his way to pay me back. Right?"

Sheila considered this for a minute. She knew when she was being played. She also knew about negotiation. Something was happening right now. It seemed innocent enough though. She decided to play along. "You know what, I think that's entirely fair. And even better, I know they are shooting today and tomorrow. Are you free to come out today?"

Victor got excited. He didn't know it would be this quick.

"Oh, I can be anywhere. I am wide open." He would have to use sick leave again, but he had some rope on Mike Guidry, so he would use it all.

"Great," Sheila said. "Come by the offices at noon. See you then."

Victor kept playing his next move over and over in his head. He didn't have a lot of time to locate The Mule, and he expected that if he found The Mule, then The PinonAstra wasn't far behind. He worried about his own welfare. Was he ready to do what he needed to do? Was he ready to be violent? Or be victimized by a violent person? He shuddered at the thought. And he really, really needed a smoke.

Victor didn't have a lot of time to get ready for The Knife. He wasn't sure if his plan would work, and, if it failed, then he would have to come up with something else, but this was his first and best opportunity. He jumped into his car and drove home. He needed to do a little internet research before he met with The Knife.

Once at home he popped onto YouTube and started searching for Bingham commercials. The funny thing about this clown was that his commercials were so over the top, so outrageous, they were almost not believable. But they were an internet sensation. He knew that. He had seen them all the time all over the internet whenever there were any stories on-line about police brutality, or car accidents, or injuries. His commercials always found their way onto his browser. It was the magic of cookies and cookies ran the internet. The Knife didn't exist on the internet when Victor hired him years earlier. He'd contacted Bingham because he saw his face on a billboard and the phone number was easy to remember: 1-800-KNIFE-ME. Not exactly a scientific way to hire counsel. Had he seen Bingham's recent goofy internet ads when he was initially searching for a lawyer, he never would have hired him. Too ridiculous to be taken seriously.

Regardless, the campy video ads garnered massive internet clicks. Like, millions. Maybe it was just because people across the country and around the world found a person like The Knife to be such a joke that they had to watch his ads for comic relief. Too bad that was the current state of the legal profession in 2020. Victor found a few that he particularly liked and copied the URLs so he could reference them back at Bingham's office. The more obnoxious the ad, the more his internet presence flourished. Bingham would actually make more money being a social media influencer than a straight-up lawyer just because his following was so big. Lord knows, he wasn't a good attorney, but he made a fortune based on volume. If he held up a can of Coke, he would probably get paid a lot more from Coke than he would ever make being a personal injury lawyer. One of Bingham's ads had actually garnered 14 million clicks. That was crazy. But it was a heck of way to communicate to people and get your message out, no matter how bizarre it was.

After his research, he quickly shaved and dug through his closet to find the most ridiculous suit he owned. He had, for some reason, an old powder blue tuxedo that he must have purchased from a Goodwill store for some 1970's theme-based party. He also had a big fringed collared shirt that had gone out of style some 40 years earlier. He quickly put on this ensemble, pleasantly surprised he was able to stuff his fat gut into the suit. Either that meant he wasn't any fatter than when he last wore the suit, or else he had been fat longer than he remembered. No wonder his dance card was empty. Thankfully, polyester had a lot of give to it.

He grabbed his sheet of paper where he crafted a carefully worded message, his white wax pencil, and jumped in the car, headed for the law offices of one Bingham "The Knife" Cutler. He only prayed that the person who had The Mule saw this message and that they were an ally, and not some crazy, lunatic Nazi sympathizer who lived in his parents' basement. Of course, what were the odds?

Chapter 31 ✳ Hollywood

The parking lot was full of film crew trucks and other equipment. Victor saw some lights set up and several people milling around near the front sign for Bigham's law firm. No one noticed him initially and then he saw Sheila Evans in a pair of black sunglasses covering her eyes, her brown hair up in a bun. She was a stunner. That was the one thing Victor remembered. She was holding a clipboard in front of her, both arms crossed over her torso. Victor walked by and she did a double-take. Good lord! Victor Jones: slightly overweight, slightly balding, middle-aged, resplendent in a powder blue suit. What was he thinking? Was this a deliberate look or a spoof? Sheila wasn't sure if he intended to look ridiculous or if that was his honest outfit. She then looked at her clipboard where she had Victor's information and an old picture from their files. He had definitely put on a little weight and his sandy hair was rapidly receding, but he still had a sweet face that appeared younger than his years. She walked up to him. "Are you about to go to your high school prom? If so, I think you're ready."

"You like it? I wore it especially for you."

"Victor Jones? It's been several years. I'm Sheila Evans." She extended her hand.

"Yes, I remember you," Victor said. "You were one of the only people I ever met with at the firm. Thank you for your hard work on my case." He was sincere in this.

"You are welcome, of course. So, what's up with the tux?"

"What do you mean? What's wrong with my suit?" He asked seriously. It caught Sheila off guard. She immediately regretted assuming the tux was a joke.

"Um, I'm sorry Victor, I...I..."

Victor let out a huge laugh. He couldn't stand teasing Sheila any longer. She let out a huge sigh of relief. She had just calmed him down from their phone call earlier in the week and she almost screwed it up again.

"I'll be honest, Sheila. I think I have an idea for a commercial."

Sheila didn't know what to say. Who was this guy and why did he think he could just write a lawyer commercial? "Well, I'm not in charge here, that's for sure. Bing and Rob usually write the commercials, but if you have some fun ideas, well, I'm sure they will listen."

"That would be great." Victor didn't have any time to waste; he had to talk fast. "But, before you grab Bingham, let him know that I am still furious about how he took advantage of me. I feel that one hundred percent in my bones. But I could look past that if he would consider my commercial ideas."

This ought to be good, Sheila thought. "By all means, I'll relay the message." She went into the group of people standing around the cameras and she started talking to someone dressed in a full Mexican mariachi suit, also known as a charro. He suit was amazing: thick, black suede with gorgeous silver buckles and clasps. The man was holding a huge sword with a giant Mexican mariachi guitar swung over his back. Those oversized guitars were fantastic instruments, they looked impossible to play, but they also made Victor giggle a little. What was it about the big mariachi guitar? It was a funny-looking instrument, kind of like the oboe or sousaphone or accordion. He had no idea what a samurai sword-wielding, big guitar-playing, mariachi man had to with personal injury cases, but it was a sight to behold. Talk about cultural appropriation!

Victor peered closer at Sheila as she talked to the guy in the mariachi outfit. With a start, he realized it was Bingham in all his glory. Bingham peered past Sheila as she explained the substance of her conversation with Victor. Bingham seemed to frown, but then he saw another man, dressed in blue jeans and a blue denim shirt. This guy was a handsome fellow with a charming smile. He seemed to laugh as he talked to Bingham. Bingham started to nod.

Sheila walked back to Victor and asked him to join the conversation. Victor was ready. He walked over to Bingham and extended his hand.

"Mr. Cutler, it's nice to finally meet you. I'm Victor Jones." Shaking Victor's hand, Bingham brushed off the slightly passive aggressive remark and smiled. Victor had to keep him off balance; he needed to get Bingham to not only agree to his idea, but to get him to run the commercials quickly.

"Nice to see you, Victor," Bingham said. "This is Rob Anderson, he produces all the commercials for me."

Victor shook Rob's hand and then looked back at Bingham.

"So, I am happy to appear in one of your commercials. But I had an idea that I hope you will agree to."

"Well, Victor, we are always looking for good ideas. I see you dressed in a costume, so I suppose this tuxedo has something to do with it?" Rob asked, casually enjoying the conversation.

"Here's the deal. Your commercials are, well, let's be fair, completely ridiculous." Bingham cringed but Rob laughed, and so did Sheila. Victor continued.

"But that's not all bad. In fact, were you aware of how many hits your commercials generate on YouTube? I downloaded some data and the more over-the-top the ad, the higher the view count. The commercial last year where you were at the Zoo and you had an imaginary conversation with the penguins..." Rob cut him off.

"That was a good one," Rob said, "difficult, but good."

"Right," Victor continued. "It garnered over 14 million hits on YouTube. I don't know how many of those people hired you, I assume very few, but to have that level of reach is tremendous. And if I'm going to be in one of your commercials advocating for you, as a satisfied former client...then I want the full chance to go viral."

Bingham considered his statements and scratched his nose where a drop of perspiration found a home. He was starting to sweat in the charro.

"Well, what are you thinking then? What does a 1970's tuxedo-wearing man have to do with personal injury cases?" Bingham asked. Victor, Rob, and Sheila all silently considered the irony of that statement from the man in a charro, but no one said anything.

"I want to play an obnoxious driver. I want to play it really hard. This was the most obnoxious suit I could find. I also got some really thick glasses to put on." He pulled an old pair of over-sized black glasses with thick lenses out of his pocket to complete the look and slid them on. His eyes seemed to magnify. "I want to be honking at someone and then rear-end their car. Then I can come out looking like this ridiculous specimen and say something like 'I hope he doesn't call The Knife!'"

Rob and Sheila both started laughing. The slicked-back hair, along with the tuxedo and glasses, made for a most hilarious look. Rob even thought it could work.

"Yes, but what about you bragging about your settlement?" Bingham asked incredulously. "Isn't that why you are here?"

"Listen Bingham, I'm here because Sheila asked me. I can't go on TV and brag about netting $10,000 on a $50,000 case. That would be damn dishonest of me. But if you do this commercial, I think it will be successful and I will let bygones be bygones. What do you think?"

This was the second blackmail of the week for Victor. It felt really good to be able to blackmail a deserving subject and have the ammunition to back it up. But he needed this to work. He didn't have other choices. How else would he find The Mule? Rob, Bingham and Sheila huddled a few feet away. Victor turned his back to them, acting like he wasn't paying attention. Victor then peered over his shoulder and shouted to Bingham, "I'll forget about any extra money if you agree to the ad." Bingham turned towards Victor with a slight frown. He went back to his group.

He heard them laugh. Bingham returned to Victor. "If your idea wasn't a good one, I would tell you to go to hell. But I actually like it. And I think you fit the bill for a stupid-looking, obnoxious, distracted driver." It was Bingham's lame attempt to try and gain the upper hand. It didn't matter to Victor if the insult went deeper than the suit and glasses. He bought it!

"But," Bingham continued, "you also have to do a normal TV spot thanking me for the help. That's non-negotiable."

Victor put out his hand to shake The Knife's hand in agreement. Victor was going full Hollywood. "Here is my second request. This needs to be shot today, now, and I need you to run it as soon as possible. Like, this week." That last part came out sounding desperate, but he didn't have a choice.

Rob piped in this time. "Well, Victor, we need to get the set designed, and production, and editing and not to mention the media buy is already done for the next month. We couldn't possibly get this on air for at least two or three months." Victor knew that wouldn't do. He was prepared.

"I think this could be shot today if we tried," he said. "I will happily drive my own car. You don't need to film a collision. You can get some stock footage of a car wreck. And I'm sure Sheila could star as your client."

They all considered the request. Victor kept pleading. "The media buy isn't that big of a deal. As long as you put it on YouTube, that's all that matters. You-Tube is key. I am sure it can be done. And it would really put my mind at rest. You know. About the crappy settlement and all."

Victor didn't plan on finding The Mule through a TV spot anyway. That was all local affiliates and the odds The Mule or The PinonAstra were in Denver were a million to one. Of course, this crazy stunt was also unlikely to lead to the owners of the other two orbs, but he didn't have any other choices. What was he going to do? Buy a Super Bowl commercial for $5 million and beg the owner to call him? Visit every antique store in the world and ask if they happened to possess the two remaining orbs that, when reunited with his orb, would open the pathway for the Dead to the true Afterlife and end the million-year fight between the Dead and the Builders? Sure, that made loads of sense. He trusted what Mark told him, to listen to his dreams and take the lead from the dreams, but the dreams were not helping him. He had only learned from his dreams that the orbs had been found and were no longer buried somewhere, and that the true owners could see a yellow hue on glass when they were in possession of the orbs. That's all he had to go on. He wasn't a police detective or an Indiana Jones treasure hunter who knew how to find ancient and valuable antiquities. His options were very limited, and he didn't have any help except for an old Alabama grandmother and a ghost who crept around the cemetery.

But Rob Anderson seemed to be an ally. He couldn't exactly figure out why. And he definitely didn't trust anyone who could produce such unbelievably inane television commercials for lawyers, but there was something about him that made him want to trust Rob. He would see how the commercial shoot ended up. At least he had managed to get this far.

Chapter 32 ∗ Not Ready For Prime Time

The commercial shoot was a complete disaster. Victor had convinced them to try his commercial idea. Once that happened, the crew set up the cars, cameras, and lighting. Victor took a few moments to go over to his window on his Honda and scrawl a message on to the driver side window of his car with the pencil and then appeared to wipe it off with a cloth. Rob observed this strange action, but he didn't pay close attention to it as he was busy with other production aspects.

The filming was a mess because Victor couldn't understand all the direction he was given and even forgot the lines that he wrote himself. After all, he wasn't a trained actor. He also had concerns that the writing on the window was not large enough. He had refused to move from the side of the driver's window while giving his performance on camera. No matter how many time Rob tried to change his staging, Victor gravitated back to the window. He obviously needed the window to be in the frame—that was the whole point of this charade. But Rob didn't know that, and it frustrated him. After several hours of awkward shooting, Rob called time-out on set to gather his thoughts.

Victor took the time to write the message again on the window in even bigger font. The message was simple: <u>If you have The Mule orb please call me at 303-456-0987</u>. Rob saw Victor doing this again and before Victor had time to wipe it off the glass, Rob approached him.

"If you have The Mule please call me?" Rob said as he stood over Victor's shoulder. Victor cursed himself for not being more careful and quickly wiped it off with the cloth.

"What's The Mule? Is that some kind of drug? Are you into something illegal?" Rob asked. He honestly had no clue what this was about.

"Um, no, Rob. Nothing like that." He kept wiping off the window, entirely self-conscious of his ridiculous get-up and insanity of thinking he could produce a viral commercial on someone else's TV production set. How stupid!

"Well, what is it then? I think I can help speed up the process and results you are looking for if you are little bit honest with me. I can tell you've been trying to highlight the window in the frame of every shot and my guess is you want this message out on the internet. Am I right?"

How could he tell? Victor didn't know how to react or what to say.

"Listen, Victor, I have been in this game a long time and believe me, I have worked with some of the stupidest people alive filming some of the most obnoxious, idiotic videos that you can imagine. But you are up to something and I can't quite figure it out."

Victor grabbed a bottle of water that was sitting beside the car. He unscrewed the cap and took a long swig. It was nearing 4 p.m. but the sun was still full and hot. "Rob, to be honest, there is some stuff going on that is bigger than me, and you and Bingham The Knife. I would love to explain but believe me when I say, and I say this with no disrespect, you would never understand, ever." He finished off the remaining contents of the water bottle and leaned against the car with his head low and his arms folded in.

Rob saw the despondency on Victor's face and in his body language. He acted quickly. "So, here's the deal, Victor, I have a commercial to shoot and you are wasting my time. I had a very simple message to produce and you have diverted our attention and made us start an entirely new shoot, which is unheard of in this industry. Now I won't have time to get my initial shoot done and you've wasted my time on this new idea. But you have Bingham all wrapped up in a tizzy and I don't blame you for that." Rob was upset with Victor, but he wasn't being a jerk. To the contrary, he was kind to Victor. He knew how to get what he needed from his actors. It was Rob's triple threat of charm, humor and good looks.

"I'll make you a deal, Victor. And I mean this. If you agree to do the simple shoot I need, I promise that tonight, when we are done, I will help you accomplish whatever the hell it is you need accomplished. Assuming it isn't illegal. Does that sound fair to you?"

Rob checked his watch and looked at the sun. He had to get this done in the next hour. Victor let his guard down and nodded. "I'll do it for you, Rob, because I trust you. But you can't let me down, and you have to trust me. And I promise it isn't illegal."

Rob didn't know Victor and had no reason to inherently trust him. But he had to get this shoot completed. "I'll trust you, Victor. I've seen some stuff in my day."

Victor smiled. Maybe he had a true ally. Maybe he would be mocked. Maybe he would be endangered. But he had to trust someone. "Okay, tell me what to do for this commercial. And Rob, have you ever heard of Aloha Senorita?"

Chapter 33 * Beautiful Bloomington, Indiana

Kitta had traced The Mule through her visions but they had not gotten her very far. She did, however, have an investigator's mind. That's what helped her track down The PinonAstra and gave her the break she needed to find The Mule.

She had long ago concluded that only chosen minions could see and understand the visions associated with the orbs. She had even had visions before she possessed The PinonAstra, but once it was in her possession, the visions grew stronger and The PinonAstra became more animated. However, if someone possessed the orbs and was not a chosen minion, the orb would only be a pretty object to look at and display on a credenza. A more discerning owner, might see these items as having a financial value. But who would buy them? The answer was easy. She had been watching TV one evening and saw a commercial for a gem and diamond exposition in Berlin. She had sat straight up from her couch and pounded her fist into her hand. Of course! Gem dealers. This bizarre group existed all over the world, but they were very well organized and usually put lots of samples into catalogues, both in paper format and on-line. It was a growing hobby that lots of people seemed to enjoy. And once in a while a casual hobbyist could get lucky and find a rare gem or diamond and retire. It was known to happen.

Kitta had visions of The Mule and she had to go with that. She posted little ads in trade magazines and in on-line forums. It was simple. "Buyer interested in rare globe-like natural cut object. Green/jade in hue and full of crystals. Size of a tennis ball. Features on object look like a horse or mule. Top Dollar paid. Email serious inquiries only with photo: KitKat98@gmail.com."

She had started this process a year earlier and she was overwhelmed with inquiries. Most people posted pictures of items entirely wrong, just hoping to persuade her to bite. She wasn't entirely sure what The Mule even looked like, but her visions helped and she knew that when she saw it, she would know. That was her promise from the Builders. After almost eleven months she had kept her postings and advertisements up and running. But she didn't have success. Until one day when she got a strange email from someone who posted a cut-out of an ancient sales brochure from some obscure gem show from the 1960's called the Ruby Ashling Gem and Diamond Show. There, on the emailed attachment, was a torn out, yellowed, advertisement that was posted by Eugene Haggerty of Bloomington, Indiana. The email sender indicated that he was an old gem enthusiast, and he collected these magazines. He saw her inquiry and remembered this old ad for a really unique piece that had horse-like features. The sender indicated that he didn't know where it is, if this was what she wanted, or if she was interested in the lead. But he thought it was maybe a clue that could help another gem enthusiast like himself.

Kitta screamed out in excitement the day she found this gift from heaven. It had to be right. It had to be The Mule. She was going to track this down as soon as she was done with an important job in Barcelona. The pieces were starting to come together. Now, she just needed a lead on the final and most important orb, The MonteGresso.

Barcelona had gone perfectly, although a little bloody, but she had The PinonAstra and now she had her best lead yet on The Mule. Kitta cruised down Highway 37, which connected Indianapolis to Bloomington. It was a typical midwestern American highway. There were fields on one side and small hills on the other. A wide ditch separated the north and southbound lanes of Highway 37. This was a stretch of road that proved that time could stand still. The small farms and stores along the small, four-lane highway were still operational. And in September most of the land had been harvested with tremendous piles of baled hay. There were the occasional billboards asking travelers to Trust in Jesus, and American flags proudly displayed on most structures one came across. It was mostly quiet country and it reminded Kitta of her home. She saw a few people standing around a John Deere dealership just off Highway 37, wearing overalls and wide-brimmed hats. The uniform of the farmer. They were looking at some baler, or harvester, Kitta couldn't be sure. The scene had a tranquil and innocent feel of a bygone era.

She sped right though Martinsville, Indiana, the former home of one Sgt. Jimmy Bilks, and kept the pedal down until she reached the bustling college town of Bloomington. The trees were starting to change in late September into their luscious hues of orange, red, and gold. The town had a nostalgic feel because she didn't see tall buildings, shopping malls and tons of chain restaurants. There was a sweet and innocent soul to Bloomington which is probably why thousands of students flocked to the limestone and ivy-covered campus every year.

She made her way down Kirkwood Avenue and found herself next to an old county courthouse that sat in a public square. It reeked of Americana and the smell was delicious. Kitta looked at the map on her iPhone and realized she was just a few hundred meters from Haggerty's store. She found a parking spot and pulled in. She reached into her case on the floor that Joe had given to her and checked to make sure the Glock was loaded. She placed this in her over-sized purse. She also grabbed one of the knives and pulled it out of its sheath to admire the gleaming metal. She then replaced it and secured it on the inside of her jacket in a specifically-designed pocket. She also opened another locked case which required a thumb print and a twelve-digit code. This case had been attached via a thick padlock onto an anchor in the car. Just in case someone broke in, they wouldn't be able to remove it or open it to check the precious cargo inside. She entered the code and opened the case. She set her eyes on The PinonAstra and rubbed her hand on it. Wow, was it magnificent. She closed and locked the case.

Kitta exited her vehicle and made sure to put more than enough money into the parking meter. The last thing she needed was for her car to be towed for a meter violation. She walked to the location where Haggerty's store was supposed to be. She found it squeezed uncomfortably between a Gap and a Starbuck's, apparently old time America was being infiltrated by the corporate giants. She found it sad. It was certainly a store of a past generation; these days it was called Hollins' Antiques. Would the current owner know about this 51-year-old posting? She had her doubts, but she had to try. She opened the door and there was an electronic beep that signaled the door had been opened. This triggered a camera that shot video of the new customer. A far cry from Haggerty's old bell on a stick.

She saw several people in the store looking at useless odds and ends, mostly older people killing time before they died. She made her way to the counter where a handsome black man about thirty-five years old stood, reviewing something on his computer.

Kitta approached the counter. He looked up from his work.

"Hi there. Welcome to Hollins. Can I help you find something?"

Kitta spoke with a soft German accent. No need to fake her nationality here. While she normally was able to convincingly hide her accent, today she felt she could speak with her normal German accent. Bloomington was, after all, a progressive college town.

"Vell, thank you. I am looking for zis store, I sink it is named CHaggertys." She really played up the guttural CH sound.

The man laughed and smiled at Kitta. Good start. "Haggerty's, you mean. Yes, this place used to be Haggerty's, but Haggerty's closed in 1985 when Eugene, my grandfather, passed away."

Kitta didn't know what that meant for her quest. "Oh, I am so sorry to hear dat. I vas looking for something from Chaggerty's."

"Well, what is it you were looking for? My father, Hollins Haggerty, opened the shop after grandpop died and I inherited the store when my father got tired of losing money. But I also found this place charming, a real piece of my family's history. I couldn't let it go. I'm Andy Haggerty, by the way." When he extended his hand with a nice bright smile, Kitta took it graciously.

Kitta's spirits perked up. "Zat is vonderful. So glad you kept it in zee family." She went into her pocket to grab the advertisement that had been emailed to her.

"I know dis iz very old, but maybe you never sold zis?"

Andy grabbed the paper and looked at it. "Wow, that is ancient. From 1969? I have to tell you, I never have seen this before. If it was in this store, I would definitely know about it." Kitta appeared crestfallen. Andy responded quickly. "But I can check our files to see if we know who bought it."

Kitta perked up quickly. She wasn't sure if she would need the instruments of death in her pocket to get the information she desired from Andy when she first entered the store, and now it seemed even less likely. This guy was just handing her stuff. Andy turned around and went into the back office. He was there for a few minutes and Kitta waited patiently. She eyed the old couple strolling through the memory lane that was Hollins' Antiques. They didn't seem particularly interested in buying anything, they were just looking and chatting and smiling. Probably killing the day. What else was there to do once you became a living antique? You get up early because you need to piss. You drink your coffee and eat your breakfast. You read the paper and maybe watch a little morning news on TV. The morning news on TV turns in to a few mindless, popular game shows, and then you make it to lunch. Maybe you hit the grocery store for something. Then back home for some really mindless soap opera or a reality TV show. Before you know it, it's time to think about dinner. Maybe a little TV before bed. Lather, rinse, repeat. And then you die. It was too depressing to contemplate.

As she watched the elderly couple, she imagined that they probably hadn't had sex in a decade and likely they didn't have much of a relationship with their children and grandchildren, aside from the obligatory holidays and occasional Sunday night dinners. But they had each other. At least for a while. And then one would wind up sick and then go to the hospital, and then probably hospice, and then there would be only one. And if it was the man, the actuarial tables dictated a male widower likely had less than five years until they had suffered the same fate. A woman would fare slightly better, maybe seven years. Either way, it looked like a bleak existence. Kitta recalled Roger Daltrey from The Who, who sang: "I hope I die before I get old!"

She had every intent of dying young. After having successfully completed her mission and ensuring that her son would be a king in the Afterlife.

Andy came back out of the office and Kitta forgot about the old couple. Andy carried a fat, old, green binder that clearly had seen better days. It was faded and coming apart at the spine. On the front and spine of the binder was a label indicating 1967-1972.

"Okay, sorry about that delay. My grandfather assiduously kept track of every purchase or sale he ever made. It was partly to protect himself if ever there was an allegation that he was trafficking in stolen goods."

"Zat is very vise."

"Yes. It helped on a few occasions. The other part was to create a mailing list for customers so he could send them updates on new items, announce sales. You understand. He was way ahead of his time when it came to marketing."

Kitta patiently nodded.

"I kept these around really for sentimental reasons. After all, wouldn't it be ironic for an antique and nostalgia store to toss old records? We save everything."

Kitta laughed. "So lucky for me."

"Okay, so 1969. Rare horse like object, let me see, let me see." Andy rifled through the pages looking up and down the columns. Turning each page slowly and using his finger to direct each line of traffic. He finally got to the last quarter of 1969 and said, "Bingo!" Kitta's heart jumped. So close! So close!

"Okay, so it looks like there was an item referenced here that says Mule orb with quartz and crystals. Sold through ITPGD."

"Vat is dat? ITPGD?" Kitta asked.

"My grandpops used all kinds of acronyms to save space. In this case, ITPGD stands for Independent Third Party Gem Dealer. And it looks like it sold for $1,000 to a Ms. Eleanor Riggs, Cincinnati, OH. Wow, $1000 in 1969 for some antique rock, pretty impressive."

You have no idea, Kitta thought.

"So vonderful. How do I call this Ms. Riggs? Is there a number?"

Andy checked the registry again and leafed through several more pages. He didn't find any contact information, which was pretty strange. But he also couldn't imagine organizing via pen and paper anymore. All of Andy's sales information was contained in an encrypted excel document.

"I'm sorry. I just don't see anything else. Hopefully, that's a good start for you."

Kitta was disappointed but the chances that a fifty-one-year-old phone number or address would even be operational or useful was unlikely.

"Sank you so much for zee help, Mr. CHaggerty. Your kindness is appreciated."

"Happy to help, and good luck." He waved at Kitta, who was already out the
door and on her way to Cincinnati.

She immediately jumped on her cell phone and called for Directory Assistance in Cincinnati. It came as no surprise that there was no working number
for Ms. Eleanor Riggs. She then googled Eleanor Riggs of Cincinnati, Ohio.
Lots of hits popped up for Eleanor Rigby of Beatles fame, but she couldn't find
anything on Eleanor Riggs. So, if the Directory Assistance showed nothing, and
Google showed nothing, maybe there was something on Facebook or LinkedIn
or some other social media feed. But it came up blank. Ugh, this was going to
be a bit frustrating, but Kitta pressed on. She made a mental note to contact the
Cincinnati Public Assessor's office as that was usually a really good way to locate
people who didn't want to be found. She didn't know if Ms. Riggs wanted ano-
nymity or just wasn't a public person. If she bought The Mule in 1969, the odds
were she wasn't even alive now. And if she was alive, she was likely ancient and
therefore maybe she wouldn't be on social media. That was the likeliest thing.

She got on to the highway for the three-hour drive to Cincinnati. She'd get
there after all the government offices would be closed, so she would have to do
whatever possible from her car to get more information. She was tempted to call
Joe Sanchez and have him start to run down Ms. Riggs, but by doing that she
would give up a critical clue. She trusted and really liked Joe, but she didn't trust
him enough to risk her child's Afterlife. No way. She'd do this herself.

She pulled into a Holiday Inn after a long drive and booked herself a room.
She carried in her special briefcases and would again find a solid anchor in her
room in which to lock The PinonAstra. She would then get on her laptop and do
as much sleuth work as possible. She had to have an answer soon. She felt close.
The interesting thing was that once she found The PinonAstra, she could see a
light glow and sensed small vibrations in the orb. But as she flew to the United
States The PinonAstra started to glow a little more, vibrate a little harder. It was
becoming more active. This had to be a good sign.

The following morning, she made her way to the Cincinnati municipal
building where all public records were kept. Kitta thought that made logical
sense. The weather was overcast that morning and she could sense summer was
definitely on its way out. She had been patiently waiting for some message, any
message, from the Builders, but nothing was coming. It was so frustrating. She
was doing this for them, the least they could do was throw her some information. Anything. She still had to track down The MonteGresso when this was all
over. She wasn't sure where that would even start. But one thing at a time.

Kitta struck gold right off the bat when she went to the public records clerk. It turns out that Ms. Eleanor Riggs died in 2015 and her estate was probated by one Mr. Dean Luiga, Esquire. That was the only drop of information she could gather from the clerk, who was a young girl, probably getting a degree in criminal justice or something along those lines. She couldn't find anything else for Kitta, but she did give Kitta the contact information for Mr. Luiga. That only posed one problem to Kitta. If she couldn't get the information she needed from Mr. Luiga, then she would have to take a finger, or maybe something more valuable. Problem was the nice clerk from the municipal office gave her Mr. Luiga's contact information. If anything happened to him, then Kitta would be a prime suspect. That's the last thing Kitta needed. She wasn't afraid to use violence, but she couldn't risk getting caught. She'd have to be more thoughtful. Hopefully, Mr. Luiga liked blonde women and blowjobs.

Chapter 34 * Visiting A Friend

The commercial shoot at Bingham's office went fine once Victor gave up on trying to manipulate the shoot. But he fully intended to take Rob Anderson up on his offer. He needed help and he needed it fast. They decided to go get a coffee after the filming and Victor spilled the entire story to him. Needless to say, Rob found it all fascinating and completely insane. He paid attention though and asked questions.

"Victor, I will tell you with all honesty and respect that you just told me one of the craziest stories I have ever heard. Beyond crazy. Mysterious orbs that will control the destiny of all mankind after they die? The battle of the Afterlife? Seeing ghosts in cemeteries? Smoking weed with them? Come on, man. Really?" He polished off his large latte and signaled to the barista/psychology major that he needed one more. Rob continued. "Listen, I love the story. And if you are a writer, then this would make a fantastic novel that I'd love to be a part of. But no way this is real. No way."

Victor assumed that would be the position of any rational person. So, he knew he would have to give a little proof. "Okay, I agree, it sounds ludicrous. And, until last week, I was the same way. I was living a normal, albeit boring, life. And this all started. I didn't believe any of it until it started happening to me."

Victor tried to find some way to establish proof aside from showing Rob the orb that was still snuggly strapped to his waist. He wasn't entirely ready to show this thing, not until he had Rob's trust. "You need some proof. I get it." He grabbed the white wax pencil. "I want you to go into the bathroom. Write anything you want on the mirror. Then I want you to wipe it off. I will then walk in and tell you what's on the mirror. The orb has given me the ability to see things other people cannot see. That's why I did what I did on the set. How's that for starters?"

Rob shrugged. Why not? Even if it was a game it would be an interesting one. He took the pencil from Victor and walked into the bathroom. He noticed he was alone, so he felt comfortable writing on the mirror: "Bingham the Knife is a complete Tool." That seemed something easy to remember. He then wiped it off completely. He looked at it from several angles. It was not visible. He turned off the light to see if there was some kind of glow. Nope. Okay, he felt if Victor could read that message then that would at least be the start of an interesting conversation.

Rob walked out. His latte was waiting for him on the table. "Okay, Victor, tell me what it says." And he sat down to drink his coffee.

"If you want to accompany me to ensure I am not cheating in any fashion, that's fine," Victor offered, but Rob waved him off.

Victor walked in and immediately saw the message highlighted by a yellow hue. It popped immediately. He turned around and went right back to the table. "Oh, I couldn't agree more. Bingham The Knife is a complete tool."

Rob sat up. He definitely expected Victor to make an excuse as to why he couldn't read it. His curiosity lifted a little.

"Well, that's a start, Victor," Rob stated. Victor smiled. "But I'm hardly sold. I'd sure like some more proof. You can understand, I'm sure. But you have me curious. Regardless, I said I'd help you and I intend to." Victor was a bit discouraged that this wax pencil skill didn't seal the deal. But he was at least still in the game. That's all that mattered. And Rob would help him, which mattered even more.

"I'll see what I can do to generate more proof. But, in the meantime, you said you'd help me. You know what I need. I need to get something to go viral quickly and I need to locate these missing orbs. I figured, if we made a funny video, millions of people would see and then I could stick a hidden message into the video. Simple, right?"

"Completely impossible is more like it," Rob said. He knew this disappointed Victor, who was desperate and wildly out of his league.

"Getting some video to go viral is an impossible mixture of doing something totally unique or funny, filming it perfectly, and then getting really, really lucky that it generates a universal audience. Even then, a few thousand hits on YouTube is not broad enough exposure." Rob was just setting Victor straight. "But there is a short cut you might be interested in."

Victor leaned forward eagerly. "Well, let me think about this, Rob, OK?" he said and laughed.

"So, I actually have a contact and relationship with a guy named Perseus the Slayer. You ever hear of this guy?"

Victor shook his head.

"No problem. Well, Perseus is what is called a social media influencer. Have you heard of that term?"

"Do you mean people without much talent or intellectual capacity who go on-line and do dumb stuff, or pretty girls who teach other girls how to apply lipstick and make huge bank solely on their name?"

"Bingo. I assume you've heard of Kasey Jenkins? Her father and mother are the actor and actress who have starred in lots of reality shows and Kasey has taken her good looks and social media savvy to pitch all kinds of products. She has made serious cash doing literally nothing but being a beautiful girl who has over two million Instagram followers."

"Who hasn't heard of Kasey Jenkins? I mean, she is pretty. But dumb, real dumb."

"Well, Victor, dumb don't matter in the social media universe. We are dumb for not being able to make that kind of easy money. Right?" Victor nodded in agreement.

"Anyway, Perseus the Slayer is one of the top video game bloggers in the world. He has over ten million followers. Everything he posts on-line goes viral instantaneously. His Twitter feed is coveted space for advertisers and marketers the world over. He gets paid a lot of money for pitching any product. And he just happens to be my nephew."

Victor got really excited. "How much will he charge me? To post a fast video?"

"Charge You? Nothing. Me? I'll figure it out. But he loves his Uncle Rob. And I bet, if I can get a little proof, he might be down with all of this.

They talked for a while about how the video should look to attract a broad audience. Rob was going out on a limb for this guy he just met and for no particular reason other than he made a promise and he kind of liked this pathetic loser, sort of like a wounded puppy. But he did admire Victor's hustle, and as Rob had been taught long ago, the world belongs to the man who hustles. He wasn't prone to hyperbole, but that stuck with him and was one of the most important lessons he was ever taught by his own father. He somewhat admired people like Victor and to a lesser degree, Bingham. Because they put their neck out of the line and were willing to get their heads chopped off. Hopefully, he could help Victor. At a minimum it made for an interesting story and it pacified Bingham who paid him a great deal of money.

Victor and Rob exchanged contact information and agreed to follow up the next day. Rob would reach out to Perseus and Victor would come up with some other ideas for a video. All in all, the day wasn't a total loss. Victor had a new ally even if Rob didn't buy the story entirely. What sane person would?

That night Victor's dreams were intense. Mark visited and gave some additional details that could help Victor convince Rob of his mission. Becky also visited, which was a welcome surprise. She encouraged him to keep pushing.

She told him she was proud of him and that his mission was pure and good. She also warned Victor of dark forces coming to get The MonteGresso and that he needed to protect himself. The end of the dream was excruciating for Victor; Beverly said she was stuck in this awful purgatory and would be forever unless Victor could unite the orbs.

Victor woke up sweating. He didn't know if he had the courage to do what was needed. Or if he had the smarts to do it. He would try and he had to get Rob to buy in. He appreciated Grandma Lucy, but she was a passenger on this ship, and he needed a co-pilot. And he had an opportunity to lock Rob in.

After a fast shower and shave, he called in sick to Cherry Knolls. It was a continuation of the illness he had been faking on and off for the last week. He didn't really care if he was reprimanded and he assumed his blackmail of Mike Guidry would last only so long. But he had limited time to accomplish his goals and he couldn't let something like his career get in the way.

He called Rob as soon as he got out of the shower and asked him if he would meet him that morning at the main entrance to Briarwood Cemetery. Rob had meetings all afternoon but said he could meet for a short time. They agreed to meet at 10 a.m.

Victor strapped The MonteGresso onto the chain in his pocket, grabbed the remaining Aloha Senorita, and jumped into his car. He could feel the object's pull. He knew The MonteGresso was alive and helping him. It was sort of like having a loyal dog.

Victor raced off to the cemetery and was glad to see Rob sitting on his motorcycle waiting for him. Rob, in black sunglasses, wore a pair of beat-up camo pants and a partially-buttoned black cotton shirt. Rob was a man. Riding a motorcycle, directing commercials, probably fighting off the women. Great hair. Confident. He was confident without being arrogant. That's a rare combination in this world, Victor thought. That was what made him so likeable. He made other people feel good about themselves. Victor realized that Rob embodied every quality that he wished he had. It was as natural as the dimples on Rob's face. Most of all, Rob was cool. He was cool without trying to be cool. People who had to try to be cool were quickly discovered to be fakers, or worse, cocky assholes. That's the thing about cool people, Victor thought, they don't come across as cocky, because no one likes cocky people. Victor loathed cocky people and was happy Rob was genuine and kind. He was glad he was helping him, and Victor was hoping that in about ten minutes he would be all in.

Victor jumped out of his car holding his knapsack. He was dressed in jeans and a short-sleeved buttoned-down shirt today. "So glad you came," Victor said. "You have no idea how happy this makes me." Victor realized that he was gushing a bit too much. Need to pull the reins on the effusive praise, he realized. If anything, Victor was self-aware.

"Glad to come," Rob said. "I don't have all day unfortunately. Lots of post-production work to get to. But happy to spend a few minutes." Rob figured he would throw Victor a bone. You never know what you will discover. But he had no interest in spending all day with Victor.

"Good," Victor said, as they walked into the cemetery. They admired the very old headstones and the history of this place. It was a beautiful place to be dead. As they started to approach Mark Levin's headstone, Victor got nervous. If Mark didn't make an appearance for Rob, then Victor would look like a crazy person and that might be the end of his new alliance.

"So, Victor, you never told me, what do you do for a living?" Rob seemed to either be genuinely interested or else he was breaking the uncomfortable silence of two men strolling through a graveyard.

"I am an over-qualified accounts manager for a chain of nursing homes. I've spent over a decade at this place and just last week I was summarily demoted and replaced with a girl, a young girl, who just graduated college. It's been a hell of a week." He gave off a nervous laugh.

"That's a drag. But I bet you make some good money, right?"

"I wish. I would love to say I've been a successful person who lit the world on fire. But to be brutally honest, I know I have been a disappointment. I know I had untapped potential but somehow, I had a few defeats in my younger years and gave in. I found a couch, food, and a television to be more my speed." Victor was surprised with how effortlessly he shared his perception of himself with Rob. Sometimes being too self-aware had its drawbacks. But Victor felt compelled to say this. He continued, "I know I just met you and I have never said that to someone before, but as long as I was brutally honest yesterday, I may as well continue my streak of brutal honesty today. Just so you know who you are dealing with." Victor felt catharsis in his self-reflection. Expressing one's insecurities to anyone out loud, especially to some stranger, was hard to do.

"Victor, no one has it all figured out. Life is complicated. It really is. We all dream of amazing things as kids and teenagers and then this thing called Life comes in and kicks most of us in the ass. Whether it's an illness, bad marriage, economic realities. Whatever. Don't be so hard on yourself. Clearly you have a mission now and that's what's important. Every single day we can push for self-improvement. It's a never-ending struggle."

"Can I ask how old you are?" Victor asked.

"Sure. I'm 55. Turn 56 next month. And to be brutally honest with you, my life has had its ups and downs and sideways. I have made lots of bad decisions, suffered huge financial setbacks, and even a divorce. But I keep pressing forward."

Somehow the fact Rob was older made Victor feel a little better. He was glad Rob had a few years on him. He trusted him more. "Thanks for those words, Rob, I appreciate it."

As Victor made his way past Abraham Huston's headstone, he looked at it. He wondered if Abraham was watching him right now and rooting for him to succeed.

Victor pointed to a series of headstones about 25 yards away. "We go right past that big Elm tree." Rob followed his direction. As they started to approach Mark Levin's grave, Victor's hands got sweaty. He didn't see anyone, living or dead, standing around the grave. This was going to be ludicrous.

They approached Mark's headstone and looked down at it. "So, this is the famous Mark Levin." Rob pronounced it *Lev-Eye-N* instead of the proper Jewish pronunciation *lev-eeen*.

"Is he standing here watching us?" Rob asked. Not trying to sound sarcastic, but it came across that way.

"I don't see him. I just remember him approaching me last time. I wasn't even looking for anything. I just sort of wandered into him." Victor scanned all around, but he didn't see anyone. He started to sweat a little. What allowed him to see Mark last time? What was he doing wrong? Then it struck him. He went into his knapsack and brought out a small pipe. "Sounds dumb but last time I saw him, I was smoking this weed that—that he really liked." As soon as he said them, he wanted to pull those words back. But they were out there.

"Victor, my man, you go ahead and smoke up. Maybe that will get old Mr. Levin to come and say hello, but I have a full afternoon, so I am going to pass." Rob watched as Victor lit the pipe and took a big hit. He blew out the smoke and started to cough. "Ouch, I still have virgin lungs when it comes to this stuff," he said. He took another hit.

Rob and Victor both sat down, leaning against a few headstones under a large birch tree. They sat there for a few minutes and listened to the wind pass by. It was light and refreshing and perfect. They sat longer and waited. And waited. Ten minutes turned to twenty minutes. Twenty minutes turned into a half an hour. Rob got antsy. Victor got nervous.

"What else you have with you today, Victor? You bring the orb?"

Victor was hesitant about showing it, but he decided it was time. He trusted his visions. This had to be part of the plan. He went into his pocket and pulled out the bag, attached to the chain, that held The MonteGresso. He held it and marveled at its form, and colors and depth. He was in love with this thing. Rob admired it from afar. He didn't immediately ask to touch it.

"Well, that is beautiful. I don't know if I believe anything else, but I think that orb is amazing. May I hold it?"

For a second Victor feared that Rob could be an agent of the Builders and might pull a gun out of his pants and shoot him. But he figured he was just being paranoid. If Rob had a gun, he could just shoot him and pick it up off the ground. He leaned forward and put it into Rob's hands. Rob put both hands on it and felt an energy pulsating from the orb. The orb glowed dimly. It sent a shiver up his spine. This thing was alive, no doubt about that.

"Pretty fucking cool, isn't it?" came a voice from behind Rob. He turned to look. It was a young man of about twenty years, dressed in a suit. "Ah, Victor, is that Aloha Senorita?"

Relief washed over Victor. Rob's face dropped. He skirted back from the headstone. Mark Levin had decided to join the party just in the nick of time.

"Pass it over here." Mark gestured towards the bowl in Victor's right hand. Victor handed it over to Mark, who took a big hit. He coughed it out and smiled. Rob sat there, aghast at what he was watching. He was trying to put it into perspective. Was this really happening? And if so, was this a ghost? And if he was a ghost, how come he coughed when he smoked dope?

"How you doing, buddy? You look like you've seen a ghost!" Mark laughed, and Victor joined him; they both watched Rob try to come to terms with what he was looking at.

Rob, trying to gain his composure, gave the orb back to Victor. Victor secured it in the chained-up bag in his pocket.

"Ssso...ssso...you are Mr. Levin?" Rob was able to stammer out, still not taking his eyes off of Mark.

"Y-y-y-ess," Mark mockingly replied and took another hit. This time he slowly exhaled the smoke through his eyes, just to give off the ghostly affect in case Rob doubted him. "And call me Mark. Mr. Levin is my dad's name." He roared with laughter.

"Mark Levin, meet my newest friend and confidante, Rob Anderson. He is a direct—" Mark cut him off. "Oh, I know who Mr. Anderson is. May I call you Rob?" Rob nodded yes.

"I know Rob writes, directs and markets some of the finest ambulance chaser videos known to man. Very pleased to meet you."

Rob extended his hand to shake Mark's hand. Then he realized that his hands were fully transparent. No skin was visible. Victor had not noticed this before. Rob pulled back his hand quickly.

"Yeah, that's the weirdest thing, Rob. The skins come and go and come and go. Fortunately, I have a face that you can see, but the hands and feet and other things"—he pointed to his groin—"are translucent almost. Creepy, right?"

Victor and Rob both nodded. "At least I can hold the ganja pipe," Mark said. Thankfully, his face was recognizable or else it would be too distracting to have a conversation with him.

"How's the smoking cigarettes thing going by the way, Victor? Did you quit yet? After all that I told you?"

Victor reached into his pocket and pulled out his Marlboros. "Hey, easy with that. I have a little pressure on me right now." Mark held up his translucent hand to acknowledge that he would lay off Victor.

Mark turned to Rob and looked him up and down. "Okay, Rob, the floor is yours. I assume you have a question or two for me that you'd like to ask before we get down to business. So, go for it. What do you want to know?"

Rob was experiencing the surreal nature of the unfolding events. He didn't know what to ask. He started with the obvious. "How do you know who I am? How can I trust this is real and not some prank?"

Mark flashed a cheeky smile at Rob. "Ah, proof. Proof is what you seek. No such thing as blind faith, I guess. That's okay with me. Well, I know a few things about you that others may not. You lost your virginity to a young lady in Tallahassee, Florida, when you were 16 years old. Was her name Amy, or Jamie?" Mark paused for effect. He continued, "How about you like ketchup and pizza sauce but you cannot stand tomatoes. Am I getting warm here?" Mark was just getting going. Victor enjoyed watching the volleys.

"Doing well so far. What about orange juice?" Rob threw him a curveball, he thought.

"Oh, you mean how you can't drink orange juice with pulp, it makes you sick. In fact, you don't care for any textures in your food or drinks. You love raisins but if anyone puts a raisin inside of your food, like a cookie or cake, it makes you have to spit it out?" Rob smiled and nodded. He waved a hand to keep going, he enjoyed this.

"Your favorite high school teacher was named Mr. Ambrose; he was a geography and American History teacher. He scared most of the students because he was loud, dressed poorly, and always had that white, crusty substance on his lips. But you found him fascinating and brilliant and he made you pursue teaching. You graduated 80th in your class from your high school in a suburb of Gainesville, Florida, and then went on to the University of Central Florida, where you received your BA in history and started teaching at a Catholic high school in Maryland. How am I doing so far?"

Rob just sat there. He was either hallucinating, dreaming or experiencing an unprecedented occurrence.

"You left teaching because you were caught sleeping with one of the administrators, went to Hollywood to start an acting career, got your first TV commercial as a man infatuated with chicken sandwiches for a national chain of fried chicken restaurants, and then eventually found a niche in production. You married and then divorced a lady from Vermont. Never had kids. You wax your chest and your—"

Rob put up a hand to stop him. "Okay, Okay, it's good. I believe you."

Mark put up his translucent hand one more time, "And just in case you are still doubting me"—here Mark put his hand up to his neck and removed his head, held it in his hands—"how's this little trick?"

Victor and Rob both jumped up and yelped. Mark was laughing as he placed his head back onto his neck. There was no blood or gore, just a simple head removal trick he was taught in Dead School.

"Jesus fucking Christ!" Rob said. "I believe you, I believe you."

"Good! Victor, I was going to show that trick to you the other day, but since you had already passed out and hit your head, I didn't want to risk it."

Rob pulled out his phone. "Just one second." He shot a picture of Mark, who smiled and placed an arm around Victor.

Rob looked at the picture on his phone. It was just Victor in the shot turning to his right to look at the invisible Mark.

Rob then called his office. "Um, hi Jennifer, it's Rob. I am going to need to have you finish up the Cutler edits this afternoon without me, something came up, OK? Good. Talk later."

Victor was beyond relieved. The dream he had the night before urged him to bring Rob out to the cemetery to meet Mark. He knew that he had to get The MonteGresso into his hand to increase the chances of him seeing Mark. And his information was spot on.

Rob looked at Mark. "Hey, stop hogging that weed. If I am going to talk with the dead, then I think that is a conversation best held when stoned." Mark tossed the pipe and lighter to Rob, who took a few hits and passed it to Victor. Victor did the same. The sun was out, and it felt good as the shade from the tree kept the temperature perfect. Rob was excited.

"Okay, so a few questions," Rob said. "To begin. Is there a god? Seems like a good starting point."

"Oh, you want to get right after it? Victor didn't even ask that question initially; can you believe it? Isn't that the first question one is supposed to ask of the dead?"

"Yeah, well, you never answered it," Victor responded.

"How about something easier. You don't want to know what Abraham Lincoln is like? Or which came first, the chicken or the egg?"

"Humor me." Rob was scared and anxious and excited all at once.

"Well, I hate to be a downer, but I don't know. In fact, no one on this side of the Divide has a clue to most of the mysteries of the universe. Is there a god? Is Allah in charge? Or Jesus Christ? Or Buddha? I just don't know. I am not only not on the other side of the Divide, but I don't even have a rightful spot on this side of the Divide because I was unceremoniously yanked out of my rightful place when The MonteGresso was improperly seeded in my grave."

Victor chimed in, "Well, how do you know so much about Rob, and I assume me, and everyone else alive?"

"Fair question. We all obtain a certain amount of knowledge when we die. We aren't omniscient, or at least I am not at this stage. If I was, I could find the other orbs. I assume on the other side of the Divide there is a level of omniscience that would make any worldly question easily answered. But not where I am. We do have the ability to view other peoples' lives in as much detail as we want. I became familiar with Rob's life the other day when I figured out Victor would need help. There are portals and avenues of exploration that are beyond your comprehension, but the amount of knowledge immediately available to a recently deceased person is immense. It's very illuminating. It's also odd to learn that your wife cheated on you with your brother, or that your grade schoolteacher watched child pornography. But none of these revelations bother us. We lose that sense of anger, or betrayal, or revenge when we die. Isn't that nice?"

It was Rob's turn. "So, is there a heaven? Or worse, a hell?"

"Ah, now we are getting somewhere. Yes. Have I been a good boy, and will I sing with angels, or am I going to be crispy and dance with the devil?"

"Yeah, something like that." Rob took another hit. Victor leaned in closely for this answer. He expected he'd be traveling to this place sooner than he had expected.

"Well, Rob, let me tell you that no one gets out of life for free. There is a price to be paid for your conduct in life. Did you murder, steal and hurt others? If so, you won't be accessing any pearly gates any time soon. But will you suffer an eternity of punishment? Nope. That doesn't happen either. Now, understand that I have limited information as I am on this side of the Divide and worse, I haven't even been truly accepted into my afterlife. But I do know that, when I died, I wasn't greeted by harps, angels and naked women, or seventy-two virgins, or whatever your concept of heaven is. But I wasn't being tortured by a horned beast shoving a red-hot pitchfork up my ass either."

Rob and Victor looked at each other and smiled. How could one not like

Mark Levin?

"But before you go thinking there are no consequences for what we do on earth, think again. For instance, a guy like Adolf Hitler, who I've never met but understand he is an incorrigible asshole, will not be able to ascend to the other side of the Divide and find omniscience for many, many years. I don't know if that's centuries or millennia or longer. But even sociopathic murderers must past through the Divide."

Victor jumped on that statement. "Well, how does that happen if the Divide is locked down?"

"Well, don't forget what I told you the other day, Victor. The Divide separates the Builders from the Dead. It isn't entirely closed off. There is a flow of the Dead that matriculate over. It just is a very slow process that keeps getting slower. However, if the Builders succeed in closing this small portal, then we will collect here, on this side of the Divide, likely until the end of eternity."

"What's so bad about being stuck on this side of the Divide?" Rob asked.

"You like going to NFL games? Or dining out in restaurants?", asked Mark.

"Sure, who doesn't?"

"Well, Rob, imagine being in line for security at an NFL stadium for years. Shuffling ever so slowly until you have a chance to enter the stadium. Or waiting for your table at restaurant for a century. Or two? No one likes to wait in line. We understand there is going to be some level of waiting. But waiting in perpetuity without the chance to gain omniscience and move on to a different paradigm of existence, well, that is Hell. I think the idea of living forever would get awfully tedious without expanding your mind, learning new things, being all-knowing."

"What about you, Mark? Where's your place in line?" Rob pressed.

"That's the bitch of all of this. Because I got all screwed over by the improper seeding, I can't even get in line. If you died tomorrow, you'd already be ahead of me. And the better you were on Earth, the closer you move up in line."

Rob was figuring this out. "So dear old Adolf is stuck at the back of the line? With Charles Manson and Pol Pot?"

"Something like that. I think Stalin is back there too. And, interestingly, so is the inventor of infomercials. Those things were the worst!"

"What? Are you serious?" Victor was shocked.

"Well, I don't know about him, but I do think the guy who started spam email definitely has his day of reckoning coming."

"Good, fuck that guy," Rob said, and all three laughed. "But it doesn't seem right that creatures like Hitler and Stalin could eventually cross the Divide and move on, but someone like you is stuck, forever."

"Well, I didn't write the rules. Life, as they say, is unfair. So is death. Enough about me. Do any of you have other questions before we get down to work? Time is ticking." Mark knew time was the enemy.

"Tell me, Mark, if Victor cannot get all three of the orbs seeded at the same time, and could only get The MonteGresso seeded, what would happen? Is that so bad?" Rob asked.

"Technically, no. It would just ensure the battle of the door of the Divide will continue for many more years, and it likely won't ever end. As more dead join our ranks, the more waiting and fighting we will endure. If, however, all three can be re-united on our terms, then there will be a cataclysmic blasting of the Divide and we will have an express train to the next paradigm." At the mention of "our terms," Mark gestured over all the dead at Briarwood.

"Yeah, well, what about Adolf and Pol Pot? Those dudes would benefit. I don't want to help those guys." Victor seemed frustrated and rightfully so.

"Everyone does a certain amount of time waiting to cross over. Bad dudes who have hurt others will continue to suffer in line. That's been determined by a power greater than you or me. Don't worry about that. And to be honest with you, once you cross over the Divide and start the process of omniscience, there is a price to pay for what you've done. Being all-knowing doesn't mean you live without realizing the pain you inflicted on others. You can become conscious of it in a very powerful way."

"So, omniscience isn't all it's cracked up to be?" Rob asked.

"Apparently, it has its drawbacks. But you must go there and deal with the stains and crimes of your life, whatever those may be. It's the nature of our existence as humans."

"And if the Divide is closed out?" Victor asked, even though he knew the answer.

"Well, that's the issue. If the Builders secure all three orbs and re-seed them on their terms, then any breach will be permanently closed over the Divide. We would literally back up here in an unending purgatory of misery. The Builders would control the vast universe of omniscience and power on an unprecedented scale. It almost seems better to avoid that risk and just keep things as they've always been, but there is a real push from the Dead to end this thing. And do it correctly. It's the big gamble. The biggest risk in the entirety of human existence."

"Great. Way to again give me diarrhea." Victor rolled his eyes and cursed the fact that he knew this.

Rob stood up and became animated. "I don't get it. If this is such a big deal and will affect all of us forever, why on earth is it being entrusted to Victor?" He looked at Victor and held his hands up, as if to say "no offense."

"No offense taken, Rob. I've asked the same thing. We should have the Army and Navy and Marines all securing the return of the other two orbs and ensuring my orb is locked away safely. The stakes are too high."

"It doesn't work like that. I don't know how else to explain other than to say the rules of the Afterlife are just different. It requires bravery. It requires a good heart. It requires kindness. There are rules. And it impacts the Builders' plight too. They can't go out and just hire an army either. This is small arms warfare being fought by the smallest of armies on the grandest of stages. If this thing became an all-out war, and it would, then the orbs would lose their power and all of us, the Dead and the Builders, could all suffer a catastrophic fate."

"So it can't get out of hand? Or else we are more fucked than we already are?" Rob asked.

"Correct, Rob," Mark said. "The world is reliant on just a small group of people. And you, whether you wanted to or not, you have joined Team Victor and we need you now. Immediately. We have a chance to get The PinonAstra and The Mule. We are sensing they are close, but we know that the Builders have their people on it, too."

Victor looked at Mark. "Are the Builders going for the full reunification too? Do you know?"

"Word down here is yes. It's all or nothing for them. They don't want any more crossing over onto their side of the Divide. It's a turf war. Plain and simple, they can't stop the flow, even if it's only a trickle, without all three orbs."

"And what about this sacrifice? Why is that needed?" Rob asked. Mark rubbed his hand through his translucent hair. "The sacrifice will have the power over the orbs," he said. "They will direct who gets the triad. That's why the minions who sacrifice must be trusted- they have incredible power if they seed all three orbs simultaneously." Victor and Rob considered the gravity of the sacrifice and the power that could be in their control. It seemed too awesome, too significant, for a couple of regular guys from Denver. But apparently those were the rules.

"Well, I accept this challenge and we need to figure out a quick and decisive way to locate The PinonAstra and The Mule," Rob said enthusiastically. "And I think we need to stop talking about this and get to work. There is literally no time to spare." He was excited and motivated but mostly he was scared. He was scared that he could die and face an eternity of misery and he had no plans to let that happen.

Mark looked at Rob. "On that point we are all in agreement. So, what's your plan?"

Chapter 35 ∗ Perseus The Slayer

Perseus the Slayer worked alone in his basement reviewing new video games that came onto the market. That was the passionate part of his job. The business part was setting up in front of a camera and lights, also in his basement, and issuing scathing reviews of the games while simultaneously playing them. He would walk his viewers through a game, or a new scene on a game, and his fans would hear his voice-over. He would sometimes find a game and give clues on how to successfully move on to higher levels. If he liked a new game, then the manufacturer of the game was set. Perseus the Slayer would give the game his seal of approval, and BAM! The game would be an unprecedented success.

The thing that made Perseus the Slayer so credible was that he truly loved video games and refused to accept the game makers' money for promoting their games. He was one of the few influencers on social media with integrity. He made a lot of money because his fans trusted him. Legions of followers meant companies lined up to use his platform to sell all kinds of goods. But when an influencer's followers amounted to over ten million, well, the money rolled in hand over fist. And he was only nineteen. Ah, what a blessing to be young, smart, and doing what one loves in life. On top of that, to be paid ridiculous, embarrassing amounts of money, well, that was a whole new level of bliss.

Perseus, aka Perry Sledge, was the son of Rob's sister Anna. He still lived at home, in Clearwater Beach, Florida, but he had purchased the house for his mom and younger brother, Harry. It was a massive house in a gated community a few minutes from the beach. He had bought all the toys one would imagine, a nineteen-year-old who could buy. A boat, a Corvette for himself, and a Range Rover for his mother. He also had a fractional ownership in a private jet. Because, well, why not?

Perry's phone dinged. It was a text from Uncle Rob.

The message: "You got five minutes to chat today? Important."

Uncle Rob was beloved by Perry. He had always been a father figure after Anna's husband died in a construction accident. In fact, Rob had helped the family financially after the death of Perry's dad, and he was the first one to buy Perry a good computer and video game console. Little did Rob know that within five years his nephew would be one of the most famous people on the internet. Rob never asked for one thing from his nephew. It wasn't his style and he personally believed that adults who profited off their children's (or nephew's) successes were the lowest of the low. He had no love for the parents of celebrity children who acted as business managers and lived vicariously through their kids. These parents often took huge paychecks for themselves because they believed they earned the money. What a joke. Living vicariously through a child was bad enough but making money off that child was unconscionable.

Rob, however, was going to ask for a huge favor from Perry and do it quickly. Perry immediately called his uncle after receiving the text.

"Uncle Rob, how you doing? It's been a while." Perry respected Rob and like most people, he was taken by his charm.

"Perseus the Slayer! I am fine. And how are Harry and your mom?"

"They are both doing great. Mom is at a yoga class right now and I think Harry is checking out a slew of new games. I'm bringing him in to help me in my business. It's really fun to work with him." Perry was happy he could share his success with his family.

"That's the best! Really proud of you. Tell them hello for me, OK?"

"You bet. So, what's up? Message sounded urgent."

Rob decided he would only share limited information with Perry. He didn't want him to think he was crazy, and he definitely didn't want to drag him into this whole ordeal and expose Perry's family to any possible danger.

"So, I need a favor. And I need it fast. Like today or tomorrow at the latest. I need you to post something to your entire YouTube, Twitter and Instagram legion of followers. I know this is a big ask but I've got money to pay you for your time and I know—"

Perry immediately cut him off. "You don't need to ask twice and never would I let you pay me for anything. I am your Huckleberry. What do you need from me, Uncle Rob?"

Rob let out a huge sigh of relief. "Okay, so here it goes..."

And Rob explained the project without explaining the context. It was simply too dangerous. They agreed to work together on this by coordinating over a video conference call. Rob would produce the segment and work with Perry to ensure maximum exposure. It was still a longshot, but they had to give it a try.

Chapter 36 ✳ Bloody Hands

Blood dripped from the end of Kitta's knife and started to pool at the base of Mr. Luiga's table. It was amazing how much blood was generated by a severed pinkie. He whimpered softly; perspiration dotted his face and bald head. Kitta didn't want to hurt this guy, but quite frankly she didn't give a shit either. Time was of the essence.

A few hours before this encounter, Mr. Dean Luiga, attorney at law, had been contacted by a Ms. Kendra Harrison inquiring about the late Eleanor Riggs estate. Ms. Harrison explained on the phone that she was a distant cousin of Ms. Riggs and was just reaching out to her late cousin's lawyer about some information related to the estate. Specifically, where did all of her assets and personal property go once she died? Poor, heart-broken Ms. Harrison scheduled an appointment with Mr. Luiga for late in the day. He had a small two-person law firm that handled estate and probate work in the heart of downtown Cincinnati.

As was the case with many estate attorneys, they tended to practice in small firms, and many were older because estate work was boring and the least sexy of the legal disciplines. Even patent lawyers found estate law to be boring.

Mr. Luiga had to have been at least seventy-five years old. He was a short, fat man who wore a bowtie and had a tight gray goatee and thick glasses. There was not a strand of hair remaining on his pink pate. His office featured many framed diplomas and mementos of Italian pride. The only other person remaining in the office when Ms. Harrison arrived was Mr. Luiga's equally old secretary, who had to catch her bus by 4:30. Dean allowed her to leave once Ms. Harrison had arrived - he didn't think this would be a very complicated meeting.

Kitta arrived at 4:15 sharp and wore a tight black skirt and red blouse. Her hair was carefully tucked under a brown Dorothy Hamill wig and she wore tinted eyeglasses. She carried her locked briefcase, which held The PinonAstra as well as a handbag containing many other items that she hoped wouldn't be needed. She greeted the short, fat, Mr. Luiga with a soft handshake and smile. They sat in his cramped conference room that was overflowing with legal binders, estate law books and treatises, as well as an old-fashioned globe that functioned as a bar. The chairs were mismatched and wholly unrelated to the conference room table that was stained with coffee cup rings.

"Thank you for meeting me on such short notice, Mr. Luiga. I just arrived in town and needed to deal with Cousin Riggs' estate as soon as possible." Kitta ditched her German accent, choosing to go with a light southern drawl. Just a little, she wasn't entirely sure if Mr. Luiga would detect it was fake.

"I'm happy to meet you, Ms. Harrison. I sure did like your cousin. A sweet and generous lady." That was a lie. She fly-specked all of his bills and called his office several times a day to complain about the language in her estate documents. Dean had learned to deal with the idiosyncrasies of wealthy people. Especially old seniors with money. They had all the time in the world to sit and contemplate their death and wanted every detail to be reviewed and analyzed over and over again.

Ms. Riggs died with a relatively healthy estate of just under eight million dollars. Because she was unmarried and had no children, the majority of her money went to numerous Cincinnati charities. Her largest beneficiary was the Cincinnati Modern Art Museum, where many items out of her personal art collection were relocated, along with a healthy million-dollar endowment. Many other charities received parts of her estate. Luiga thought highly of donating to art museums, but he always preferred to have donations go to human aid charities like The Red Cross, The American Heart Association, or the Salvation Army, organizations which were on the front lines of humanitarian crises. But it was Ms. Riggs' money, and she could with it whatever she wished.

"Ms. Harrison, how were you related to Ms. Riggs?" Kitta expected this question. "Oh, Eleanor's mother and my grandmother were first cousins. Which made us second cousins."

"Actually Ms. Harrison, that would make you third cousins. But I'm sure you were very fond of her."

"I can't say that I knew her well. I lived in Atlanta and never made it to Cincinnati. So it's been many years." That seemed like a safe lie.

"Well, tell me what can I do for you?"

Kitta straightened up in her seat and gave a cute smile. "So, Mr. Luiga, I realize my cousin was a collector of many rare antiquities and art. There was one piece in particular that I believe belonged to my mother and somehow came into possession of Cousin Eleanor. I just wanted to find out where it went. It means a lot to our family."

"I see. So, were you a listed beneficiary of the estate? I don't recall your name." Dean rifled through a manilla file folder.

"I wasn't. That's the problem. I believe I have a valid right to one of the items."

"I understand. But the problem is that I still represent the estate of your cousin. Even though she is dead, I am not authorized to disclose the contents of the estate other than what's on file with the court clerk." He placed the file down on the table and removed his reading glasses.

"Well, listen Mr. Luiga, I'm sure that I could hire a lawyer and file a lawsuit to find out where some of these items are. But it would cost her estate money, which I assume is all gone. And I would pay whoever came into possession of the item. I'd be happy to, even though I don't think I should be obligated to, considering it's a family heirloom that belongs in my family."

Luiga was getting frustrated. He really didn't have to explain this again, but he went through the concept of attorney-client privilege, and the privacy of estate documents. He wasn't even sure if this person was who she said she was. As far as he knew, she could be pulling some scam. He had seen it happen before. They went back and forth for a few minutes. She tried to be seductive and even leaned over the table so he could see the outline of her healthy cleavage and the moistness of her lipstick as she licked her lips.

As her flirting wasn't getting her anywhere, she accelerated. "I'm sure I could do something Mr. Luiga, to help loosen your pants and give me just a peek inside that file. I'll take care of it lickity-split." She placed her hand on his thigh from under the small conference room table.

Luiga stood up, not only fully unaroused, but quite frankly angry. "Ms. Harrison, I am gay, you see, and I am quite certain that my husband would not care for me violating my marital oath. I would ask you to leave and if you want to hire a lawyer to get into this file, then you should hire one." He pointed to the door.

Kitta stood up and smiled. Well, I prefer beating up this little munchkin to sucking his dick anyway, she thought. As she started to walk out of the conference room, she brushed by Luiga, who held the door open. She then turned to him and, with an open hand, slapped him hard across the right side of his face. Stunned by the blow, Dean stumbled over, hit the chair and fell to his knees. As he tried to stand up, Kitta kicked him in the chest and he bowled over in apparent agony.

Gasping for air, he looked up at Kitta. "I assure you that I will be calling the police. This is highly impro—." Bam! Kitta kicked him square in the jaw. This was fun for her. A waste of time, but fun, nonetheless. He rolled over, blood trickling from his forehead and mouth. He must have hit the table. She didn't want him passing out though; she needed crucial information from him first.

"Now, Mr. Luiga, why don't we just resolve this my way? I promise I don't want to hurt you."

Luiga crawled away from her; when he was steady enough he stood up and grabbed the file folder. But she was blocking the entrance. He went for the phone on the far side of the conference table, but Kitta reached it first and ripped the cord out of the wall.

"Jesus Christ, you dumb old Dago. Give me that file and this is all over." She then went into her handbag and pulled out her new blade. It glimmered in the lights of the conference room. Luiga considered the blade. He didn't want to die for this old client, but damn this evil woman. He was an attorney and he had duties to clients, living and dead.

"I am not sharing this with you," he said as he held the file aloft. "Are you really prepared to kill me for a look inside this file? Most of the information you are seeking isn't even in this file."

Wrong thing to say. Now she knew she would have to torture this guy to get the right file. She moved to her left and he followed suit, trying to get away. The room was so small he didn't have a lot of maneuverability and she was definitely stronger and more agile. She turned course and he ran right into her. With the blunt end of the knife, she punched him in the back of the head, and he went down, again. She pulled him up into a chair and grabbed the telephone cord hanging lifeless from the phone. She wrapped him up in the cord and cinched the knot as tight as possible. Fortunately for Kitta, the cord was long enough.

She then grabbed his left pinkie and put the blade to it. She didn't cut him. Yet.

"Listen old man. I need this file. You can either give it to me with ten fingers or nine. But it's coming with me."

Luiga looked at Kitta and spat a mouthful of blood onto the conference room table. "You are an evil person, and you can go to hell!"

With that she sliced off the pinkie with one simple movement. Blood shot out onto the old, wooden table. Dean screamed in agony. She secretly wished the conference room table was made of glass so he could really see the mess he was making. But she was pretty sure he understood that he was in a precarious position. She grabbed the thin file and rifled through it. He was correct. This didn't contain much of anything. There had to be a bigger file somewhere. She knew she had little time to dig through his office, but she didn't have much of a choice. Time was getting tight.

"Now, Mr. Luiga, I think I have been polite, thoughtful, and courteous to you. I could have started with your nose, or an eye, or your dick. But I am a good girl, and that's just not lady-like. So, pretty please tell me where the full file is."

Luiga could see little hanging pieces of flesh and bone where his pinkie used to be. He did see the pinkie on the floor, covered in blood and quickly collecting more blood. This woman was both evil and sadistic. She seemed to take pleasure in her work. He had no doubt she would continue with the torture. What to do? What to do? His cleaning personnel usually didn't arrive until at least 6:30 p.m. so they wouldn't be there to save him. His partner was gone on a cruise somewhere in the Pacific. It was just him versus this sociopath, who seemed to be getting enjoyment from this.

"What's it going to be, Mr. Luiga? More fingers? How about the left eye to go with the left pinkie? I have limited time here."

He groaned in pain. After the adrenaline started to wear off, the throbbing started but the blood had not started to clot yet. What a mess. "Please, Ms. Harrison, you need to understand the rules. I promise if you go now, I will not report this. I swear!"

She grabbed the bleeding hand and swiftly sliced off the adjacent ring finger, which had a lovely gold band. She didn't realize gay people solemnized their marriage vows with wedding bands too. But she was acutely aware of the lovely mess on the floor beneath him.

Luiga was whimpering now. He actually was crying. Kitta was a bit concerned he might pass out. She found a bottle of water and put it to his lips. He drank some. She then shook it over his head to keep him conscious.

"I am clearly not fucking around here. The next thing that goes is your cock. Do you understand!" She didn't yell it loudly, but she was stern. She pointed the red, dripping blade at his genitals and with the tip of the knife cut a swift tear into his wool pants. That did it.

"The file is in my office. In the far right filing cabinet. You are a terrible person." He was defeated. Kitta knew the sound of a defeated person. She ran into one of the two offices. His had a light on so she guessed that one. She saw the filing cabinet. "Which drawer, loverboy?" she called out. How could she be so whimsical, Luiga thought?

"The bottom drawer," he said weakly.

Kitta opened the bottom drawer and found the fat Eleanor Riggs file. She rummaged through it quickly. She didn't know what she was looking for. She brought it out to the poor man suffering in his own conference room, bleeding terribly from his left hand.

"I need to know where her art exhibits went. Specifically, some small items." She dumped the file in his lap and yanked off the cord so he could use his right hand. He looked through the file. He put his glasses on, which were smeared with blood and sweat, But he saw the letterhead from the auction house where almost all of her items were sent. The letter was attached to a long list of numbered items, the price paid and the name of the purchaser. She stared over his shoulder. Bingo, she thought.

She yanked it out of the file and flipped the pages. Wow, there was a lot of shit this woman owned. Then, on page three, she saw it. Line item 67: "Small glass object (quartz?), crystal, green with pink and gold hues, face of horse." That was it alright! She grabbed the entire file just to be sure.

"You see, that wasn't so bad. I'll tell you what, you put those fingers on ice, I bet they can do something with them. And I know you are going to call the police. But Dean Luiga, Esq., I know where you work, and..." She pulled him up out of his seat, yanked his wallet out of his pants and pulled out his driver's license. "I know where you and your husband live. If the police are called, I will come and I will cut off your husband's dick and shove it down your throat. So, when you are in the emergency room, you think really hard about how much information you want to give them. I suggest you tell them you were not careful near your paper cutter, or maybe a circular saw. Either way, don't make this evil bitch come back and finish you off." At least Luiga was relieved that she leaving and he was alive. That was all the mattered.

She gave him a small squeeze from behind. He was too weak and lightheaded to do anything back. She then crept behind him, grabbed his hair and yanked his head back. She slit his throat from end to end. She made sure to hold him firmly so he didn't turn and get blood all over her. He managed to spray the office, but Kitta remained spot-free. Being covered in blood was never a good thing when trying to avoid being noticed.

Not wanting to risk the elevator, she walked patiently down the staircase, three stories to the outside exit. She walked out the side door to avoid the lobby. The fewer witnesses and cameras the better. She had some blood on her skirt and blouse, but it blended in. She quickly turned the corner and scanned the surroundings. It was quiet and she didn't see anyone. She pulled off her wig and her red blouse. She had a camisole on underneath, but it was black and didn't show off too much. She dumped these in a sidewalk trashcan and slowly walked another two blocks to her car. She unlocked the door and sped off. Her destination was a small town an hour northeast of Memphis, Tennessee, named Jackson.

Chapter 37 * Jorba The Beast

Victor and Rob sat in front of Rob's computer monitor in Rob's office. It had been a full day working with Perry to get the video to look just right, and they were both exhausted. It was already 11 p.m. Denver time, which meant they had been producing this video for almost twelve straight hours. It wasn't anything super or dramatic, but if it was done correctly it would be effective. The video was going to launch in just under one hour and they had to be ready for any and all inquiries. Victor had gone to a convenience store to buy a cell phone that had a number to be used exclusively for the launch of the video. It was charging at an outlet next to the computer monitor.

They each reclined in an office chair, cold beers in their hands. It was amazing to Victor that he had only known Rob for less than forty-eight hours, but their friendship was strong and real. Yes, there was the common purpose that united them, specifically saving all of mankind from a tortuous hell of an afterlife, but they genuinely liked each other. Rob was neither patronizing nor dismissive towards Victor. He didn't care that Victor was fairly unaccomplished and dull. Maybe Victor wasn't that dull after all and it just took a good person to really understand him. All the cards were on the table and there had been so much honesty between them already that if Rob had asked him his most private secrets, he would have likely divulged. Fortunately, he didn't have any dark and deep secrets.

Rob went back to play the video one more time and he used his computer program to alter the color scheme a little more, change the tone on the volume slightly, and reduce some of the glare. Rob was a perfectionist. If he could make a person hire a goofball lawyer on TV, then this would be a breeze.

"Rob, I think it looks perfect. The hue coming off the screen is perfect. I can read it without any problem."

Rob squinted tightly at the image on the TV screen that Perry was holding in the video. He could not make out anything. "Okay, I can't see a thing, but you are saying it's clear as day?"

"Clear as day. It looks really good. I couldn't ask for a better shot at fishing in these waters. We've done all we can to get a bite, if any fish are out there." Victor was antsy. He sensed time was running out.

"Well, I never had the patience for fishing, seems I always got my line tangled and lost my bait. But I agree, we need to get moving." Rob finalized the video and emailed it back to Perry in a compressed format due to the size of the file. He then got on the phone. Perry picked it up immediately. "Uncle, I see the link, you good with this version? If so, I can go live as soon as you give me the word." He was on speaker so Victor could hear as well. Victor gave the thumbs up sign and then crossed his fingers.

"Perseus the Slayer, go to it! We have faith it will work and appreciate what you have done. One day, when we are a little older, I will explain what this was all about."

Perry jumped on that. "That's the deal, Uncle Rob. But until then you keep your secrets. Perseus the Slayer is always here to help. Any information I get I will forward to you, although I think the person you need will reach out directly to you."

"That's the hope. Thanks, buddy. Talk soon."

"Bye." Perry hung up. He then uploaded the video to his Perseus the Slayer website, YouTube, Instagram and Twitter accounts. He hoped his reach was global enough to find who they were looking for.

A few minutes later Rob's Instagram account and Twitter feed showed a new post from Perseus the Slayer. Victor pulled up the YouTube channel and saw Perseus the Slayer's new video going live. It was happening.

On the video Perry sat in front of a large Perseus the Slayer black banner featuring a picture of the legendary Perseus of Greece who slew the evil Medusa. The mythological creature with serpents as hair whose look would turn a man to stone. His banner was designed with Perry's face on top of Perseus's body, clad in Greek tunic and a winged helmet, holding Medusa's severed head highly in his left hand, a dripping bloody sword in his right hand.

Perry sat just to the right of a large TV at his feet with another monitor on top of the TV. The TV was on, but it was just a black screen; the computer just had Perseus's logo bouncing around. Perry used the TV as a prop and spent the next three minutes addressing his worldwide audience.

"To all of my fans and followers, it is I, the great and mighty Perseus the Slayer. I want to thank all of you for the wonderful comments and suggestions you sent in regarding the new GameCo selection of the month, *Battle the Beast*. I think this is GameCo's best, even better than 2017's *Normandy Invasion*. Unless you are a tremendous pussy and are scared of the vivid action scenes and gore, you will have hours of fun. While I refuse to reveal all of the secrets to defeating

Jorba the Beast, and there are several, I have had over one million people begging me for help. I've read countless theories, but you are all wrong. I know GameCo is going to be pissed off with me for sharing one of these secrets because it is without a doubt the biggest surprise in the gaming industry, and GameCo will probably try to sue me, but I don't care. This is one way to defeat Jorba…"

Following his introduction, Perry turned on the computer monitor and started up the immensely popular *Battle the Beast* video game. The game had over 23 million downloads and was likely the most popular video game on the planet. No one could defeat Jorba the Beast. And his many fans were begging for advice. Perry wasn't planning to air the secrets to defeating Jorba for at least another month, and he knew when he did, he would get major hits on his social media feed. That meant lots of advertising money. But this was the perfect time to release his secret to killing Jorba, and he hoped whoever Rob was looking for was also interested. It was worth a shot.

When he turned on the computer, he also turned on the TV below him to a dull, white screen. On it he had used a white wax pencil and wrote in big, booming letters:

"DO YOU OWN THE MULE? A SMALL GLASS-LIKE OBJECT. THE SIZE OF A BASEBALL. CRYSTALS ARE INSIDE IT. THERE IS A FACE OF A MULE OR HORSE ON THIS. CALL 303-871-0009 IMMEDIATELY. YOUR LIFE IS IN EXTREME DANGER!!"

To those without the vision it was just a white TV screen, but to those few people with the vision it was a flashing neon sign.

It was just after midnight in Jackson, Tennessee, when Frank McDuffy's iPhone got a notification from one of his favorite game bloggers, Perseus the Slayer. He saw a small post underneath that said, "Secrets revealed to solving *Battle the Beast*." That was earlier than he expected, and he was psyched. Being an adult male, living in his parents' basement and unmotivated to do much except fantasize about killing Jews, Muslims, and illegal immigrants, Jorba the Beast was a pleasant momentary distraction. He reached into a mini fridge he kept in the basement near his computers and TVs and grabbed a cold can of Blast Off, an energy drink. If Perseus had the answers to solving the Jorba riddle, he was ready to stay up all night!

He rotated his chair in front of his massive 54-inch monitor and put on his headphones, which attached to a video game console. He could watch normal videos through this set up as well as play video games and interact with other gamers around the world. Even though he knew lots of these other gamers were probably camel jockeys from the Middle East or black thugs from Compton, at least he didn't have to see their actual faces. That would ruin the experience for him. Being a bigot was complicated.

He settled into his comfortable gaming chair and clicked on the Perseus link. He could still see that annoying yellow hue on his screens, but it didn't really bother him anymore—or diminish the enjoyment of killing zombies or aliens. Frank dimmed the overhead lights. He entered his login name and password, and immediately saw the Perseus the Slayer insignia which slowly faded out. Then there was Perseus himself, sitting in front of a large TV screen with a smaller monitor placed on top. The Perseus logo was on a black banner behind him. Perseus was no more than 20 years old, blonde-haired, and blue-eyed. He looked Aryan through and through and that made Frank feel good.

Perseus was wearing a dark T-shirt and small silver chain around his neck. He had on a massive Rolex that was simply too big for his little arms, but hey, when you have millions in the bank you may as well buy some bling. Frank couldn't argue with that. He listened to the opening statement from Perseus and then, once Perseus had turned on the TV and the computer monitor, Frank sat in dazed silence. He completely tuned out everything Perseus was saying and doing on the computer. He could have cared less about defeating Jorba. He was only cued in on that secret message that he saw on the TV screen below:

"DO YOU OWN THE MULE? A SMALL GLASS-LIKE OBJECT. THE SIZE OF A BASEBALL. CRYSTALS ARE INSIDE IT. THERE IS A FACE OF A MULE OR HORSE ON THIS. CALL 303-871-0009 IMMEDIATELY. YOUR LIFE IS IN EXTREME DANGER!!"

He dropped his can of Blast Off and immediately started to sweat. He jumped up out of his seat and ran to his safe where The Mule was housed. Jesus Christ, Jesus Christ was all he could think. Was this the thing that Perseus was mentioning? He grabbed The Mule. It had been over a year since he'd seen it. Now it glowed and vibrated gently. He had never seen that before. How long had this been going on? Considering Frank didn't buy this trinket until 2015, it had been inactive. It had only re-activated a few weeks earlier once The MonteGresso's forty years of dormancy ended, and all three orbs went into search mode.

It felt warm to him, although that was probably his imagination. He ran back to his seat and read the message again. Yes, this object in his hands definitely looked like a mule. It was the size of a baseball, almost a perfect size, and it had crystals throughout. If this was what Perseus was discussing, how did he know that Frank would be watching? How would he know how to get a message out to him via the special yellow hue that made that secret message pop? Could anyone see that message? Perseus did not say one thing about the message at all, as if it was left there as a secret message just for him. And most disconcerting of all: why was his life in extreme danger? It didn't make sense. This was just some trinket he bought from an estate sale. He bought stuff all the time. There was nothing particularly unique about this item. Or was there? He then started to put some things together. His vision problems started at about the same time as the purchase of that trinket. He also had those constant annoying and frightening dreams about the end of the world and hell, and purgatory and he always felt people were trying to talk to him in the middle of the night. He knew this all started right about the time he bought this item.

He was imagining all of this. Surely he was. That was just a clue to the game, right? He was just lame old Frank McDuffy from Jackson. A part-time computer technician and full-time video and gaming aficionado. He didn't have many friends or aspirations aside from wanting to kill lots of non-Christians and brown people. And even that was more of a fantasy than a reality. He had never even spray-painted a swastika on a wall or punched some random black guy. Adolf Hitler would be so disappointed in him. He was not special. His little trinket was not special. And he was certainly not the person who was supposed to be receiving this message. But what if no one else could see that message? If everyone could see that message, then thousands of people would be calling that number. Yes, that's right, this was a message for the masses. It was not for him. There must be a million trinkets that look like his orb. There must be. This was all part of Perseus the Slayer's *Battle the Beast* video. It had to be.

He decided to call one of his few buddies, Derik Losh, who also followed Perseus's channel. He   would most assuredly be awake following the step-by-step instructions being provided right now.

Derik answered on the first ring. "Frank, what the fuck dude, are you seeing this?" Frank felt a wave of relief wash over him. "Yes, Perseus's channel, right? That's why I'm calling. Do you see the message?"

Derik responded as if he was bit high, "Dude I totally hear the message. This Perseus dude is incredible. Such a boss gamer." Frank started to feel bad again. "What about the message on the screen below the computer. On the TV screen, do you see it?"

"Dude, what the fuck are you talking about? Are you drunk? Aren't you watching the computer monitor that Perseus is using? He is only a few levels away from torching Jorba. I can't belie--."

"Derik. Shut the fuck up for a second. Look at that big TV screen below the computer monitor. Do you see that?"

"Yes, what do you think I'm blind? What about it?"

"Do you see a message on that screen? Does it say something about a mule? Or that someone's life is in danger?" Frank's heart was racing. Please, oh please let Derik the idiot see that message.

"Dude, you drinking moonshine tonight? That TV has nothing on it. It's just a white screen, like snow, there is no message or video playing. But, dude, check out Jorb—"

Frank hung up. He was officially about to have a panic attack. He decided as a last resort he would wake up his mother. She had to work early in the morning, but he needed someone else to see what he saw. Maybe it was just on his monitor. Yes, that had to be it. As Perseus continued to rattle on about how to win the video game, Frank ran up the stairs two at a time and made his way to his mother's room. She slept separately from Frank's dad, who worked a night shift and snored like crazy.

He whispered in her ear, "Mom, I need you to wake up and see something." He gently nudged her shoulder. Mrs. McDuffy startled awake, a moist string of drool connecting her face to her pillow. "What? Frankie? Are you okay?"

"Mom, just come downstairs and look at something really quick."

"Oh, Frankie, I'm fucking tired, honey. What is it?"

"Just please, I'm asking you to look at something, please." His voice shot up another level and Mrs. McDuffy could sense he was panicking. He was thirty-years old and a social moron, but he was still her son. She worried about him constantly. He was kind of going nowhere in life, but as a loving mother she pandered.

"Okay, okay, let me grab my slippers." Frank grabbed them from under the bed. He was in a rush. "Come on, please."

She followed Frank down into the cool basement, a bathrobe wrapped around her shoulders. "Mom, look on that screen, do you see anything on that TV screen?"

"All I see right now is a can of Blast Off soaking into my carpet!" She bent over and picked up the can. And then walked to the monitor. "Where am I supposed to look?" Frank pointed his finger right onto the screen, and he read the message word for word, pointing at the screen. "Do you see those words?"

Mrs. McDuffy grabbed some reading glasses in her bathrobe pocket and got within inches of the monitor. "Frank, I don't see anything but white snow on that TV screen. What dangers are you talking about? Are you in trouble? Have you been fired? Are you still smoking that weed? You know only niggers smoke weed."

At least Frank knew where his bigotry came from. "No, mom, I'm not smoking no weed. Okay, go to bed, forget it. Sorry to bother you."

"You okay, my little Frankie Boy? You stressed out? I know we have some bad stuff going on in this state. Fucking communists are taking over our government. Is that bothering you? Take one of my pills. You'll sleep better." She handed Frank a pill out of a bottle she kept in her robe pocket, along with her reading glasses. "I'm going to bed. Love you, sweetheart."

"Love you, too." Even bigots loved their mommies.

Mrs. McDuffy trudged back upstairs and closed the door. Frank decided he had only one choice. He grabbed his phone and dialed the number.

Chapter 38 ∗ A Fish On The Line

"Hello? Who is this? What's going on?" Frank asked into the phone.

"Who is this?" Victor replied.

This was the only phone call Rob and Victor had received in the thirty minutes since the Perseus video went live. They didn't have high expectations for any calls and certainly not within thirty minutes of posting the video. They figured if lots of people had this vision enhancement then the phone would be ringing off the hook. The fact that they only received this one call was significant.

Victor put the phone on speaker setting so Rob could listen in. Despite the fact they were dead tired, a surge of adrenalin lit through both of them like lightning and they sat eagerly on the edges of their chairs.

"My name's Frank. I saw your message."

Victor had to play it out a little and make sure he had the right person.

"You did? What did the message say exactly?"

Frank stood up and looked up at the screen, which was frozen allowing him to read the message directly from the Perseus the Slayer post. He recited it verbatim. Victor and Rob gave each other a high five and continued to question Frank.

"Frank, do you have the Mule? Can you describe it to me?"

Frank was suspicious, but he didn't see any threat in giving the details of what his object looked like. He   described it in minute detail. That had to be it, Victor thought. It was precisely as he had envisioned it and almost identical to what Mark Levin described. Wow! They were close.

"That sounds like the Mule. But let me ask you a question."

"Go for it."

"How long have you been able to see strange yellow hues on glass?"

Frank let out a sigh. He felt some relief that someone else knew what he was going through. "Honestly, since I bought this thing you call the Mule five years ago, I've always had that vision. I always called it the horse ball, but if you're telling me it's a mule, I reckon I can see that."

From his southern drawl and the fact that he used the word "reckon," Victor figured this guy was American and from the south.

"So, tell me, partner, what's your name? You know my name. You know I have this mule ball, and you know I can see special hues on glass. So, what's your name and I reckon you can see special too?" Frank asked.

Rob and Victor looked at each other. They expected if someone called in, they had better be ready to answer some questions without giving out specific information about their location. If they gave out too much information to the wrong person, they could be on the wrong end of a gun and cast off to an eternal purgatory. They couldn't risk that. But they had to give out enough information to get the Mule into their possession without violence and without losing The MonteGresso.

"Fair question, Frank. My name is Robert Victors. I am in Denver. I came into possession of the brother of The Mule. There is a third sibling out there named The PinonAstra. The owner of The PinonAstra is desperately looking for The Mule and this person will stop at nothing to get that from you. This person, or people, will not hesitate to kill you and I believe they know where you are now, and time is ticking to get you to safety."

Frank, light-headed, sat down on his couch. He started sweating profusely. Was this person telling the truth? Maybe this person wanted to kill him. How did he know? He wished he had paid attention to those crazy dreams that haunted his sleep night after night. He didn't remember the specifics, but the one thing he recalled was that people would be coming for his Mule. He knew it had something to do with life and death and some battle raging in the Afterlife. But those were just dreams. Not reality. Who was this Robert Victors guy? Was this some set-up?

"Hello? Frank, you still there? Have you had any strange dreams to accompany your newfound vision? I know you have. If so, then you have to trust me."

Frank waited. What if this guy was telling the truth? He sure as shit had no plans to die. And how did he know about the dreams? He chose to play it out. "Yeah, I'm here. So, what are you think'n I should do?"

"I think you need to get to Denver immediately. Like tonight. Where do you live? Actually, don't tell me. I want to protect you. I want to buy The Mule from you. That will get this target off your back and put some cash in your pocket. But time is wasting. Can you get to Denver immediately?"

Frank had to think about that. He had a job, but he also could take a vacation. He was entitled. He also had $1,000 of emergency cash in his safe. He had to make some fast decisions but when he thought about all the dreams, the colors, the messages and The Mule, he knew he had to take this opportunity. At a minimum he needed some answers, and at best he needed to make some money and save his life. "Okay, Robert, I'm willing to meet you."

Victor smiled at Rob and made a fist of victory. "Frank, we want to save your life and when you get here, we will explain how we will do this." Rob looked at Victor and immediately Victor mouthed the word FUCK. He'd said "we." Maybe Frank missed that.

"Who's WE?" Frank quickly responded. He didn't miss anything.

Victor stammered for a second "We as in the colloquial we."

"The what? What are you saying?" Frank stammered. Victor started to panic. Did he just blow it? Shit! Then he figured, if Frank was a southern boy, he probably was a religious person, so he gave it a shot.

"I meant we as me and the holy god Jesus Christ. I apologize for startling you, but wherever I walk I walk with Jesus. I'm sorry. I am not preaching or trying to convert you if you're not a Christian, but that's how I talk." Victor looked at Rob and held one hand up in a helpless gesture.

Frank thought for a moment. "Well, it just so happens I am a god-fearing Christian and son of Christ, so I understand what you mean."

Rob mouthed "Thank Christ" to Victor, who shook his head and realized they'd dodged a bullet.

"How soon can you get to Denver?" Victor said. "I don't even know where you live. Just tell me the general vicinity, not your city or address. That's for your own safety."

"I'm in southwest Tennessee, so I'd say if I left at day-break I could be in Denver by tomorrow night. You reckon that will be okay?"

Victor looked at Rob with a questioning expression. Rob nodded and gave a thumbs-up. If they were too aggressive and pulled too hard, the fish could jump off the hook and be gone forever.

"It would probably be better if you jumped on the first plane out, but I have no idea how complicated that would be so tomorrow morning makes plenty of sense. No need to drive without getting sleep. If you are able to sleep tonight." He just prayed that no one would come for him in the next twenty-four hours. Victor wouldn't feel safe until The Mule was close and under their protection.

"Also, let me recommend, however, that if you have a gun that you keep it close by and lock your doors tonight. Make sure The Mule is locked away in some lockbox when you leave with it. Never, ever let it out of your sight." Victor added for good measure. He knew the line about owning a gun would create an ally out of Frank. What Christian from Tennessee didn't own a gun? If Victor only knew who he was dealing with, he wouldn't want this race-baiting, violent bigot anywhere near a firearm, but that was a detail Victor didn't know. Yet.

Frank went into his gun room while he was still on the phone with Victor and pulled a shiny .357 Magnum out of his gun locker. It was a heavy piece of equipment, guaranteed to put down any threat with extreme prejudice. He cradled it in his arm. "No need to worry 'bout that, Robert. I am well outfitted."

Rob and Victor made a mental note. When this guy arrived in Denver he'd be strapped. Of that there was no doubt.

Frank thought for a moment. This was a negotiation. A strange negotiation, but a negotiation, nonetheless. "Mr. Victors, I had no intention of selling The Mule. So, if you plan to buy it you will need to properly compensate me for this beautiful object." Victor had expected this. "Don't worry, Frank. We will discuss a more than fair price for you. But none of that will matter if you are dead. So, keep your eye on the prize."

Victor then went on to explain that, once he crossed the Colorado border, he should call the number again and he would be given instructions on how they should meet. Victor and Rob did not want to give up any information about the power of the Mule or where they were located just yet. That would have to wait for everyone's safety. Frank agreed with the plans and gave Victor his cell phone number. He would try to get some sleep and make his way west at the crack of dawn. By Frank's rough estimations, Denver was about an 1,100-mile drive from Jackson. Conservatively, if he left at 7 a.m. and took quick breaks, he could be there by 10 p.m. He would just have to avoid the state patrol and anyone else who might want to kill him.

They agreed to talk again at 10 a.m. Denver time. Until then they would remain radio silent. Victor hung up and turned to Rob. "I hope this Frank fellow is the real deal and doesn't try to get any ideas about stealing The MonteGresso and screwing up our plans." Rob knew people like Frank, he could read him like a book. "Victor, let me tell you something. Frank is an idiot, through and through. He is a simple person. And you can't turn a simple person into a complex person. He wears his heart on his sleeve and, hopefully, we can get this done for some cash without him ever reading too much into this. At least I pray we can." With that they both opened one more beer.

Back in Tennessee, Frank felt tremendous relief that he began to understand the value of the Mule, and that he likely was not going crazy. Someone else out there was dealing with the same issue he was dealing with. He was cautious but committed. He had every intention of selling this thing and getting it out of his life forever. If this Robert in Colorado was that desperate for this thing, and people wanted to kill for it, he'd be safer selling it and getting himself out of anyone's cross-hairs. Frank had no idea that The Mule didn't work that way.

He ran up to his room to pack a bag. He loaded in the .357, as well as a few other weapons of choice and ammunition. He grabbed the Mule and placed it in one of his gun totes that was hard plastic and lockable. He needed to keep this item safe. He also grabbed the $1,000 in cash he had stashed there. He would definitely need cash.

He carefully organized all of his stuff and wrote a brief note to his parents that he had to make a fast business trip out west but would call from the road. He knew that if he left at 7 a.m. both parents would be sleeping so he could avoid an in-person discussion. He didn't want to have to explain himself. After he organized all of his items, he decided to walk outside to his truck to remove some stuff he didn't need in there and confirm that he had plenty of gas and a spare tire. It was approaching 1 a.m. and it was dark. The ambient light off his front porch failed to illuminate a blonde-haired woman sitting behind the wheel of her car about three houses down. When she saw Frank walk outside, she made her move.

Chapter 39 * Jackson, Tennessee

Kitta had driven non-stop from Cincinnati to Jackson after she finished her discussions with Mr. Luiga. The Riggs file had all of the information about the disposition of the estate. She was able to locate the name and address for one Mr. Frank McDuffy. The last known possessor of one of the most important items in the existence of all of mankind. He had no clue of the power of the item he possessed.

As she drove through the dark two-lane roads outside of Jackson, she remembered the details she had learned in high school about the American Civil War. It was always interesting to drive through culturally significant areas and realize the history of the land. While much of Jackson had been developed, there was an eerie sense of the past that haunted this area. She assumed the same could be said for most of the South. How many slaves had been traded or sold right there in Jackson? Did any of them make it to the safety of Cincinnati via the Underground Railroad and stop for a rest in the woods of Jackson? Did Confederate generals use Jackson as a place to maintain a siege against the Union troops, or was it run over completely by General Grant's army? If the old trees she saw dotting the side of the road could talk, what would they say?

She figured that, if she dug deep enough in the soil along the tree-lined roadway, she'd unearth some old remnants from a battle. Over the course of the past few years, she had become very interested in historical relics. Before her child died, she could have cared less about antiquities and historical events. But now she was fascinated by the tales told by artifacts found in historically significant locations. That was one of the benefits of her quest.

While Kitta was no fan of the negro or the negro's enabler, the Jew, she also found the concept of slavery abhorrent and uncivilized. She maintained some of the Aryan blood in her veins and believed that she was superior to many other people. She drove in silence thinking that America was once great and foreboding and invincible, but those days were waning. The political divisiveness in this country was over the top and she sensed another civil war was not too far off in the distance. It wasn't the North versus South any longer, the battle lines were all over the place. It was Democrat versus Republican. Progressives versus Conservative. The growing divide wasn't just about race any longer. No, it encompassed a host of issues tearing the heart out of the American giant. Religion, economics, guns, immigration- the list went on. And it wasn't just one side versus the other side. There were divisions within divisions. The war for America's soul was a messy battleground and Kitta knew blood would be shed sooner rather than later. The pot of water was simply boiling over. And that would mean many more people would die and she would rule them all. She did respect the United States, though, as an amazing experiment in democracy that endured despite the increasing tension, and every part of the fabric of the country, even the rural parts of Tennessee, helped make America great. But what made America great, was also destroying America. The irony was as thick as Southern grits.

On that note she saw a Cracker Barrel restaurant sign from the side of the road and realized this quaint country diner was the perfect American enterprise. It allowed fat Americans to eat caloric-rich country foods and experience it in the setting of an old country general store, just like in the late 1800's or early twentieth century. But how could one be nostalgic for a time in which one never lived? How could country fried steak and gravy be romanticized? Or was it biscuits and gravy? Either way, she was starving and decided to try out some biscuits and gravy and maybe some ham steak too. Why not? She had traveled a lot and was weary and had a date with a Mr. Frank McDuffy very soon. Although he had no idea.

Kitta had earlier contacted Joe Sanchez up in Buffalo Grove to have him do some research on Frank McDuffy. What she learned played right into her hands. Apparently, Mr. Francis McDuffy was a fourth generation Volunteer state resident who loved video games, worked on computers, and just so happened to have an alias on the internet under Duffy Franklin. Duffy Franklin was a real son of a bitch who liked to post long diatribes against Blacks, Jews, Gays, Mexicans, Catholics, abortion providers. No one, or nothing was spared. It was amazing that with some of the vitriol he spewed, he had not somehow surfaced on an FBI watchlist. Although, it was likely he was tagged.

There was nothing illegal about posting nasty, bigoted material on-line here in the U.S. of A, but in Kitta's hometown of Frankfurt, she could face a variety of criminal sanctions because it was illegal to deny the existence of the Holocaust as well as to promote hateful, racist ideas. Mr. Frank McDuffy, aka Duffy Franklin, had also joined a variety of fringe, right-wing, extremist organizations, such as Stormfront and the KKK of southwest Tennessee. But he didn't appear, per Joe's research, to have committed any criminal acts or even participated in-person. He was probably some socially awkward loner who had been raised in a culturally isolated place with many generations of bigots in front of him. She did have Joe forward her a picture of Frank. He was a pleasant-looking man of twenty-five to thirty years old, average height, dark hair and blue eyes. He did have a beard in the picture she had, but she wasn't sure if that was currently on his face. She also confirmed that his address was still the address she had on file from Mr. Luiga's office. He drove a blue Ford F-250 truck and when she parked down the street from his residence at about 11:30 that evening, she saw the truck parked in front of his house.

With her belly full of good old-fashioned country fare and strung out from a long day of torture and driving, she decided to close her eyes and wait until morning to connect with old Frank McDuffy. She hoped to avoid torture. Maybe he would sell her The Mule. That is, if he still had it in his possession. She had every sense that it was with him as she dreamed in her car. Her dreams didn't confirm he had it, but she felt its presence. She felt it so strongly, in fact, that she awoke with a startle at about 12:30 when she could see a glow coming from her lockbox containing The PinonAstra. That was something she wasn't expecting but it had to signal that she was close. She opened the box and saw that The PinonAstra was warm, glowing auburn, and vibrating. She suspected the closer these orbs got, the louder and more animated they became. That means The Mule was warm and glowing too. There must be something about proximity between the orbs that caused them to react.

As she held The PinonAstra in her hands and explored its majestic beauty and depth, she lost track of time. She looked up to see a man walk out of Frank's house and head to the Ford truck. He shuffled through some stuff in the cab and removed some items. She looked closely and the man did resemble Frank. There was no time like the present. She placed The PinonAstra back in its lock box, grabbed her Glock, and slowly exited her vehicle, closing the door very quietly. She didn't want to scare him, but anyone creeping up on someone at one in the morning would definitely cause a startle. If he was holding a weapon, which was certainly possible, then she could quickly find herself in a precarious situation. She walked as quickly and silently as possible. Based on her training, she knew that quick lateral movements in a dark environment were the best options. He had not spotted her. She found a large southern red oak tree that allowed her cover. Kitta waited until he was bending deep into the back seat of his truck when she was able to silently run up behind him and place the tip of the Glock into the base of his spine.

"Mr. McDuffy, if you wish to live, I suggest you immediately put your hands on your head and slowly take three steps back." She used her full German guttural tones, hoping that he would recognize that she was from the land of the

Third Reich and maybe, just maybe, elicit some quick sympathy.

"Who are you? Who are you? Don't shoot me. Please don't shoot me," he whimpered. Clearly, he was of the pussy genus, despite all of his tough talk online. His hands immediately went to his head. Kitta used her free hand to pat him down. He appeared to have no weapons. His .357 was in his bag inside.

"I have no plans to hurt you, Mr. McDuffy. In fact, I am here to help you. But if you make any sound, I will not hesitate to put a hole in your spinal cord. Do you understand?"

Frank was now crying. He was actually crying. But that wasn't unusual. Most people had never had a gun put to their back and had their life threatened. She was surprised he hadn't pissed himself yet.

"Stop your blubbering, what are you a child? I thought you were a warrior for the white race. Isn't that true? I thought I was going to talk to a fellow warrior for white justice, not listen to a little faggot boy cry for his mommy." She was laying it on thick. She needed to dominate this process.

"I'm sorry. Yes. I am a warrior for the white race, what are you doing here? Are you here for The Mule?"

Kitta almost lost her balance. How did he know about that? This couldn't just be a coincidence. He knew something. Was he having intense dreams and was expecting her to come? She didn't know but she kept playing along.

"Is The Mule here? I want to see it."

"P-p-please just move the gun and I'll show it to you. Just don't shoot me. The guy told me that you'd kill me."

The guy told you I'd kill you? Kitta thought. That was definitely interesting. What guy? Was this another missing clue? Was this all coming together perfectly? She got excited. She needed to remain calm.

"Listen, Mr. McDuffy, I am not here to hurt you or kill you. Whoever told you that certainly has told you a lie. I need you. I need your help. I am going to take three steps backwards and I want you to slowly turn around. Then we are going to walk to my car over there across the street. It is the dark blue sedan. You will open the front door and sit down. I will get in the back seat and we will have a little discussion. If you want to live, I suggest you agree."

"Of course, yes, I see the car."

Kitta took a few steps back and ordered Frank to turn around but keep his hands on his head. He saw a perfect blonde Aryan standing in front of him. She was a few inches taller than he was and she definitely looked tough as nails. She was also gorgeous and he, for some unknown reason, became aroused. Maybe because of the excitement of the day, maybe because of how attractive and tough she was, and maybe because he hadn't been laid in almost a year, and he paid for that one.

Kitta could sense his pleasure because he had a large grin as soon as he saw her. "Settle down, Mr. McDuffy. I might be a woman, but I assure you I will kill you without a second's thought. Do you understand me?"

"I do. I'm sorry. You just look and sound like a perfect vision of a pure German Aryan. I didn't realize they made them so pretty in Germany."

"Again, Mr. McDuffy, I don't wish to deal with your charms at this moment. Walk to the car please."

Frank walked towards the car, occasionally stealing a glance over his shoulder at the woman trailing him by about ten feet. He decided he could try and run, or try to turn around and subdue her, but something told him that any attempts would be met with a bullet, and she definitely appeared qualified to use that Glock. But more importantly, he was intrigued by her and thought maybe she was an ally and the man in Colorado was the enemy. Maybe he was about to drive right into a trap in Colorado. He didn't know. He decided he would have to wait and see.

They entered the car and the interrogation began. Kitta learned all about how he obtained The Mule and the dreams he had tried to shut out of his head. He explained about Perseus the Slayer and the yellow hue on glass as well as the phone call with someone named Robert Victors. He told her his life was in danger and he needed to meet with Mr. Victors in Colorado. So, he planned to head out first light. He didn't tell her that he planned to sell The Mule to this Mr. Victors. He held that detail back.

Kitta leaned back in the seat, keeping the gun aimed directly at Frank's head. She contemplated her options. She could put a bullet in his head and search his house, kill whoever was in there, and then leave. That, however, seemed messy and pointless. She could have Frank as an ally, for all he knew they both were on the same side. If she killed him now, how would she ever connect with whoever was in Colorado? Maybe that person very well was in possession of The Monte-Gresso. If so, she needed Frank alive. Otherwise the Colorado person, or people, would be on edge and never connect with her. Yes, she would have a good sense of where The MonteGresso was, but Colorado was a big state and if this Mr. Victors got spooked, he could just re-seed The MonteGresso by itself and then this would all be for nothing.

No, she had to keep Frank alive and make him her ally. She needed him. Without Frank McDuffy her penultimate plan would fail.

After several minutes of silence, Kitta lowered her gun and placed a hand on Frank's shoulder. Her touch made him quiver. Was he going to be that easy? She whispered into his ear, "Listen my friend, if you go to Colorado by yourself you will die. If you stay here long enough, they will hunt you down and kill you. You almost walked into a deadly trap. And due to my good, analytical thinking, I found you first. If I wanted to kill you, you would be dead already. You agree?"

Frank nodded. Of course, he agreed.

"Good. I want to work with you. And let me just say if we work together, we can take out a large network of people who believe in a perverted way of life. It is an organization rife with nigger lovers, and Jews, and lots and lots of queers. The Mule is very valuable and does have some powers that they will use to promote their agenda. It is worth a lot of money and will help them keep spreading their disgusting message. It's all a big socialist conspiracy." Kitta was making this up as she went. She knew that people like Frank McDuffy were easily moved by conspiracy theories. If this situation didn't sound like some crazy conspiracy, then what did?

Kitta knew she had him. She knew human nature and Frank was putty in her hands. She decided to seal the deal.

"Listen Frank. I'm sorry for scaring you with the gun, but I had to be sure you were safe and were not lying to me. But if we are going to work together, we must trust each other. We have to work as one. As a unit. Will you do that?"

Frank could feel her warm breath on his neck and the soothing words she uttered. He was fully erect and she could see the bulging in his jeans. "Frank, let me take care of that for you."

Chapter 40 * We Need Cash Fast!

The plan was in place as to The Mule. If Victor and Rob played their cards correctly, they would have The Mule in the next twenty-four hours. Once they had two of the orbs, they would be in control of this game. But how to find The PinonAstra? There was a second Perseus the Slayer video coming out the following week that would contain similar language for The PinonAstra minion. They specifically decided to only seek The Mule initially because it might be a battle just to handle the owner of The Mule. Considering The PinonAstra was likely in possession of a Builder minion, it was likely going to be much more dangerous to handle. This Frank McDuffy could also be a Builder minion, but he genuinely seemed too stupid to be dangerous. So, one thing at a time. The Mule, then The PinonAstra.

For two consecutive nights Victor had visions that once he had two of the orbs, the third missing orb would send off signals, to allow them to be reunited. He wasn't sure if that was going to happen, but his dreams had gotten him this far. He assumed that, once The Mule and The MonteGresso were together, he might get new visions and they would focus all of their attention towards the third and final orb.

Victor and Rob spent the greater part of the morning preparing for how to handle this character, Frank from Tennessee. They did some on-line research and they quickly discovered his stupid alias Duffy Franklin. Clearly, he was a race-baiting moron, but they didn't see anything particularly violent about him anywhere. They would remain vigilant. They would offer him straight cash for The Mule and hopefully that would appease him. They had no intention of filling him in on the whole Afterlife issue. If he wasn't aware of the significance of this object at this stage, then this was going to be a simple transaction.

Victor had been sitting on some money and realized that he could give $5,000 for The Mule. But that wasn't likely to generate a sale. Frank might try to sell this on the open market, especially after their conversation the night before. Some dealers might offer more. Of course, he couldn't envision anyone paying serious money for this item because it simply didn't have much intrinsic value aside from the aesthetics. But if Frank took it to the open market, he would likely draw the attention of one of the Builders' minions and it could be lost forever. They had to make an overwhelming financial offer to Frank.

Rob had another $3,500 he could put into the bucket if needed. But they both knew $8,500 just might not get this guy motivated. They needed an obscene amount of money that no one could refuse. Putting $100,000 in cash in front of a loser like Frank McDuffy would certainly get The Mule into their hands, but neither had that kind of money. But they knew who did.

"Hi Sheila, it's Rob. Hey, I need a big favor from Bingham. Is he in?" Rob sat at Victor's kitchen table and held a cup of coffee in one hand and a cell phone in the other. It was worth a shot. Could he manipulate Bingham into giving him some cash? It was unlikely but who knew?

"Hey, you," Sheila said. "Before I call Bingham, what in the hell is going on with Victor Jones? That was a weird thing he did the other day."

"Bizarre is more like it," Rob inserted. He knew she'd be curious. He continued, "But not as crazy as you may think. I make you a promise, Ms. Sheila, I can't explain all of this now, but I promise I will. It will make a great story one day." Rob just prayed he'd be alive to tell a story with a happy ending.

"I'm holding you to that. Bingham is in and he has tried to get you a few times. He wanted to know when the dailies would be ready on his latest swashbuckler ad." Sheila giggled.

"Dailies? What does he think this is, Hollywood? Good grief. Okay, I'll fill him in."

"Just a second." While Sheila put him on hold, Rob got to listen to recorded message from Bingham telling people how hard he worked, how he always netted the maximum amount of money for his personal injury clients, and how scared insurance companies were of his tactics. Listening to that verbose airbag talk, while waiting to speak to the actual airbag, was pain on top of pain.

A few minutes later Sheila patched him through to his Highness.

"Rob, hey buddy. How's the new shoot coming? I want to see the dailies. Can you send me a link I can download? That Victor Jones dude, what a trip! Hey, I was thinking I need to get a bigger sword though. Couldn't stop thinking about it for a few days, a bigger sword. And I also think I should wear a mask, and then tear off the mask and reveal myself as the person who slayed the dragon. Kind of like Zorro. I thin…"

Rob cut him off. It was too painful. "Slow down, Knife. Slow down. We can look at other options. I think the sword size was perfect, and Zorro never removed his mask. Kind of like the Lone Ranger." Rob rubbed his hand through his hair that hadn't been washed for several days. "I want to discuss that video too. But right now, I have a more critical question for you."

Bingham was playing with a samurai sword while he had Rob on speaker phone. He was swinging it wildly and vanquishing many invisible enemies. He sheathed the sword. "Sure thing, Rob, what do you need from me?"

"I need $100,000 in cash." Why fuck around?

Bingham plopped down in his chair. He wasn't sure he heard that correctly. "What?"

"I need $100,000. To borrow. I'm not asking for a gift. I'm asking for a short-term loan. I can't get into the details right now, but I will pledge all my camera equipment as collateral if needed."

"You're serious? Why? And why me?"

"I can't tell you that right now, Bing. You have to trust me that it isn't for anything illegal. Far from it. I have a business opportunity that is expiring in the next forty-eight hours. Without the money I can't compete. I don't have time for a conventional loan."

Bingham rubbed his chin and looked at his teeth in a small mirror he kept on his desk. He hated when friends asked to borrow money. Did anyone know how hard he worked for his money? Dammit.

"Bing, you there?"

Bingham resisted another minute. "Yeah, I'm here. Why can't you tell me about this investment? Maybe I'd be interested."

"Oh, well, I didn't think of that. Honestly, it's entirely confidential. I can't even discuss what it is. I'm good for it, Bing. If I don't repay you, I will shoot videos for you for free until it's all paid up. But I assure you it will be paid."

Of course, that was complete bullshit. If Frank took the money, Rob would have no way of paying that amount of money back. He would then maybe ask Perry for a loan, but the idea of borrowing money from a kid was unthinkable. He didn't care what Bingham thought of him. He did care what his nephew and sister thought of him. Better to ask for forgiveness than permission.

"Rob, you know I like you a lot. You've helped create this amazing image for me and all bu—"

"Bing, do you think I'd do this if I had another choice? Yes, I have helped you. I've always delivered for you, isn't that right?"

Bingham nodded to himself behind his desk. "Yes, you have. No doubt. But $100,000 is a ton of cash."

"Bingham, I know you've got access to that in your safe, along with tons of other investments and cash holdings. This is nothing to you. I swear it will be returned. I swear."

Bingham had no idea that Sheila was eavesdropping on another line. She knew something was up, something serious. Rob would never pull any shenanigans, especially with one of his biggest customers. She wondered what was up. He definitely didn't sound the same. There was an urgency there that made her very nervous.

"Rob, I'm going to need to think about this. Would you give me a few days?"

"Bing, I don't have a few days. If the answer is no, then I'll just have to ask a few of my other customers. But I thought of you first since we have such a close friendship and I thought you, of all the attorneys I work with, would trust me and help me. But no worries, I'll just call Felix."

That might have done it, Rob thought. Felix was one of Bingham's competitors and a complete lunatic. He refused to be one-upped by Felix "Fat Dollar" Friedman. Plus, Bingham liked the idea that Rob thought of him not just as a customer, but a friend, a close friend. People loved to be liked. And Rob made Bingham feel special.

"Give me a few hours."

"Thanks, buddy, really appreciate. Call me soon." Rob hung up. The idea of begging Bingham for cash was awful, but he didn't have a choice in the matter. And he knew Felix wouldn't even take his call, let alone loan him money. He hoped Bingham would talk it over with Sheila. She would definitely have his back.

That's precisely what Bingham did. He called Sheila into his office. Because Sheila heard the urgency in Rob's voice and knew him to be a man of integrity, she wholeheartedly backed the move. "Bing, you've known Rob for years. He is partially responsible for all the money you've made. He needs your help, and he doesn't want to embarrass himself by giving out details."

"Yes, but I'd like to know about this business opportunity. It's a lot of mon—" Sheila cut him off.

"Jesus Christ, Bing. Just give him the money. I'm sure there isn't a business opportunity. He probably has a personal issue and is embarrassed to disclose it. He could be in danger for all we know. Are we done with this conversation?" She stood up to leave his office. Bingham thought about this. Maybe his house was being foreclosed on, or maybe his mother was sick. But more likely he was in danger. Whatever it was, for a friend, a close friend, he would be there. He stood up as well, went to his safe in his office and pulled out the money requested. He put it into a steel, reinforced locked briefcase and sat down to draft a quick promissory note for Rob to sign. If he didn't get this money back, Rob would be his slave.

He called Rob back within the hour and gave him the good news. Rob would come in later in the day to sign the promissory note and pick up the cash. Bingham did place a discreet tracking device on the inside panel of the briefcase. Just in case. Just in case.

Chapter 41 * Denver Or Bust

Kitta's Honda screamed west on I-70 at 85 miles per hour. She had two ra-
dar detectors attached to her dashboard and had only encountered a little police
presence outside of Kansas City. She was making great time. Frank dozed comfortably in the passenger seat, oblivious to the serious nature of their adventure.

Frank had made the call to Robert Victors at 10 a.m. Denver time just to
prove he was heading west and was still alive. He obviously didn't mention Kitta
was right next to him. Kitta thought it was smart to stick to the plan to call in
and keep other details minimal. She had Joe try to get the location of Perseus
the Slayer, who definitely had some inside knowledge, but according to Joe,
Perseus was a hell of a computer expert and his location was entirely locked
down. Finding his location would be infinitely harder than tracking down the
person to whom Frank spoke to in Denver. Kitta assumed that this person was
in possession of The MonteGresso. That had to be the case. If so, then she had
all three orbs within her reach. She confirmed that Frank did have The Mule
and it rested silently in her protected lockbox. It was as beautiful and interesting
as The PinonAstra. As soon as she placed it next to The PinonAstra, they both
started to glow an identical red hue, different from their earlier colors. And they
vibrated and throbbed in unison. It could almost be heard when the lid was
locked, and they were stored away. As she headed west, the tempo of the vibrations increased. She was getting close. She could feel it.

Hours had passed since Frank made the call to this mysterious Robert Victors. Kitta had driven non-stop since Jackson and covered over 800 miles. She
was drinking coffee and taking amphetamines. No way was she trusting this
idiot next to her, who was passed out and drooling, to drive any part of the
trek. She could easily have taken out the young Mr. McDuffy at any point, but
she had to assure Robert Victors that Frank was still alive. If he was dead, then
Robert Victors, and any accomplices he had, would likely disappear. Definitely.
These were vicious people, and the stakes could not be higher.

Sleepy racist boy started to open his eyes and sit up. He wiped his mouth
and tried to straighten his hair. He was totally under Kitta's spell.

"Hey, buddy, you have a good sleep? You feeling fresh?" Kitta asked, completely uninterested in his response.

Frank issued an expansive yawn that only made Kitta more fatigued. "Yeah, that felt great. I'm ready to drive whenever." Kitta momentarily thought about it, but she would never be comfortable.

"No, thanks. I'm feeling great. I think when we get to Colorado maybe we get a hotel room and relax a little, sound good to you?"

Frank got horny again and started to paw at Kitta's right arm. She pushed it away but gave him a come-hither look. "Relax, we got time." Truth was she needed to get a few hours of sleep as the next 12 hours would be the most significant of her life. It was about 3 p.m. and the traffic heading west was light. Eastern Kansas was probably the most boring, flat, lifeless area she had ever seen, with the exception of a few deserts she had worked in while in the German special forces. It was amazing to her that, once upon a time, the great plains of America had buffalo herds so massive, they painted the landscape black. The native Americans roamed these areas for centuries. The great Comanche nation dominated Kansas, Oklahoma and Texas, right where they were. The Comanche were the last of the great American warrior tribes and this their turf. It wasn't until the Texas Rangers developed the Colt six-shooter that they even stood a chance against the Comanche. If she could only go back in time and witness the majesty of these amazing horsemen riding roughshod over the vast prairies, that would be a sight. This was definitely sacred ground.

As they continued to approach the Colorado border, Kitta scanned the horizon for a motel where she could get a little sleep. They also needed to call this Robert Victors again and get details from him on where to meet. Then Kitta had to plan how she would steal The MonteGresso, kill this moron Frank, take The Mule, find a place to immediately re-seed the three orbs and then finally, finally, see her child again. She was starting to get emotional just thinking about the reunion.

"Hey, there is a decent hotel off the next exit, why don't we go there?" Frank pointed this landmark out on his cell phone.

"Sounds good. Are you ready to call and get further instructions? Let's go through the plans."

Frank scratched his ear and scrolled through a few notes he had stored on his phone. "So, I think I just tell them I am in Colorado and ready to meet. Ask where he wants to meet and then you would drop me off and set up as a sentry a few hundred yards away."

"Sounds good. Then what?"

"Well, uh, I, uh, wait, let me scroll through this a little more."

Kitta rolled her eyes, steered the car to the side of the road and slammed on the brakes. She had to re-assert herself as Top Dog. Frank slammed into the dashboard and his phone went flying into the back of the car. "What the fuc—"

"Now you listen here! This is serious shit we are walking into. Your life and my life are on the line. I don't know what kind of student you were in high school, but it is time to study and pay attention! If there is even the slightest fuck up, we could both be tortured and killed. And I for one am not losing any fingers or toes on account of your inability to recall these simple plans. Do you understand me?!!"

Frank rubbed his head where it had collided with the dashboard. He knew Kitta was not someone to fuck with. "Yes, yes. I understand. I'm sorry."

"Don't be sorry! Be informed, be prepared, be on alert. Don't be sorry. Got it?!" She merged her car back onto the road and spotted the exit for the hotel. "Now what happens next?"

Frank closed his eyes and gathered his thoughts. The sunlight streamed through the car window and partially illuminated his face. Kitta couldn't tell if this made him look wiser or dumber. Dumber, for sure, she decided.

"Okay, so I will meet this person. I will negotiate a price. And then I will try to find a discreet location to make the transaction. You will have my location pinged at all times via my cell phone, but you will try to stay within visual distance."

"And??" Kitta demanded.

"And I will also require this person to show me The MonteGresso. Let this person know I have had recent visions of The MonteGresso. That I refuse to part with The Mule until I know it will be safely reunited with The MonteGresso, and that this Mr. Victors works for the Dead." He stopped talking for a moment and sighed. "Of course, you realize I don't understand any of this. It makes no sense to me. It sounds like some science fiction movie."

Kitta turned toward Frank with an icy glare. "Just continue."

"Then, once he shows me this orb, you will make a move to come in from behind, use a stun gun to partially subdue him, and then we take off with the orb."

"Correct, you need to insist on seeing The MonteGresso before you hand him The Mule. That's critical."

"Yes, that's definitely understood. And I need to ask for cash too, right?"

"Yes. He has to consider this a purchase and sale. Once you're rid of The Mule, he should assure you that you are no longer on anyone's hit list. That's when you'll know he plans to kill you."

"Wait. What? You think that once I hand him The Mule he'll kill me?"

"Well, I can't be certain, but I'll have your back. We hold the element of surprise." Kitta had no plans to help Frank, but he felt comfortable knowing she had his back.

Frank pointed to the hotel across the highway. "Well, as long as I'm slated to die in the next day, how about we try out that hotel?"

Yuck. She was repulsed by this simple country bumpkin. But as a soldier she had taught herself to do many things that turned her stomach. Frank was just another one of those. Plus, the more she gave of herself, the tighter her control was over The Mule.

"The hotel is at the Colorado border anyway. Go ahead and make the call. Then, then…" and she rubbed one of her hands over her breasts.

Chapter 42 * Motels And Plans

Frank sat on the edge of the bed in the hotel room, a towel around his waist. Kitta sat up in bed, her bare foot rubbing Frank's shoulder. They were both exhausted and they had to get some needed sleep.

Kitta made Frank review the notes from his phone call with Robert Victors so they could be prepared for that evening. It was 4 p.m. If they slept until 8 p.m. and drove straight through to Denver, they would be there by 11 p.m. Plenty of time to try and locate this Robert Victors and stake him out. They were set to meet with him the following morning at 6 a.m. at a diner that was open twenty-four hours a day. Victor had planned on a crowded diner that attracted a heavy early morning crowd for their initial meeting. Victor hoped that would work. Frank had written down the location of the diner where they would meet. Frank and Kitta had agreed that it would seem unrealistic not to demand cash for The Mule. If he didn't try to sell it, they believed that would make Victor suspicious. Of course, Frank had his own plans to get paid for *his* orb. He would handle Kitta later.

Before he hung up with Victor, he let him know he had thought long and hard about selling The Mule and decided if they could agree on a price, he would sell it and rid himself of the curse. That was music to Victor's ears. Victor and Rob were prepared for that. Plus, it wasn't as violent as having to hurt Frank. They definitely didn't want violence but were prepared to use it if absolutely necessary. Frank left Victor with a request that they could discuss the value of The Mule in person and if everything was agreed to, they could make the exchange that morning and conclude their business. Victor replied that he would have cash accessible immediately if they could come to a price. The whole thing could be done at the diner. For Rob and Victor, it seemed almost too good to be true.

Kitta had secretly developed her own plan. She knew it wouldn't be as easy as Frank thought. Plus, despite the ploy they had concocted, Frank had every intention of selling The Mule, and Kitta knew that. She didn't trust this idiot as far as she could throw him.

On the contrary, it was going to be staying with her as Kitta never planned to sell The Mule. She had to find out who this mysterious Robert Victors was and, more importantly, where he lived and with whom he was close. She seriously doubted he had given his real name to Frank. Frank was a dumb ass and provided his real name. So, by now it was evident this cryptic Robert Victors would likely have done some basic research and determined they were dealing with a potentially violent person. She doubted this would be a financial transaction, although that would be nice. If, however, this Robert Victors was in possession of The MonteGresso and planned to re-unite the orbs, then he would most likely take The Mule by force if necessary. She knew Frank would never leave Colorado alive.

 Kitta realized she would have to get the jump on this character. Find out who he was and beat him to the punch. By the time their clandestine meeting at the diner was scheduled to have happened, Kitta planned to be in possession of all three orbs. What's more, at least two men would be dead. If everything went right.

She had Frank give her Robert Victors' cell phone number as soon as they left Tennessee. She then got on the phone with Joe Sanchez to have him do some research into the number. Joe was able to ascertain that the number was registered to a business called Cherry Knolls Senior Care, LLC. There was no person's name listed, but there was a credit card assigned to the phone that ended in 0090. Joe determined that Cherry Knolls was a senior residential facility located throughout the United States, but their corporate headquarters was in southeast Denver and he gave Kitta the address and phone number. That was all he could find out. It was perfect for Kitta. It was obvious this Robert Victors didn't want to use his own name or credit card information to buy the phone, but foolishly used a corporate card that was easily traceable.

She asked Joe to call this facility and see if he could get the name and address of the employee who purchased the phone. Despite a good ruse that he was a police officer searching for a suspect who had stolen a credit card, he could not get the information he needed. Mike Guidry's assistant explained there was a requirement to go through their in-house counsel to give out any information to law enforcement, and that she would need a copy of his badge and an incident report number to verify. She was a smart one. Joe indicated he would get all that to her, and then hung up. It was worth a shot. Kitta would just have to get the information the old-fashioned way, which she didn't really mind.

Kitta determined that, once they got to Denver, they would pay a visit on Cherry Knolls, after hours, of course, and see what information they could dig up on that credit card. Once she had that information, she would find a home address and the rest would quickly, and painfully fall into place. She set her phone alarm for 8 p.m. and set it on the nightstand. She cocked her finger at Frank. Even though he was a country bumpkin and dumb as a pile of rocks, he was aggressive, bordering on violent, in the sack. She could use one more.

Chapter 43 * No Turning Back

It was midnight and the parking lot at Cherry Knolls was empty except for a few vehicles, probably nurses or security. They pulled into a parking spot that was not well lit. Kitta exited the car, Frank was ordered to remain. They each had a gun and several knives. They didn't expect much resistance, but one never knew. They would have to come in strong and forceful, time was not on their side. Frank had a meeting planned at 6 a.m. with Robert Victors and Kitta wanted to get to him first.

She put on a hat with a long dark-haired wig underneath it and pulled the brim down tight. There would obviously be video surveillance cameras everywhere and she needed some disguise. While she had a high degree of faith she was mere hours from securing The MonteGresso and completing her quest, there was still a chance she wouldn't and she did not need her photo in the hands of law enforcement. Her rental car was rented under an untraceable alias, so chasing down the rental car license plate would yield nothing.

Kitta walked under the lit portico entryway. The well-manicured grounds and low shrubs reeked of either an extended-stay motel, or a senior living facility. Kitta figured the same architect probably designed both of these atrocious, very American-style structures, that were littered across the country. Cheap and easily replicated.

Kitta tried the front door but it was locked. There was a speaker box to talk to the security guard she could see inside at the front desk. Billy Stine pushed the monitor button from his desk. "Can I help you? We are currently closed."

"I'm sorry, sir. My mother toured the facility this morning and she left her inhaler somewhere in the lobby. I am so sorry, but I must get that to her tonight." Kitta poured on the emotion, and used a southern accent, in hopes of softening up her image. Billy Stine was not aware of any late night pick up he was supposed to handle.

"I'm sorry ma'am, but there is nothing here for a pickup," he told her through the intercom. "You'll have to call tomorrow."

Kitta started to cry. "I'm so sorry to do this, but I believe she left it in one of the restrooms or somewhere in the lobby. No one set it aside for us, I was just hoping I could do a quick check. May I please come in for one minute and look? I cannot get her a replacement at this time of night. I am begging you, sir."

Billy contemplated this damsel in distress. She looked and sounded harmless. He stood up from his desk, clad in a light blue security guard shirt, navy blue pants, and army boots. He had a small plastic badge on his left lapel, and he wore a holster with a flashlight and a radio. Oh, this poor man, Kitta thought, he had no idea what was coming. Never bring a flashlight to a knife fight.

Billy pulled one of the keys on his keychain looped around his belt and unlocked the first entry door. This led to a small entryway where he started to unlock the second door. Kitta gave him a deep thank-you look and strong puppy dog eyes. The key was connected to a retractable chain. There were at least a dozen keys connected to the chain. He opened the door and Kitta stepped in.

"Thank you so, so much for this. If I could just look quickly, I'll be out of here in just a seco—" That's when she silently and deftly inserted the knife into his belly and pulled vertically upward as deep as she could. She intentionally inserted the knife away from his superior epigastric artery so she wouldn't get splattered with blood. It took the wind out of Billy Stine. He dropped to his knees, unable to gasp for air or say anything. He collapsed on his side and Kitta quickly summoned Frank, who was watching from the car. He put on a face mask and ran to her aid. They quickly moved Billy into a storage closet where she turned the knife several more times and let the blood flow. She was able to expertly avoid the splatter, just like with Dean Luiga in Cincinnati. Billy was as dead as a stuffed moose hanging on the wall. He didn't suffer, much, Kitta thought. She held no ill-will against anyone she killed, and Billy Stine was just a means to an end.

She yanked the keychain off Billy's belt, and they locked the front doors and shut off the feed to the lobby security camera, which had to have caught the entire escapade on film. Whatever was on film was on film. Her disguise was still in place and she felt comfortable no one could identify her. Frank wore a mask so he could not be identified at all. If all went according to plan she would be dead in a few hours anyway. Her only goal at the moment was to find the owner of that credit card.

She and Frank didn't see any other personnel in the front hallway and saw a sign indicating executive offices about fifty feet from the security desk. There was a large sitting area in the lobby behind the security desk filled with numerous plush chairs, artwork and potted plants. There was also a stone fireplace and massive native American rug which really pulled the room together. This must be where loving family members would sit and wait for a salesperson to show them around and make them feel good about leaving old grandpa here to die.

They tried the door to the executive suites. It was locked, but they could see a few lights on in some of the offices. They didn't see anyone walking around so they figured it would likely be safe. Kitta tried several of the keys and finally found the one that fit. She quickly unlocked the door and she and Frank entered. They would start with the bookkeeper's office as that's where it was likely the credit card information would be stored. Once they walked past the front office reception desk, they heard voices coming from the office to the immediate left. That office door was open wide enough that they had to investigate as there was no way to sneak around and not be seen. Kitta gave a "hold tight" sign to Frank by holding up her arm midway with a fist. He gave a quizzical look. Then she mouthed "STOP." That he understood.

Kitta slowly pushed open the door to President Michael Guidry's office, as was indicated on the brass name plate on the door. Ah, this was a nice sight. President Guidry was balls deep into some young lady as he had his pants around his ankles and was hammering her from behind on his couch. She was young and beautiful. They both looked up at Kitta, who started laughing. Their faces froze and President Guidry quickly exited his employee (or whoever she was) and yanked up his pants. The girl's face, who Kitta would learn was named Jerri Hughes, flushed full red and she rolled over and slid her panties up and pulled her skirt down.

"Who the hell are you? Get out of my office!" Mike yelled. No one, not even Mike Guidry, was intimidating when caught with their pants around their ankles. Kitta started to laugh and pulled out her Glock. Frank heard the commotion and came in to check. He started laughing too.

Seeing Frank in his mask made Guidry turn white. "What do you want?" Mike said in a shaky voice. "Take what you need and please leave. We have twenty-four hour a day security here." Kitta could still see he had an erection which was fascinating to her. This guy just experienced a series of highly intense emotions in a matter of seconds: having sex in his office, getting caught clearly doing something wrong, and then having a gun pulled on him. Kitta realized he must have taken a Viagra; there was no other way a dude could experience a boner at this point in time.

"President Guidry I presume?" Kitta played with him. "You *did* have twenty-four hour a day security here. You *don't* currently have twenty-four hour a day security. Maybe once the new shift comes on, you will have security once again. Get my drift?" Mike swallowed hard. Poor Billy Stine: he always covered for Mike's indiscretions over the years, but Mike always rewarded him with a good holiday bonus. Kitta eyed Ms. Hughes looking anxiously at her phone, which was just a few feet away on a side table.

"Oh, young lady, let me explain to you the problems we will have if you even think of touching that phone." Jerri retreated and stood right next to Mike. She would have climbed inside him if she had that ability.

Kitta looked at Frank, handing him two zip ties. "Come over here and cuff these two, face to face, I'm sure they won't mind being that close." Frank zip-tied Mike's right hand to Jerri's left hand, and Mike's left hand to Jerri's right hand. Mike stiffened up and wouldn't let Frank finish the second tie, so Kitta went over to Mike and smacked him in the head with her Glock. A huge gash opened up on Mike's forehead and he fell to his knees, causing Jerri to fall down as well. Frank finished cinching the zip ties good and tight. Frank was impressed by Kitta's aggression and violence. She didn't pause to consider the risks. She clearly had already thought this through. She did what needed to be done.

"Now that we have your undivided attention, I assume you'd like to survive this evening. Am I correct?" Kitta stated as she squatted down on her haunches to address them. Mike was too groggy to respond and his left eye was flooded with temporal blood. But Jerri indicated yes, she wanted to survive. Jerri was crying furiously and Kitta whispered in her ear, "If you don't stop crying, I'll give you something to cry about. Do you understand?" Such a parent thing to say, but it worked. Jerri muffled her crying, but she still gasped and wept, although in a much quieter tone.

Kitta stood up. "Good. Now, I need to know something easy. One of your employees here used a Cherry Knolls credit card to purchase a cell phone the other day. I simply need this person's name and address and then I'll be gone. Sound good?"

"Yes," Jerri quietly sobbed. "I can help you." Clearly Jerri didn't give a rat's ass about who would be hurt or likely killed by this maniac, she was only concerned with getting out of there alive. While many people dream of being heroes, Kitta knew that almost no one actually can be a hero when it counts. This little young thing sobbing, would be signing someone's death warrant and could not care less.

"Wonderful. Now where do we get the information?" Kitta asked.

"It's in Andrea's office, she's the bookkeeper. All the credit card information is there."

"Well, what are you waiting for? Stand the fuck up and take me there," Kitta demanded. She motioned to Frank to get them up. He yanked at Mike's arm and he slowly stood up, his knees still weak. Blood everywhere. It was dripping onto Jerri's shirt and cute little skirt that only a few minutes ago was up around her torso.

Mike and Jerri awkwardly shuffled to Andrea's office, which was a few offices down. Kitta read "Andrea M. - Bookkeeping" on her placard. She tried the door. Locked. "Which key?" She held up the whole keychain to Jerri, who seemed to be in control as her lover was just a bloody mess. Jerri pointed out the right key; Kitta unlocked the door and the automatic lights turned on.

Jerri motioned with her head where the filing cabinet was with the credit card information. "It's probably in the top shelf under credit card accounts," Jerri told Kitta. Kitta rifled through the files, found the credit card folder and yanked it out. She started looking at all the different card numbers and tried to find a match with the last four digits being 0090. On page three of the document, she found it. The card was in the name of Victor A. Jones.

"Ah, here we go, Victor A. Jones. Do you know him?"

Mike Guidry lifted his head and came to life for the first time since the pistol whipping.

"Yeah, I know him. He is our accounts management supervisor," Mike stated and then Jerri quickly interrupted, "*Assistant* accounts management supervisor. I am the accounts management supervisor." Kitta chuckled that even as this little spoiled twat was dangerously close to being the recently deceased accounts management supervisor, she had to make sure her boss, President Mike Guidry, knew that all that ass came with a price.

"Well, that's nice to know. What's his address and phone number?" Kitta asked politely, easing the tension.

"Look at the bottom filing drawer," Mike said. "His information will be there. The cabinet is unlocked." Kitta immediately bent over, popped it open and went to the "J" tab. She found Victor Jones and pulled out the file. She saw the name and address and Social Security Number. This was the best chance she had of getting The MonteGresso. She had chills. She was so close.

"You know that Victor Jones is a real troublemaker. He was about to be fired for insubordination and poor performance. I wouldn't trust him. I wouldn't trust him at all," Mike volunteered. It wasn't just that Mike was trying to save his own ass; he was actively trying to hurt Victor Jones. Kitta figured that Victor Jones must have had some dirt on Mike Guidry, and from the compromising position she caught him in, she assumed Victor Jones knew all about this torrid love affair. He probably black-mailed Mike Guidry too. How delicious.

"Really, you don't say," Kitta said. "Well, I need some information from him. You think he will be forthright and helpful when I ask him my questions?"

Mike thought about it. He knew he needed something to keep himself alive. "Well, I know something that will help you, but I want to have some assurances you won't hurt me." Jerri gave him a cold look. "I mean us. If I tell you this information, you won't hurt us. We promise to say nothing."

Kitta mulled this over. "Okay, you give me the information and I promise I will not hurt either one of you. But you need to do it right now."

Mike grinned. "He has a very close relationship with one of our residents."

"Oooh, do tell? He's nailing one of the senior citizens?" Kitta laughed.

"No, I don't think so. He's just very close with one of the residents named Lucy Black. I'm sure if he knew she was in trouble he'd give you anything you needed." Jerri looked up at Mike. She was disgusted that he would subject poor old Lucy Black to these horrible people. He didn't even need to do that. Although if it saved her ass, she would look the other way.

"Well, that's perfect, what room is she in?"

"218, just up the back stairs at the end of the main corridor," Mike told them.

"Well, Mike Guidry and whatever your name is, thank you for your help. As I told you, I won't hurt you." She looked at Frank. "Frank didn't promise anything though." He knew exactly what Kitta wanted and didn't hesitate. Frank grabbed his knife and slit Jerri's throat; a stream of blood shot onto Mike. Mike tried to pull away, but Frank went behind him and finished him off. It was exhilarating to Frank, who had only dreamed of this. He never knew he'd have the guts. But Kitta had prepared him for the fact he might need to kill someone, and she had not hesitated with the security guard. He proved a very apt pupil. He didn't want to wimp out, he was trying to impress his lover and teacher. Kitta smiled at Frank and then they ran out of the office and down the corridor to Room 218.

Chapter 44 * A Friend In Need

Grandma Lucy awoke with a start. Her heart was pounding, sweat poured down her neck and her back. Her nightgown was soaked. She sat up in the dark and her eyes tried to adjust to the darkness around her. Her digital clock said 12:08 a.m. She reached over to grab her water glass on the nightstand. She couldn't feel it, so she turned on the lamp instead. She leaped back. Sitting across from her on the two small chairs were Beverly and some older black gentleman.

"Don't scream, sugar. We need to talk to you." Beverly's soothing voice and mild tone immediately set Lucy straight.

"Wha...wha...what are you doing here?" Lucy managed to spit out. She wasn't scared. But she was startled. Although it would have seemed more appropriate to be scared shitless.

"Lucy, sugar, I want you to meet someone very special to me. This is my father Samuel Griffin. You've heard all about him." She then looked at her father and extended an arm towards Lucy, palm up, in manner of introduction, "and father, this is my friend, Lucy Black."

Lucy sat up straight in her bed but pulled her covers up to her chin in a defensive manner. After all it wasn't every day you were introduced to a ghost by another ghost. Chills ran up and down her spine, but she was calm.

"Hello, charmed to make your acquaintance." Lucy managed to push the words out of her mouth. Was she dreaming? The goosebumps on her arms let her know this was real.

"Miss Lucy," Samuel began in monotone, "you must go and help re-seed the orbs. Now. Miss Lucy, you must help avenge my error from forty years ago. You must help Victor and Rob; they cannot do this alone." Samuel's eyes were white, no pupils at all, although his skin and hair and body looked fine, young, vibrant. But his eyes were dead. Beverly's eyes were alive, and her hair was on fire. She looked older than Samuel. That didn't make sense to Lucy. Why would a daughter look older than her father? She didn't know, she didn't care. She just wanted them to go. After all, it was creepy, even if they were friends.

"Lucy, you have to leave this place," Beverly said. "It isn't safe here. Someone is going to be coming for you right now. Find Victor. Help Victor. Help us defeat the Builders. You Lucy are a chosen one. Help us bridge the Divide." Beverly's voice was fading quickly. Lucy vigorously rubbed her eyes. She reached out to Beverly, whose image was also fading. Was she dreaming? This had to be a dream. "Who, Beverly? Who is coming for me? When?"

"Lucy, leave…don't delay, they are coming right now. Help re-seed the orbs. Help us all," Beverly muttered before she and Samuel vanished completely.

It was a quick and startling first experience interacting with a ghost. She trusted her instincts. Her instincts had gotten her to this ripe age. She jumped out of bed and ran to the bathroom to splash cold water on her face. She grabbed a towel and dried off quickly, and then put on her jogging suit and sneakers. She pulled the loaded pistol out of her bathrobe pocket that sat next to her bed and placed it into her jacket. She knew she was not a prisoner at Cherry Knolls but walking out the front door at midnight without a car waiting for her was not permitted either. There were rules. She was allowed to leave. And she needed a ride. Where would she go? She didn't want to alarm her family and she knew she had to get to Victor. But she didn't have his phone number. How stupid was that? She walked down the hallway and saw her favorite nighttime nurse Vivian. She remembered that Vivian and Victor were pretty friendly from what she remembered.

Vivian was reading a paperback novel at the nurses' station when Lucy arrived. It startled Vivian because usually residents didn't walk around at midnight.

"Well, hello there, Lucy, why are you up so late?"

Lucy had a plan. "I just couldn't sleep. I was hoping to get a little late night exercise in. Walking the halls!" When Vivian winked at Lucy, Lucy smiled back.

"Oh Viv, I know you are friends with that delightful Victor Jones who works in accounts. Right?"

"He's my favorite down there, but don't tell him or he will get an inflated ego." Vivian laughed.

"Would you happen to have his cell phone number? I wanted to give his name to my grandson, who needs a little career advice. Victor said he'd be happy to talk to him. But I misplaced his number." She abhorred lying, but these were not ordinary times, and the lie wasn't going to hurt anyone.

Vivian reached into her white nurse's smock and pulled out her cell phone and toggled through it. She found Victor's number and jotted it down on a piece of paper. "Here you go, Miss Lucy. Tell him hi for me."

Lucy grabbed the paper. "You bet. You have a good night, Vivian." Back in her room, she dialed the number. Victor answered the phone on the first ring. His voice was groggy, but it was him and she was relieved he was alive and that her call was answered. As soon as she heard Victor's voice, she told him to wake up.

"What's going on? Lucy? Are you Okay?" Victor asked as he sat up and quickly became alert. Before she had the chance to answer him, she heard something in the hallway. Some type of argument. She peaked out of her room and saw Vivian lying in a pool of blood and saw two people running towards her room. "Victor, they are coming, Victor, be ready!!" She quickly closed her phone and put it into her pocket, next to her gun, but she didn't have time to use it before the door broke open and she saw two people staring at her. One wore a mask. They had blood stains on their hands and clothes.

"Lucy Black, I presume?" Kitta snarled. Lucy shivered and nodded. "Aren't you up late? How about we go for a ride?" Frank and Kitta lunged for the little woman.

Chapter 45 ∗ Get Out Fast

Kitta and Frank bound Lucy's hands and legs and put a gag in her mouth. She was a tiny thing and they decided just to carry her out. Time was not on their side. There were four dead bodies and people would soon discover the carnage. Frank took the top half and Kitta grabbed the legs. Lucy didn't really struggle. Lucy was actually quite calm. She had been alerted by Beverly who was looking out for her.

They exited Cherry Knolls and dumped Lucy into the trunk. They couldn't risk having her in the back seat. It was late and since there were not a lot of vehicles on the road, they would be easy pickings for a police officer.

They looked at themselves in the car mirror and saw the blood splatters on their faces, hands and clothes. They quickly wiped themselves down and threw on new shirts. That would have to do. It wouldn't be obvious that they just brutally murdered four people, but if there was a muffling in the back seat, all bets would be off. That's why the trunk was the best bet. Lucy would certainly be useful in dealing with Victor Jones. Kitta was trained to bring her pulse down quickly, but Frank was a mess. "Calm down, Frank. Take a few deep breaths. Be calm." He tried, but his hands were shaking.

Kitta slowly exited the parking lot and had Frank key in Victor's address into his GPS. Of course, this was the right guy. What alias did he give himself? Robert Victors? Um, yeah, this was certainly the right guy. Kitta looked down at her lock box and the glowing from the two orbs was definitely intensifying and beams of light were clearly exiting the cracks of the case. These two orbs sensed they were getting really close to The MonteGresso. It had to be in Denver. It likely was in Victor's possession.

It only took about twenty minutes to get to Victor's street. At 12:45 a.m., the street was fairly dark except for the few houses with front porch lights on. His address, 3344 South Niagara Way, was just two houses down. Kitta told Frank to be silent and stay in the car as she exited and made her way to the house. She closed her door softly and stayed in the shadows to the extent possible. There were lights on at Victor's house and she hid to the side of the front porch until she felt comfortable there were no cameras or alarms. She saw there was a chair sitting right in front of the front door. There was a basket resting on the chair. She stole a glance in the basket. There was piece of paper taped to a polaroid picture. She pulled out the paper and picture.

"I assume you are looking for this. I assume you have hurt people to get this far. I am going to re-seed The MonteGresso in one hour unless we can come to a fair financial arrangement. Meet me at Briarwood Cemetery, near section 18. If you
fail to come by 1:30, The MonteGresso will be re-seeded and that will be the end of that. Be well. V.J."

There was a picture of The MonteGresso. There was no mistaking it. This Victor Jones knew exactly what the score was. She had no doubt that, if he felt the heat was coming, he would have to re-seed the orb. Victor could not take the chance that this person, who had just threatened Lucy, and maybe killed her, would do the right thing with The MonteGresso. In fact, he knew this person had to be associated with the Builders. Kitta was despondent. Lucy Black must have sent a warning call to Victor. Dammit! She had gotten to Lucy's room one minute too late and now things were not in her control. She had lost the element of surprise. But, she still had a few tricks up her sleeve.

Rob and Victor had to move fast after Lucy sent the distress call. They originally believed that just poor old racist Frank McDuffy would be coming to sell The Mule and that it would be a fairly easy and straight-forward transaction. But the emergency call he got from Lucy made them realize that Frank was either dead or else working with some trained killers. Frank didn't seem to have the wherewithal to track down Lucy. But a true minion of the Builders would. Which made them realize that The PinonAstra was also within their grasp - it had to be. It was very exciting but also incredibly nerve-racking. The MonteGresso had been purring and glowing intensely for the past 24 hours and its responsiveness only increased by the hour. Something strange was afoot.

Kitta grabbed the paper and picture and ran to her car. Whether Victor was serious or not about re-seeding The MonteGresso, she didn't know, but she couldn't take a chance. If Victor re-seeded the orb, that would be the end of her chances to see her child and become a hero for the Builders. She wouldn't have the power in the Afterlife and who knew what would happen to her dead child's soul? Victor was definitely playing the same game she was playing and only one of them could win this game. She couldn't afford a tie. If Victor got nervous, he could tie the game and hope someone, far in the future, could fix it. But it wouldn't be her and that was too heartbreaking to even consider.

She opened the door. "Was he there?" Frank asked.

"Shut up and don't say anything! Get me GPS to Briarwood Cemetery. This shit is about to go down." She checked her Glock and chambered a round. Frank immediately shut his mouth and keyed in the cemetery's address. It was now 12:50 and she had 40 minutes to find the cemetery, find Victor and steal The MonteGresso. She was freaking out. She slammed the accelerator and fishtailed it down the road.

"Slow down, Kitta!" Frank demanded. He had no clue what had happened, but he knew he was an accomplice to four murders, and he didn't feel like getting arrested because of a speeding violation. Kitta eased off the gas but drove leaning into the steering wheel. She didn't look or talk to Frank for several minutes.

"Okay, Frank, this is what we are going to do. We will only have one shot at saving your life and protecting The Mule." She went on to explain the plan. Frank still banked on a financial transaction occurring, and he didn't care what Kitta planned to do. However, the price just went up considering all the blood spilled that night. Kitta still had not explained the true issues at play, and as far as she was concerned there was no reason for him to know. He chose to disregard his dreams and visions and had avoided learning about the valuable item he had luckily purchased from an estate sale, why should he have any more knowledge than needed? Even though she doubted he would hurt her and gather all three orbs, it was still a slight possibility. Nope, she had to keep him in the dark until Victor killed him, or she did. The only thing she knew is that Frank had a short life expectancy.

As she was driving for her rendezvous with Victor Jones, she was oblivious to the car that was driving behind her and had followed her to Victor's house.

Chapter 46 * Briarwood Cemetery

Kitta turned onto Briarwood Drive and saw the imposing cemetery. It appeared even larger than she expected. Three quarters of the massive cemetery was surrounded by wrought-iron fencing that was a minimum of twelve feet tall. There were dense trees and bushes that surrounded the grounds. They pulled to the back of the cemetery, which was up a small hill and sat along a broad, twenty-foot wide earthen canal. This canal had a well-maintained biking and running trail that ran along the south side of the cemetery grounds and was not enclosed by the fence. Tall cottonwood trees and thorny bushes grew adjacent to the canal and provided excellent cover. Kitta assumed the canal fed water to the grounds of the cemetery, although it was a deep dirt canal that likely lost two gallons of water for every gallon it supplied to the cemetery. They would approach the cemetery from the south, so they didn't have to climb a fence or try to burrow underneath. She also assumed that Victor had to do the same thing, although he wasn't going to bring a bound and gagged 84-year-old with him.

Kitta grabbed a knapsack and opened the lockbox. It was the first time Frank had seen how the orbs were both glowing in rhythmic hues. Pink, green, red, yellow, white. They seemed to be pulsating and even humming or purring. It was a beautiful sight. Mesmerizing. She put the orbs in her knapsack and threw it on over her left shoulder. Her Glock was in her jacket pocket and her knives were situated throughout her person.

"What's happening to them?" Frank asked, looking at the majestic colors of the orbs.

"I think they are alive and ready to play," Kitta responded. "So, let's play, what do you think?"

They opened up the map of the cemetery from Frank's phone and located section 18. It appeared to be about 200 yards directly north. There were hundreds of large elm, evergreen and cottonwood trees. Frank had never seen a cemetery so big, except for that one time when his parents took him to visit Arlington National Cemetery. But this was something entirely different. At Briarwood, headstones of every shape and size dotted the landscape, along with numerous crypts and large obelisks marking family plots. Because the moon was full, there was decent vision, although Kitta regretted not having night vision goggles. That would have been perfect. She could have been able to easily sneak up on Victor.

They untied Lucy's legs and pulled her out of the trunk. She remained gagged and bound at the hands. They started to walk north through the cemetery. Silent. Kitta took Lucy and they separated from Frank, walking in a north-easterly direction. Frank continued due north and would approach Victor by himself. Kitta was willing to sacrifice him.

Frank walked slowly. His hand rested comfortably on his gun inside his vest. Feeling the cool metal of the gun soothed him. There were so many old headstones he saw. He was creeped out being in such a huge cemetery at night, especially with all the really old dead people who likely haunted this place. He saw one headstone that indicated a woman had died in 1912. Wow. He wondered if she voted for that son of a bitch Abraham Lincoln. He spit on her grave, good riddance commie. Of course, he didn't see that she was born in 1883 so that would have been impossible.

He got close to section 18. He heard some heavy breathing and saw some figure in the dark ahead of him approximately 50 yards away. His palm began to sweat on the grip of the gun.

"Who's there?" the voice shouted. And then a flashlight lit up Frank's face. He stopped and didn't move.

Kitta could easily make out the location now due to the flashlight. Victor was about one hundred yards away from where she stood with Lucy. Kitta noticed that Lucy was very compliant. Her calmness was unsettling to Kitta. Maybe she knew something Kitta didn't.

"It's me, Frank," Frank yelled.

"Well, Frank, put your hands up and let me see that you don't have a weapon," Victor called out.

"I do have a weapon. You told me someone was trying to kill me. So, I will hold this weapon, it's just a knife, it won't hurt you if you don't hurt me," Frank lied.

Victor changed his tone. "Frank, I'm the one who warned you that your life was in danger. I'm not going to hurt you. I just want The Mule."

"I know you do. I want money if you want The Mule." They cautiously approached each other.

"At least put your knife on top of the headstone to your left," Victor said. "If you keep the knife, I'm not negotiating with you."

Frank considered this option and decided that Kitta had his back. He removed his hand from the .357 in his vest, but he could feel the reassuring weight of it close by. He effortlessly pulled out a knife that was also inside his jacket and placed it on top of old Dr. Redman Van Hubert's tombstone. Born 1899, died 1980. That's a nice run, Frank thought.

"Thank you, Frank. Come closer now, slowly." Frank obliged and came within ten feet of Victor. Victor was wearing a black baseball cap, black pants and a gray hoodie. He held a flashlight.

"Before we begin, Frank, I need to know what happened to Lucy Black. Where is she?"

"She's safe. Just a little insurance in case you try to hurt me. If you hurt me, Lucy will die tonight."

Fucker. Victor was worried. This was not something he and Rob considered before, but he appreciated the warning phone call from her. He still didn't understand how they found Lucy. Then all of a sudden it came to him.

"Ah, my credit card. That's how you found her. I'm sure of it."

"Bingo, Robert Victors, or shall I call you Victor Jones?" Frank felt like he was in a spy movie.

"Very well Frank. I used an alias. Sue me. I just needed to make sure it was safe. And from the sound of things, it isn't. I hope you haven't hurt her. If you hurt her, you'll answer for it." Victor tried to sound tough, but this was virgin ground for him. He thought he just sounded nervous. He sized up Frank McDuffy, but due to the bushes and concealable shadows it was hard to make him out clearly.

"She's fine. Don't you worry. But we are here to cut a deal. You never stated your price on the call, but I assumed this little baby ball is worth a lot to you. So why don't we start the negotiations?"

"Happy to. Let me see it," Victor responded. He didn't have a weapon on him. He felt naked.

"In good time. It is stashed away safely. If we reach a deal, I'll let you see it. Sound fair?"

How could Victor argue? "Fine. I've got $10,000 cash for you now. That's probably one hundred times what you paid. Sound reasonable?"

Frank and Kitta had planned this out. Frank needed to smoke out this other orb, The MonteGresso, according to Kitta. He didn't understand it, but he had to trust her.

"Just $10,000? That can't be close to the value of this little guy. I'd consider $150,000. But I want to ensure that if I sell this to you, it will be re-united with its brother. I assume you have his brother? The MonteGresso, I believe, is his name?"

$150,000! That wasn't going to be possible. More concerning to Victor was that Frank knew about The MonteGresso. How did he learn about it so quickly? He had to have been tipped off to its existence and was going to make a play for his orb. Victor had to think quickly. Frank couldn't be a die-hard believer. How could he be convinced so quickly? He thought, incorrectly, that he could pay for The Mule. Usually people were swayed by money, lots of money.

"Frank, there isn't any MonteGresso. But I am willing to give you $100,000. Now. Tonight. I have it in a case close by. Deal or no deal?" Victor said. He was worried what would happen if he and Frank had to get physical. Frank appeared to be about his size, but he had no doubt that if they were to fight, Frank would lay him out.

"NO deal," Frank insisted. "I want to know The Mule will be safe with you. I need to know. If you let me see The MonteGresso, then it's a deal at $100,000."

What did he have to lose at this point? He just knew he couldn't risk Lucy's life. Even though the stakes were much larger than Lucy Black, and she knew blood had be spilled, Victor couldn't be cavalier about her life. He wasn't wired that way. "I need your word that Lucy will be turned over safely," Victor pressed. "I need to see her before I show you the orb."

Frank considered this. He told Victor to wait. He walked a few yards away and got on his phone. He texted Kitta, who had been waiting patiently. She had to decide when to make her move. She was holding steady until she saw The MonteGresso. The text read: Send Lucy, he will show me the orb if he sees her.

Kitta didn't mind that. She would stay concealed. She whispered into Lucy's ear, "Lucy, if you wish to survive this night you will walk over to Frank. If you make any attempt to run, or talk, I will put a bullet in your back. Do you understand?"

Lucy nodded but tried to talk. Kitta momentarily removed the gag so Lucy could speak. "I won't try to run or say anything." The gag was replaced. Lucy started to walk but immediately fell down; her balance was off and affected by the bound hands. Kitta helped her to her feet. Lucy walked a few more paces and stumbled and fell again. "Get up, you cow!" Kitta warned. Lucy mumbled something and Kitta removed the gag again. "I'm sorry, I'm losing my balance. I need my hands for balance. I'm an old woman." Lucy appeared to be crying. Kitta considered the risks. They were minimal. She untied Lucy's hands but reinserted the mouth gag and tightened it. "So be it. But if you remove the gag, or warn Victor, or you attempt to flee, I will put a bullet in your head and I will kill Victor one second later. Do you understand?" Lucy nodded. Kitta watched Lucy walk slowly towards Frank. Kitta's eyes were getting more adjusted to the darkness and she could see better.

As Lucy made her way to Frank's side, Kitta saw something, or someone, furtively moving about 20 yards directly to Victor's left. It had to be his helper. That's probably where The MonteGresso was being held. No way Victor had it on him. That would have been foolish. Kitta quietly started to walk to her right. She would come up and flank this person, who would never hear or see Kitta. She would then have what she needed, and she could take off. She was so close.

Frank sensed Lucy approaching and turned to see her. He grabbed her arm and pulled her in close. "Here she is, Victor. No worse for the wear. Now let me see the money and let me see your orb and we can close escrow." Frank had always wanted to use that term. He heard it once in a movie. He had no idea what it really meant, but it sounded cool.

Victor looked at Lucy. "You okay, Lucy?" She nodded yes. He could tell her mouth was gagged. She must be scared to death. But Victor didn't sense any fear from her. Tough old broad.

"Fine, Frank. Let me go get the money." He had Bingham's steel suitcase hidden a few headstones away. He grabbed it, opened it, and tilted it forward, putting his flashlight on all the bills so Frank could see the money. He closed the suitcase and started to walk closer to Frank. "I'll obviously need to see The Mule now."

Frank pointed to the east. "It's sitting in a burlap sack exactly 25 feet east of here next to the large crypt with the pointy roof, you can't miss it." Frank kept fingering the gun in his vest with his other hand. Victor held up the suitcase. Frank may have been smitten with Kitta, but he damn sure was more smitten with money. He locked his eyes on the case. That money could help him do so much with his revolution. He forgot about Kitta.

Victor started getting antsy. "Frank, I am not turning this money over to you without seeing The Mule. You will need to get it."

At that point Frank pulled out the gun from under his vest, grabbed Lucy from behind her neck, nearly pulling her off the ground. Frank was abandoning Kitta's plan now that he was close to his pay-day. "Here's the deal, Mr. Jones. You throw that suitcase over here, and you toss me the orb, and I won't blow Ms. Lucy's brains all over this place. And that's non-negotiable." His voice was animated. Even though it was still late at night, and they were in the middle of a vast cemetery, the volume of his voice was too loud. Victor had one move left. "Bad call, Frank. You kill Lucy and my friend Rob will gun you down. He's had a scope on you since you left your car." That wasn't true at all. Neither he nor Rob had a gun, let alone a rifle with a scope.

"I call bullshit, you motherfucker! Now show me the orb and toss me the case!" Frank was riled up. Victor reached into his backpack and looked at The MonteGresso. It had been pulsating and glowing blue and yellow; now it also flashing red and orange. It was on fire and breathing. If it had a temperature it would have scalded Victor's bare hands. Even Victor was surprised at how animated it had become. He knew that had to mean The Mule and The PinonAstra were close. He couldn't expose it though - to do so would be a death sentence.

"Frank, I'm warning you, let her go. If not, I will bury this thing right here, right now, and we all lose!" Victor dropped the knapsack on the ground and pushed some fresh dirt on top of it with his foot. Of course, Frank didn't know what that meant. He laughed, "Fuck you faggot!" And he pointed the gun into the air and pulled the trigger. The sound ricocheted off the headstones. "That was for show. Now toss the money and the orb or this second one will take off your head!" He lowered the barrel and took aim at Victor, who still refused to throw the money to him. Frank started to squeeze the trigger. He only stopped pulling it when he felt a blade go through his back. Looking down, he saw the other end of the long sword came out of his belly. Stunned and silent, he started coughing blood. He dropped the gun and Lucy.

He looked at the dripping end of the impossibly sharp object protruding out his belly when part of his intestines collapsed onto the ground. "What..wha... wh..." were his final words as he collapsed on the ground, his face colliding with Dr. and Mrs. Reinhold Bozeman's double headstone. He: 1890-1972; she: 1899-1982. A good run for the Bozemans. Blood smeared their marker and the grass became wet with Frank McDuffy's insides. He: 1990-2020. Not a great run for one, Frank McDuffy.

Bingham "The Knife" Cutler put his foot on Frank's posterior and yanked the sword out. Sheila Evans grabbed Lucy and pulled her away. Victor was astonished at what he had just witnessed. Bingham The Fucking Knife, he finally did something commendable with his life and his knife.

"Bingham?" Victor cried as he ran to Lucy, Sheila and Bing. "What the hell, holy shit! And thank you!"

"I thought maybe Rob was in serious trouble the way he begged me for that money. I didn't know what was going on. I had to protect him and my investment." Bingham was shaking and he turned to the side and vomited. "Wow, that was intense." He wiped his mouth with the back of his sleeve.

"Are you okay ma'am? Sheila asked Lucy, who was working to ungag herself. Lucy immediately turned to Victor. " Victor, there is an evil woman out there." And she pointed in the general direction of where Kitta left her. "She is coming for The MonteGresso. She's still out there. Be careful."

"Shit! Rob!" Victor screamed and he turned to run to his friend.

Chapter 47 ∗ One Down, One to Go

Kitta turned to see what was happening when she heard Frank yelling. Was this idiot about to ruin things for her? She was so close to this dark figure standing behind a monster Poplar tree she could almost touch him. He didn't see her at all. This had to be Victor's backup. And she had no doubt The MonteGresso was in his possession. Her orbs were going crazy in her backpack, she was surprised this person couldn't hear them. As she was about to put her gun to his back, her attention was diverted by the sound of Frank's gun. Fuck! What had that fool done? Did he have The MonteGresso? Dammit!

Rob had been behind the tree ready to provide Victor backup if Frank got violent. He couldn't see that Frank had pointed a gun at Victor until he discharged the mighty weapon. That's when he caught sight of the flash and made a move to aid Victor. He quickly turned to run and saw Kitta just to his left. He saw her gun drawn. He had no choice, so he made an immediate decision to dive at her. It was the only thing he could think of. Rob was a strong man, but he wasn't a killer. He had been in a few fights in his life, but he had never seriously hurt another person, let alone killed anyone. Kitta had killed several people just that evening.

Rob brought Kitta down on her left side and she hit the ground hard. She just missed hitting her head on a headstone. Her backpack with the orbs rolled under her and her Glock dropped out of her hand. Rob put his left knee into her stomach and tried to plant his right fist into her face as she lay on the ground. She rolled hard right, and Rob put his hand into the ground, breaking several bones in his hand. He cried out in agony as she kneed him in the groin and used a double fist punch to the left side of his face. He went down and rolled to his right, in extreme agony. She bent over to grab the gun and she as pulled the trigger, he kicked at her ankle and swept her down to the ground. The shot went wild. The Glock dropped again. This time as Rob tried to stand up, Kitta pulled out her knife and swiped it at Rob's chest, slicing through his shirt and drawing blood. She then kicked him in the face and circled up behind him. She put the blade to his right side and inserted it under his armpit. It wasn't a fatal wound, but it was bleeding profusely and had knocked the wind out of him. She then dove for her Glock and pointed it at him. She ordered him to put his hands on his head, even though his right arm wouldn't move more than a few inches.

"If you move one more inch, I will put a bullet in your head, do you understand me?" Rob was in agony. He had lost. She ordered him to start walking towards Victor, Frank and Lucy. She wasn't aware that Frank was dead and that several more people were on scene. She missed that excitement when Rob attacked her.

Victor, Lucy, Sheila and Bingham had heard the Glock discharge right after Lucy warned them about Kitta as they had started to make their way to him. They saw Rob, a bloody wreck, marching towards them with his left hand on his head and his right arm dead on his side, blood pouring out of his shirt.

There was a striking, tall blonde woman a few feet back with a gun pointed at them.

"Drop that weapon immediately or your friend is dead, and put your hands up," she motioned to Bingham, who quickly obliged. She had no idea who the other people were, but she didn't have time to conduct interviews. "Where is Frank?" she demanded. Lucy pointed to his lifeless body crumpled on the ground.

"Fool," Kitta muttered. "Which one of you is Victor?" She asked looking at Victor and Bingham. Victor quickly raised his hand, as he wasn't going to endanger Bingham. She couldn't see The MonteGresso anywhere though. "I presume you are the Builders' minion?" Victor asked.

"Very nice. And I am done with this game. I know you or this man have The MonteGresso," she said as she pointed at Rob. "Give it to me or you are all dead. Do you understand?"

"Do you know what will happen if you re-unite the orbs for the Builders? We will all suffer an eternal purgatory. You are human. You must have dead family. You will die one day. You re-unite these orbs incorrectly and you have sealed the fate of every man, woman and child in this world for the end of eternity. Please, I beg of you, don't do this." Victor was close to tears.

Sheila and Bingham looked at each other. Neither had a clue what he was talking about.

"Mr. Jones, I am not going to negotiate with you, I'm not going to be talked out of this!" she yelled. "I am going to kill all of you if you do not turn it over now!" He believed her.

"Well Miss...?" He was trying to ascertain her name and stall for a few precious seconds.

"My name is Kitta Schultz. My child died several years ago. The Builders have promised me that he will be a king of kings if I re-unite the orbs. This is the only thing I care about. Do you think you will say something to me that convinces me that I treasure your Afterlife more than my child's? So stop stalling and hand it over!"

"Well, Miss Kitta Schultz. You win. May I bend down and get it?" Victor's hands were still on his head. Kitta smiled; she was about to win.

Victor stood back up and he held Frank's .357 in his hand. Kitta was unaware that it was laying there in the dark grass. He put the gun under his chin. Everyone shrieked. Kitta froze even though the gun was not pointed at her.

"Okay, so I placed The MonteGresso in the ground, right here. The ground has softened up with your friend's blood. If you don't drop your gun right now, I will put a bullet in my head, and I will be a sacrifice and I will fall on The Monte-Gresso and that's all she wrote for you and your son. So how about you back the fuck off!"

She didn't think this fat American had the guts to shoot himself. Never. She pushed Rob aside and held her gun within twelve inches of Victor's face, oblivious to everyone else around her.

"Drop your gun, Victor, and give me the orb!" Spit flew out of her mouth. She was enraged. She had bloodlust in her eyes. She could faintly see The MonteGresso at Victor's feet glowing, but inside a bag and partially covered with dirt. She knew that if he sacrificed himself as he threatened then The MonteGresso would be re-seeded, solo, again, and forty more years would pass before the orbs could be actively re-united.

No one made a move. "I can't, Ms. Schultz. I care about the fate of humanity too much. You can't be that selfish. I beg of you." Kitta pressed her Glock into Victor's forehead; he could feel the barrel burrowing into his skull. He pulled the hammer back on the .357, its large snout pressing into his chin. This was an ugly game of chicken; it was now or never. Was this how he was going to go out? He realized it was time to play it safe. For the third time that night, the .357 was cocked and the trigger was being depressed. And then a shot rang out and blood covered Victor's face. His ears were ringing, and he thought he had been shot.

Lucy had put her pistol to the back of Kitta's head and fired. Kitta's face erupted all over Victor. Blood streamed down his chin and onto his shirt. Kitta never thought to check a grandmother for a pistol that she might have secreted in her jogging suit pocket. Rookie mistake. Victor dropped the gun and fell to his knees, sobbing uncontrollably.

Lucy ran over to Victor and hugged him tightly. They had won.

Chapter 48 * Reunification

Sheila and Bingham helped provide first aid to Rob and stopped the bleeding. They all knew they had witnessed something extraordinary that evening. But currently there were several shots that had been fired and two dead bodies on the ground. They knew the police would be there very soon and Victor and Rob knew they still had work to do.

As Rob sat against the Bozemans' headstone being attended to by Sheila, Victor grabbed Kitta's bag and opened it. The Mule and The PinonAstra were both there. They hummed and kicked off an elaborate color show. Bingham looked in the bag. "Wow, that's some cool stuff. What is it?" he asked Victor. Victor couldn't take his eyes off them. "That's called eternal salvation for all of you. But we still have work to do."

Victor stood up with Kitta's bag and placed The MonteGresso inside. As soon as they all touched, they simultaneously glowed a strange purple hue and the bag began violently vibrating. Then Victor saw that the orbs opened up and the crystals merged into one; no longer were there three orbs, but they fused together into a troika, pulsating a brilliant blue. It was time.

Victor had them all gather around Rob, who was immobile. "This is the end of one incredible journey. A journey and chase that has lasted throughout humanity's existence. I don't want to sound corny, but this is the most important event happening right now in the history of our planet. And we need to finish it."

Rob piped in, his voice weak, but he used all of his remaining strength to talk. "Victor, let me do this. I am injured anyway, and you have sacrificed so much. Please, let me do this."

"What's he talking about?" Sheila asked.

"The orb must be seeded with a human blood sacrifice. A selfless sacrifice that Rob has offered. And Rob, you are wonderful to offer, but I have no life here any longer. I have no career, few friends, and I have accomplished very little in my time on this planet. I remember telling my parents many years ago that I thought I would do something significant in my lifetime. But I didn't. I never amounted to anything. I never applied myself and never tried very hard. I got exactly what I deserved. You, Rob, are a beautiful, wonderful person who helped me when I didn't know what to do. You are needed now on this Earth. Now, more than ever." Victor was crying heavily at this point and everyone, even Bingham, wept. Bingham didn't know why, maybe the shock of the last twenty minutes was simply overwhelming.

Victor grabbed a shovel that they had brought to the cemetery in the likely event that this would happen. He dug a small ditch next to Frank and Kitta's bodies. It wasn't nearly deep enough to bury the bodies, nor was it intended to happen that way. He really wasn't even entirely sure what he needed to do next. But he knew there needed to be some type of grave for this to work.

He hugged Sheila and Bingham and knelt down to hug Rob. Tears flowed. "Don't be sad for me. This is a journey I need to take. I never had blind faith before. I thought it was a silly construct. But the events of the last week have shaken me to my core. I have faith now. I have seen the light. Please tell my parents how much I love them. They won't understand that I did this for them, but please tell them I helped when I was called upon."

Victor then turned to hug and say good-bye to Lucy. A braver woman he had never known. As he turned to look for Lucy, he saw that she had stepped into the shallow grave that he had dug and held the new unified orb in her left hand and the pistol in her other hand.

"No!" Victor screamed. "You can't, Lucy, you aren't supposed to. You can't! This is not your responsibility! Lucy, remember what happened forty years ago. Jeannie ruined it. She wasn't supposed to bury the orb, even though she thought she was doing the right thing to help her friends. Don't make the same mistake," Victor pleaded with her.

"Oh sweetie, do you think this was all a coincidence that I ended up at Cherry Knolls living with Beverly? Beverly and her father came to me tonight. They warned me about the imminent danger. They saved us all. And they told me I was chosen. You think it's a coincidence meeting you, calling you to warn you tonight, bringing this pistol? Oh, you are a sweet child, Victor Jones. You can say whatever you want about how you haven't fulfilled your destiny and haven't made your mark on this world. But the Dead would never have chosen you to help *me* if they didn't see something special in your soul." She was a chosen one too. She didn't really know it until that very minute.

"You are an extraordinary person who will live a wonderful, long life and you deserve all the joys on this Earth," Lucy continued, "and I can promise you that you have big things to look forward to when you die. But not for many, many years. You are needed here." Lucy was the only person not crying.

Lucy went on, "I've got the instructions for what happens next, I need to shepherd the orb to the Divide and end the Builders' reign. I'm excited to see Beverly again, and my parents and even meet President Lincoln. Interesting fact, my great-grandparents weren't too fond of Old Hickory, you know. I want to thank him personally for what he did." She gave a short, nervous laugh. "My love to you all."

She put the pistol to her head. Victor tried to lunge at her, but Rob jumped up and pulled him back. "Noooo!" Victor screamed. And then the pistol went off. Lucy's body fell into the small ditch. The unified orb fell under her. As soon as it hit the ground the entire grave lit up in a bright light, so powerful they all had to shut their eyes. Her body was quickly absorbed into the dirt, along with the orb, and all of the light and vibrations coming from the shallow grave quickly stopped as if a refrigerator door had been slammed shut. Victor, Rob, Sheila, and Bingham all stood there trying to wrap their heads around what they had just witnessed. Victor took a knee. A few moments later they all felt the Earth shake. It was a powerful tremor that caused the few who were still standing to crouch down and cower tightly with the others. Several trees toppled over in the cemetery. They could hear far off car alarms blare and sirens blast. If they were initially worried about the police coming due to the gun shot blasts, they definitely had some time because the police would be busy with one huge earthquake that not only ripped through Denver that evening, but vibrations could be felt around the world. It wasn't the same type of earthquake that devastated Montemurro in 1857, but it still packed a punch strong enough to bring down the wall. The Divide had come down, the Builders had lost, and the Dead could make their way towards salvation.

Epilogue

(Six weeks later)

The crane sat next to the grave ready to remove the concrete vault that had sat atop Mark Levin's coffin for the past forty years. There was also a small backhoe that sat at attention waiting for the ceremony to conclude. Rabbi Stan Berenbaum, now eighty-two years old and carrying a small oxygen cannister, said some brief blessings in Hebrew and gave a short statement to the dozen or so people assembled. He spoke about the concept of grieving, how this is a process and not a means to an end. And even after forty years, the grief process is still very real and alive and that all people must challenge themselves to honor their loved ones by being so kind to the living, so forgiving of petty disputes, and so open to helping those in need.

The tears were not flowing as they were forty years earlier; they had been replaced with contented smiles on the faces of Kenny Levin and his wife, Veronica, as well as Rachel Levin and her wife, Shoshana. Bingham and Rob stood next to each other, slightly stooped beneath the small canopy, while Sheila and Victor stood a few feet away, holding hands.

It had been a whirlwind of activity since that eerie night six weeks earlier and things were settling down. The Denver Police Department had determined that Kitta and Frank, despite their disguises, were solely responsible for the deaths of all of the people at Cherry Knolls as was evidenced by the clear video that was never erased. They also found that Bingham was justified in using deadly force on Frank, due to the testimony of Victor and Sheila. Bingham had been continually tracking the money that he gave to Rob. He had begged Sheila to come with him that night. When they saw Rob and Victor at Victor's house they had no idea what Rob was doing with the money. When Rob and Victor ran out of the house with the briefcase of money late at night, Sheila cautioned Bingham to hold back for a bit before chasing off behind them. Just as they were about to leave and follow the tracking device they saw Kitta pull up to Victor's house. As soon as Kitta dashed off they decided it was time to follow and see what the hell was happening. They hadn't seen Lucy get pulled out of the trunk or else they would have just called the police. But they did see some furtive movement that concerned them both. Fortunately, Sheila grabbed the sword that she saw sitting in the backseat of Bingham's car and pressed it into his hands. It was no longer a prop and Bingham finally put that to good use.

The mystery of Lucy Black was more peculiar.

Lucy had fallen into the grave and they had all witnessed the ground swallow her, along with the unified orb. When the earth closed on the grave, the orb and Lucy were gone. It would be several days before her body re-surfaced in a small quarry approximately one mile from the cemetery. The evidence was consistent with a suicide and her pistol was found next to her body. The gun found by Lucy's body matched the ballistics of the weapon that killed Kitta and ended Lucy's life.

The four survivors decided to come up with a story that Kitta was dead before they arrived and that they never saw Lucy. That explained Kitta's gunshot wound and the fact that Lucy was nowhere to be found. As for Frank, they kept that story exactly as it happened and that seemed to be enough for the police. The fact that a mysterious death in Barcelona, as well as the torture and killing of Dean Luiga, Esq., all pointed to Kitta's handiwork made it easy for the police to put an exclamation point on the whole ordeal and turn the page. Two bad, bad people were wiped off the face of the Earth and the story of survival played well.

That same bloody evening as Victor, Rob, Sheila, and Bingham were leaving the cemetery, Victor spied someone strolling through the headstones, looking spry and giddy. Victor recused himself to say hello.

"So proud of you, Victor. So, so proud. You have helped more people than you will ever know. You're a hero, a real hero, and I for one would love to shake your hand. That is, of course, if I had hands." Mark looked at his now fully translucent hand and mocked shaking Victor's hand. He couldn't even hold a pipe to smoke weed any longer. He appeared to be fading away. They both laughed.

"What happens to you now? Everyone is starting their journey to the Divide; can't you talk to someone?" Victor asked.

"Sure, I will submit a complaint with the customer service department, I'm sure someone will be happy to change the way the Afterlife works just for me." His jubilant spirit seemed darker now, even though the Divide had come down. "I am likely just going to fade away. In a few months I'll be gone, but that's okay. I feel my job is done and that makes me smile." His toothy grin was hardly noticeable.

Victor felt for Mark. Mark was the only reason he was alive and that the Divide had come down. Surely there was something he could do. Think, Victor, think! "Varanasi!" Victor exclaimed. "Varanasi!" Mark smiled.

It would take several weeks of negotiating and pleading but somehow Victor was able to convince Mark's sister, Rachel, that Mark needed to be re-located. Victor found Rachel through one of Bingham's investigators. She no longer resided in Denver, but she was still the trustee of the family estate and maintained total authority over what would or could be done with Mark's remains. He appealed to her sense of spirituality and was pleasantly surprised when she was open to discussing the impact Mark had on Victor's life. He wasn't entirely forthright, but he explained that he had visions of Mark on a regular basis, and these visions told him to re-locate his remains to the holy Indian city of Varanasi. He was loaded with enough intimate details of Mark's life, that even a cynical person would have to think twice about the veracity of Victor's statements. It could have been due to Rachel being a deeply spiritual person that Victor's pleas resonated with her. Or maybe it had something to do with Mark infiltrating her dreams asking for her help. But it probably mostly had to do with Bingham offering to apply $100,000 towards a foundation that Rachel and her wife started to help homeless animals. Or maybe it was a combination of all those things.

Whatever it was, Rachel agreed to allow Victor to disinter Mark's remains and take them to Varanasi to be placed onto a funeral pyre and gently released into the Ganges. She would, of course, require a Jewish ceremony for the disinterment and Rabbi Berenbaum's approval. Rabbi Berenbaum was a pragmatic man, and he was less constrained by strict Jewish dogma than he was with the concept of souls being freed.

Victor held Sheila's hand tightly as Rabbi Berenbaum wrapped up his thoughts and prayers. They had fallen for each other immediately after the events of the night six weeks earlier. It happened quickly and deeply, and it was the happiest Victor had been in his life. He sensed his life had meaning and a purpose. Victor had formally decided to leave the Cherry Knolls corporation after that night, despite the national leadership pleading with him to stay. His particular facility would be shut down for at least six months due to the tragic murders, but he couldn't stand the thought of going back into that building again.

Victor started working with Rob in his small production company, which seemed to be busier than ever. News that Bingham had saved someone's life with his sword catapulted him overnight to cult-like status. He was still an awful lawyer, but he was a viral sensation far more than he ever was before. That triggered significant new referrals for Rob's production company, and therefore Rob needed more help. Victor was the perfect person. It was as if something magical had caused it all to come together perfectly for all of them.

Once the ceremony was over, the crew would unearth the remains and place them into a heavily sealed casket. Victor and Sheila would remain with the casket the entire journey to India to personally ensure that Mark could escape his own forty-year dungeon and seek peace and omniscience along with every other soul that had walked the face of the Earth.

As the sun was quickly fading and the grounds crew got to work, Victor felt his jacket pocket and found a half-empty box of cigarettes. Mark's warning about cigarettes flashed through his mind. He looked at Sheila, who wrapped her arms around him. He tossed the package into a nearby trash can. He had lots to live for now. He had plenty of time to experience his Afterlife; right now he wanted to enjoy living the rest of his life.

THE END

Acknowledgments:

"The world belongs to those that hustle." February 8, 2010. Artofmanliness.com.

"Congregation" written and performed by the Foo Fighters from the Sonic Highways album.

Thanks to the following for helping me work through this first novel. My wife Becky and kids Rex, Lucy and Ozzie. During the pandemic you never bothered me in the basement plugging away (of course would it have killed you to check on me from time to time??). You are the BEST a guy could ask for. To my parents Steve and Joyce Foster who read the manuscript and gave me lots of feedback (they think this novel is the greatest story ever told...got to love your parents!). To my brother David Foster, sister Debbie Foster, and sister-in-law Ali Foster, for their thoughts and encouragement (I may have moved up in the child rankings). To my father-in-law Bob Hetzel, and mother-in-law Sue Pitt, thanks for all of your thoughts and ideas. To Laura Lieff, Jim Miles, Joel Bahr, Jena Skinner, and Nicole Magistro for all of your help getting this finished! And to all my peeps at Foster, Graham, Milstein & Calisher, LLP I am still OTMF! I love all of you!

I would also like to note that 100% of any of the author's profits from the sale of the paper edition of this novel will be donated to the extraordinary *Make a Wish Foundation*. Visit Wish.org to learn all about the amazing things they do for terminally ill children.

About the Author:

Danny is a first time novelist, but long time personal injury attorney in Denver. He enjoys skiing, scuba diving and terrorizing golf courses. He loves the Denver Broncos, Indiana Hoosiers, springer spaniels and red licorice. He is lucky to have a beautiful family that he adores.